MY GENES DON'T FIT

AMY JARECKI

Rapture Books

ISBN Hardcover: 9781942442530

ISBN Paperback: 9781942442523

ISBN e-Book: 9781942442547

ISBN Amazon Paperback: 9798328300148

Dedication

To my daughter, Moriah, who battles illness every day and still manages to be an amazing mother. And to her son, Calum, who has proved he has the same fighting spirit as his mother. I am immensely proud of you both!

To my husband, Bob, who is my rock of salvation when things are at their worst.

Also, a heartfelt shoutout to all the doctors, nurses, and technicians who negotiate the murky waters of rare diseases. You are the heroes.

FOREWORD

Though this is a work of fiction, all of the doctor appointments are actual representations relayed from the patient's point of view.

CHAPTER ONE

JANE

S *ydney, Australia. Twenty-nine years ago*

My chilling scream pierced through dreamless sleep. Grabbing my stomach, my eyes snapped open while every nerve in my body frayed, torturing me with spasms of agony.

Oh, God. Oh, God. Oh, God. The baby!

I doubled over as if a demon clawed the inside of my uterus with steel talons.

"Eeeee!" I squealed, covered with sweat, panting faster than a dog shut in a hot car while I curled around my pregnant belly.

The relentless contraction gripped my abdomen as if trying to turn me inside out. "God!" I had a high tolerance for pain but my eyes were rolling back, my entire body shook, and my mouth started watering like I was going to puke.

I reached for the controller to ring for the nurse, my stomach roiling, the back of my throat burning with the contents of my empty stomach.

"Help!"

I gagged. Heaved. Yellow bile spewed onto the sheet as I jabbed my thumb on the red dot. I'd been in the hospital for observation for three days and was scheduled for a cesarean in the morning.

At the moment, seven o'clock was a lifetime away. So was my absent husband.

Rocking back and forth, I clutched my arms around my stomach. "Nurse! God dammit!"

The blood pressure cuff encircling my arm began to inflate. The mere pressure brought on another urge to hurl. I tried to rip open the Velcro but collapsed with the torment of the cramping tourniquet gripping my gut.

This might be my first full-term pregnancy. But after a stillbirth at twenty-seven weeks followed by a miscarriage, I had a pretty good idea labor was not supposed to be like this. It should come on gradually with contractions becoming more frequent, but since I opened my eyes I've been in the throes of one continuous, murderously excruciating contraction that felt more like being ripped in half than squeezing something the size of a beach ball down to the size of a walnut.

The blood pressure cuff released and immediately restarted. I glanced at the monitor. My breath stopped. Holy shit, the reading was 187 over 122. I've never had high blood pressure in my life and, though I wasn't an expert, I was pretty damned sure with a reading this high, the machine was about to explode.

My panting sped faster. For the love of God, no one had responded to my call. And if I didn't get help in the next five seconds I was going to die.

That absolutely could *not* happen.

Not now.

Not before my baby was born.

"Nurse!" I screamed, sliding my feet off the bed while hot liquid gushed down my legs.

When the door opened, a flood of light blinded me followed by a high-pitched gasp. "We need to get you back on the bed *now!*" she said so fast, the words slurred together.

The nurse shoved me by the butt as she reached for the red phone. "Code green, room three-twelve. I repeat, code green, three-twelve!"

I managed to get one knee on the mattress as I doubled over with my everlasting contraction. "I'm gonna die!"

"Not while I'm here. No, no, no," she said, injecting something into my IV.

As a calming effect hit my bloodstream, I rolled to my side, the room filling with a myriad of hospital personnel. Tears made the tubes flying around me appear distorted and liquescent, the conversation short and filled with so many acronyms I had no idea what was being said.

I didn't care. "Save my baby!" I yelled as I clung to consciousness.

The soiled sheets disappeared before an orderly rolled my bed down the hallway at a run. One fluorescent light after another blurred past on the ceiling above.

They pushed me into a cold room where the lights were too bright and everyone was wearing green scrubs. "Hi, Jane," said a woman, her face appearing above mine. She wore safety glasses, a face mask, and a blue hair net. "I'm Dr. Prendergast and I'm going to perform your emergency cesarean."

I nodded, my consciousness waning, but I fought the drugs. I had to hold on for a few seconds more. "Please tell me my baby will live!" I tried to shout but my voice only managed a slurring whisper.

The doctor's face filmed over. "That's our goal."

The last thing I heard were two words: *ruptured uterus*.

Chapter Two

Jane

*D*enver, Colorado. Twenty-nine years later

"Hey, Curt, what's today's challenge?" I answered my cell, turning my chair toward the floor-to-ceiling windows of my corner office. A flock of geese flew past, moving in graceful unison, their focus determinedly set on the horizon.

"I wish I could say nothing," replied the Philadelphia plant manager for Bethany Plastics. When it came to Philly, the news was rarely good.

I talked to Curt several times a day—more than any of the other seven plant managers under me, mainly because his facility was not only the largest, it posed a colossal thorn in my side. We were always battling something from the price of electricity to union takeovers to blow molder machines that didn't produce to manufacturer specifications.

As the geese continued on, vanishing from the picture frame of my window, I wondered what it might be like to be able to fly...with a flock of geese...*today.*

I checked my watch. "Come on, out with it."

"It's bad," he groaned, sounding like death.

My hackles stood on end. Curt was tough. He'd seen just about everything in this business and if he opened with "it's bad" then I most likely didn't want to know why. Except I was the boss—the woman with the ultimate responsibility, bad or good. I leaned forward and cradled my head in my hand. I was leaving for vacation with my daughter in two days and I didn't have time to deal with a crisis. "What happened? You okay?"

"Hydroade just called. Um..." Curt's shaky inhale hissed over the line. "Well...*ahhhh*...they found a bottle with goose shit in it."

My mouth dropped open, then my tongue went dry as dozens of possible explanations fired across my brain neurons. It couldn't have come from one of my plants. Not from one of my employees. It had to be from a competitor, right?

Damn.

No one in the beverage packaging industry ever wanted to hear anything that resembled contamination, let alone tampering. "One of *our* bottles?" I asked barely louder than a whisper.

"Yes."

Throbbing pain thundered at the back of my head, threatening to bring on another one of my miserable migraines. We had an exclusive contract to supply Hydroade a million plastic bottles per day. "Was it filled?" The only thing worse than a contaminated empty bottle was one that went through the customer's filling line.

"God, no. Their inspection equipment caught it right after depalletization."

I still couldn't believe it. Except there were geese all over the grounds at the Philly factory. Then again, there were geese everywhere. I'd just seen a flock fly past my window and I'm in Denver. "Do they *think* one of our employees tampered?" I swallowed down three ibuprofen with the dregs of cold coffee.

"There's no doubt. They had to shut down the line and sterilize the entire plant." Curt paused while the faint sound of mouse clicks came over the line. "I just sent you a photo—didn't want you to see it before I got you on the phone."

I refreshed my email twice before the message hit, then it took me about two seconds to open the jpg.

Fuck! If only I'd left for vacation yesterday.

"Unbelievable." The haunted tenor from my voice gave me chills as I stared at a picture of the bottom of one of our bottles—facing the foot was an embroidered patch from a Bethany uniform. Our trademark *B* was front and center, strategically placed beneath a bunch of goose droppings—a blatant statement of contempt.

I grabbed my stress ball, squeezing until it split open. "Disgruntled employee?"

"Looks like it."

"Who?"

"Hell, I don't know. That's the million-dollar question, isn't it?"

Even though I was sitting in an office over seventeen hundred miles away, I winced as if I'd been on the receiving end of a sucker punch between the eyes.

This was tampering on a criminal scale.

And it happened in one of *my* plants.

On *my* watch.

I threw the ball in the trash so hard it bounced out. "Who knows about this?"

"The folks at Hydroade, me, and now you."

"Damn!" I balanced the phone between my cheek and shoulder, grabbed my briefcase, and started packing up my laptop. "Where's the bottle?"

"Hydroade still has it. I'm heading to Allentown first thing in the morning."

"I'll go with you. Then we'll keep the bottle hidden. Do *not* tell anyone what it contains. We need to conduct an investigation and the less people know, the more likely we'll be to find the culprit."

"Should I call the police?"

"Probably. But hold off until we have the evidence."

"There's more," Curt said.

I yanked my power cord out of the wall. "Seriously? Goose shit in a beverage bottle found at the filling plant of our largest customer isn't enough?"

"You need to know Hydroade is out for blood."

And we all might be filing for unemployment tomorrow. "Do you blame them? I'll be on the next plane."

I grabbed my briefcase and threw my purse over my shoulder, dashing out of my office and shouting at my admin assistant as I walked past, "Get me on the redeye to Philly. I need to grab a bag and swing by my mother's place. Text me with the flight info."

"Sure thing, Jane," she said as I ran down the stairs and out the door, dialing the CEO of Bethany Plastics and making a beeline to my car.

Leon Worthington was a son-of-a-bitch, and this news wasn't going to be received well. But just like Curt had called before anyone else could notify me of this disaster, I needed to fess up to my boss immediately.

The phone call with Leon hadn't lasted long, though his message to me was clear: do everything possible to keep the incident away from the media and "bury it." Of course I'd make sure the disaster was contained. That's why he hired me for this job. Because I'm fast, efficient, and I don't take bullshit from anyone.

However, in this case it was goose shit.

I zipped into the parking lot at Mom's assisted living facility, grabbed her bag of adult diapers, and hustled inside.

Sarah, the director, approached from my right, weaving through the maze of couches. "Hi, Jane. Have you got a moment?"

When it came to my mother and this facility, that was the dreaded question. It wasn't the staff—they did a thankless job and were topnotch. What did Mama do this time? Shout at the caregivers? Spit out her medicine? Sing at the top of her lungs during the afternoon movie?

Trying not to cringe, I stopped. "A minute? Please tell me my mother has been a model senior citizen ever since my last chat with her."

Sarah laughed, her gaze shifting down the hallway to the dragon's lair. "It's not too bad this time—no bruises at least."

Thank God for small miracles...I hope. I tried to smile, but only managed to grimace.

"Your mom's showing everyone a picture of her with a man and telling them the fellow is her husband. She even told me that you're buying her a new bed so he can come over and have..." Waggling her eyebrows, she made quotations with her fingers. "A 'good time.'"

If I were thirty years younger, I'd probably be embarrassed, but I've been looking after my mother for too long to let anything faze me. But, jeez, the idea of my ninety-year-old mother having sex with anyone was just wrong. "She isn't?"

"I wish I could say no, but she's been quite loquacious about it." Sarah glanced at the enormous fish tank that spanned the wall of the entrance. It usually had a calming effect, but presently did nothing to ease the knots boring into my neck. "Oh, and there are two children in the photo—a boy and a girl. If memory serves, there's a Christmas tree in the background."

I gulped, the photo Mom kept beside her bed coming to mind. "I'm sure that's the one of me and my brother with our parents. Mom divorced my dad when I was a junior in high school."

"Is your father still living?"

"No, he passed away years ago—aneurysm. And it's been seventeen years since my mother's second husband died of cancer." Only a month after my stepfather's death, Mom's Alzheimer's had come on with vengeance.

"So, how do you recommend we set her straight?" Sarah asked.

Unfortunately, my mother's grasp of reality had faded into oblivion. If any of the employees at Ridgeview told her she'd lost her mind and her ex-husband wasn't only not coming to visit, he was dead, she'd be likely to explode. The vision of Mama using her walker to shatter the glass of the beautiful fish tank gave me heartburn. "It's a good thing I'm here. I'll have a chat with her now. She'll be less volatile if she hears it from me."

"You're a lifesaver." Sarah patted my elbow, her shoulders visibly relaxing. The poor woman, she had a thankless job. "Thank you."

Honestly, I should be thanking Sarah. I should be kissing her feet. I tried bringing my mother into my home for a couple years—hired a part-time caregiver as well. Needless to say, it was an exercise in grandiose self-flagellation. First of all, as the Vice President of Operations for Bethany Plastics, I travel a lot for work. My absences on top of my mother's irascibility meant we cycled through caregivers before she managed to learn their names.

"Hi, Mama." I forced a smile, slipping into her studio apartment which was mostly tidy aside from the assortment of half-finished crossword puzzle books strewn atop every surface.

"Jane!" she said as if she hadn't seen me in weeks even though I'd visited three days ago.

She held up the Christmas picture which had been on her bedside table. "Do you see this?" She smiled lasciviously, her legs up on the footstool of her recliner. We kept Mama's hair short because she rarely combed it and today it stuck up at the crown, a sure sign she'd slept on her back. I had her blue eyes but hers had become rather vacant of late. How I longed for the caring mother who'd flown to Australia and had helped to take care of my newborn daughter while I spent two weeks in the ICU after nearly dying from a ruptured uterus.

With little time to sugarcoat anything, I carefully slid the frame from her fingertips. "I'm very familiar with this picture." Regardless of if my heart was presently twisting into knots, I used my gentlest voice and pointed to my younger self. "This is me."

Confused devastation filled my mother's blue eyes. "That's you?" she asked, voice suddenly childlike. Mama did still recognize me as an adult, though it seemed she had forgotten what I looked like as a tow-haired five-year-old.

"It is." My finger slid to my brother. "See, that's Roger. And next to him is Dad. You divorced him—five years before he passed away from a ruptured brain aneurysm."

Rather than give me sass, Mom leaned back in her recliner, the corners of her mouth drawn downward in an utterly deflated frown. "Oh."

This woman had been an awesome mother. She'd driven me to my ballet lessons, and baked cookies for a gazillion school functions. She'd always been there with a comforting embrace whether I had a scratched knee, was heckled by the kids in junior high for winning a debate or when I broke up with my sophomore boyfriend. She had always been my rock even though I didn't appreciate her during the rebellious years. Seeing her fragile, lonely, and unable to remember who my dad was or what I looked like as a child tore me apart as if I'd failed her.

Regardless of how little time I had, I pulled her into my arms, squeezing my eyes shut against unshed tears. Of course, I had mastered the art of not crying thanks to my brother Roger, but if there was a time to cry, this was damned close. "I'm sorry, Mama." Damn, it took a huge breath to keep my voice from cracking. "I think when you see old pictures you sometimes don't remember what happened, so you make up stories."

"I know," she cried, her shoulders shaking.

I rubbed my palm in circles over her back and held her close as long as I could. "I love you." I kissed her forehead, my heart in shreds. Old age wasn't supposed to be like this. It should be filled with grandkids and sugar cookies, quilting clubs, and bingo games. "I have to catch a flight, but I'll be back soon, okay?"

Mom nodded, reaching for the Alzheimer's remote control. It only allowed her to turn the TV on, adjust the volume, and change the channels.

It broke me up to leave her dazed and confused, but she couldn't keep traipsing around the old folks' home telling everyone she was going to do the dirty with my deceased father. Alzheimer's was a wicked disease, stealing not only the sufferer's memories, but turning them into souls who were, at best, shadows of their former selves. Her doctor told me I was lucky because Mama still recognized me. In my opinion, I would have been luckier if she were ninety years old, in her right mind, and full of vim and vigor.

Even with my stopover to see my mother, I waited for my flight for an agonizing three hours. I made use of the time in the airline's membership lounge, tidying up loose ends, making phone calls, and responding to emails, diverting inventories of bottles from New York to Hydroade, holding the phone away from my ear as I took an ass-chewing from my counterpart at the same company.

I sipped a glass of wine and managed some meditative breathing before calling my daughter, Margaret Lehn Corley, who nearly always went by Meg. She was my miracle baby soon turning twenty-nine. Honestly, I was also Meg's miracle mom because I managed to survive her birth.

"Why did I get a bad feeling as soon as I saw you on the caller ID?" she asked rather than answering with her usual cheerful greeting.

Closing my eyes, I dropped my head forward and groaned. The last time I had to cancel a vacation with her, she was in college, but Meg wasn't one to forget anything. I suppose I'd had to cancel a long weekend last year, but that wasn't a huge deal. At least she didn't seem to be upset about it at the time. But my daughter knew me too well, maybe better than I knew myself.

"There's been a development in Philly," I explained. I'd been looking forward to this getaway for a year. The cruise to Bermuda was her twenty-ninth birthday present. I had paid for a suite.

"Oh, really?" Meg didn't bother to hide her sarcasm. I didn't blame her. "When isn't there a development in Philly?"

"Yeah, but this one is...unbelievably bad." Nope, I wasn't even going to fess up about the goose shit to my own daughter. "I'm sorry, Sweetie. I promise I'll make it up to you. Why don't you go without me? Take one of your friends."

"It won't be the same."

"No, but it ought to be a lot more fun than going on vacation with your mommy in tow."

"Excuse me? Is that supposed to make me feel better?"

She didn't have to say more. My daughter didn't exactly have the perfect childhood. And though she'd come into herself, occasionally her deep-seated resentment would rear its ugly head—especially when I did something as thoughtless as cancelling a vacation at the last minute.

She blamed me for working too hard. She blamed me most of all for leaving her father. Of course, I'd never told her the reasons because I firmly believed it wasn't appropriate for one parent to complain about another, even though my ex didn't adhere to the same values. He complained about me plenty, his nickname for me being The Bitch from Hell (yeah, great Jack, really original, so glad you taught that one to our daughter). Regardless of his immature, pathetic name-calling, Meg didn't need to know the bastard had been on a seven-year bender, contributing nothing to the family when I finally gave up and divorced him.

I crossed my ankles and sat back in the vinyl low-backed armchair. "Ask someone nice to go with you. I'll pay the change fees. Most of all, I want you to have a good time. I want you to have a great birthday."

"Right. I'll be the pathetic woman sitting alone in our suite, toasting myself with a double tequila sunrise." Meg chuckled. "Maybe I ought to take Dad."

Uncomfortable chair or not, my spine shot straighter than a bow staff. Dozens of retorts were only suppressed by pursed lips. The asshole still lived in Australia and I sure as hell wasn't about to pay his fare to the US. Nor did I relish paying her father's share of the cruise where he'd most likely drink to excess and ignore Meg. I inhaled deeply and forced myself to smile. "Do you think he'd go?" I asked carefully.

She snorted. "You know as well as I do no one can take him away from his precious horses, not even me."

Meg was right, of course. The only good thing that had happened to my ex-husband since we divorced was inheriting a horse stud farm in Queensland. As far as I knew, he was happily drowning himself in copious amounts of alcohol while collecting stud fees. "Maybe take someone your age? A love interest perhaps?"

"Love interest? What happened to the word boyfriend? Which, by the way, unless you've come down with Alzheimer's in the past few days, you know I do not presently have a *love interest*!"

The boarding announcement text for my flight popped up on my phone. "I stand duly corrected."

"You need to quit that job before it kills you."

"I know."

I slid my laptop into my briefcase. I had thought about it, but I was only fifty-nine. And I'd been single for twenty-two years. Being a VP of Operations was my life. After divorcing Meg's father I'd poured myself into my career and fought my way to the top. What would I do if I left Bethany Plastics? Fall into another vice presidency somewhere? One thing was for sure, there were no easy VP jobs in corporate America. At least none I knew of.

And if this disaster ever leaked to the media, I doubted there'd be a company anywhere on the planet that would hire me.

CHAPTER THREE

MEG

Contrary to what my mother believed, it proved impossible to find anyone to go on an all-expenses paid cruise to Bermuda at the last minute. My father had never come to see me in the United States, even though I couldn't resist yanking Mom's chain when she called to cancel. My friends worked. Some had kids. And no matter how much my bestie Elaine and I tried to convince our boss to let us both take off at the same time, the answer had been a humorless no.

But traveling alone aside, as a self-proclaimed introvert I didn't mind having a luxury suite to myself, the ship's staff catering to my every whim. I didn't have to wake up early with Mom. Nor was I pressured to go to fitness classes before breakfast. My mother was the athlete in the family and incredibly driven. The woman earned her black belt at the ripe age of fifty-eight. A five-foot-one dynamo, she was in great shape and wore a size two. About the only thing I inherited from her was red hair and blue eyes. Unfortunately, I didn't inherit her athleticism, nor was I petite. For exercise I enjoy long walks, don't mind shoveling snow, and can chop wood like a mountain man (thanks to Dad). Organized fitness? I'm allergic.

So, I got to relax.

I went to the spa for a massage.

Twice so far.

I ordered room service and struck up a conversation with the bartender on the Lido deck who told me about his wife and kids back home. And I read.

A lot.

What can I say? I'm a librarian. Reading is my elixir.

I didn't even step ashore when the ship stopped in Nassau because I had just started reading Kristan Higgins' *Out of the Clear Blue Sky* and couldn't put it down. I also had an aura in the center of my vision which was an indication I was about to get smacked with a migraine. I've had headaches all my life, but I got a leg-up on this one with a cocktail of acetaminophen and ibuprofen, and, of course, a fantastic book.

This morning when the ship arrived at King's Wharf on the Bermudian island of pink sand, it happened to be my twenty-ninth birthday and, after indulging myself for three days, I was ready to go forth and act like a tourist. I slathered sunscreen on my freckly and fair skin. I also packed a couple of waters and a granola bar into my mini backpack and headed for the gangway, taking the stairs as my exercise for the morning. The excursion I chose for today was a tour of the Crystal Caves.

I'd given deep sea diving a miss.

Am I afraid of sharks?

Sure am—and anything else that might sting, bite, or eat me.

I had a spring in my step, wearing a wide-brimmed straw hat, sun-flower-shaped sunglasses, pink shorts, and a frilly boho tunic swirling with purple, lime green and blue. I might be a librarian, but I also love color which, according to my colleagues, made me eccentric. You should see what I did with the kid's section at the main library. The entrance looks like the door of a hobbit hole surrounded by book trees—similar to a money tree, except with brightly colored book covers. Inside, the walls are painted with scenes from classic stories like *Where the Wild Things Are, The Wind in the Willows,* and *Charlotte's Web.* Of course a children's section wouldn't be complete without a white-bearded wizard wielding his wand and presiding over the center of everything.

The salty smell of the Atlantic washed over me as I stepped onto the pier. Warmed by the Bermudian sun, I smiled broadly, snapping a selfie with the ship and the ocean in the background. I quickly posted it on Facebook with the caption, "Mom doesn't know what she's missing!" Then I found my shuttle bus, spotting a woman wearing a turquoise shirt who waved a "Crystal Caves Excursion" placard over her head.

By the time I climbed aboard, most of the seats were taken, but I found an empty one near the back. "Anyone sitting here?" I asked the guy in the window seat who was scrolling through his phone. He glanced up and grinned—one that gave my stomach a zing.

Whoa. I hadn't zinged in a while.

He was hot in an unkempt sort of way, appearing as if he might have rolled out of bed, riffled his fingers through his hair, and called it good. He gestured with an upturned palm. "Be my guest."

"Thanks," I said, taking off my backpack and sliding in beside him, our shoulders slightly touching. *Bring on the zing*.

I didn't try to shift away. "Where are you from?"

He returned his attention to his phone while one shoulder twitched up. "Ohio."

"Cool. I'm from Wisconsin. We're practically neighbors."

The dude blanked out his screen, giving me a sideways glance like he was checking me out but didn't want me to notice. He slid his phone into a pocket of his khaki shorts which were as wrinkled and disheveled as his hair and t-shirt.

I didn't care. He smelled like Ivory soap and that was nice, especially since I couldn't shift aside far enough not to press up against his shoulder.

"Wisconsin, huh?" His warm thigh pressed flush against mine as well. "Are you a Badger fan?"

"Sure am—got my master's at UW Madison." I tried to scoot away, but the contour of the seat just made me slide right back into him.

"A brainiac?" The dude offered his hand. "So, I'm Lance."

I shook it. "Margaret but everyone calls me Meg."

He grinned wider this time—I mean dazzling white teeth, the incisors crossed slightly. If I had to assign a word to his lazy smile, I'd choose *magnetizing*. "Meg it is."

I think I melted for a moment, but when Lance looked out the window, I remembered to breathe. "Did you go to Ohio State?"

"You mean *The* Ohio State University?" he asked, putting the emphasis on the "The" like the starting NFL football players do when they're announced at the beginning of games.

Being from Wisconsin, I wasn't a fan of emphasizing the word "The" because the pros sounded so disgustingly arrogant, but the dude smirked as if he knew he was being a brashole. I rolled my eyes. "Yeah...did you study there?"

He nodded just as the bus started off and the tour guide interrupted us with a welcome and a spiel about our destination. She pointed out the Commissioner's House and Museum, as well as a dolphin sea pool. She continued to mention points of interest, then said something about taking a detour through the town of Hamilton with its brightly painted buildings. The word "bright" got my attention, of course.

The sound system grated with static and, as I strained to hear, Lance tapped my sunglasses. "Cute shades."

"Thanks." Any guy who complimented an item of my unconventional attire was an ace in my book. Maybe my fashion sense skipped a generation because my father wore nothing but jeans and button-down shirts. Mom? Well, she must have been born in a business suit.

"How has your cruise been so far? Having fun?" asked Lance.

"It's been awesome," I said, turning my ear toward the speaker.

"What has been your favorite part?" He obviously wasn't even trying to pay attention to the guide.

If I told him about the plot from the last book I read, he'd probably never speak to me again, so I shrugged. "The food has been amazing."

"It has." His hazel eyes lit up. "Oh, my God, did you have the lobster last night?"

My gaze trailed to his arm, slender and peppered with dark hair—same color as on his head. "Sure did...melted in my mouth."

"And the chocolate volcano dessert?"

Sheepishly, I scraped my teeth over my bottom lip. "I went for the fruit plate."

"Who eats fruit when there's an eruption of molten chocolate?"

I laughed. The guy was super thin but he talked like he ate as much as an offensive lineman. Did he have any idea how difficult it had been for this chocoholic to resist the volcano? "Maybe I'll try it next time it's on the menu."

"I noticed that, too. Especially with desserts—if you miss it one night, there's a pretty good chance you'll be able to get it later."

I pulled out the bottles of water and handed him one. "So, what has been *your* favorite part of the cruise so far?"

"Lots of things." He guzzled the entire bottle, then dropped it on the floor which I tried to catch with the toe of my daisy sandal, only managing to push it farther under the seat. I was a stickler for recycling, especially plastics because my mother was adamant that if people were more vigilant about recycling the millions of bottles her company produced, the oceans would be less polluted. "Last night's comedian was pretty good. And I really liked the show with all the singers and dancers."

"The shows have been great," I agreed, though I'd given the comedian a pass.

I finally trapped the bottle with my heel and leaned out into the aisle to pick it up.

"I won the basketball contest," Lance offered.

"Seriously?" My gaze slid to his knees now propped against the seat in front. Was he tall? "Did you play in college?"

"High school—guard." Lance looked aside. "Um...there wasn't enough time to play sports when I was in college."

I stowed the empty bottle in my backpack so I could drop it in the first recycle bin I found.

"What was your major?" he asked while the tour guide gestured to the buildings along the main street, reminding me of Disneyland with pinks, corals, yellows, and blues.

I glanced to the dude and grimaced. "You'll think it's boring."

"Me? No way." Lance nudged me with his elbow. "Come on...what? Basket weaving?"

I nudged him back. "Contrary to what someone from *The* Ohio State University might think, Wisconsin does not offer a basket weaving major."

"So, what then?" He looked at me as if my answer might be the most important tidbit of information he'd heard that day.

I think I liked this scruffy guy. Sort of. "I majored in biology, then got a masters in librarianship."

"Biology to librarianship? Is that a thing?"

"It was for me. I worked in the library when I was an undergrad, and decided it was the perfect place for a girl with a profound love of books who was about as sociable as a Hobbit."

"Books, huh?" Lance sounded intrigued as if reading were his favorite pastime, too. "So, I take it you're a librarian? Are you still at UW?"

"Yes to the first question—though I'm now an *assistant director* and I work for the La Crosse Public Library."

"La Crosse?" He narrowed those hazel eyes. "Where is that?"

"West side of the state. On the Mississippi." The bus had taken a turn down a winding, narrow road, every so often giving us a glimpse of a pink sandy beach while Lance and I swayed in tandem. "How about you? Where did you land after you got your degree?"

"A little hospital in Nowheresville Ohio."

"Are you a doctor?"

"Ah...yeah." A bit of pink tinged his cheeks as if he was a little shy, either that or he was afraid I was going to start talking about some awful affliction and ask him a bunch of questions.

But go figure, the dude wearing wrinkled khaki shorts and a Pabst Blue Ribbon retro t-shirt was an MD. One thing was for sure, the saying "you can't judge a book by its cover" certainly applied to Lance.

I took another sip of water then twisted the cap back on. "What's your discipline?"

The static from the speakers spiked with a grating crackle and he reverted his attention out the window. "What?"

"Did you specialize or are you a general practitioner?"

Lance pulled a ball cap out of his back pocket and jammed it on his head. "Definitely a generalist—emergency room stuff. That's where it's real, you know?"

"Well, I'd imagine so."

By the time the bus arrived, we friended each other on the ship's app which had everything you needed to know for the cruise. The best thing about the app was it worked at sea where there wasn't cell service. We followed the procession of tourists inside the gift shop and then to the cave's entrance. The temperature cooled noticeably as we descended the steps into a cavern as enchanting as a fairytale.

From the parking lot, no one would have guessed the beauty hiding underground, with ancient stalactites dangling like icicles from the ceiling. A wooden dock meandered through the center of the cave, the shallow aqua-blue water shimmering with iridescent lights. It was magical and ethereal. How incredible to think the formations began over thirty million years ago by one drip of water at a time.

I took a couple of selfies with Lance and posted the one of us on the bridge on Facebook because it was so perfect, we looked like we were in a dreamland. I bet that photo was going to make my mom happy—and sad because she hadn't been able to come along. Was I rubbing it in?

Probably.

If I were being honest with myself, it burned that she cancelled on me. All my life, she'd put her job first. As a teenager, I was more than a little resentful. As an adult, I do my best to insulate my feelings. I love her, but I also love myself.

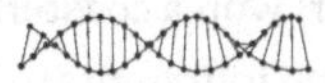

After the ship left Bermuda, Lance and I taste-tested a sampler in the ship's martini bar. We'd had a bottle of wine with dinner, so Miss Lightweight here was already buzzed. I gaped at the rack of six shot glasses in front of me. "Tell me again what each one is."

Lance leaned in, his shoulder nudging mine. "The clear one is the classic, then espresso, appletini, cosmo, lemon drop, and chocolate."

I handed the classic to him. "You have that one. It doesn't look sweet enough for me."

"All right." He sipped.

I took the chocolate, tapped his glass with mine, and we drank. "Oh, my God, this is better than a milkshake."

Lance licked his lips, setting down his empty glass. "I thought you'd like that one."

I pushed the rack toward him. "You choose the next round."

He took the espresso and gave me the lemon drop, which was almost as good as the chocolate, though I doubt anything would top the milkshake.

We each shared sips of the appletini and cosmo. I'd had a cosmopolitan before, so I knew I'd like it. I wasn't as keen on the apple-flavored liqueur, though. "So, what's next?" I swayed in my chair. "Anything but more booze."

Lance slung his arm around my shoulders and nuzzled into my ear. "Anything?" he asked, sounding like hot sex.

I shook the disc that was my room key. "You want to hook up?"

He kissed my earlobe, using just enough tongue. "I thought you'd never ask."

Oh, my effing God. Did I mention hot sex?

It might have been a while since I last slept with a man, but I certainly remembered how it was done—learned a few new moves as well. Three times. Before noon we managed to order room service. By one o'clock we decided to find the Outback Lounge to play a *Harry Potter* themed trivia game—which I won because, well, I'm a librarian. Lance came in a close second, but this Ravenclaw girl won a coaster.

After that, it took a whopping four hours to solve the murder in High Seas Heist, but of the three thousand five hundred people aboard, Lance and I won! And for our efforts we each received a cruise line hat and tote bag.

On the final night of the cruise, we went to the theater for a Broad-way-themed show during which he held my hand, kissing me, nuzzling my ear. By the time the production was over, I was ready to get naked.

He laced his fingers through mine. "Let's go to the bar for one last drink."

A better idea came to mind. "How about going to my suite and ordering room service?"

"Hmm," he ran kisses up my arm. "We did that last night. You pick the bar, okay?"

"If that's what you want. Let's go to the Skylight Lounge at the top of the ship because not only is there a fantastic view of the ocean, it's always quieter up there."

We sat at the bar and Lance ordered two old fashioneds, paying with his room fob. Because all my drinks were free, we'd been using mine, but he insisted on paying this time. Honestly, I appreciated the gesture.

"When do you have to be back at work?" he asked.

The bartender put the old fashioneds in front of us. "Monday. How about you?"

"Monday as well."

Tomorrow was Sunday, which didn't give us much time to get home and unwind. "I guess we'd better not have any flight delays—especially you."

Lance pushed one glass toward me and picked up the other. "Why just me?"

"Well, missing a shift when you're an ER doc is a whole lot more critical than it is for me at the library. I mean, it's not the end of the world if I don't show up for work on time, but with your job, people could die."

He took the swizzle stick and pulled the maraschino cherry off with his teeth. "Yeah. There is a lot of stress."

"But that's why you get so much time off, right?"

"Yep." He kissed me on the lips. "I need to use the little boy's room. Be right back, okay?"

I watched him saunter away while sipping my drink. This was probably the second old fashioned I'd had in my life and I was still trying to decide if I liked them or not. I usually preferred sweeter drinks with clear alcohol or wine.

"Is everything good here?" asked the bartender, tucking Lance's receipt under his glass.

"Yeah. Great. I can't believe we're already at the end of the cruise."

"Time flies, huh?"

"Sure does."

I glanced at the receipt peeking out from under Lance's glass. The first name was Virgil.

Virgil?

I slid the glass away, but the condensation from his drink had blotted out the rest of his name. I guess it didn't matter. He'd told me his last name was Lovell before we left Bermuda.

Was Lance his middle name?

If my name was Virgil, I'd probably use Lance as well. Glancing back to the doors, I took another sip, shrugging off the alarm bells. Lots of people went by their middle names. Heck, I used a nickname. I'd been Meg as long as I could remember. Any time someone other than my mother called me Margaret, it took me a beat to realize they were talking to me.

As I turned my stool, Lance strolled back inside. I pointed to the receipt. "Hey, I—"

"I wanted to talk to you, too," he interrupted, sliding his fingers through his hair. I raised my eyebrows, encouraging him to continue. "Um...I have a super early flight, and well, my life is so busy I wanted to make sure I thanked you for the good time, okay?"

The temperature in the bar suddenly went from freezing to unbearably hot. My pits stung. My face burned like I'd just been slapped.

Holy shit, I know we hadn't labeled our fling, but was he breaking up with me? Then again, if we were only casual, could we really breakup? Was this one of those micro-breakups I'd seen all over Instagram?

"Okaaay...?" I said, my mouth deciding this was the time to become inarticulate. "D-did I do something wrong?"

"No way, you're totally amazing." Lance's damned hand landed on my shoulder, his fingers squeezing. "Thanks for the good times, Meg. I had ton of fun."

"But what about—?"

As the bastard all but sprinted out of the lounge, I glanced at the bartender out of the corner of my eye. Thank God he was across the room and hadn't overheard. I'd just been micro-ditched by a guy who not a half-hour ago was necking with me during a Broadway show. Ohio wasn't that damned far away from Wisconsin. We could have at least *pretended* we were going to stay in touch.

I finished the rest of my drink, not quite ready to move yet. If I tried, my legs might give out. Was micro-ditching a thing?

Dammit, I was having such a good time, and now I'm going home pissed!

Chapter Four

Jane

Dear God, my brain-drain had me on the verge of turning into the Wicked Witch of the East. I was wound so tightly, it was all I could do not to bite anyone's head off for asking something as trivial as the time of day. I'd spent the past three weeks in a quagmire of hell, leading the Philly team and working around the clock as we all but summoned miracles to keep Hydroade from dropping us and moving their business to the competition. Curt's warning that the customer was out for blood had been an understatement. With their every demand, my people jumped through miniscule hoops, performing feats of greatness, only to be met with yet another outrageous request.

The problem was they'd all but incinerated our contract and we were dangling over the abyss of Mount Doom, about to turn to ash.

I personally interviewed the thirty-two employees who had come in contact with the contaminated bottle with no success. I met with the police and attorneys (ours *and* theirs). All the while Hydroade kept ramping up their mandates. The last one? Fire all thirty-two hard-working employees. And my idiot boss Leon actually told the CEO of Hydroade I'd take care of the mass termination without discussing it with me first. They were all good employees. One who worked in maintenance was a single father and could fix anything. Another was a single mother who took extra shifts to feed her kids. Leon didn't care, but I cared, God dammit.

If only I'd shirked my duty, taken my well-earned vacation, and gone on the cruise with Meg, my limbs might not be dragging as if I'd been put on a medieval rack and stretched to within an inch of my life.

In desperate need of a break, I flew home for the Fourth of July weekend. Today was the first full day I'd had to myself in what felt like forever. Though I'd worked out every morning in the hotel fitness room, my muscles were weighed down like they'd coagulated into lard. When I wasn't in "firefighting" mode at work, I usually arranged my schedule so I could be home on Wednesday and Thursday nights for advanced karate classes.

But tonight I called my sparring partner Renee to meet me at the dojo for a real workout. The studio was in a strip-mall and was long and spacious. One wall was lined with mirrors and there were six seven-foot punching bags at the far end. I was about halfway into my warmup when Renee pushed through the door with a grin. She was a good six inches taller and had two teenage daughters who were naturals.

"Where are the girls?" I watched her in the mirrors, both of us dressed in black gis and pants with our prized black belts knotted around our waists.

Renee joined me on the mat, jogging around the circumference. "Are you kidding? Ever since Molly got her driver's license, they're always out with their friends on Saturday nights."

Molly was the youngest. "When did she turn sixteen?" I asked, throwing a roundhouse at a punching bag.

"Whoa, you really have been burning the candle at both ends." Renee ran to the center of the mat and did a few jumping jacks. "Her birthday was a month ago."

I made a mental note to order a belated gift card. Renee was a single mom and worked for the post office, so I tried to remember her daughters' birthdays. We'd started taking karate classes about the same time, and we were fairly close in age, so we were always paired together...

Okay, I was eighteen years older but that's nothing when you're an adult (if only I really believed that).

When I was a white belt, I jumped into the sparring ring with a green belt who was about twenty and a good fifty pounds heavier than me. It only took one strike and I went down with a concussion—not just a concussion. One little bop on top of my noggin and I was out cold.

I awoke in an ambulance with a screaming headache throbbing at the back of my head. Needless to say, I wasn't happy—asked the medic to give me some smelling salts and turn me loose. He didn't listen, but the ER doc did. After shining a light in my eyes, he told me to take some ibuprofen, and sent me home with concussion info.

The doctor did caution me, however. He said that at my age it was best to avoid strikes to the head. *My age?* I wasn't old then, and I still don't consider myself to be even though my hair has turned gray and started falling out. Because I went gray early, I had used the same strawberry-blonde dye for decades. One day my follicles suddenly decided they couldn't take it any longer. And now it's only getting thinner. I wear my hair long so I can style it in a bun with a comb-over which hides the thin spots (so embarrassing).

Fortunately, after the concussion incident, my sensei paired me with Renee who is savvy enough to only hit me with light taps. In our discipline, a strike is a strike no matter how hard or soft and, since I started working opposite her, I haven't had a single concussion.

Renee faced me in the center of the mat. We'd become such a team, neither of us had to utter a sound before we launched into a routine of strikes and kicks.

She parried away my jab. "Your job has you traveling too much, huh?"

I blocked her side kick. She didn't know the half of it. "It's been relentless."

"I have no idea how you cope."

After we'd gone through our routine twice, we bowed to each other. "Did we cover anything new?" I asked.

She began a series of random strikes, which I parried and blocked. "Nope. Since we're getting close to the tournament, we've been perfecting our forms and sparring."

We bowed again before turning toward the mirrors. "At least I was able to get up early and practice every morning."

She stretched her arms before bending over and touching her toes. "You going to be able to make it to the test?" she asked.

"Yep," I replied, my voice confident, though doubt needled its way under my skin.

Who knew where I'd be in a month? I had terminated the thirty-two souls who had come in contact with the contaminated bottle. Of course, to avoid litigation, we'd given all of them nice severance packages along with placement assistance to help them find new jobs. The problem was we weren't any closer to finding the real culprit. The police didn't get anywhere with fingerprints and the film from the security cameras was useless, especially since there were only cameras on the doors. At least that's what my IT guy said—then I made him give me a flash drive with the footage, not that I had time to watch six months of film.

Renee and I went through our kata form—the one we'd been practicing ever since we'd earned our black belts. Next month we'd be testing for our second-degree, and no matter how much I'd practiced in the hotel fitness room, I hadn't had the benefit of our sensei's scrutiny in weeks. I wobbled a bit here and there, not sure why my balance was off. Maybe it was the stress of everything? Who knew? At least I had the moves down.

"How are you doing with the fitness part of the test?" asked Renee.

I eyed her in the mirror. "You would ask that, wouldn't you?" I glanced back at myself, noting the dark smudges under my eyes and the gray at my temples. Jeez, when did middle age creep up on me?

Renee stood with her feet apart, her hands gripped under her chin. "Let's go. One hundred and twenty-five squats."

"Bring it!"

I clenched my fists, willing the goddesses of youth to fill me, and motivating the pair of us by calling out the count of each. These weren't old-lady squats, these were deep knee bends, making my butt nearly touch the floor. By the time we reached ninety, my thighs burned, I was sucking in air, and the back of my head started pounding like it did whenever a migraine was coming on. I forced myself to keep going. Even though my voice wasn't nearly as powerful for the last twenty-eight, I got through them. I'd been doing three sets of fifty squats in my workouts, but I was going to have to start forcing myself to do all one hundred twenty-five from now until the tournament.

I shook out my legs, taking a few deep breaths. "You ready for pushups?"

"Thirty?"

We'd earned our black belts with twenty-five but the next level was thirty. In my book the pushups were tough, but not as grueling as the squats. I dropped into the plank position. "One!"

This time, Renee and I called out the count together, but no matter how much prep work I did, at number twenty-two, my arms started shaking, about to give out. The throbbing at the back of my head punished me with a tsunami of a migraine, pounding in my skull with the force of a ball peen hammer.

I gnashed my teeth and bent my elbows for number twenty-eight. Halfway down, my head exploded as if someone had smashed open my skull and started tightening a tourniquet around my brain with an iron wrench.

The room went black.

Ice pulsed through my veins.

Dropping to the mat, I shrieked, "Ow, ow, ow!"

My breathing sped. The torturous, unbearable pressure gripping my skull was as relentless as a boa constrictor's vise. God save me, I've been plagued by migraines my entire life, but this was pain beyond pain, beyond tolerable.

Far worse than breaking my hand or tearing my adductor muscle, or having my brother slam the car door on my ankle.

On my belly, I pressed the heels of my shaking hands against my temples. "I can't see, I can't see!" I screamed, the pressure so intense, I was positive my gray matter was about to burst out my eardrums.

"Ow! Ow! Ow!" I gasped again, my breath coming in short staccato spurts. I blinked over and over. I squeezed my eyes shut, willing my vision to come back.

Now!

"Oh, my God, Jane!" Renee was by my side, her hand on my shoulder. "What happened?"

All I could do was suck in air, staring at the mat and seeing only blackness while a cold chill snaked up my spine. What the hell was happening?

"Are you all right?"

I wasn't anything close to being all right. I was in the most excruciating pain I've ever experienced in my life and I still couldn't see. I clenched my fists and shuddered. What if I ended up blind forever?

"Give me a minute," I finally said, rolling to my back.

As suddenly as the blindness had come on, my vision returned, the experience surreal, as if someone drew open the curtains in a theater. The halogens above glared, contrasting hazily with the black ceiling.

Renee kneeled over me, her eyes enormous and filled with worry. She pointed to her phone which was safely stowed by the mirrors. "Should I call an ambulance?"

I blinked, slower this time. The pounding in my head eased a bit. I might have been pretty damned dazed, but I was confident that my vision was as clear now as it had been before I collapsed—at least it was close.

No ambulance. No way! "I think I'm okay."

The last time I ended up in an ambulance had been an utter waste of time. On top of that, about ten years ago I'd had a similar sudden, screaming migraine and went to the ER where they didn't even bother to draw blood. They gave me Benadryl and Tylenol and a printout about migraines (yet again). I swear, going to a doctor about thunderous, screaming head pain was totally useless. They'd take one look at me, mumble under their breath that it was a typical woman who complained about every little ache and pain, then they'd roll their elitist eyeballs and tell me I was imagining things.

"Seriously?" She gawked at me as if I were delirious. "I've never seen anybody go down like that. What exactly happened to you?"

I tried to sit up but when the room began to spin, I eased myself back to the mat. "The mother of all migraines came on." God, my words garbled like a drunk. "Suddenly I felt like someone had tied a tourniquet around my brain and was cranking it so tight it made me go blind."

She patted my knee. "Whoa, that's scary. You should go to the doctor, lady."

It was late. It was also the eve of a holiday. The emergency rooms across Denver were probably all filled with kids who'd been mishandling firecrackers. I made myself sit up, still a bit woozy, the room rocking like a ship at sea.

My gaze shifted back to the ceiling. "I don't know..." Jeez, I hardly recognized my voice.

"You want me to drive you?"

After spending the past few weeks in hell, I just couldn't deal with going into a hospital and having some resident treat me as if I'd imagined everything. "Nah, I'll be okay in a minute."

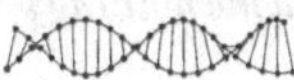

"What do you mean you didn't go to the doctor?" Meg shrieked over the phone.

I shouldn't have told her about the incident Saturday night, but I'd mentioned it because this was Monday and I still felt dazed. And though I was no stranger to headaches, I'd never completely gone blind before. "You know I have an aversion to doctors."

I did. Medical practitioners were always so belittling.

"Yeah, but this is different. You said you collapsed. You said you went blind for about a minute. That's not normal, Mom."

I put the kettle on to make a cup of tea. It was nine o'clock in the morning and I was still wearing my nightie—very unlike me. "Maybe it's just all the stress at work."

"I'm sure it is, but you have the day off, right?" Meg asked. "You need to go to urgent care."

Ugh!

I loathed doctor appointments. Did everyone else leave their doctor's offices feeling as if they had not been heard? Maybe misdiagnosed if not undiagnosed? Possibly judged?

In my experience, it never failed when, after being ushered into an exam room and explaining the reason for my visit, a pronounced furrow would form in the doctor's brow and he or she would regard me with a quizzical expression as if I had to be insane. Either that, or I might have been inept at describing the reason for my visit because, time after time, I left their hallowed offices feeling foolish as if those well-educated practitioners of medicine considered me to be a hypochondriac.

Which I most certainly was not.

"Yeah," I replied. "I do have today off since Independence Day was Sunday, but I need to fly out tomorrow."

"So what? You have to be seen. Should I catch a plane to Denver and drag you to the ER?"

I sighed. Meg could be so emotional at times. "No."

"Then promise me you'll at least go to urgent care."

I pulled off the lid from the canister of English breakfast tea. "I don't—"

"Promise me!" she demanded.

"Okay, I'll go." *Then they'll tell me nothing is wrong and I'll leave gulping back my bruised pride.*

"I'll be calling you tonight and I want to know the results."

⫸⫷

I barely made it in the door of my executive town house when my phone buzzed with a call from my daughter. I answered and tossed my purse on the white leather couch. "Hi, Meg, it's not evening yet."

"Please tell me you went to urgent care."

"Total waste of effort." Dear God, how many times did I need to be told I suffered from migraines? "The doctor at the urgent care sent me to the ER where they did a CT of my head followed by an MRI of my head, and then pronounced me perfectly fine...aside from a touch of double vision."

"You didn't tell me about the double vision!"

I dropped onto the couch and reached for my Yorkshire Terrier tapestry pillow, clutching it across my stomach. I'd really like to have a dog, but with my hours, pets were out of the question. Jeez, I couldn't even keep a potted plant alive.

"I swear the doctor had two pointer fingers on his right hand. But he was adamant he only had one." Honestly, he moved his finger all around the room as if I might see the damned finger more clearly if I looked at it from different angles.

"They didn't find *anything* with all those tests?"

I set the pillow beside me. "Nope. They said if I had a TIA or something, there was no sign of it by the time I went in."

"You should have gone in immediately."

That's what they told me at the hospital.

"I don't think it's normal to go blind from a migraine," Meg added.

I didn't think so either, which is why I agreed to be seen, but what did I know? I wasn't a doctor. Moreover, I had no time to be sick right now. If I'd had a stroke, it would have been an unmitigated disaster. "Well, at least they didn't find anything, so I'm clear to fly to Philly tomorrow morning."

"Philly again? Why is that plant so awful?"

I could go on about the tampering incident and Hydroade's outlandish demands, or the fact that we had a multi-million-dollar contract on the chopping block and everyone involved was cosmically stressed. Top that off with a new union takeover (very poorly timed if you ask me), and I'd never been in this much shit in my life.

"You know Philly," I said in my sweetest voice, looking at the Yorkshire Terrier on my pillow which now seemed to have four eyes. My head pounded and, even though I hadn't gone on the cruise, the room would not stop swaying from port to starboard. "It's my Achilles' heel."

Chapter Five

Meg

As soon as I had decent cell service, I found Lance Lovell on Facebook but not on any other social media. His profile said he lived in Darbydale, Ohio, which I Googled. The population was only seven hundred ninety-three and they didn't have a hospital, but being close to Columbus, there were several within driving distance.

I'd been home from vacation for two weeks and two days. Today, I sat at the library's main desk and scrolled through Lance's Facebook photos. He looked like a surfer dude in his profile picture, just as he did the first time I saw him on the bus. His pictures were gorgeous and all from his travels—rainforests, Iceland, Europe, Mexico. There was one of a Bermudian sunset, but I wasn't in it. Actually, his pictures either were solo selfies or of landmarks. I wondered if he always hooked up with a willing female when he was on vacation.

Probably.

Maybe that's why he never posts pictures of anyone besides himself?

"Hello," said a deep voice from across the library's counter.

I glanced up from my phone and plastered on my friendly librarian smile. "Hi! How can I help you?"

The man facing me wore glasses, his expression serious and inquisitive, his dark-chocolate-colored hair cropped and neatly combed, making me wonder if it was always that perfect or if it was ever mussed like Lance's. "I've recently moved to La Crosse—bought a Victorian on Tenth Street and wanted to do some research about it."

I nodded reassuringly. After all, customer service was a crucial part of public librarianship. "Well, you came to the right place."

He shoved his hands into his jeans' pockets as if he might be shy. "My realtor said you'd be able to help?"

"Absolutely." Alas, my cue to push up from my chair, put my phone away, and step out from behind the counter. "You'll find everything you need in the Archives. There's a section of the library exclusively for historical research—even the City of La Crosse uses us to store their documents." I beckoned him. "It's upstairs. If you'll follow me, I'll introduce you to the archivist."

He fell in step, his lips twisting. "Can't *you* show me the documents?"

Was he flirting? *Nah.* "Nope," I cheerfully replied, flicking my hair. "Otherwise I'd be upstairs sitting at Monique's desk."

The man was taller than Lance—about six feet two. He looked fit, like someone who might be into biking or hiking. "Thanks."

I glanced at the computer processing icon on his black t-shirt with the tag line, "I'm thinking." *Does Amazon sell those in pink...maybe chartreuse?* "Where'd you move from?"

"Madison."

What a perfect place for a techie geek to be from. "Madison is nice, but it has grown too big for me. What brings you to La Crosse?"

"Work."

I arched my eyebrows, but he didn't volunteer anything further and I wasn't about to press the man. I'd already pegged him as a techie type—though judging by his Tag Hauer smartwatch and trendy haircut, he was a high-end geek. Maybe he was the head of technology at Trane or one of the larger companies in town.

I stopped outside the Archives department and gestured to the woman sitting behind the L-shaped desk inside. "This is Monique. She'll be able to assist with the research on your house."

The man glanced her way, then back at me. He had soulful gray eyes and our gazes connected for a tad longer than was comfortable. "Thank you."

Being a redhead, I was prone to blushing and my face burned as I smiled at them both. "I think you'll like living in La Crosse. It's a small town, but if you ask me, it has everything you need. Both Monique and I did our undergrads here and then went to Madison for our masters."

He glanced at the back room with the rows of shelves barely visible through the doorway, then Mr. Geek again met my gaze—goodness, he had intense eyes. "What do you like most about it?"

I looked at Monique while a gazillion things riffled through my mind. "The historic downtown. Great theater and local musicians. The changes of season. The mighty Mississippi and how all living things rely on the river, even humanity. There are awesome hiking trails around Grandad's Bluff. You'll never be at a loss for something to do here."

Monique's head bobbed in agreement, her eyes wide.

"Here?" he asked.

"Hey, it's a college town. I don't lie. Just check *explorelacross.com*, there's bound to be something to interest you." Before I made a stupid remark like offering to take him on a Friday night pub crawl along our infamous Third Street, I gestured to the archivist. "Well, I'll leave you in Monique's capable hands."

Heading down the stairs, Elaine had taken my spot manning the counter. I considered changing directions and going to my closet-sized office to work on next month's schedule, but her face lit up as she caught my eye, beckoning me with both hands. "Who was that?" she whisper-shouted as I approached.

I suppose I should have introduced myself to the man and asked his name. But then again, we had a lot of visitors come into the library whom we never saw again. "A new La Crosse resident. He bought a Victorian and wants to do some research."

She batted her eyelashes, which made me snort because Elaine's glasses magnified her green eyes to comical proportions like Disney's Honey Lemon. "He's kinda cute."

I glanced back up the stairs, my stomach fluttering. I ignored it. God knows what happened the last time I opened up to a cute dude. "Ya think?"

Elaine adjusted her headband—light brown hair, flawless skin. Yep, she could totally pull off playing Honey Lemon in a local production of *Big Hero 6*. "Hey, what gives? You still haven't spilled any details about the stud in your Facebook posts."

"Lance?" I tried to sound like I hardly knew what she was talking about. Maybe I was also trying to convince myself that he was as insignificant as a gnat. And I did delete the pictures with him, obviously not before all my friends saw them. "Didn't I say we agreed what happens on a cruise stays on the cruise?"

"Yeah, but that's not your style." My bestie pushed the glasses up the bridge of her nose.

"Maybe not, but that's how we ended it." I busied myself by straightening the lane stanchion across from the checkout desk. "Besides, long-distance relationships never work."

"Damn shame." Elaine tapped the keyboard of her computer. "Hey, you're still going to the symphony with me Saturday, right?"

"I wouldn't miss it," I replied, welcoming the change in subject.

"I'll pick you up—it's my turn."

"Sounds good. Six-thirty?"

"Yep."

As I headed for my office, I lit up my phone. It was still opened to Lance's Facebook page. Interestingly, he hadn't posted any pictures since Bermuda. What was he doing now? I hovered my finger over the "friend" button and held it there. Sure, he didn't want to have a long-distance relationship. How could I blame him? He was a doctor. The dude was super busy with a stressful job. Hell, I was busy, but that was no reason not to be friends on social media.

Right?

I tapped the damned button and turned off my screen. If he didn't friend me back he was a total douche. If he did friend me back, then...

Who knows what might happen?

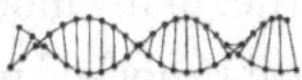

I lived in one of La Crosse's old houses that had been converted into apartments. Mine was on the ground floor and had a beautiful, south-facing bay window which let in a lot of light. It was cozy, with boring white walls and hardwood floors. My furniture was wicker and I'd decorated the couch and chairs with Bohemian pillows and throws in a riot of color—put a boho carpet on the floor in shades of oranges, reds, pinks, and blues. Sure, my walls might be white, but I wanted color in my life. A lot of it.

I've been saving like a fiend to buy my own place, especially since the dude who recently moved in upstairs cranks up the bass on his stereo so loud it not only rattles my eardrums, it shakes the entire house right down to the foundations. As Elaine pulled up outside, the plates in my cupboard clattered. I swear, the bass was so overpowering, I couldn't even hear the music—just the deep thump, thump, thump pounding in the back of my head.

It had now been two weeks and six days since I got home from the cruise and right before my neighbor's music interrupted my lovely quiet, I got a notification saying Lance had accepted my friend request. I didn't message him immediately because that might make me look too needy. Besides, Elaine and I had a date with the symphony and I wasn't about to sit through an entire concert looking at my phone, willing it to light up with a reply from him. When her horn tooted, I slipped my feet into my bright red heels, grabbed a scarlet shawl, my purse, and managed not to twist an ankle as I dashed for the car.

"Have you called the cops about that dude yet?" Elaine asked while I slid into the seat of her Mini. "I can hear his sound system over the rev of my engine."

I fastened the seatbelt, looking up to the second floor. I wasn't good at confrontation—at least not with people I didn't know. Mom or someone like Elaine who I'd known for years—no problem. The hairy beast who lived above me? That was going to take some strategizing. "It's on the list."

She snorted. "You're not going to call the cops are you?"

"No!" I smacked her arm with my purse. "I'd rather talk to him first."

Elaine put the car in gear and turned down State Street. "Okay, when?"

"What do you care?" I asked, making a mental note to march up the stairs and pound on his door the very next time he wasn't playing music so he'd be able to hear me. I bit the corner of my mouth. Maybe I shouldn't pound. Perhaps he'd be more receptive if I knocked politely?

Before Elaine answered my question, a car came racing up Eighth Street and ran the stop sign. Elaine slammed on the brakes, the wheels screeching.

"Argh!" I screamed, my body lurching forward. As I was stopped by the seatbelt, my head whipped back against the headrest.

"Asshole!" Elaine shouted, continuing through the intersection.

With my next breath I doubled over shrieking, the pain excruciating as if a vampire hunter had driven an iron spike into my neck and up into my brain. My hands flew to my head. "Ow, ow, ow!"

"Meg!" Elaine shouted, the car lurching as she swerved to the curbside.

I dry heaved with the jerking motion. "Ow!" I screamed, cringing, and squeezing my eyes shut, trying to make the pain go away.

She put the car in park. "What's wrong?"

Opening my eyes, I stared straight ahead, but everything was blurry. I blinked and opened wider. Holy shit, I'd gone blind in my right eye. "I can't see!"

"But I just braked hard," She patted my shoulder. "Nobody hit us."

God dammit, I'd never been in this much pain in my life. "I-I don't know, my head snapped back, and now I swear my brain is about to explode out of my skull!"

Elaine waved a hand in front of my face. "Can you see this?"

My hands shook and my heart was beating so fast, my blood pressure had to be in the ozone. I blinked against the tears welling in my eyes. "O-only out of my left eye and i-it's blurry."

"Crap!" She put the car in gear, peeling rubber as she pulled onto the street, the sudden acceleration making stars dart through my vision. "Hang on! I'm taking you to the hospital."

Chapter Six

Meg

"The CT scan of your neck indicates that you've dissected your right carotid and right vertebral arteries," said the ER doc who looked nothing like Lance and more like a blurry grandfather. "Though your brain scan is clear, your symptoms indicate you've had a TIA. And your blood pressure is too high. I'm going to have to admit you."

Dissected arteries? I didn't know arteries could be affected just because a car braked hard. And what had he said? TIA?

I'd heard that term before but couldn't recall what it stood for. In fact, I don't think my mind was firing on all cylinders. "What's a TIA?" I asked, sounding a bit garbled and spaced out.

"It's an acronym for transient ischemic attack—a mini-stroke—one that doesn't necessarily leave you paralyzed."

Oh, no. People my age didn't have strokes. "I don't think I had a TIA."

Nonetheless, I was confused, totally dazed, my head still pounded. The whole experience was unreal. When we arrived at the ER door, they had to put me in a wheelchair because my left leg gave out. But it couldn't have been a stroke. I was way too young. "Wait a minute. I think my mom had this same thing last week but they told her she just had a migraine."

Please be a migraine.

"Did they do a CT of her neck and head?" asked the doctor.

"I think so." What was it she'd told me? She'd been in the ER and had both a CT and an MRI. But I'm positive she only mentioned her head. Good thing Mom didn't have high blood pressure, I guess.

The doctor patted my shoulder. "Well, I can't speak to what happened to your mother, but you are lucky because your friend acted quickly."

"Good morning," said the overly chipper nurse who came into my room before dawn. "I need to take some blood."

No wonder people complained about not being able to sleep in hospitals. Couldn't the bloodletting wait until after breakfast? I held out my arm, feeling like vampire fodder. I could swear they'd taken a pint of blood since last night.

After I was admitted, I called Mom. Of course, she wanted to hop on a flight immediately, but there was a lightning storm in Denver and all the planes had been grounded, which was probably a blessing. My mother had hardly been home in the past several weeks, and she needed some down time—the woman needed to go on the cruise for some mega destressing, but that didn't happen because she was married to her damned job.

"When can I go home?" I asked while the blood pressure cuff on my other arm started inflating.

I winced as the nurse inserted the needle and drew the plunger outward. "I'm not sure. The referring doctor recommended you be seen by a neurologist and a vascular surgeon."

"I don't need surgery, do I?"

Once the vial was full of dark-red blood, she pulled out the needle and wrapped my arm. "That's probably best answered by the doctors. At least I can say you're not scheduled for surgery."

The blood pressure cuff deflated and the monitor read 140 over 89. Damn. I'd been having trouble with high blood pressure since graduate school. My father suffered from hypertension as well, not that he ever complained about it much to me. I guess I'd have to let him know about this incident—later. After I was home and back to one hundred percent. I didn't want him feeling like he had to fly across the Pacific Ocean or anything.

Not that he would. I was always the one who flew to Australia.

I lit up my phone—the battery had fallen to ten percent. First, I sent a text to Elaine, politely asking her to bring in a charger.

Next, I held my breath while I opened Facebook. When the bubble indicated someone had messaged me, my heart jumped onto a treadmill, beating out of rhythm, and making the machine beside my bed beep erratically. I clicked open messenger while taking deep breaths to settle back into a steady beat that wouldn't send the nurses charging in here with a defibrillator.

Still, my hands were shaking and if I weren't in the hospital, I'd jump out of bed and launch into the Electric Slide. I knew the connection we had on the cruise in Bermuda meant something!

Lance: *Hey, Meg, thanks for friending me. I've been thinking about you a lot and feel bad about how we left things. I didn't mean to be a jerk. Glad we're still friends.*

I reread his note, mentally accepting the apology, thrilled about being friends. I guess given the six hundred miles between us, that was better than zilch. Besides, neither one of us made any promises. Maybe we could be friends with benefits? Alternatively, maybe I just had a TIA and still wasn't thinking straight?

I replied: *Hey, great to hear from you. I'm sorry to bug you but I'm in the hospital—dissected carotid and vertebral arteries. The ER doc said I had a TIA. I'm sure you probably hate hearing from friends about health stuff, but can you give me the inside scoop about this?*

Of course, he didn't respond right away and by the time Elaine showed up with a charger, my phone was dead.

She took charge of plugging it in. "How are you doing?"

The usual came to mind—scared, freaked out, and anxious about when or if I'd get another message from Lance. My head was still pounding as well, but not wanting to sound like a complainer, I replied, "Aside from my brain being in a fog as if I'm in the Twilight Zone, I'm great. Ready to run a marathon."

"Right. When was the last time you ran anywhere?"

I snorted. "I think I ran to the bathroom a week ago."

She slid into a guest chair that looked like a recliner. "TMI, girlfriend."

"You asked."

"Is your mom coming?"

"She couldn't get a flight last night, then I told her not to. I mean, I'm sitting up and my vision is clearer. Besides, she's so stressed at the moment, the last thing she needs is to worry needlessly because of me."

"You're her only daughter. She's predisposed to worry and now you're in the hospital. Grave concern is appropriate in this case. Heck, *I'm* still gravely concerned."

A doctor came in and introduced himself as a neurologist. Elaine slipped out, saying she had to get back to work. I watched her leave. Damn, why didn't I ask her to trade places with me?

He took me through a series of tests, including the ability of my arms to resist pressure up, down, in, out. He used a penlight to look into my eyes. I told him I'd had some blurriness and had lost sight in my right eye for a few minutes last night. He had me walk across the floor, which I did without any problem. Thank heavens my left leg was back to normal.

He studied the notes on his tablet. "Do you routinely suffer from migraines?"

"Yes."

"What do you take for them?"

I took the same thing my mother did. "Two ibuprofen and two acetaminophen. If that doesn't help, I take two Benadryl and go to bed."

"Have you ever taken migraine medication?" he asked.

"Nope. I've never seen a neurologist, either."

"Interesting. Well, there's a new medicine available that is effective for patients with vascular issues. I think you might see an improvement if you'd like to try something new."

Now I've been classified as having vascular issues? God! "Sure, if you think it will help."

"I'll write a prescription," he said, reading again. "There's a note from the ER doc that says your mother had a similar incident about a week ago?"

"She did—not from whiplash but hers happened when she was working out."

"Did she have carotid and vertebral dissections as well?"

I was thinking a little clearer now, and I was positive she said the ER in Denver only scanned her head. "They didn't find anything with Mom, but last night the doctor in the emergency room said dissections would have shown up on a CT of the neck, right?"

"Correct. At least yours were in the neck."

"I'm pretty sure Mom only had her head scanned."

"Hmm." The doctor tucked his tablet under his arm. "I believe we might better understand your situation if we knew if your mother had a dissection or not. Do you think she could get a CT of her neck...*today*?"

I shrugged. My mom abhorred doctor appointments, but neither of us had a run-of-the-mill headache. "I could call her and ask."

"Good. Let me know what she says—as well as her results."

"How do I reach you?" I asked.

"You can send a message to my office through the patient portal. In the meantime, I'm going to order some blood tests."

I glanced at the purple bruise where they took blood last night. "For what?"

The neurologist stepped toward the door like he had somewhere else to go. "Just some standard tests to rule out the big things like Lupus and protein imbalances."

After he left, the nurse drew more blood. My phone had enough charge for me to call Mom and ask her to get a CT of her neck. Of course, she balked, so I told her it was an emergency because the neurologist desperately needed her results right away to help with my diagnosis. I also reiterated that I definitely did not want her to fly to La Crosse. She'd been pretty sketchy about what was going on in Philly, but I could tell by the sound of her voice that she was more stressed than usual. At least she was home for the weekend, and that's where I wanted her to stay.

Thank God she agreed rather than charge up here in her battle armor.

When I checked Facebook, Lance had messaged me again.

His reply: *A TIA is caused by a sudden blockage of blood flow to the brain and doesn't last long. It sounds like they're taking care of you. I hope so. Miss U.*

Me: *I'm dazed and my head aches, but I want to go home, so that's a good sign, right?*

I waited, noticing there wasn't a green dot by his name, so he had to be offline.

Smiling, I typed another line: *Miss you, too.*

After I ate a French dip for lunch, the vascular surgeon came in. The man hardly looked at me and didn't refer to his tablet like the neurologist. He told me he wasn't convinced that I'd had arterial dissections and that he disagreed with the ER doc about the TIA diagnosis.

In his estimation, since I suffered from migraines, the little bit of whiplash from Elaine's hard braking made a mega headache come on and I ought to be fine in a day or two. He had the audacity to roll his eyes and tell me a braking incident definitely would never cause simultaneous dissections and that the radiologist must have been mistaken. Then he decided to discharge me with some minor restrictions—such as no hard braking when riding in a car, and no amusement park rides...

"Just to exercise caution," he said.

I squinted at him, a ping pong ball bouncing from one side of my brain to the other. How could two doctors have such differing opinions within the span of a couple of hours? Since he was a vascular expert, did his diagnosis override the other two docs?

Did he expect me to tell all the bad drivers out there not to run stop signs? "Do I need to follow up?"

"Not with me. You'll get discharge instructions from the nurse," he replied, walking out the door.

I stared at his vanishing white coat. He didn't even ask me if I had questions. His visit couldn't have lasted more than five minutes and now I was totally confused. *But what about the neurologist who insisted Mom get the CT of her neck? Don't these doctors talk to each other? This guy didn't even ask me to describe the event or the pain or the numbness in my leg or the blindness in one eye. Did he even read the notes? Did he look at the CAT scan images?*

It stung like a slap to the face to have the surgeon walk into this room, take one look at a healthy young adult female and decide I was one of those women who complained about every little ache and was not to be taken seriously. Furthermore, I could swear on a Bible I had just been victimized by medical gender bias!

My face burned as I stared down at my hospital gown and the white cotton blanket over my lap. Mom always complained that doctors made her feel like a hypochondriac, and right now, sitting here alone with machines beeping behind me, I knew exactly what she meant. I'd just experienced the most frightening and painful incident in my life and it seemed as if nobody could agree about what was wrong with me, or at least nobody knew how to treat it. If it weren't for the IV in my arm, I might have walked out right here and now.

What really happened in the car last night? What had caused so much excruciating pain? The blindness in one eye and the weakness in my left leg? Had the ER doc been mistaken? Was the radiologist's report way off? If so, why was my brain still foggy and hanging out in the land of Aquarius?

Since Lance hadn't responded to my latest Facebook message, I Googled "TIA."

At the very top of my search it read: *"A transient ischemic attack (TIA) is a stroke that lasts only a few minutes. It occurs when the blood supply to part of the brain is briefly interrupted. TIA symptoms, which usually occur suddenly, are similar to those of stroke but do not last as long."*

The following line stopped my breath, chills slithering up my arms: "*TIA's are often ignored which is a critical mistake.*"

CHAPTER SEVEN

JANE

If Meg needed me to have a CT scan of my neck, by God, I was going to get one regardless of if I had to cancel "vital" meetings in Philly. I drove to the same urgent care I'd been to a week ago—the one with the doctor who'd sent me to the ER. To my chagrin, that doc wasn't on shift. When I explained everything that had happened both to me and Meg to the new physician, he sat with his elbow on the desk and his chin in his palm. He stared at me without an inkling of empathy, his expression dull, judgmental, and condescending.

He didn't need to open his mouth and utter a word. The man had already pegged me as a neurotic, health-obsessed female. Nonetheless, I swallowed my pride and persevered. "My daughter's neurologist said it is crucial for me to get a CT scan of my neck immediately."

The man straightened and groaned, shifting his eyes to the wall as if this was the hundredth time he'd heard a woman ask for a needless CAT scan today. "Honestly, I don't believe it's necessary. You seem perfectly fine now."

Mother-effing asshole!

How did he know if I was fine or not? Aside from shaking my hand when he entered, he hadn't touched me.

I hated.

Abhorred.

Absolutely loathed being judged as a hypochondriac wimp—being gaslighted as if having a vagina made me too dumb to know my own body. As if being a woman put me in a category of patients who were never to be taken seriously.

I'd spent hours reading every credible article and web post I could find about carotid and vertebral dissections. They were absolutely scary and I was not about to take no for an answer. "Please." I resorted to pleading. "I'm not asking for myself, I'm asking for my daughter who is an inpatient at

Gustafsson Hospital in La Crosse, Wisconsin and, as I said, her neurologist insists it's critical for me to be scanned *immediately*." I grabbed my phone and held it up. "We can call them if you'd like."

After a great deal of hemming and hawing, the man finally agreed. "If it will give you peace of mind…"

By this stage, I'd kiss his feet if he told me that's what it would take to get the damned test. "Yes. I need peace of mind, thank you." So did my baby, and if I couldn't be in Wisconsin holding her hand and making sure the doctors were giving her the proper care, I was going to help in any way I could—screw the eye rolls and my hypochondria paranoia. I absolutely must have the arteries in my goddamned neck looked at.

When I took a moment out of my frenetic schedule to think about it, I still wasn't back to being my normal self. I'd swallowed as much ibuprofen and acetaminophen as the labels would allow. I was still dizzy and a little nauseated, but I drove myself to the facility where the urgent care sent patients for non-emergency scans. Once I'd checked in, the imaging took about ten minutes, after which I was told the results ought to show up in my patient portal in a few hours.

I headed back to work, where no sooner had I turned on my computer when Leon Worthington slid into my office guest chair, a taut frown etching the deep lines around his mouth. My boss was seriously intense—gray hair, black eyes that never blinked and bored through everyone like a drill. Usually, the man called me on the phone when he wanted to talk. Sometimes he asked me to go up to his office on the top floor. Rarely did he ever come down to mine.

"What's the latest with Hydroade?" he demanded, crossing his knees, tipping up his square jaw, peppered with a hint of gray whiskers.

"Nothing new." My butt cheeks clenched. "We still have people at their facility inspecting every bottle as its depalletized even though we're taking them from the lines to the trucks. The investigation will be ongoing for weeks yet."

"Then why are you sitting on your ass in Denver?"

I looked at my coffee mug and wondered if it would shatter if I threw it at his head. "I had a doctor appointment I couldn't miss this morning. I'm flying out tomorrow."

He tipped the chair back and crossed his arms. "Should I be worried?"

"Of course not." There was absolutely no way on earth I was going to tell him about collapsing while doing pushups. I wasn't even going to volunteer

Meg's issues. He expected me to be Superwoman and this was no time to tell him I wasn't. "It was just routine."

"You couldn't reschedule a routine appointment?" He glared at me, narrowing those hawk-like eyes. "Should I put someone else on this?"

Exactly what did he mean? After years of driving unprecedented profits to the bottom line for this company, I wasn't allowed a few minutes to go to the doctor? Hell, I was the VP of Operations—in charge of all eight plants. It stung to have Leon insinuate I wasn't cutting it.

"The situation is contained." Every fiber of my body tensed as I fought against the urge to explode. "We've done everything Hydroade has asked us to do. Believe me, six months from now, this will all be ancient history."

"If they don't pull our contract."

Our gazes collided with an electrically charged moment of unspoken doom. I didn't breathe. Moreover, I refused to flinch because if I showed an iota of fear, my boss would eat me alive. If there was one thing I'd learned from working for this man all these years, when it came to the business, I never sugarcoated anything with him. "Would you be surprised if they didn't?" I asked—my way of feeling him out.

"I would."

I heaved a sigh, making my head spin all the more. "So would I."

"We lose that contract and we'll have to close down Philly."

My butt cramped from the tension, damn him. "I know."

"We can't lose Hydroade, Jane."

We could, though it would require some major restructuring. "I've already asked sales to go after Muscle Juice."

Leon stood and looked out the window—another flock of geese flew past—*oh, the irony*. "Yeah, but that's half the volume."

"It is. That's why I also told the CFO to run shutdown scenarios for me—top secret of course, but we need to know all of our options before and *if* Hydroade pulls the pin."

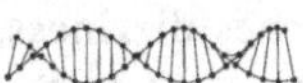

After Leon left my office, I got on the phone. Making sure I had all my bases covered, I pushed the CFO for his report. I also asked him about the status of filing an insurance claim but he said Leon had that covered—dear God, the man was a total micromanager.

Late afternoon, I discovered I'd missed a text from the patient portal and quickly logged on, expecting my usual clean bill of health. The pulsating rush I'd been having in my ears turned into a pounding boom as if my heart were beating in the back of my neck while I read the CT findings listing normal lymph nodes, salivary glands, thyroid and more. With each normal result, I breathed easier until I got to the middle of the second page:

IMPRESSION:

    1. *Beaded appearance of the bilateral cervical ICAs compatible with fibro-muscular dysplasia.*

    2. *Small short segment dissection of the distal right cervical ICA, measuring 4mm in length.*

    3. *Minimal atheromatous plaque in the proximal right ICA without hemodynamically significant stenosis.*

I reread the results, my mouth agape, a tight pinch between my eyebrows. Was something wrong? What the heck was fibromuscular dysplasia? Holy Pete, I'd never seen terms like *atheromatous* or *hemodynamically significant*.

I Googled everything.

First of all, I should have realized ICA stood for internal carotid artery. But the rest was nothing with which I was familiar.

The Moya Clinic's website reported: "*Fibromuscular dysplasia is a condition that causes narrowing (stenosis) and enlargement (aneurysm) of the medium-sized arteries in your body. Narrowed arteries can reduce blood flow and affect the function of your organs. Fibromuscular dysplasia appears most commonly in the arteries leading to the kidneys and brain. Fibromuscular dysplasia can affect other arteries, including those leading to your legs, heart, abdomen and, rarely, the arms. It's possible to have more than one affected artery. Treatments are available, but there isn't a cure...*"

Toward the top of my search was a website called the Fibromuscular Dysplasia Society of America. I clicked on the symptoms and signs, some of which I didn't have, but headaches, dizziness, and a whooshing sound in my ears were all things I lived with on a daily basis.

I couldn't believe what I was reading aside from the good news that I did not have significant narrowing of the neck arteries...*yet*. Evidently, I did dissect my right carotid when I was doing pushups.

There was no follow-up communication from the urgent care doc who'd ordered the test, so I emailed a copy to my GP and one to Meg as I was dialing her phone.

She answered on the first ring. "Hi, Mom."

"How are you feeling?"

"Not sure. They're now basically saying that nothing's wrong with me and I'm waiting for the nurse to remove my IV so I can go home."

"*Nothing's* wrong?" I was on the verge of spitting my teeth across the room. "But you had two dissections!"

"I know. It's okay. They said there's no reason to keep me in the hospital—just told me not to do anything too strenuous for a while. Frankly, I'm relieved because I can't get any sleep in this place."

Dammit, I should have gotten on a flight to La Crosse. My baby needed an advocate. "Are you okay to go home alone?"

"Yeah, I might be a little dazed, but I'll be fine. Besides, I have a follow-up appointment with neurology."

I could relate to her use of the word dazed. Heck, I was still woozy. "Will you be seeing the neurologist who wanted me to get the CT scan?"

"Uh huh—that's the one...um...were you able to get your neck looked at?"

"I was." Maybe I should have started with that. "I just received the results—not sure what it all means, but I did have a dissection. The report also says my carotids have a beaded appearance, compatible with something called fibromuscular dysplasia."

"Fibro-what?"

"I emailed you the report. Show it to your doctor."

"Okay. God, Mom, it's really weird that we both had dissections one week apart."

That was an understatement. "Scary weird."

After printing the radiology report, I called my GP's office. She never had openings on the spur of the moment, but I didn't give a damn because I sure wasn't going back to urgent care and that son-of-a-bitch who belittled me like I was important as a gnat.

Initially, the receptionist put me on hold, making me suffer that godawful synthesizer music in frequencies that rattle your brain. Drumming my fingers, I amped up my fighting spirit. I swear, if she tried to tell me I couldn't be seen for a month, I'd go over her head.

Somehow. It was never easy to sidestep a doctor's receptionist.

"Ms. Corley?" said the woman as the hold music cut out.

All right. I breathed in, ready to plead my case. After all, this didn't only concern me. "Yes?"

"The nurse is hand-delivering your report to Dr. Panda. How soon can you come in?"

I blinked.

I didn't need to be assertive? This was new, except I wasn't exactly filled with joy—not because she didn't kick back, but because I sensed urgency in the receptionist's tone. "As soon as possible. Five minutes?"

"The nurse said to come when you can and we'll find a way to squeeze you in."

Once I arrived at the clinic, I sat in the brightly lit waiting room with its familiar paintings of the Front Range and pictures of The Rockies' peaks.

Only a few minutes passed before the nurse took me back to an exam room, checked my vitals, asked the standard questions, and then I waited about half an hour for Dr. Panda to come in. She was about four-foot-ten, had long black hair and was a tad unconventional. She was the only doctor I'd ever been to who used acupuncture needles to loosen tight muscles. "Jane, how did you dissect?"

"Pushups—number twenty-eight. Needless to say, I didn't make it to thirty."

She had a printed copy of my report and flipped through it. "Hmm. FMD?"

"Have you heard of it?"

She put her stethoscope in her ears and pressed it against my chest. "It's on the list of rare diseases. I'm going to refer you to a vascular."

"Another doctor? Ugh."

Urging me to sit forward, she listened to me take a few breaths. "It might take a few weeks to be seen, so make an appointment today, okay?"

If I had more time, I would have complained about the fact that urgent care hadn't even bothered to contact me, but I just gave a nod. "All right. Anything else? I need to head back to the office."

"Are you still taking your cholesterol meds?"

"Yes, of course."

"Good." She draped the stethoscope around her neck and started typing on the computer's keyboard. "I'm sending you to Dr. Vaughn upstairs. You ought to pop up there now and make an appointment."

I checked my watch. I had a meeting with HR in an hour. "All right."

She held a very pointy finger under my nose. "And don't push yourself too hard when you exercise. I'm sure no one needs to tell you what happens when a dissection actually ruptures through the outer artery wall."

I gulped. All my life I'd tried to stay in shape. Who got dissected arteries when they did pushups? I'd never even heard of dissections before Meg called. Why had it happened to me? And Meg wasn't even in a real accident. Why did hard braking nearly kill my precious baby?

Filled with questions, I walked past the elevator and took the stairs up to Dr. Vaughn's office, who happened to be the only vascular surgeon in the building.

However, the greeting I received was far frostier than the one downstairs. No matter how fiercely I tried to argue, the receptionist said the earliest appointment was in two weeks and I ought to be thankful to be getting in that early.

My mind boggled at the inconsistencies in the medical profession. When I'd walked into Dr. Panda's office, it seemed as if my situation was akin to a medical emergency—but the vascular specialist's receptionist didn't seem to believe so. Her nonchalance was almost a relief because I didn't have the luxury to worry about my health at the moment. Curt and I had to meet with Hydroade in Pennsylvania tomorrow. I'd already wasted enough time.

Chapter Eight

Meg

Once they released me from the hospital, I took the rest of the week off even though I felt a little guilty. It wasn't as if I could say I broke my leg or I actually had a TIA because some doctors thought I did and others didn't. I wasn't only confused, I wondered what I did to cause the problem in the first place. Was there anything I could have done differently? Whatever happened, I never wanted to be in that much pain again.

The whole experience had been terrifying. The fact that I actually might have had a small stroke made me think hard about what I was going to do with the rest of my life. I'd been coasting for too long, working in the library, going out with friends, being a doggie mom to Maya. The problem was I wasn't really taking care of *myself*, at least not my future. I wanted more out of life than to become an old-maid librarian and lose my identity in my career like my mother. I wanted kids, a husband, and a house with a big garden.

Maybe I had a little PTSD because I didn't want to drive my car and I sure as hell didn't want to be a passenger in one. Most of all, I didn't want to talk to any of my coworkers and try to explain what happened. They'd all think I was nuts.

Maybe I was nuts. Maybe I'd just imagined the whole thing. The vascular guy seemed to think so.

Was Mom imagining things, too?

Holy kamoly, what if we both needed to see psychotherapists?

No wonder my mom abhorred going to doctors. They couldn't even agree on a diagnosis.

I sat at my home-office desk in a nook of my apartment tucked away behind purple boho curtains depicting the tree of life. Maya, my tiny Chihuahua, curled up on my lap while I scrolled through listings of houses for sale. Perhaps I'd start from the bottom of my goals and work up. At least a girl could dream.

We both startled when my phone beeped with a Facebook voice call. Maybe I wasn't up to talking with anyone at work, but Lance was a different story. My heart performed a swan dive as I swiped up the icon. "Hello?" I answered, trying not to sound too anxious, too needy, or too excited.

"Hey, Meg. How're you doing?" he asked, his voice filled with concern.

I let out a long sigh as if he'd reached through the line and rubbed my shoulders. "I'm pretty good—wish I could give you a hug."

"I know, right? I'd love to hug you back."

I reclined in my chair and put my feet up on my desk, crossing my ankles, scratching my little dog behind the ears. "That sounds delicious."

"I did some checking and wanted to make sure your doctor gave you a blood thinner."

"Yes. They're having me take low dose aspirin and they've changed my blood pressure meds."

"Good. Um...excellent."

"Are you at work?"

"I'm on break. Why?"

I lowered my feet and clicked the next page of house listings. "You just sound a little distracted is all."

"Me? I'm never distracted."

"Of course not," I agreed, finding a cute little brick house—one I could see the two of us living in, raising kids, growing a vegetable garden. Maybe we could do the whole off-grid solar thing. "Did you know there's a Moya Clinic branch in La Crosse?" Yeah, I was trying to be stealthy, but also cringing because he just might see through my not-so-innocent question.

"Really? I thought you said you were at Gustafsson Hospital."

"I was because that's where Elaine took me," I explained, even though that's not why I brought it up. "Have you ever considered moving to Wisconsin?"

Did I really say that out loud? My cringe morphed into a grimace.

"Nah. I'm an Ohio boy through and through."

"*The* Ohio State, huh?" I asked, all but smacking myself upside the head. It was way too early in our relationship to start up any conversations about moving, especially since as of the last night on the ship there was no relationship. Before I could shove my proverbial foot all the way into my mouth, I shut down my web browser and resumed petting my dog.

"So..." I said, changing the subject. "I'll bet you hate it when people ask you medical questions."

"Yeah. Pain in the ass...um...except from you, of course."

"Seriously, you don't mind?"

"Well, yeah. I'd love to have you in my arms right now," he repeated.

I didn't care. I could listen to him repeat himself all day especially if he was talking about giving me a much-needed hug. "There's no place I'd rather be, too." I bit the corner of my mouth. "Um...there is one professional question I wanted to ask you if it's okay."

"Sure, anything."

"What do know about FMD?"

"FM what? Huh?"

"Fibromuscular dysplasia." I'd messaged him about Mom's CT scan but he hadn't replied yet. "Anything?"

"How do you spell it?"

Maya started to fuss so I set her down. "F-i-b-r-o-m-u-s-c-u-l-a-r."

"What was the other? D-something?"

"Dysplasia."

"Yeah, can you spell that, too?"

Maybe he hadn't slept well. I was used to people asking me how to spell difficult words, but it was odd to have a doctor ask. Nonetheless, I spelled dysplasia for him, then he asked me to wait while he looked it up on his medical network.

"Just reading about it now," Lance said. "It's a rare vascular disorder with twisted and torturous arteries. You don't have that do you?"

"I don't think so, but my mom does."

"Huh," he mused.

I looked at my phone and shook my head. "Did you get enough sleep last night?"

"Oh, yeah, slept great."

Well, I couldn't expect him to be an expert in FMD or even know about it. After all, it was super rare. "That's good."

Lance chuckled. "My mother tells everyone I'm the world's greatest sleeper."

Interesting. "I guess as an ER doc, you have to nap when you can, right?"

"You got it, Babe." He cleared his throat. "I sleep on vacay. I'm thinking about cruising to Belize next."

I mentally added Belize to my bucket list. "That sounds amazing. When?"

"Not sure—got to wait until I can take some time off again." The sound of a truck engine rumbled over the line. "Hey, I gotta run. Later, Babe."

Chapter Nine

Jane

A good six-feet-four-inches tall and forty-ish, the vascular surgeon, Dr. Vaughn, sauntered into the exam room as if I hadn't been sitting there for over an hour.

He smiled as he took his seat on the rolling stool. "It's good to see a younger patient for a change."

I didn't mind being referred to as young, but seriously? What prompted the man to say such a thing, let alone as a greeting? "I take it most of your patients are elderly?"

"Mm hmm." He turned to the computer screen, typing in his credentials. "So what are we seeing you for today?"

Though I'd explained everything to the nurse, I summarized the pushups and the CT scan finding FMD as well as the dissected carotid artery.

With his nose to the monitor, he skimmed through my notes. "I see." He clicked to to Google and typed in *fibromuscular dysplasia*. Then he took a moment to read an article, but from my position I couldn't see the fine print. "I'm not sure you have FMD. It's extremely rare."

"Oh? Did you look at my scan?"

He changed the screen to the radiology results highlighting my neck arteries. "Here's the s-bend twist in your left carotid…and the appearance of a string of beads." He pointed to a frayed bulbous mass on my right. "Here's where you dissected. You must have been pushing yourself too hard."

That was an understatement. "Nothing more than I'm used to, but I have been under a lot of stress at work."

"Ah huh." He turned off the monitor and stood. "Well, you don't need any stenting because you have mild to moderate stenosis. Your dissection will heal in a couple of months. Until then, go easy on the pushups."

Stenting? Because the doc was moving toward the door, I stood as well. "So, that's it?"

"Yep."

"Do I need to follow up?"

He shrugged, putting his hand on the knob. "It's up to you. Maybe come back in a year?"

"But what about my bruit—the whooshing in my ears?"

He gave me a look much the same as the one I received from the urgent care doc I had to plead with in order to get the CT. "Bruit? What? Did you read about bruits and pulsatile tinnitus on the internet?"

"Of course I did. It's one of the symptoms on the FMD Society of America website."

"You know, many of my patients often read things on the internet, and when they have a few symptoms that are similar, they convince themselves that they are sick." He smiled, except there was no warmth in his grin. "I only needed to look at you to know you're not sick."

My face burned hot as I followed him out the door, wishing I could grab his arm, twist it up his back, throw him to the ground, then dig my knee into his bicep and let him know exactly what I thought about his diagnosis. "Tell me, are most of the patients to whom you're referring women?"

"Believe it or not they are." The bastard pointed to the exit sign. "The lobby is that way. Have a good day."

I stormed past the receptionist's desk and out to my car. There was no way in hell I was ever going to make another appointment with Dr. Vaughn. I wove through traffic on the freeway, gunning my way back to the office. When will I ever learn? I shouldn't have gone to see the damned vascular specialist. Once he actually came into the exam room, it took him a record two minutes to throw up his wall of medical gender bias.

Why in God's name would I imagine something like a thundering pulse in my ears?

Why in God's name did my imaginary bruit hammer so loudly it sometimes woke me up at night?

Asshole!

Most of the time I'd deal with being completely brushed off by focusing on something else. But I'd done quite a bit of research and I didn't think my "torturous and twisted" carotid arteries ought to be discounted as unimportant.

The FMD website listed a number of clinics that specialized in the disease, almost all of which were on the east coast. There was only one doctor in Colorado who specialized in FMD and when I called his office, they said my PCP had to send in a referral, but the specialist was presently booked out eight months.

I figured by the time I got ahold of Dr. Panda's office and she submitted a referral, it would probably be a year until I got in to see the guy. Was I blowing things out of proportion? Was I overreacting because of the data I'd read online, even though I was accessing credible sources? Maybe Dr. Vaughn was right, I didn't have anything to worry about, and everything would heal on its own. I mean if he, a vascular surgeon, wasn't concerned, then why should I be?

The FMD website did indicate that most patients who had the disease could lead normal lives with a few modifications, like no martial arts and no car accidents. I'd already informed my sensei I wouldn't be at the test for my second-degree black belt. He wasn't surprised because Renee had told the whole class about the pushups.

Moving into the right lane, I signaled for my exit. Then I barely made it through a yellow light, sped for the office, and zoomed into the parking lot, telling myself to put all this health business behind me.

Curt and I had negotiated a satisfactory deal with Hydroade and things were looking up in Philly. I needed to give my other plant managers some TLC for a change. I'd have my admin book flights and tour every plant within the next few weeks—make sure we were meeting all of our housekeeping and safety goals before I pushed them to submit their budgets.

I made a resolute decision as I marched toward the building. I was fed up. I was going to forget about FMD since Meg didn't appear to have it. There was far too much on my plate to worry about a little artery dissection that would heal. By the time I walked into my office, I had a renewed sense of purpose and none of it centered around my heath, thank God.

Except Leon Worthington was sitting in my chair. "You're late," he boomed, those black eyes as humorless as a rattlesnake's.

My heart jolted while I glanced over my shoulder. "Sorry. I just had a follow-up appointment and I'm happy to say I have a clean bill of health." I set my briefcase on the desk, steeling my nerves for bad news. "Is something wrong?"

"Shut the door."

The harsh edge in his tone prickled the back of my neck. I did as he asked, then slid into the guest chair, gripping the armrests. "If this is about Hydroade, Curt and I met with the VP and ironed out an agreement to supply pallets direct from line to truck until—"

"You only *thought* you had an agreement."

"Thought?" I shook my head. "They said they were happy with every-thing we've done and—"

Leon threw a newspaper in front of me. "Read the fucking headline, Jane."

I looked down. *"Bethany Plastics' Contamination Blunder."*

My breath stopped, turning to fire in my lungs. "Oh, shit."

"The VP was fired this morning."

My mouth drier than the Mohave, I sat back.

"I'm sure it won't come as a surprise to hear the CEO of Hydroade called me this morning with a new list of demands."

I didn't like the way Leon glared at me—as if he had a six-shooter pointed at my heart under the desk. "But we already fired thirty-two employees and—"

"You've done a decent job up until today." Leon jammed his pointer finger on top of the newspaper. "Now I'm backed into a corner."

He didn't have to say another word for me to figure out what he was planning to shoot me with. I tried to breathe. I tried to talk. I tried to look away, but all I managed was to freeze, still gripping the armrests of the chair, my knuckles white.

Holy shit, holy shit, holy shit!

The rims of my eyes stung. "Are...are you firing me?" I finally asked, my voice haunted. I'd given the last twenty years of my life to this company. Aside from a couple of doctor appointments, I came in at seven and left when the job was done—almost always after the dinner hour. He couldn't just write me off!

"You're close enough to retirement."

I crossed my arms and squeezed. Hard. For the love of God, Leon was five years older than me. "I didn't put the goose shit in the damned bottle."

"No, but someone under you did, and that makes you culpable." He sliced his hand through the air. "It doesn't matter. You're still entitled to your stock options and you'll receive a substantial severance package equivalent to five years' salary—minus unearned bonuses, of course."

I didn't care about the money. This was untenable. Worse, the damned twisted veins in my neck pulsed with mind-numbing pain, threatening another dissection. An aura spun in my vision blurring Leon's scowl like I was looking through a kaleidoscope. This was going to be one mother of a migraine—one I absolutely did not need right now. "If you do this, I'll never work again."

He pushed an envelope toward me. "You won't need to."

My entire body shook. I couldn't think straight. Hell, it took enough effort to breathe. Five years' pay was a lot—more than I needed to retire comfortably, but that's not what I wanted.

Still, I knew how this worked. The person on the chopping block had no say in the decision. I picked up the packet. "So this is it?"

"Yep."

"Can I ask who my replacement is?"

"Nope."

"Are you going to close the Philly plant?"

Leon rolled up the newspaper and slammed it on the desk, making every nerve in my body jump. "I'll give you a half-hour to clean out your office."

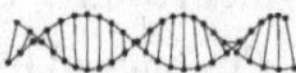

I saw a movie once with a man in a straitjacket thrashing and screaming in a padded, soundproof room. I don't recall why the man had been restrained, but if he wasn't already insane, he would have been by the time he was released.

I now knew exactly what it was like to be that man. Except I was doing all my screaming and thrashing on the inside.

A hundred times or more I'd replayed my last meeting with Leon—his cold voice haunted me, made goosebumps rise on my arms. I was fifty-nine years old and washed up.

Humiliated.

Damned for something over which I had no control.

How could I show my face in public?

How could I tell anyone?

How could I tell Meg?

I'd been lying on the couch in my pajamas for three days, hugging my doggie pillow, not even bothering to take the five-second walk down the hall when it was time for bed. The taste in my mouth was sour. Stale. I stank. I don't remember the last time I'd eaten.

I wasn't hungry.

I didn't care.

What in God's name was I going to do now?

If only the damned dissected carotid artery had killed me.

I picked up my water bottle and sucked on the straw, drawing in nothing but a gulp of air. Groaning, I threw it across the room, hitting the television's blank screen, and clattering to the tiled floor.

I ought to go see my mother. But it was hard enough to leave the couch when I had to pee. I ought to call Meg. At least she'd be happy because I no longer had a reason to cancel our vacations.

Except I don't want to be seen as a failure in my daughter's eyes.

I picked up my phone. *Shit.* I had no service. Obviously, my number had already been cut off by Bethany Plastics. I didn't have a landline either.

Around midday, I got up and stumbled to the bathroom, taking a good look at myself in the mirror. I stretched the skin around my mouth and let it drop back, sagging into jowls that seemed to appear overnight. God, I looked old. My eyes were bloodshot, my hair was smushed on one side, the part showing a wide, thinning swath where my scalp glistened with oil.

Blech.

Grabbing my toothbrush, I refused to scrutinize myself for another second as I cleaned my teeth. Then I turned on the shower and stood under a pelting stream until it ran cold.

On my way back to the living room, I stopped in front of a picture of Meg taken when she was a sophomore in high school—when we lived in Wisconsin. At the time, I'd been a plant manager near La Crosse. Honestly, of all the places Bethany had moved me, I think I liked Wisconsin the best. At least every month aside from January and February.

Still, those months were tolerable if a person dressed for the cold. And nothing beat good old Midwest values. Wisconsinites not only worked hard, I'd say they were the friendliest people I'd ever met.

I touched Meg's smiling face. Jeez, she was beautiful—deep blue eyes, all that red hair, and the cute freckles across the bridge of her nose. She thought she was too heavy, but she was just curvy in a very feminine way. I used to look at her and marvel that she'd come from me—the living stick woman.

A cavern swelled in my chest.

I missed her.

Why had I spent so much of my adult life pursuing the corporate dream? I'd never been satisfied, always setting my sights on the next promotion—making plants more profitable, proving myself. And for what? Why did I push myself so hard as if I never measured up to my superiors' expectations?

Yes, Jack had been awful during the divorce. He'd soured me toward marriage so much that afterward I'd pushed men away at the first sign a relationship might get serious. But, jeez, the past twenty-two years had been lonely.

My stomach growled.

My slippers scuffed over the tiles as I made my way to the kitchen and opened the fridge. It was empty.

I needed a phone.

It was time to swallow my shame and face the world.

Chapter Ten

Meg

"You're buying a house?" asked Elaine as we walked along Ninth Street toward Cass. It was a sultry mid-August Saturday and we'd both pulled a shift at the library. The sun was shining with cotton-ball clouds sailing overhead. But no matter how dreamy the weather had looked from indoors, as soon as we stepped outside, my clothes instantly stuck to my skin thanks to the sweltering humidity.

My skirt glued itself to my thighs. My shirt looked as if I'd peed out of my armpits. At least I was with Elaine who was as sweaty as me and couldn't give a fig.

I stubbed my toe on the uneven sidewalk, ungracefully stumbling forward, recovering my balance before I ended up doing a face-plant. "Not me," I replied. "I don't quite have enough money saved for a down payment yet."

She groaned. "I'll never be able to afford a down payment because my student loans are akin to the national debt."

I shouldn't ever talk about money to Elaine because my mother had paid for both of my degrees and the only debt I had was for my car and my credit card which I paid off monthly.

My bestie wiped her brow with the back of her forearm. "So why are we going to see a house?"

I guess there was no use skirting around the truth because it was going to come out sooner or later. I'd asked her to come along as we were both walking out the library door and hadn't explained anything. "My mother was fired from her job because of something she had no control over and now she wants to move to La Crosse."

Mom had called me last night using a number I didn't recognize and I hadn't picked up. But once I listened to her voicemail, I called her right back, afraid she'd had a stroke because it didn't even sound like her in the message. Well, it was her voice, but I'd never heard Jane Corley sound vulnerable or depressed.

Once I got her on the phone, I couldn't believe she held it together while she explained about the horrid goose shit incident in Philly. And then her jerk ex-boss used *my mother* as a patsy, the bastard!

Elaine stopped and clapped her hands over her heart, her eyes enormous. "My God, Superwoman got fired? What the hell happened?"

"You don't want to know. All I have to say is my mother was a victim of grandiose injustice and I'm glad she's finally done with that place."

"Seriously? From what you've told me, I thought your mom loved her job so much she wouldn't retire until she was eighty." Elaine led the way across the street. "So, how do you feel about her moving here?"

I plucked a leaf from the branch of an enormous hackberry tree shading the sidewalk. When I was growing up I always felt like Mom was judging me—as if my grades weren't good enough, or I wasn't polite enough, or skinny enough. I certainly was never fit enough. I settled in La Crosse to start my own life without her constant scrutiny. In my opinion, the distance between us was ideal. I had my space, she had hers and we got along really well as long as she showed up for our planned vacations. "I'd be lying if I didn't admit to being a little freaked out. I mean, I have no idea what she'll be like without a job."

"She's intense, huh?"

"That's an understatement. I just hope she doesn't drive me crazy with her micromanaging tactics." I stopped at the crosswalk on Cass Street and looked both ways. I always loved the Victorian mansions lining this street. Back in the late nineteenth century, this was where the "in" crowd lived—now, too, I suppose. My favorite looked like a gothic castle, complete with imported masonry and a conical turret. "And she's bringing my grandmother who doesn't recognize me anymore. I love her…I love them both, but what's all this change going to do to my precious free time?"

"Kiss it goodbye, I guess." Elaine gave my shoulder a sympathetic pat. "Is Granny going to live with her?"

"Oh, no. Mom already tried that and it was a disaster. The best thing is to set her up in an assisted living facility where she'll receive the care she needs—three square meals every day and all that goes with it. In fact, I've already emailed Mom with some options."

Once we reached Cameron Avenue, I spotted the real estate agent standing by a for sale sign, the dingy white house in back of her looking haunted. The lawn was brown and the bushes were overgrown. And as we approached, I could see the paint was chipped and peeling in places.

"That's it?" Elaine whispered, wincing as if she just drank a glass of sour milk. "I thought your mom was loaded."

"She's not loaded, she's comfortable." But this place looked like something out of *The Addams Family*. My mother wouldn't like this house at all. "She'll probably find something else that better suits her even though she won't be happy unless we go inside and take pictures."

"Aren't those on the realty website?"

"Of course they are, but my mother doesn't trust them."

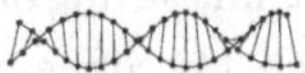

Everything was happening too fast for my comfort level, which wasn't difficult to believe when it came to Jane Corley. After losing her job, my mother might have initially been depressed, but once she had a plan, the woman attacked it like I'd attack a new Jodi Picoult novel. Every time Mom had set her sights on something, it was always accomplished with speed and efficiency. Six weeks had passed since I looked at houses for her and today I've been cleaning my apartment like a fiend, shuffling around with Maya on my heels doing her best to get in my way. When one has a three-and-a-half pound Chihuahua, one learns to shuffle because a single misplaced step could result in a fatality.

I flushed the toilet and returned the scrub brush to the holder just as the doorbell rang. Maya shot through the apartment, her high-pitched barks verging on hysteria, her tail whipping like a windmill.

I pulled off my rubber gloves as I followed the dog, spotting Mom's red Volvo SUV parked on the curb outside the bay window. Plucking Maya from the floor, I opened the door.

"Mom!" I said, unable to stifle my gasp. Holy crap, she'd aged five years since I'd seen her at Christmas. Sure, it had been nine months, but now she was grayer, frailer.

I don't think I'd ever used the word frail to describe the female equivalent of a spark plug.

Her makeup was scant with a hint of blush and mascara. Mom's hair was pulled back in its usual tidy bun, but I swear it was thinner, her face drawn and etched with lines.

I forced a smile. "Goodness, I didn't expect you until dinnertime."

She hugged us both while my Chihuahua squirmed and emitted a pathetic growl—it always took three days for Maya to remember she loved my mother. "You know those roadside hotels. No one can ever sleep in them."

I led her inside. "Are you okay with the front bedroom?"

With one finger, Mom gave Maya a scratch under her chin. "Anywhere is fine, dear. It's only for a few days."

"Can I get your bag?"

"We can bring it in later." She glanced toward the kitchen. "Do you mind if I make a cup of coffee?"

Mom made the best lattes I'd ever had. She'd even bought the outrageously expensive Breville machine sitting on my countertop, but for some reason she had the magic touch. My coffees were merely passable. "You're on if you make one for me, too."

She jumped right in, remembering where I kept everything, thank God. After seeing her at the door, for a second I was afraid she might be getting senile like Grandma.

I slid onto a seat at the breakfast bar. "I can't believe your town house sold on the first day it was listed."

"That's what prime real estate in Denver will do. It's also a seller's market." She grinned over her shoulder. "I'm meeting the realtor here and doing a walk-through of the house in a couple of hours. Want to come with?"

"Absolutely. Can you still get out of buying it?"

Mom worked the stainless steel pitcher up and down as the milk frother began to hiss. "Why would I want to do that?"

"Because the place needs a ton of work."

"And I need a project so I don't drive you insane." She measured the grounds and started the espresso. "Besides, I grew up in a Victorian. I've always wanted to live in one, and now I have my chance."

"Yeah, but the basement floor is dirt. And some idiot built a plywood bar in the dining room. And the kitchen is a nightmare. It looks as if they tried to remodel it in the sixties and failed."

As deftly as a barista, Mom filled two of my colorful "tequila sunrise" mugs with coffee and topped them off with frothy milk. She even made a heart in mine. "All of which can be fixed. It's going to be magnificent."

"If you say so." I sipped, then licked the froth from my upper lip. "This is delicious."

Mom sat on a stool beside me. "How is that guy doing...the one from the cruise? Are you still in contact with him?"

I was glad she brought him up. "Lance." I repressed my urge to shimmy my shoulders. After his Facebook phone call, we'd kept in touch on-and-off for about a month, then out of the blue, he called and said he had a few days off and wanted to visit me in La Crosse. "Actually, he's coming for Octoberfest."

"Oh, my. When is it, exactly?"

"It's a week later than usual this year, so he won't be here until October sixth."

Mom sipped her coffee and emitted a blissful sigh. "Thank goodness my house will be closed by then."

I savored another sip. "Yeah, but do you really want to move into that place right away?"

"I certainly do. If the bedrooms are anything like your pictures, they're in decent shape. Besides, I've arranged for the moving truck to deliver my furniture the day after closing."

"Are you sure the roof doesn't leak?"

"Positive. I paid for an inspection. I might have wanted a project, but I wasn't about to buy a house that was on the verge of being condemned. The people who foreclosed were only in the house for a few years, thank goodness. Before those yahoos moved in, it was owned by a responsible couple. The roof was replaced five years ago, the foundation is sound, and the electricity is up to code. Even the boiler is fairly new. Everything else is cosmetic."

I picked up Maya and put her on my lap, the three-and-a-half-pound princess turning in a circle and curling up. "I have no idea where you get your energy."

Mom slumped a little. "I wish I had more."

Robo-mom was slumping? This was so not like her. I wondered if she even realized how much the disaster with Hydroade had taken its toll. Nonetheless, buying a house to tackle an enormous renovation project wasn't far off the mark for the human spark plug, but was Mom's energy really starting to wane? She had to still be reeling from being fired. "Um...you haven't said anything about karate lately. Did you make it to the test for your second-degree?"

She sighed, her focus shifting to the window. "I've put it on hold for now—well, most likely forever. The FMD website lists karate as taboo and, to be honest, the physical requirements push me to my limits. I sure as heck don't want to cause a dissection just by doing pushups."

"You actually chose not to push yourself?" I snorted, my sarcasm showing. How many fifty-nine-year-old women did thirty pushups on a daily basis? "Wow, that must have been hard."

Mom's face pinched with her sniff. "Don't get cheeky with me. It was a tough decision to make, but it doesn't mean I'm not going to work out. I've already signed up at the Y, mind you."

"Why am I not surprised?" I smoothed my hand along the curve of Maya's back. "But I know exactly what you mean. I never want to have a dissection again, either. In fact, I've been walking a whole lot more just so I don't have to ride in a car."

"Good for you. One of the reasons I chose the house on Cameron is because it's close to town and I can walk almost everywhere."

"Are you going to get a dog?"

Mom used her spoon to scoop the dregs of the froth at the bottom of her cup. "I've always wanted one, but I think I'll hold off."

"You? Wait?" Now I had absolute proof. Hydroade had majorly messed with my mom.

"Yes." She collected both of our cups and headed for the sink. "I'm waiting. Life isn't a race, you know."

As she dropped dollops of dish soap into each cup, from behind, she looked far too thin, her leggings baggy. Knowing Mom, she probably lost weight from all the stress. I wish I had her genes. The more stress I was under, the more I ate.

I hardly remember the divorce, but I do recall her losing weight then, too. Even at the age of seven, I'd worried about her. Now, my parents rarely spoke. Mom never talked about it, but I know Dad didn't let her off easy. She wasn't hostile toward him, but cold was an understatement.

And no matter how much both of them denied it, I had always been the one stuck in the middle. Until I was eighteen, I was the kid who had to travel to Australia for my summer break every year, which meant I had to endure two winters. I guess with my lily white, freckly skin, it was probably best that I stayed out of the sun. But who wants to put up with winter all year long even if they have red hair?

My childhood monumentally sucked. Sure, I love my mother fiercely. And I don't deny that she is the rock forming the foundation of my character, but that never made her leaving my dad any easier.

To be honest, I had no idea why they hooked up in the first place. He drank too much (though he tried to hide it from me whenever I visited) and was laid back—the complete opposite of my overachieving mother. The only thing my parents ever had in common was me.

It was still hard for me to forgive and forget all the winters as well as all the moving around we did as Mom climbed the corporate ladder. I came back to Wisconsin for college because that's where I'd spent high school—all but the end of my senior year when she moved to Denver. Yep, I graduated with a bunch of kids who were basically strangers.

Mom was disappointed that I hadn't returned to Colorado, but after she finally landed her dream job, she was almost never home. Yet another reason for me to establish my life in a small town that I could call my own—a place I'd come to love. La Crosse on the Mississippi River with idyllic snowy winters and quintessential summers.

I wasn't joking when I'd told my mother to quit her job. I hated Bethany Plastics almost more than I'd hated being a pawn in my parents' divorce.

Mom turned from the sink. "So, can I take you out for dinner?"

Popping back to the present, I grinned and nodded. "That sounds wonderful."

CHAPTER ELEVEN

JANE

During the past month and a half I'd managed to hold it together by keeping myself so busy there was no time to think. I didn't go to bed at night until I was so exhausted I crashed. Even then I had nightmares—they weren't all about work disasters either. It seemed every horrible thing that had ever happened to me in my life decided to attack my subconscious.

I awoke most nights in a pool of sweat, then booted up my laptop and stared at the security camera footage of employees going to and from a warehouse. Why? Because after I came out of my slump, I cleaned out my purse and found the flash drive the IT guy in Philly gave me. The police may have looked at the film, but I was convinced they must have missed something. I wanted to nail the bastard who was responsible for getting me fired. I wanted to pick up the phone and tell Leon who to go after. I'd be vindicated, completely in my rights to thump my chest like Tarzan's Jane.

But Bethany Plastics aside, whenever my life imploded and fell apart, I did everything in my power to fixate on something else. Presently, buying and selling houses, as well as packing up and moving consumed most of my time. Unfortunately, I didn't have any control over my unawake hours.

While I drove from Denver to La Crosse, I'd passed the miles with Madeline Miller's debut audiobook, *The Song of Achilles*, which I'd enjoyed immensely thanks to my librarian daughter's expert recommendation. Except it ended three hours too soon and I spent the remainder of the drive singing loudly and badly. Music helped a little, but my mind wandered too much. By the time I arrived at Meg's, my spirits were again analogous to a dirty washrag, wrung out and flapping erratically in the wind.

My daughter had a wonderful eye for home décor. I'd never be able to pick such brilliantly outlandish colors and make them look fantastic together. She had two 1920s lamps with colorful glass shades, their fringe dripping with beads. On every surface there were vases of silk flowers in colors of vermillion, magenta, bright yellow, and cornflower. In one corner was a coffee table supported by a statue of an elephant—I gave that to her a couple of birthdays ago after she'd picked it out, of course. I never bought anything for Meg unless she chose it herself. My tastes were too "eighties" (her words, not mine).

Nonetheless, entering her living room always dealt me with a brisk slap in the face. Yep, every single time, I got a shock, even though I knew it was coming.

After she left for work, with a cup of coffee in hand, I studied Meg's wall of framed photos—the frames were beautiful, each one a colorful and unique work of art. Sure, I'd seen them before but I always hoped they'd contain different photos. She did update the pictures from time to time, but it seemed as if her memories with me weren't worth keeping.

I sighed, pushing away my dark thought. I'd had far too many of those of late and it wasn't in my nature to be depressed even if I'd recently walked through hell.

Maybe Meg didn't need to be reminded of the memories we made together because I kept photo albums and she looked through them whenever she came to visit. I don't know why she treasured so many pictures of her father. Perhaps it was because she didn't get to visit him as often whereas she and I got together at least twice a year. Hopefully, we'll see a lot more of each other now.

I studied a picture of Jack and Meg riding horses with eucalyptus trees in the background. Jack looked natural in the saddle. Meg as well. There was Jack on his front porch, his fingers wrapped around a beer. Meg in her cap and gown at her college graduation—I'd taken that one. There was another of Jack with his two brothers in front of the Yelarben Pub. No surprises, all three of them had beers in their fists. There was Jack in his kitchen, Jack sitting in an easy chair, Jack with two-year-old Meg on his shoulders—I'd taken that one, too.

In the far corner was the only picture with me in it. It was the first time I'd been allowed to hold Meg in my arms, my lips pressing against my baby's crown. I'll never forget waking up in the ICU a week after she was born. The doctors told me that I had unusual veins at the bottom of my uterus as well as a rupture, and had I not been in the hospital for observation, neither I nor Meg would have survived.

As a thundering noise shook Meg's apartment, I jolted from my revery and clapped my hands over my ears. For Pete's sake, I could barely tolerate the sound. Was her neighbor deaf?

"Hey, Mom!" Meg yelled above the ear-splitting subwoofer still coming from the upstairs apartment. My daughter stepped inside while Maya greeted her, turning into an ecstatic, tail-wagging cyclone of fur. "Whatcha doing?"

Pursing my lips, I turned from my laptop on the kitchen breakfast bar and pointed. "Looking up the city ordinance for noise violations."

Meg cringed, her gaze drifting up to the swinging chandelier, her entire apartment vibrating like a 1960s fat-jiggling machine. "That guy is so annoying."

Understatement.

"Have you ever asked him to stop?" I shouted, my head pounding so hard I'd developed another one of my psychedelic auras akin to a child's kaleidoscope. If this kept up, I'd have to get a hotel room until my house closed.

"I've been meaning to," she replied, setting her purse on the counter. It was so like Meg to avoid confrontation. Sure, she had no problem when it came to me, but she couldn't stare down a fly if it was outside her close-knit circle of friends and family.

Not me, however. I relished confrontation, especially when it came to the peace and quiet of my personal space. I held up my phone. "Well, today's the day. I downloaded a decibel app. Even down here the reading is eighty-five, and it's been going on for over an hour! That's cause for a call to the police."

"Ugh." Meg fished her phone out of her purse. "I'll call them now."

"No." I hopped off the stool and marched toward the door. "It's only fair to give Mr. Subwoofer a warning first."

"Ya think? I'll bet he won't hear you even if you bang on the door."

"No?" I asked, stopping.

Meg picked up her dog and followed. "At least give *me* a chance to talk to him before you bare your fangs."

I scoffed at her melodrama. "Have you looked up the ordinance laws?"

"Well...no."

"Then I'll handle this. Besides, if he gets mad then he won't take it out on you." A twisty idea popped into my head—one the subwoofer types probably wouldn't be able to resist. "Hey—why don't you put a handful of chocolate chip cookies in a Ziplock bag and bring them up?"

"You baked?" She sidled into her galley-sized kitchen but I didn't wait.

Determinedly, I continued on my quest, taking the stairs two at a time. I pounded on the man's door, giving myself a couple of bruised knuckles that immediately started to swell, thanks to my thin skin. "Hello?" I shouted at the top of my voice, kicking the door to avoid further injury.

The rap music cut off just before the door swung open. "What the hell?" blurted an angry, enormous man who looked as if he could have doubled for a hairy Big-Time wrestler. The guy had to be at least six-feet-six and three hundred and fifty pounds.

My first sparring match came to mind, the one where I'd been clonked on the head and awoke in an ambulance with stars darting through my eyes.

I squared my shoulders. Dammit, I wasn't going to let this man's size frighten me. I'd earned my black belt. I knew how to defend myself no matter the immensity of my opponent. "My daughter, Margaret, lives in the apartment below yours and has suffered your incessant noise for..." I turned just as Meg started up the stairs. "How long?"

She'd left the dog behind and now carried a bag full of cookies, eyes wide, mouth drawn, obviously terrified. "Since h-he moved in about a year ago."

I held up my phone. "The decibel reading of your music in her apartment is eighty-five. I checked with the city ordinance and we would be within our rights to call the police, however—"

"Who do you think you are?" the man barked, his thick eyebrows slanting downward and forming a unibrow.

Not a good look for him, I'd say.

To his outburst of aggression, my training kicked in. *The first action is not to react.* I took a deep breath and looked him square in the eyes. "I am a mom and a very nice lady." I jammed my phone in my pocket and widened my stance a little, bending at the knees, ready to fend off an attack. If this guy so much as laid a pinky on me, I was going to take out his knee with a wicked roundhouse kick, then I'd back Meg down the stairs making sure he couldn't touch my daughter. "I also have one helluva headache because of the noise booming from this apartment."

He jabbed his thumb into chest. "I got rights."

"Yes, you do." I also pointed to my chest. "As do I. We didn't come up here to make you angry..." I bit my lip, thinking fast. "Tell me something, sir. Do you prefer it when people treat you with respect?"

He peered over my shoulder, scowling at Meg as if he didn't trust her. "Damn straight."

I gave him one of my VP of Operations, "I'm in charge and I'll take no bullshit" stares, ticking up my chin. "Well, that's why I'm here, because it is respectful for me to tell you that your noise is causing me a health hazard."

"A what?"

"A blessed migraine," I rephrased a little sharper than I'd intended to sound, pressing the heels of my hands to my temples. "Presently, the silence is soothing, don't you think so?"

"Huh?"

I sighed for effect. Obviously, not all of us appreciated peace and quiet. "I'm asking you politely to keep your music below fifty decibels, if you please."

Glaring, the man ran his fingers down his overgrown beard. "What if I don't?"

"Oh, dear, we really would prefer not to involve the police, but if that thundering bass continues to rattle the plates in my daughter's kitchen, then we'll have no recourse but to take up the matter with the cops." Before he had a chance to cogitate my message, I added, "Did you know you could download a decibel app?"

"I can?"

"Absolutely." Deciding this guy wasn't going to try to give me a sucker punch, I pulled out my phone and showed him. "See? You don't want to upset your neighbors, do you? Especially nice neighbors like Meg who are super friendly and who would never hurt a soul."

The man didn't reply, but he did pull out his phone. "An app, huh?"

As he opened Google Play I said, "By the way, I'm Jane. What's your name?"

"Ripper."

Why wasn't I surprised? "Pleased to meet you. I baked today. Do you like cookies?" I asked, moving in for the kill. In my book, in order to encourage someone to do something for you, a little kindness was the key to success.

His eyes widened, making him appear almost friendly. "Homemade?"

I took the bag from Meg and handed it to him—he didn't need to know they were slice-and-bake. "Fresh out of the oven."

He opened the bag and reached inside. "Uh, thanks."

"No, thank you. Don't forget to download that app. If you do, you might not be deaf by the time you're fifty."

"Thanks, Ripper." Meg leaned around me, giving him a little wave. "Your Harley is awesome."

The man actually grinned—maybe he blushed as well? Nah. He was just red in the face from my little scolding.

Meg and I returned to her apartment where Maya went batty, acting as if we'd been gone for hours. "Thanks for not practicing karate on his face." My daughter's laugh bubbled through the air. "God, Mom, you were over a foot shorter than that guy."

I glanced at the paper towel where the cookies had been cooling. Jeez, Meg had given Ripper all but two. "The first rule in karate is to walk away—to do everything in your power not to fight."

"What's the second?"

"To apply the appropriate amount of force."

She shrugged. "Which means?"

"Allow me to give a little demonstration of what I call the Drunk Uncle Maneuver." I faced her with my hands on my hips. "Let's say your Uncle Roger is soused at a wedding and making an ass of himself—maybe he's in someone's face and the situation is about to get ugly."

"Okay."

I grabbed the top of Meg's hand, twisted up and out against the tender sinew in her wrist, then started escorting her toward the bedroom—it was an easy maneuver, but effective because it caused enough pain to be able to lead the drunken person anywhere. "Come on, Roger. It's time for you to take a break."

"Ow!" Meg complained, tugging her fingers away. "That hurt."

"Sure, a little, but I didn't cause any damage because the situation didn't require it." I rubbed my palms together. "However, if your neighbor upstairs would have tried to attack me after I politely told him his music exceeded the city ordinance, I might have taken out his knee."

Meg backed away. "God, that's awful."

I held up my hands in surrender, offering an innocent grin. "Better than crushing his larynx and rendering him unable to breathe."

During my week at Meg's I settled on an assisted living facility for my mother and made arrangements to move her. The closing of my Victorian house was executed without a hitch, most likely because I'd paid cash. Afterward, I spent a day cleaning the floors, bathrooms, and countertops. And the following morning I was as excited as a ten-year-old when the truck delivered my effects.

Searching, I read the labels I'd written on the boxes stacked from floor to ceiling in my entrance hall. The worst thing about moving was unpacking. It was always faster with extra hands but I didn't ask Meg to help me because Lance was coming to town tomorrow and she needed some time to prepare. I also was hell-bent on unpacking, because there was no way I wanted my daughter's boyfriend in La Crosse without having him over for dinner. You could learn a lot about a person when you broke bread with them.

By the end of Lance's visit I'd have the house tidy enough to host a meal even if it killed me.

At least that was my plan.

First, I needed a functional dining room, a fact which put unpacking on hold for a moment.

"Aha," I said, finding the box with my tools at the bottom of a stack. Even though I'd invested my severance and rolled over my 401K, I didn't want to use any of my nest egg on the house. I'd made enough money selling my place in Denver to use the profits for renovations I had planned. I wanted to buy some antiques as well. It was a sacrilege to own a Victorian house and stuff it full of modern furniture.

In fact, the only furniture I'd brought with me was my bedroom set, a Mission-style dining room table and chairs, and the comfy white couches from my living room. This old house had five bedrooms. Thanks to the movers, one was now occupied with my couches where I planned to watch TV. Since all of the closets were tiny, I'd earmarked the smallest bedroom to convert into a dressing room which I was going to have a heyday designing.

I'd make everything in this house as historically correct as possible—the draperies, the Persian carpets, vintage replica faucets for the two claw-footed bathtubs. I'd already started combing the local antique stores in my quest to find a vintage dressing table. Maybe I'd add some red satin drapes and a portrait of a Gibson Girl—though they were technically Edwardian.

After shifting all the boxes off of the one marked "tools," I used my pocketknife to slice the tape, opened it up and pulled out a hammer. The first thing I was going to do was remove the hideous plywood bar in my dining room.

The previous owners had forfeited on their loan, a testament to their lack of judgment, I suppose. But because the house was in need of repair, I purchased the place for the balance they'd owed the bank and the realtor's commission. Yes, it was a steal. My undergrad was in accounting. I had analyzed the numbers, factoring in all the repairs I wanted to make, and this little gem truly was a windfall. Even if I went over my budget by a whopping one hundred percent, it would still be a good investment.

And I intended to make this place mine—to turn it into a showplace where I'd be proud to host parties (if I so desired). Sure, for a million dollars I could have purchased the mansion on idyllic Cass Street, but in my opinion, Cass had too much traffic, even if the entire populous of the city of La Crosse considered Cass Street to be the shizzle.

After everything I'd been through, I didn't want to make a spectacle of myself. I wanted to be left alone. I hadn't looked at the news since I left Denver and didn't give a rat's ass. And aside from a cursory glance or two, I hadn't checked my email, either.

I still had a driving need to find the culprit who was ultimately responsible for getting me fired. So, I spent countless hours staring at the warehouse footage in the middle of the night. It added new meaning to the saying "watching paint dry."

In my dining room, holding my hammer, I closely examined the plywood bar which had been erected in front of a gorgeous built-in oak China cabinet. It had Corinthian columns extending to the ceiling, and the sides of the cupboard were inlaid with an intricate fig leaf pattern. The drawers were all functional, though they needed proper pulls, rather than the cheap copper ones someone must have installed around the 1930s. The drawer pulls in the butler's pantry were ornate and original Victorian and I planned to find something similar. The piece should be polished and on display, not the backdrop to a bar that looked like a teenager had thrown it together in his parents' basement.

There was only one nail attaching the eyesore to the wall, so it took but a few swings of my hammer to dislodge it. To my joy, the oak paneling underneath wasn't terribly damaged and would only need a dollop of wood putty, a little sanding, and a touchup of stain to cover the hole.

I hauled the plywood out back to break it down into pieces small enough to fit in the fire pit. The effort to swing a hammer felt good, though bending over made me dizzy. I managed not to wobble too much while I took out twenty years of pent-up aggression from kissing Leon's ass.

Aside from desperately needing fresh paint, there were so many things about this house that I adored—the rose marble hearth in the drawing room, five stained glass windows that ushered in sparkling light which varied at different hours of the day. The entrance hall was spacious and welcoming with vaulted ceilings and the original woodwork of the main staircase was still intact, though it needed a new carpet runner to show it off. Persian of course, maybe red, maybe gold. I'd know once I picked the paint colors.

All the hardware on the doors was original brass, etched with incredible details of leaves, urns, and flowers. Even the hinges had been embossed. Everywhere I turned I discovered something new, treasures that weren't in any of the pictures I'd seen, things that gave this house its very own charac-ter—including a Steger and Son's piano which had been left in the library. It was a gorgeous upright with inlaid oak, and ionic columns supporting the keyboard. They were incredibly similar to those in the dining room china cabinet. However, to my chagrin, the piano sounded like a wounded cat when I played it. As soon as I got the chance, I'd call a repairman and have it tuned.

I took a few lessons when I was a kid and I'd always wanted to start back up again. Now that I had a vintage piano in my vintage house, I planned to enjoy it.

After demolishing the bar, I spent the afternoon unpacking boxes when the brass knocker on the enormous front door boomed, making me jolt.

"A moment!" I hollered, weaving my way through the clutter of wadded paper, boxes, and bubble wrap.

On the front porch, a bearded man faced me, his expression serious. About my age, he was solidly built with a tanned face, contrasting with his thick, nicely trimmed gray beard. his shirtsleeves were rolled up, flaunting a pair of well-muscled, hairy forearms. He wasn't terribly tall, but still had a good five inches on me.

"Hi." He gave a friendly nod and smiled, making the corners of his shiny green eyes crinkle. He wore a University of Wisconsin ball cap and work boots. "I'm Bob Anderson. You called about some landscaping?"

"Oh, yes, absolutely." I stepped out onto the wooden porch and closed the door on the mess behind me. "My yard needs a complete makeover. How soon can you start?"

"Well, let's not get ahead of ourselves here. You do realize we're already into October and we'll be lucky if it doesn't snow before Thanksgiving?"

Undaunted, I led him to the edge of the porch, where the shrubbery was overgrown, some of which had already started to turn brown in anticipation of autumn. "Come spring, I want this place to look amazing. I'm thinking a well-cultivated English garden would be ideal."

He pointed to a clump of spindly looking bushes. "Well, you'll want to keep these lilacs. All they need is a bit of pruning and they'll fill out nicely."

I liked this guy already. "Perfect, and what do you think about planting some wisteria to grow along the top edge of the porch?"

Bob removed his cap and scratched his shiny bald head, several shades lighter than his tanned face. "Wisteria takes a lot of work and if you don't stay on top of pruning the vines, they can damage the wood and cause rot."

The wood on my clapboard house had already been subject to enough damage. "What do you recommend?"

"Well, if you want to plant a wisteria vine, you ought to build a trellis and constrain its growth there rather than on your house's wood."

I glanced over the side of the rail to a pile of rocks with moss growing on them. "Can you build a trellis?"

"Yes, ma'am."

"Excellent." I led him down the steps to a brick walkway that wasn't in bad shape. "So, in preparation for winter, how do you suggest we start?"

"If this were my house, I'd prune everything back pretty aggressively now. As you said, it's overgrown. With a good fall pruning, come early spring we'll be able to see what we have to work with—build your trellis and plant your wisteria." Bob pointed to a flower bed—at least I think it used to be a flower bed. "There you have a mess of untamed tiger lilies. If you don't get those under control, they'll eventually strangle every plant in your garden."

I almost suspected the lilies had already gone wild. "We don't want those then, do we?"

"No, ma'am. In my opinion, tiger lilies are a lazy man's flowers. They grow fast and take over."

I stooped down and tried to pull one, but only ended up with a handful of spindly leaves. "I'd rather have more variety. Let's take them out while we're trimming."

By the time Bob left, we had not only started to sketch out plans for my new garden, he'd given me phone numbers for a painter, a boiler service repairman, and a basement floor specialist, all of whom I called immediately.

The painter could start on the outside of the house in June, the boiler service repairman would be here next week to winterize my heating system, and the basement floor would be poured in two weeks. It must have been my lucky day because the basement guys had a cancellation, otherwise I would have had to wait six months or more.

In my opinion, moving day was a win. Not only did I get half of my boxes unpacked, I met Bob who seemed to be clever and honest—the salt of the earth. When it came to contractors, they always had the best connections and it was better to ask them for referrals than to comb the internet, calling people who might or might not be reliable, no matter what their star rating was on Google.

Because the kitchen needed an upgrade immediately, I didn't bother shopping around and calling contractors. The day after I arrived in La Crosse, I'd gone straight to the big box hardware store with the dimensions and sat with a consultant to design my kitchen. I chose an oak veneer for the cupboards which would coordinate nicely with the Victorian character of the house, but this was the twenty-first century and I needed modern conveniences when I cooked. Tomorrow, I had a new gas range and a side-by-side refrigerator being delivered so I could make dinner for Meg and her boyfriend.

With luck, the kitchen would be finished by Thanksgiving. If not, at least I'd have a decent oven in which to roast a turkey.

CHAPTER TWELVE

MEG

"**D**ammit!" I cursed, running my hand under a stream of water in the kitchen sink. The stupid knife slipped while I was slicing cauliflower for a vegetable tray. It barely pricked the heel of my hand, yet I was bleeding as if I'd slashed myself to the bone.

I grabbed a paper towel and wrapped it around the cut, applying pressure as I dashed to the bathroom to my mega stash of Band-Aids. I went through them like most people go through tissues. I guess I was a bleeder—and tiny cuts took so long to heal. Once Elaine and I showed up on the same day with Band-Aids wrapped around our pointer fingers. By the time my cut scabbed over, Elaine's had already healed.

She had all the luck.

But today, I wasn't about to let a little owie slow me down. Lance ought to be here any minute. I dabbed on some antibiotic ointment and covered the wound with a Band-Aid, waited a few minutes for the blood to overflow, repeated the process like I always had to, then finally I finished the veggie tray and set it on the coffee table.

Everything was ready. Ripper had even been pretty good about keeping his music bearable. The fridge was stocked, the apartment was spotless. I'd already touched up my makeup five times and was getting whiplash from twisting to look out the window, but I didn't want to just stand in front of it and wait for him to drive up...or did I?

Thank the stars, my internal argument didn't last long because an older model, gray Toyota Corolla came to a stop alongside the curb.

A Corolla, huh?

My dad always said Toyotas were reliable. I wasn't disappointed, but I guess I expected something a little more original, like a Jeep or one of those GMC trucks that have all the bells and whistles in the commercials.

When the driver leaned forward to cut the engine, my estrogen levels went into overdrive, my fixation on his Corolla forgotten. Who cared about a car when the man of my dreams had just arrived? I couldn't help my squeal or my frenetic jogging in place complete with girly flapping hands.

Before I even started running for the door, Maya launched into a cacophony of barking. "Hush!" I shouted. Of course, when the Chihuahua ignored me, I headed outside, shutting the door in her adorable wide-eyed, somewhat crazed face.

"Lance! You made it!" I cried, dashing down the steps and to the curb.

As he closed his car door, he grinned at me, his clothes a rumpled mess, his brown hair a riot of curls and spikes. Yep, this was the same dude I met on the cruise three months ago. He came around the Corolla and opened his arms. "When I found out La Crosse had Octoberfest, there was no way I'd miss it. After all, I have German roots *and* a thirst for beer."

It wasn't exactly the greeting I'd been imagining, but I fell into his embrace and breathed him in—the scent of Ivory soap with an overtone of French fries. "You're lucky this year. Usually Octoberfest is a week earlier."

He gave me a peck on the lips. "I'm always lucky, Babe."

My hands trembled as I led him up the porch stairs to my apartment. Inside, Maya had barked herself to the verge of hysterics. I held up my palm to Lance as I reached for the knob. "Stay there while I corral my attack Chihuahua."

He laughed as I opened the door, but scuttled backward as she shot outside, barking and growling, her fur standing on end. The imp grabbed his pants leg and shook her entire body. "Whoa, you weren't kidding!" he said, kicking his foot, trying to dislodge her dagger teeth.

I twisted my dog away and scooped her into my arms. "Sorry! She's a real sweetheart most of the time but isn't overly fond of guests."

"Aw, she'll like *me*." He held his finger beneath her nose. Maya bared her teeth and growled. Lance snapped his hand away. "Will she bite?"

One must never assume anything when it came to Maya. "Once we're inside, she ought to keep her distance. Just don't provoke her."

Because Miss She-Devil Princess was still growling, I kept her in my arms as I showed him inside my colorful, Bohemian-inspired hideaway. The interior might look like a thrown together mismatch, but it took a lot of time to create the perfect combination of controlled chaos.

Lance turned full circle. "Whoa, this place is gnarly." He looked at my office nook, framed by the tree of life on a purple background. "It reminds me of you."

"It's homey." I kissed the top of Maya's head and gave her a gentle rub under the chin with my pointer finger. "Did you stop for lunch or eat on the road? Are you hungry?"

He brushed off his shirt, making a few grains of salt flutter to the floor. "I grabbed a burger and fries, but I can always eat."

I set Maya down and she skulked to her bed in the corner of the living room, keeping her eyes on Lance, growling at him if stepped too near. Such a little charmer.

We nibbled on the veggies I'd set out and drank iced tea while Lance raved about the Ohio State football game he'd listened to on the way up. He had the audacity to complain because once he'd crossed into Wisconsin, he was forced to listen to the Badgers which I had showing on the TV while I was cleaning. Maybe later I'd remind Lance that UW was my beloved alma mater—after we had a chance to reacquaint ourselves.

He checked the Ohio State score on his phone—like he needed to. They always won, which was boring. I'd rather watch a Badger game any day because the outcome wasn't a for sure thing.

Tapping my foot, I leaned in and watched his thumbs fly across his keyboard. Was Lance ignoring me? Was there something wrong with the pink paisley dress I was wearing?

Holy kamoly, I'd been waiting for this day for weeks, yet if his preoccupation with the score was any indication, Lance was indifferent about our reunion. As for me, I sat twisting a lock of hair around my finger, my lips twisting with all the things I might say next.

Wasn't he as excited to see me as I was to see him? Not that I expected Lance to immediately jump my bones. But as soon as he stepped out of his car, he acted as if he were meeting an old college buddy rather than a fairly new girlfriend with whom he'd been communicating long distance. Well, the communication had been off and on, but I knew how busy he was.

"So, where's this Octoberfest? I thought you said we could walk to the grounds from here." He held up his empty glass of iced tea and clinked the ice. "I need something stronger than this."

I couldn't help but glance at my watch. It was only two o'clock in the afternoon—way too early to start drinking. A vision of my father drunk and passed out on the couch shot through my head. Of course, I shook it off. My dad was a big drinker, but he usually didn't crack open a can of beer until late afternoon—most of the time. But then again, Octoberfest was a major holiday in this town, and if we paced ourselves, we ought to be okay.

Was I overreacting? Was my deflated ego dramatized? Why shouldn't I be a little hurt since it appeared as if Lance had come to party at the festival rather than to see me? On the other hand, why did I always worry excessively? He probably wanted to do both.

I grabbed my purse and donned my favorite purple jacket with pink and blue flowers and a green border. Maya bid us farewell with a round of howling that we still heard a block away.

Lance held my hand, his stride longer than mine, making me shuffle faster than usual.

"Are you in a hurry?" I asked.

"You bet." He gave me a wink. "You wanna race?"

"What, are we ten?"

He nudged me forward. "I'll give you a head start."

Only this morning I'd read an article about how looking at the world as a child and living in the moment helped to rekindle a sense of wonder into an adult's life. Sure, I was a little quirky, but I was no runner.

"How about we skip?" I countered. After all, I was wearing ballet flats, not exactly as sturdy as his sneakers.

He gave me a quizzical look, but I wasn't going to wait. I giggled and surged forward.

At least in my opinion I surged. The dude passed me after the first block, grabbed my hand and practically dragged me onward.

Polka music shook the sidewalk before the fairgrounds came into view. And once we were inside the gates, Lance bought two boot-shaped steins filled with frothy beer. I must have started a thing with the skipping because he proceeded to link arms with me and skip toward the stage, leaving a trail of beer in our wake. A polka band was holding forth while couples dressed in lederhosen and dirndl costumes spun around us.

Lance put our boots on the stage before grabbing me by the waist and launching into the most raucous step-together-step-hop I'd ever done in my life.

Who was this dude?

Sure, I knew he was spontaneous even though we'd only slow danced on the cruise. I had no idea he was so enthusiastic about polkaing, but he whirled me around the floor like he was in a contest and hell-bent on winning. Between sets, he guzzled the beer in his boot. I nursed mine, finishing it about the time they shot off the fireworks from Grandad's Bluff—a high point on the western cliffs that looked out over the city.

I'd lost count of the number of boots Lance had consumed.

It was after midnight when he held my hand and we walked—more like wove—our way back to my apartment, met by my poor traumatized Chihuahua.

When I came in from taking Maya to go potty, the dude was already out cold, snoring on the couch.

My head dropped forward as I rubbed the back of my neck. *So much for a romantic evening.*

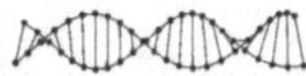

The next morning, I awoke to the gentle caress of fingertips brushing my scalp. I sighed, stretching, and opening my eyes. Lance held up a Bloody Mary—his hair combed back and wet, his face shiny and clean as if he'd just stepped out of the shower. "Last night was amazing, Babe."

What had I missed? I glanced at the pillow beside me but that side of the bed had been unused. I don't think I'd ever met anybody so psyched about Octoberfest, even if he was of German descent—but Lovell wasn't even a German name.

"Sure, last night was something else," I replied, gently pushing the drink away. "I'm more of a coffee in the morning girl."

I don't know why, but his smile warmed me just like it had on the day we met. "Thought of that, too." He reached for a steaming mug on the bedside table. "You like it with cream, no sugar, right?"

I scooted up and leaned against the headboard. "You remembered."

"I remember everything about you, Meg-a-licious." He nuzzled into my neck. "I'm sorry I flaked on you. I guess the drive took it out of me. You deserve better than that."

I sipped my coffee, the apology and the peace offering doing a great deal to ease the doubts I'd gone to bed with last night. After all, Lance had driven all the way from Ohio just to spend the weekend with me.

His lips trailed beneath the collar of my V-neck t-shirt. "Tell you what, why don't we stay in bed all day—make love—watch movies."

I closed my eyes and indulged myself in his kisses. "Mm, that sounds amazing. I even have a copy of the *Kama Sutra* in my bedside drawer. We could cuddle up and read it."

"Reading is way too boring." He slid onto the bed beside me, kissing his way under the covers. "I like to watch."

Chapter Thirteen

Jane

During the week I'd spent at Meg's, she and I had found a little Victorian settee at an antique shop in Sparta, just east of La Crosse. It was perfect for my parlor and I'd placed it in front of the large street-facing window, but since it was the only piece of furniture on the main floor aside from my dining table and chairs, the parlor looked rather stark, as did my empty drawing room.

Lance didn't seem to mind. He'd come right in and made himself useful by opening a bottle of wine he and my daughter had brought. At first glance, the young man didn't look like Meg's type. She usually dated guys who were on the nerdy spectrum—guys who tinkered with computers or who were talented musicians. But Lance reminded me of a sun-kissed surfer—at least someone who preferred to spend his time outdoors.

Though my brother Roger was no longer practicing medicine, he was a doctor, and Lance didn't seem like the type to put up with all the years of school. Roger was serious, studious, and contemplative. I couldn't exactly put my finger on it but my first impression was to peg Lance as the sort of man who never left his childhood. Maybe he reminded me of my ex—immature and always hankering for a party.

I hoped not, for Meg's sake.

For dinner, I made chicken fajitas including guacamole and *pico de gallo*. Fresh ingredients were always better, and now that I had time on my hands, I didn't mind making things from scratch.

Meg rolled up her flour tortilla and took a bite, her eyes rolling back. "Oh, my God, Mom, this is delicious."

"Yeah, it's better than going to Chili's," Lance agreed, taking a sip of his third glass of wine.

Fortunately, I'd also bought a bottle, which Meg's boyfriend had been more than happy to open after the first disappeared. I'd opted to drink water and gave him a nod, the corners of my lips reluctantly turning upward. "Thank you."

I took my first bite and savored it. Goodness, it did taste good. "How long was the drive from Ohio?"

Lance's prominent Adam's apple bobbed with his swallow. "A little over nine hours."

"Wow, that's quite a distance." I was well-versed in geography, though I needed to make small talk, so I added, "I'm surprised you didn't fly."

"Driving relaxes me."

"Wonderful, if you can afford the time." I pursed my lips. When I was working for Bethany Plastics, whenever I went on vacation I wanted to get to my destination as soon as possible. Driving was a waste of precious minutes. Moreover, with my salary, I could afford to fly and rent a car. I was absolutely positive a single doctor earned plenty of money to do the same.

"What are you planning to do now that you've moved to La Crosse?" Lance asked.

It was difficult not to read into his words...*now that you've been fired*. Sure, Meg would have told him why I'd moved here and bought a house close to her. I hadn't asked her not to. The bile in my gut churned. Would I harbor an inadequacy complex for the rest of my life?

Probably.

I'd put a lot of thought into my future, and though I didn't *need* to work, I certainly wasn't about to let Leon Worthington take the wind out of my sails for good. Of course, that damned newspaper article had all but doomed me from ever working in the beverage industry again. Moreover, I still hadn't seen movement during my late-night security camera footage watching vigils.

Meg and I exchanged glances as I replied, "I'm taking a bit of time to refurbish this house, and once that's done, I'll start weighing my options."

Lance piled guacamole on one end of his fajita, licking his fingers where it had overflowed. "Cool."

I decided to take the lead of this question-and-answer session. "So, what made you want to become a doctor?"

"Uh..." Lance shrugged as he took a bite. Chewing, his mouth full, he replied, "I wanted to help people."

I almost laughed at his standard answer. Was he fobbing me off? "I'll bet everyone who goes into medicine initially does it to help people. But I'm guessing there's more. Isn't there?"

"You don't have to answer that." Meg shot me a dagger-eyed look. Yes, my daughter knew what I was doing. "Helping people is incredibly virtuous."

"But don't most employees help people in some way?" I took a tortilla and began to load it up. "Meg, you help people at the library all the time."

"Yeah, but that's different."

I dropped a dollop of sour cream on top of my creation. "How so?"

Meg reached for the *pico*. "I'm not helping people recover from illnesses."

"Maybe not directly," I took a drink of water. "But isn't reading calming? Doesn't the library carry any number of books about self-care and what-not?"

"Of course we do, but I don't listen to patron's hearts and test their cholesterol. Good grief, Mom, all doctors are heroes in my book. You're just tarnished because of the bad experiences you've had."

Maybe she was right. Perhaps I'd let my aversion to MDs taint me.

I bit into my fajita, chewing and swallowing before I posed my next question to the scruffy but handsome doctor from Ohio. "Did you have an experience in your childhood where you helped someone and that cemented your decision to become a doctor?"

Meg groaned and looked to the silver Victorian chandelier above. "Mom, enough."

"Sorry." I didn't regret my questions at all. Instead, I was overjoyed that I owned a home abounding with historical relics like the chandelier. "I asked your Uncle Roger the same question not too long ago. He said he made his decision when he had to have his broken arm set." I inclined my head to Lance. "Roger fractured his radius playing basketball in the eighth grade. He said the doctor had a calming bedside manner—talked to him about basketball and made Roger forget about his arm. That was the moment my brother decided he wanted to be just like that doctor—he wanted to guide patients through the scary moments."

Meg sighed. "I love Uncle Roger."

Of course, she did. Everyone loved my brother especially in small doses. He lived in Washington state and couldn't bear to see our mother because it tore him up too much. However, I wasn't convinced his feelings justified the fact that he hadn't been to see Mama since I'd been forced to put her in assisted living. I wasn't sure how I felt about Roger's choice to remain absent aside from a little resentful because our mother's care fell solely on my shoulders.

"Yeah," Lance rubbed his belly and belched. "Now that I think about it, the ER doc who sewed up the stitches at the back of my head when I was nine was awesome—made a real impression on me. I'll never forget how cool he was."

Wonderful, my daughter was dating a surfer-dude doctor who lived six hundred miles away. But maybe the distance wasn't such a bad thing. After all, absence made the heart grow fonder...or gave it amnesia.

I grinned at him. "How about we play a game of Scrabble?"

CHAPTER FOURTEEN

MEG

Lance had been gone for two weeks. We'd texted a couple of times but hadn't established a date for getting together again. And the more time droned on, the stranger our relationship seemed. I mean, the morning he'd brought me coffee in bed, sex had been amazing. He'd apologized for overdoing it at Octoberfest, which I really appreciated. But there were little quirky things about him that were weird. When I dug right down and examined my warring emotions, our fondness was lopsided. When he arrived, I wanted to kiss and cuddle and show him how much I missed him. Lance? He wanted to polka and drink beer.

Was I over analyzing? Mom certainly made her opinion clear, but she'd compared Lance to my uncle, saying that he wasn't the doctor type.

Type?

Did there have to be a type?

"He misspelled siren," I said, explaining about our Scrabble game at Mom's while Elaine and I worked to catalogue a box of new books, sitting at a study table behind the fiction section.

"So?" She peered at me through her thick lenses. "Lots of people are bad spellers."

After adhering a library label, I closed the book and put it on the cart. "Doctors?"

"Sure, smart people can be bad spellers, too. Even math geniuses."

"Do you know any math geniuses?"

"No, but I'm trying to make a point here."

I stuck a label to the inside of another book and rubbed it flat. "I appreciate your candor. I know there are a lot of people out there who aren't good spellers. I just don't expect a doctor to be one."

Elaine reached inside the carton and pulled out a thick novel. "When you add it all up, how much time have you spent with the dude? And I don't mean texting and talking on the phone. How much time have you physically been together?"

"Well, there were four days on the cruise where we were inseparable. Then just the three days he was here."

"And he drove an old Toyota Corolla?"

"Yeah, but that's a decent enough car. He doesn't need to have a new SUV to impress me."

Elaine gaped with those enormous eyes. "Aaaand he drinks too much?"

I'd told her about that, too. On the ship, I hadn't really considered his drinking to be excessive. After all, adults tend to imbibe in copious amounts of alcohol when they're on vacation. I didn't realize he might have a problem until he bought the beer boots at Octoberfest and subsequently passed out on my couch—the unconscious part I hadn't told Elaine because if I did, she'd tell me to dump him and run. Nor had I mentioned the Bloody Mary he'd downed the next morning...or losing count of the glasses of wine he drank at Mom's. But now when I took a moment to look back at the cruise, we both did an awful lot of drinking, though he'd definitely consumed substantially more than me.

As far as Elaine was concerned, I'd told her the sex was amazing and I wasn't going to say anything else about that part of our relationship. Nonetheless, since she mentioned it, Lance and I really hadn't spent all that much time together even though we'd technically known each other nearly four months. No wonder I was having doubts, especially since it wasn't unusual to go days without hearing a peep out of him—sometimes weeks.

I pulled a new library sticker from its backing and managed to get it stuck to my shirt. "He does drink a lot when he's on vacation, but who knows what he's like when he's home."

She snorted. "I'll bet he's as sober as a tree."

I stripped off the sticker and flicked it into the bin. "A tree?"

Elaine shrugged, putting the novel onto the cart. "A stick? I don't know. As sober as a nun?"

I laughed. "At least he's amazing at dancing the polka."

"Then he'll fit right in around here."

True, but Lance had professed to being an Ohio boy. He even openly hated my Badgers. He may have enjoyed Octoberfest, but he didn't mention anything about moving to La Crosse. On the other hand, I didn't talk about the possibility of me moving to Columbus either, which would be a colossal disaster. My mother would have a cow. She'd not only bought a house here, she'd moved my grandmother all the way from Colorado just to be close to me.

I dropped my forehead into the palm of my hand. What the heck was I doing dating a party animal who lived three states away?

"Something's really bothering you." Elaine clasped my shoulder and squeezed. "I can tell, and it's not Lance's drinking or his spelling. What is it?"

"I don't know." But as soon as the words left my lips, I did know. "Um…"

"What?" she pressed.

"He not only would rather watch movies than read, while we were watching *The Hunger Games* series, which he said he loved, he confessed that he'd never read a single one of the novels. He also admitted he's not much of a reader altogether—but on the ship he told me he had read all the time." Wasn't that akin to lying? Was he trying to impress me because I'm a librarian?

"Seriously?" Elaine grabbed the last book out of the box and shook it under my nose. "Who hasn't read *The Hunger Games*?"

"Lance Lovell, evidently." I twisted my ponytail around my finger. "But he's still a huge fan."

"Look." Elaine opened the hardback, carefully pressing the pages downward so as not to break the spine. "I might have been a believer with Scrabble, but not *reading*? You're a freaking reader on steroids."

I shrugged. "Lots of people aren't readers."

"Stop for one minute and listen to yourself." She threw out her hands. "You *love* to read."

Yes, I did, but Lance and I could have lots of varying interests—didn't most couples? "So? That's me."

"You're also surrounded by books of all types with computers at your fingertips."

I groaned, would she just let it go? "Duh."

"No, what I meant to say is that you are an expert at research." She put the hardback on the cart and stuck her googly-eyed face an inch away from mine. "Have you looked him up?"

"Sure—well, I searched social media profiles. I also found the little town where he lives in Ohio and whatnot." But damn, I didn't even know the name of the hospital where he worked.

"Not good enough." Elaine thrust her finger toward my office door. "Go forth and collect data And for the record, I think the dude is awesome. After all, he got you to dance a polka, didn't he?"

As I headed off, I gave her a wink. "I suppose, but I got him to skip all the way from my apartment to the Octoberfest grounds."

She stood and grabbed the cart by the handles. "Don't skirt around it. You enjoyed yourself."

I hated it when she was right.

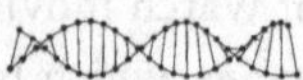

I did have a great time at Octoberfest with Lance. Polka dancing was not an activity I'd choose for myself, but once I realized no one was watching us and he didn't seem to care how many times I stepped on his toes, I just went with it.

But no matter how much I wanted to ignore all the stupid voices in my head filling my mind with doubts, I just wanted to fall madly in love with the man. Doing so would fit in ever so nicely with my plans to get married, have kids, and buy a house. However, what woman wouldn't have doubts when trying to maintain a long-distance relationship with a guy with whom she'd only spent a cumulative sum of eight days?

Why couldn't I just roll with it rather than overanalyzing everything? On the other side, how could I ignore my inner voice of caution? Was Lance an alcoholic? Was I one of those women who fell for men like her father? Why did he drive an older Corolla? Because he spent his money on vacations? Why did he sometimes ignore me for weeks? I hated to be ignored.

Oh...and how could I forget how he dissed me the last night on the ship?

God, I'm gullible.

Of course, he'd misspelled siren, substituting the "e" for an "i" when we were playing Scrabble at Mom's. Interestingly, she didn't correct him—she just gave me a knowing look which needled at me, too.

It didn't take a psychic to know Lance did not endear himself to my mother after he drank all but one glass of the two bottles of wine served at dinner. Maybe he *was* like my dad. Could I be drawn to him because of some sort of underlying daddy complex?

God save me. The last thing I needed was to fall in love with an alcoholic.

Sitting at my desk with the door closed, the first thing I Googled was Dr. Lance Lovell. The search came up with a dentist in Wyoming, a PhD who was a consultant in Montana, and a lawyer born in 1960 who also lived in Montana.

The skin across my entire body prickled with heat.

I pulled up the website the Ohio State Medical Board and typed Lovell and found there at least were no complaints lodged against his last name.

I then started methodically bringing up the websites of hospitals within fifty miles of Darbydale, the first one being The Ohio State University Wexner Medical Center. I clicked on *"Find a Doctor,"* typed in Lovell, and got *"There are no providers who match your search criteria."* I typed the name Virgil and got the same result. I repeated the process at the five other hospitals within a reasonable driving distance.

When those searches turned up nothing, I went back out to Google and searched for Dr. Virgil Lovell, found an obituary for a farmer, and another for Dr. V.C. Lovell who passed away in 2012.

I went to Facebook and examined Lance's profile—his picture with his messy hair wearing a wrinkled t-shirt and the name Lance Lovell, M.D. beneath his photo. In his feed he'd recently added some stunning images of La Crosse including a selfie of him with the bridge in the background. I didn't remember taking him down to the river. In fact, we'd been so busy at the Octoberfest grounds, we hadn't made it to Riverside Park, but that's where he must have taken the shot—or else he'd photoshopped his handsome self into a stock image.

Maybe he drove by the park on his way out of town?

Weird.

Still, his post didn't mention anything about meeting up with this great girl he got to know on his cruise to Bermuda. Was he embarrassed by me? He was so perfect, and I...*wasn't.* Sure, he told me he liked curvy girls, but did he really?

I hadn't ever confronted him about his first name. I suppose I should have said something, but we hadn't really been together long enough to talk about such a trivial thing. And I wasn't exactly good at confrontation. "I saw your receipt says Virgil and the last name is blotted out, so what gives?" I could have asked, but that wasn't me. I was more the type who kept things inside and waited to find out if I ought to worry or not.

I'd chosen not. Sort of.

For the hell of it, I typed Virgil Lovell in Facebook's search. I didn't use "Dr." or "M.D." A bunch of Virgils with the last name Lovell appeared. I scanned the list and even opened a couple of profiles, but none of them were Lance, or whatever his name was.

Not about to give up, I grabbed my cell phone and did a Google search of his image from one of the selfies I'd taken.

Google gave me the thinking circle, but after what seemed like ages, it came up with two exact likenesses, both of them from Facebook. The second was the dude I'd been communicating with, Lance Lovell. The very first image was also my Lance, but his name was Virgil Klein.

Klein is a German last name.

I gulped. The condensation from his glass had made the last name unreadable on the receipt I'd seen on the ship.

My hands shook as I opened Virgil Klein's profile.

There was no reference to Lance. No reference to Lovell. No middle name was listed.

By this stage, I shouldn't have been shocked by what I saw.

But I was stunned, rendered dizzy, and straining to breathe.

Why hadn't I done this sooner? I was a researcher, yet I'd just blindly trusted some dude I'd met on a ship's excursion. I'd blindly believed everything he said, kissed him, slept with him.

Virgil Klein's Facebook header displayed a picture of him with a woman—a gorgeous brunette. They were happy, laughing, and on the deck of a pristine white cruise ship. His posts were almost entirely pictures of him with her—Christmas, Thanksgiving, on a beach somewhere.

His profile said he went to East High School in Columbus. It didn't mention college. He was married to Jocelyn Klein and he worked for the Solid Waste Authority of Central Ohio.

My head spun and my fingers trembled as I moved to the mouse and clicked on Jocelyn's profile. She was an entertainer for Cutter Cruise Lines.

Holy shit.

Everything unraveled in front of me. I'd heard a big truck rumble to life when I was on the phone with *Virgil*. The two-timing bastard was a garbage man and he messed around behind his wife's back when she was at sea, performing on cruise ships.

He drove an old Corolla.

He wasn't a doctor.

He wasn't honest.

He has been stringing me along over the past several months and I've been too blind to realize he has blown smoke in my face since the moment I sat beside him on that damned bus!

Chapter Fifteen

Jane

For weeks I'd been patching plaster walls and painting and it was getting difficult to see the blue denim through all the splatter covering my overalls. Of course, I washed them all the time, but the paint never came out.

I'd used Victorian colors recommended by the man at the paint shop, and every room had its own personality—though I'd yet to buy much furniture or artwork. I was holding off until the walls and floors were finished, then Meg and I were planning to hit every antique store within a hundred-mile radius.

Fresh paint made the walls come to life. The parlor was a wedgwood blue for daytime tea parties and the drawing room, which the Victorians used for withdrawing after dinner, was a deep burgundy. I painted the dining room a medium hue of gold to coordinate with the chandelier shades I'd ordered from Amazon. The library was a sage green, and the color of the entrance hall reminded me of seafoam.

The bedrooms were an array of colors from salmon to linen to rose madder, and yellow ochre. I'd saved my dressing room for last, for which I'd chosen a soft shade of pink. After taping the molding, floorboards, and doors, I climbed the ladder with my paint can and brush to carefully apply a line of paint beneath the upper molding.

As soon as I dipped the bristles into the thick latex, the front door knocker clapped loudly. I jolted, making the paint can teeter, my brush slipping from my fingertips and smacking me in the face. "Dammit!" I swore, climbing down, the wire handle of the can cutting into my fingers.

After I set the paint on the tarp, I swore again, this time at the purple bruises swelling on the inside of my fingers. I had such ridiculously thin skin, I even managed to break blood vessels when I clapped my hands. Jeez, I hated it when that happened.

The knocker sounded again, and I grabbed a rag, making sure I didn't have any paint on myself that might rub off onto something as I hurried down the stairs. "Coming!"

Before opening the door, I swiped the cloth across my face.

Leaning against porch rail with his ankles crossed, Bob grinned...I swear he was doing a terrible job of not laughing. "Did I catch you at a bad time?"

"No." I touched my cheek with the tips of my fingers. Was it still covered with pink paint? "I was just starting in on the dressing room."

He straightened and dropped his arms to his sides. "You need some help?"

"I thought you said you don't paint?"

"Not for a living, but I'd do it for a friend."

I tried not to smile too broadly. The man had done an amazing job trimming back my bushes and had just spread fall fertilizer over the lawn. And hell yes, I could use a friend. "You want to come in for a cup of coffee?"

He looked at his clothes—grass stained, though in a lot better shape than my overalls. "I'm not really dressed for it."

In my opinion, he was a whole lot cleaner than me, paint-splattered face and all. "Neither am I. We can sit on the stools in the kitchen. It's a disgusting throwback to the sixties—but my espresso machine works."

He agreed and I led him through my starkly-furnished house and into my grungy kitchen offset by my brand-new stove and refrigerator.

"When are the guys from Menards going to start installing the new cupboards?" Bob asked, sliding onto a stool.

"Next week, thank goodness." I pulled the milk out of the fridge and turned on my espresso maker. "Sorry, I forgot to ask if you like latte."

"Never had one."

I gawked at him. "Then you haven't lived."

"Well then, enlighten me."

I chuckled. Bob didn't come across as a typical yard guy. Sure, his skin was sun-bronzed and he had those incredibly well-muscled forearms that come from hours of hard labor. But he used big words like grandiose and floriculture.

The machine started frothing the milk while I measured the espresso. "Have you always been a landscaper?"

"Oh, no. I'm retired."

"Aren't you kinda young to be retired?" I put a few slice-and-bake chocolate chip cookies on a plate. When Meg was little and needed to take snacks to school, I quickly learned that slice-and-bake cookies were the closest thing to homemade a working single mom could manage.

"Aren't you?" he countered.

"Touché." I poured the coffee, topped each cup with the frothed milk, then joined him, sitting on the second stool. "So, what did you do before you became my extraordinary yard guy?"

"I was a pharmacist. Got burned out when COVID hit and decided to hang up the white coat once and for all."

"Was it awful dealing with the pandemic?"

"Yes. It changed how we did everything. They didn't just change something here and there, either. The powers that be threw new stuff at us *daily*. Of course, the pharmacy stayed open when the country shut down and we were trying to help patients yet were constantly required to be on phone calls and Zoom chats with corporate."

"Which took you away from your job." I knew all too well what it must have been like. I'd been in the middle of a firestorm at Bethany at the time.

Bob shook his head. "Technicians quit in droves, then we couldn't hire people, so those who were left had to take extra shifts. I worked six months without a day off. That's when I decided I'd had enough."

He sipped his coffee while his eyebrows shot up. "Mm. This is good."

As I drank, warmth meandered all the way down to my stomach, but for some reason, I doubted the sensation was caused by the coffee. "Thanks."

"So, what's your story?" he asked.

I hadn't talked to anyone but Meg about the disaster with Hydroade and I wasn't about to start. Taking a deep breath, I looked to the ceiling fan above. "Well," I said, wanting to be truthful, yet not wanting him to look upon me as a complete failure. "I was a high-level executive at a Fortune 500 corporation based in Denver. It was stressful, not that I didn't relish the challenge, but after years of excessive hours and little thanks, like you, I'd had enough."

"But why La Crosse? You don't have a Wisconsin accent."

"My daughter does—we lived here when she was in high school. After she got her master's degree she settled in this lovely town. I decided I wanted to be closer to her. On top of that, my mother was—*is* suffering from Alzheimer's and moving here allows me to spend more time with her, as well."

He looked from one wall to the other of my dilapidated kitchen and rubbed the back of his neck. "So you bought a fixer?"

"Yep." I dipped my chin and gave him an innocent smile, though not flirting. Definitely not flirting. "I need a big project to keep myself out of trouble."

"Really?" He sipped his coffee, licking the foam from a full bottom lip. "What are you going to do once it's done?"

I regarded my disgusting mustard-yellow cupboards. "I don't think it will be for a long time," I said, avoiding his question. "As soon as I finish painting, I have to start on the floors."

"Big job—sanding, staining, applying the finish."

I glanced at the linoleum that had been worn through to the floorboards in places. "At least there's solid oak under that awful lino."

"You need a hand?"

I couldn't help but shift my gaze to his left ring finger. It was bare. Was he flirting or just being friendly? "After we finish painting my dressing room?"

"Sure. Business is winding down for the season, and I need an excuse to get out of the house—it's too quiet there."

I spooned a bit of froth off the rim of my cup. "Do you live alone?"

"Yeah. It's been twenty-three years since my wife left me—"

The back door burst open. "Mom!" Meg cried, falling into my arms, bawling hysterically. "H-h-he's m-marrieeeeed!"

Bob took his cup to the sink, then moved a box of tissues beside me. "I believe this my cue to disappear," he said, backing away and showing himself out.

"W-who was that?" Meg asked, wiping her eyes with her hand, which did no good at all. She was hyperventilating with sobs. Tears welled and spilled onto her cheeks as I reached for a tissue.

"Just Bob. He's my yard guy." I wrapped her in a tight embrace. "Tell me what happened, Sweetie. Is this about Lance?"

Meg cried so hard, she couldn't answer at first. The lout was married? I should have realized he was a scoundrel the moment I set eyes on that smug bastard.

All the emotion of motherhood coursed through me with Meg perched on the stool between my legs, my lips caressing her forehead as I whispered soft words, "That's right, Baby, let it all out. Let all that pain and hurt burst forth. You're safe here. You'll always be safe here."

Was I wrong to sense a tad of triumph to have my daughter in my arms? To finally live close enough to provide a shoulder for her to cry on? I gave her another tissue.

As Meg's hiccups subsided and she gradually regained control, she told me about her research—that the charlatan had lied about being a doctor. Not only that, he worked for solid waste. Meg told me about his wife's Facebook profile—that the poor woman was a cruise ship entertainer and her husband obviously played around when she was away at sea.

Meg blew her nose. "No wonder he ignored me so much. No wonder he never posted a picture of me on his fake Facebook page."

Every muscle in my body clenched, my lips curled. "I wish he were here so I could practice karate on his face."

"Would you?" Meg managed to let a sad smile shine through her anguish.

I snarled, molten blood pulsing through my veins. "Damn straight. Anyone messes with my kin, and I'll taser their eyeballs!"

"Whoa, Mom. I've never heard you sound so savage."

I squared my shoulders, though I wasn't going to take back my words. I wanted that man's head. "I think we all have a bit of savagery inside of us. We've just learned to tame it. I know I have."

Meg moved to the stool where Bob had been sitting and dropped her head into her hands. "What am I going to do?"

Send out a hit squad? Deflate all the tires on his car? Put a wild badger in the cab of his garbage truck?

I gulped back my vengeful thoughts. "You need to confront him."

"Sure, but a guy like that is pathological. It's not going faze him when I tell him he's a scumbag. I'll bet the jerk knows he's a slimebucket and he thinks it's cool."

"I wonder if his wife has any idea what he's up to while she's working. I'll bet she makes a lot more money than he does, too." Visions of my ex sitting on the couch drinking beer while I worked shook me to my core. It was a damned good thing Meg found out about this now before she wasted her time pining for a guy who was already married. "I'll bet he lives pretty comfortably because of her—gets to go on cruises for free. The contemptable, advantage-taking fraud!"

Meg curled over, a wail erupting from the back of her throat. "I can't believe I'm so gullible."

"You? You're not at fault for any of this." I pounded my fist on the counter. "He's the prick. Do not for one second blame yourself."

"But I'm such a loser when it comes to men. What am I, a dickhead magnet?"

"No!" I said emphatically, yet I'd given her a lousy example. After Meg was born, her father hadn't worked, mooched off me, and I'd put up with his laziness and excuses for seven unbearable years. Once I won the majority custody in the divorce, I took my daughter and moved back to the States where I'd married myself to my job. "There are nice men out there."

"Like whom?"

"Well, I guess Bob, my yard guy is pretty nice."

"Oh…" Meg glanced through the butler's pantry, leading through the house. "Did I interrupt something?"

"Absolutely not. We just took a break for coffee and that was all." I gestured to my overalls. "Look at me, I'm not exactly dressed to impress."

Meg chuckled and shook her head. "I don't want Lance…Virgil or whoever he is sailing to Bermuda and hooking up with unsuspecting librarians ever again."

"You said his wife is on Facebook?" I asked, an idea forming.

Meg's bottom lip pushed out like she was about to burst into tears again, but she just hid her face in her hands. "Yes, and she's gorgeous, and skinny."

"Well, you are gorgeous *and* voluptuous. In my book you win over the Barbie dolls every time."

With a huff, my daughter opened her fingers wide enough to give me a sober expression of disbelief. We'd been down this road too many times. No matter what I said, in her opinion I was petite and skinny and had no right to make any comment about her figure whatsoever.

I drank my last sip of coffee. "I think you ought to friend the wife on Facebook."

Meg's breath hitched as she dropped her hands. "Seriously?"

"I would."

Her puffy eyes widened. "And then what, tell her I've been having an affair with her husband?"

"I don't think you need to be quite so direct. Maybe just ask if she's seen Lance's other profile."

"You mean Virgil's other profile?"

A grin slowly stretched my lips. "Exactly."

"Um…" Meg looked out the window as if mulling over the idea. "If I friend her, she might see a couple of selfies I've taken of us."

"Hmm. You could always bury them or at least make sure you have a few innocuous photos at the top of your recent feed." I took my coffee cup to the sink and rinsed it. "You decide what is best."

<h1 style="text-align: center">Chapter Sixteen</h1>

<h2 style="text-align: center">Meg</h2>

I didn't do anything right away, aside from posting a few pictures of La Crosse and friend Jocelyn Klein because I had no idea if she'd friend me back or how long it might take. Otherwise, in typical Margaret Lehn Corley form, I had to enhance my misery by stewing for days. I'd shown up for work when scheduled, but I can't say I was engaged. I basically went through the motions, doing the easiest chores, checking books in, checking books out, pretending to be a good librarian when all I was doing was staring off into space while a burning swath of anger slowly consumed my soul.

After a very long pep talk standing in front of the bathroom mirror this morning, I decided that today I was going to take action about the Lance disaster once and for all...of course by the time I was dressed, it was time to walk to work.

I didn't look up when someone entered through the front door, though it was impossible not to notice the whoosh from the glass and the way it sucked the warm air out into the vestibule. The weather had cooled and I'd donned a fall sweater the same day I realized Lance was a backstabbing bastard.

"Hello again," said a deep voice, one faintly familiar.

I glanced up to see the geeky guy who'd come in last summer. "Hi. Back for some archival work?" I asked, anxious for him to go do whatever it was he'd come in for and leave me alone.

"Actually, no." He shoved his hands into his pockets, looking as awkward as Ron Weasley when he was trying to ask Hermoine Granger to the Yule Ball. "Monique put together a very thorough research packet on my house."

"That's wonderful to hear. She's good at her job."

"Yes." He didn't move on but stood there staring as if he might be waiting for me to introduce him to the next bestseller.

Darn it, I really wasn't in the mood to be congenial today. "Is there something I can help you with?"

"You have DVDs here, right?"

I nodded, my librarian smile waning. "Yes, and audio books."

"Well, my niece is coming to visit for a few days and I was wondering if the library might have a copy of the complete set of *Harry Potter* movies."

"Of course we do, but they're almost always checked out. You can also stream the movies on Peacock."

He craned his neck, looking toward my monitor. "Is it possible to see if they're in the library now?"

"Sure, sorry. I should have done that right away." I sighed loudly as I quickly logged on to the computer and performed a search. "Oh, dear, they're out, but they're due back in three days."

"Okay, thank you." He still stood there, though now the dude was scraping his teeth over his bottom lip. Sure, he was cute, but I had donned my armor this morning and was on the warpath.

I pointed to the DVD section. "You might want to take a peek at what we have on the shelf. There are dozens of movies for kids of all ages."

He glanced in the direction of my finger, then gave me a nod and disappeared, thank God. Determined to end things with Lance in order to reclaim my soul, I left the counter in the hands of another librarian and sought the solace of my office.

I brought up Facebook on my phone. Jocelyn Klein had accepted my friend request. My palms perspired as I deliberated over what I was about to do. Ever since I decided to friend her, I'd written about twenty-five notes to the woman and hadn't been satisfied with any of them. On one hand, I didn't want to break up their marriage, but on the other, if I were married to Lance (aka Virgil), I would want to know if he cheated on me.

So, I clicked on "message" and typed: *I took a cruise to Bermuda and met a man who said he was Lance Lovell. He told me he was single and he was a doctor who worked in the ER. We hit it off and a couple months later he came to visit me during Octoberfest. Later, I discovered there is no Dr. Lance Lovell anywhere. This led me to dig deeper where I learned that Lance is actually Virgil Klein, your husband. I felt it important for you to know what is happening behind your back. You can find out more on Lance's Facebook page.* I inserted a link to the backstabber's profile.

Next, I typed a message to Lance, the fake doctor: *Hello, Virgil. How Is Jocelyn? Never try to contact me again. You are dead to me.*

I waited a few minutes then unfriended fake Lance. I'd make sure Jocelyn saw my message, then I'd unfriend her as well.

There. The ugliness was finished.

I hoped.

But why did I still want to crawl into a hole and die? I grabbed a tissue and dabbed my eyes. I hated being put in this position. For all I knew Jocelyn was a perfectly nice person and I might have just ruined her marriage. But who would want to be married to a scumbag? Maybe I just gave her the impetus she needed to divorce the lying bastard. Was there anything positive somewhere in all this awfulness? Nah, finding anything good in this whole disaster was about as likely as me ever meeting a man who was actually a decent guy.

Nonetheless, why did doing the right thing slay me as if I'd been a Judas? I didn't outright tell Joycelyn that Lance was cheating. I just inferred the bastard was a douche.

A light tap sounded on my door and Mr. Geek popped his head in.

Dammit, can't I get a moment to myself?

"Hey, did you find anything your niece might like?" I asked, surprised I was still able to conjure my friendly librarian voice.

"Maybe I'll subscribe to Peacock." He smiled apprehensively. I'm kind of a sucker for shy geeks, but this one was going to have to focus his cute grin on some other nerdy girl. "Um...you look like you could use an ice cream."

Suddenly self-conscious, I ran my hand over my ponytail, hoping I didn't have a gazillion flyaways, which happened whenever I forgot to use hairspray. I loved ice cream no matter if it was fall and chilly out. "Is it that obvious?"

"Yes." He smiled again, a bit bolder this time. Did the dude have to be wickedly hot? Dammit, I didn't give a whit if his face was hideous. Men were all in the dungeon as far I as I was concerned. "When do you get off?"

I glanced at my watch. "Not soon enough."

"When?" he persisted.

"Five minutes."

"Then I'll see you at the front door in five."

Before I could refuse, he left. Cripes, I didn't even know his name. How the hell was I going to get out of this? Elaine thought the dude was cute, maybe he could take her instead.

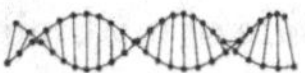

After finding out that Elaine had left early for the day, I zipped up my sherpa jacket as I looked longingly at the back doors—the ones facing the parking lot. I could make a run for it, but that would be cruel, and I wasn't cruel. Even if I might have just destroyed a cruise ship entertainer's marriage. Besides, I needed chocolate. Copious amounts of it.

Geeky Guy was there as I pushed out the front. "You're here," I said because I sort of thought he wouldn't be. I mean, I'd just been strung along by a cheating fiend. Why would a shy geek keep his word?

He glanced at his Tag Heuer smartwatch. "And you're on time."

I crossed my arms and faced him. "First of all—"

He offered his hand. "I'm Mike. Mike Reynolds."

"I'm Margaret Lehn Corley, but please call me Meg." Of course, I shook his hand—it would be rude not to. "You should know right off the bat that I'm recovering from a hellacious breakup and I don't think I'll ever want to date again in my life."

"Okaaay." He gestured down Main Street. "You still want an ice cream?"

"I should say no." But chocolate beckoned, making me bite the corner of my lip. "The Pearl Ice Cream Parlor?"

"Is there any other place in La Cross that serves it creamy and homemade?" he asked, smiling. Damn him for having an enamoring smile.

"All right, then. I'm getting a chocolate dipped cone with two scoops of Mississippi Mud." *There. Judge me by my voluptuous bod and see if I care.*

"Only two?"

I gestured to my hips. "I might look like a glutton, but two scoops is my limit."

"Wait. First of all, even though you're only doing this out of pity, you most definitely do not look like a glutton. Secondly, if you just broke up with your boyfriend, you deserve more. After all, a standard ice cream scoop is only four ounces. In my book, major heartbreaks definitely qualify for an entire pint."

I tried to glare at him, but a snigger shot through my nose. "I like how you think."

"Thank you." Mike offered his elbow. "Shall we walk, or would you prefer to travel by electric motorcar?"

Though a voice in the left side of my brain told me to keep my hands to myself, the right insisted it was rude not to. Regardless, I still wasn't fond of riding in cars and only drove when necessary. "Walking would be nice."

Once my fingers were gripping his rather well-muscled arm, I relaxed a little. "You have an electric car?"

He shrugged. "A Volt. Doing my part to help combat global warming."

"Commendable," I said, recalling how Lance had discarded his water bottle on the floor of the bus in Bermuda. That should have been a major red flag right there.

Along the way, I discovered that Mike Reynolds wasn't only a techie guy, he was the Chief Information Officer at UW La Crosse. He grew up in Madison and had an older sister who still lived there. His niece was seven and wasn't coming to visit until her Christmas break, but he needed an excuse to pay a visit to the library.

Damn. Why did the dude make it totally impossible not to like him?

He had the most beautiful pair of gray eyes I'd ever seen—deep, soulful, maybe a little guarded as if he'd been hurt before. Interestingly, he didn't yammer on and on about himself. He just answered my questions, then he asked one in return.

"Do you have any family in town?" I asked as we slid into a booth, me with a pint, him with a waffle cone.

"Nope. How about you?"

"My mom just moved here. We found a nice assisted living facility for Grandma, too. Like you did, my mother bought an old Victorian except hers needs a lot of work."

He licked his cookies'n cream. "Who said mine didn't?"

"Oh, no. You bought a fixer, too?"

"It's not horribly run down, but there are a few things I'd like to do to modernize a bit."

"You're not restoring back to the olden days?"

"Nope. I'd have to gut the place. It already has wall-to-wall carpeting and conventional heating and air conditioning." He licked his lips, making them shiny. "What about your dad?"

"He lives in Queensland, Australia." I loved him, but as the years passed, I saw him less and less. Now that I paid my own airfare, I couldn't afford to fly as much as I did when I was a kid.

"Whoa, that must be a story."

I took another bite of Mississippi Mud and savored it. "A tale of woe and too many winters."

I ended up glossing over my childhood and the fact that I'd been born down under, quickly moving on to more interesting topics—La Crosse and how much he loves it here. We talked about football and how well my beloved Badgers were doing this year. It was refreshing to learn he was an avid fan—not an Ohio State follower like the asshole who must no longer be named. Mike had actually read all of the *Harry Potter* books as well as all of the *Percy Jackson* and *The Hunger Games* series. He liked to fish and putter in the yard. He had made it his quest to hike all the trails around Grandad's Bluff. And this winter, he thought he might give skiing a try.

He took a bite of his crunchy waffle cone. "Do you enjoy classical music?"

"Love it. I played the oboe in my high school orchestra."

"Played? What about now?"

"No time, I guess." Also, by the time I hit college, blowing on a double reed instrument gave me a dizzying headache and I'd had to quit. But that sounded lame even if I didn't care about impressing any man at the moment.

He used a pink napkin to wipe a dab of ice cream from the corner of his mouth. "I'll bet you're amazing."

I was passable. "Definitely not a protégé. I'm a far better librarian."

He chomped another bite of his cone and a big piece dropped onto the table which he cleaned up with his napkin. "Well, I know you're not wanting to date or anything, but there's a Bach recital at Christ Church—across from the library. It's Saturday at seven."

"So you've discovered things to do in La Crosse?" I asked because I'd been the one to tell him about the events website.

"Yep." He popped the last of his cone in his mouth. "So, you want to be my sidekick?"

"I love Bach," I replied before I could catch myself. What was it about this guy? First he buys me the best ice cream in town and now Bach?

"Then you'll go?"

Did the man's eyes have to be so tempting, so difficult to ignore? "I can't."

"I mean it's not a date or anything," He leaned his chin on his hand, reminding me of the brainiac coach of the Miami Dolphins, and totally pulling off the sexy-nerdy-I'm-into-sports-but-not-a-jock look.

Why now? Why today after I finally got up enough nerve to eighty-six Lance?

Mike seemed like a real sweetheart—a prime catch. The problem was me. I didn't trust myself to ID a nice guy in a room full of them. After all, I'd thought Lance was a decent human being—a doctor who wanted to chill and be scruffy while he was on vacation. At the moment, I was too wounded and too discouraged to let Mike Reynolds charm me no matter how much my ovaries disagreed.

I opened my mouth to refuse when he gently touched my arm, making tingles skitter all the way up to the back of my neck. "Please?"

My head swam. It seemed the word "no" had escaped my vocabulary. "How about if I meet you there?"

Chapter Seventeen

Jane

It was after three o'clock in the morning when my brain registered a blur on the security footage playing on my laptop. Instantly wide awake, I bolted upright and rewound the video. The camera angle was focused on the back door of the warehouse which wasn't used by the employees, or at least it wasn't supposed to be used, even though it could be accessed by a key.

When I again saw the dark figure approach, I paused and zoomed in on the grainy image. The intruder wore a baseball cap, but when he inserted the key and looked over his shoulder, I got a decent view of his profile.

Is that Leon Worthington?

I slowly advanced the film, taking note of the date and time—twelve sixteen a.m. on April seventeenth.

Wasn't that when the board of directors visited Philly for a plant tour?

I took my laptop down to my office and checked my calendar. I was right. Not only was Leon there, so was I and the CEO of Hydroade who also happened to be a member of the board.

At least a dozen times I watched the six-second footage, more and more positive that the man entering the building was my ex-boss. I saved a clip of the video, then shifted to the inside camera pointed at the same door, on the same date and time. The intruder partially unzipped his bomber jacket and reached inside, pulling out something but he stopped as he looked directly at the camera.

My blood turned icy as I stared into the unmistakable black eyes of the bastard who fired me. I zoomed in to his jacket and was almost positive I could make out the faint outline of a Hydroade bottle.

Holy shit!

What did this mean? Why would Leon sabotage his own company's inventory? The inventory was insured, but the payout wouldn't be enough to take such a risk.

Or would it?

The CFO had told me Leon was handling the insurance claim. That seemed a little odd at the time, but not out of the realm of possibility because of my ex-boss' innate desire to control everything.

But now I knew differently. Leon had a more sinister reason, and my guess was his partner in crime just might be the CEO of Hydroade.

I Googled Bethany Plastics news. The headline of the first article that came up was: *Plastics Giant Files for Bankruptcy.*

And then another idea sparked from the recesses of my memory. Several years ago, everyone on the board of directors was given preferred shares right after the stock split. If Bethany filed for bankruptcy, creditors would be paid first, and I highly suspected that Leon had used his dirty tactics to ensure there would be enough left over to pay out the preferred stock, leaving the common stockholders in the lurch. Furthermore, the board members' preferred stock value was more like a bond. It didn't go down with drops in the market, but the value sure as hell went up. All the common stockholders would lose everything while Leon and his comrades walked away with millions.

Was I being paranoid? Why the cover up when Leon could retire and walk away with his preferred shares? What about his divorces? He'd complained enough about getting fleeced. Moreover, what else was going on in the boardroom that I didn't know about?

By the time I looked up from my computer, it was six in the morning. I thought about calling Curt, but he was further removed from the machinations of the board than I had been. Honestly, with Leon's penchant for control, I didn't know if I could trust anyone at corporate, and if he found out I was snooping, who knew what that asshole would do next?

After I went through my morning routine and made a cup of coffee, I decided what needed to be done. It took about a half an hour to get through to the FBI's business and fraud prevention office, but once I got a woman on the line, I told her everything and emailed her the security footage. I asked that I remain anonymous unless it was absolutely necessary to release my name. She agreed and said she'd be in touch if she needed anything more.

By the time I hung up the phone, I was so drained I felt like I'd lost a pint or two of blood. I was dazed, but certainly not confused. The best thing was that I no longer felt like I had failed. I had been framed. I was used. I was mercilessly fired because Leon saw me as a threat. I must have been getting too close to the truth and he couldn't have me blowing the whistle.

Except he was wrong on that count. The bastard.

A few days later I walked from my house to the local Moya Clinic for a doctor appointment. I know. I'm a glutton for punishment, but since karate was no longer allowed, to keep myself in shape, as soon as I moved to La Crosse I started taking fitness classes at the local YMCA. I bought a smartwatch to log my progress. I was so damned competitive, I tried to keep up with women thirty years younger than me, but once my watch started recording my heart rate at astronomical levels, telling me to slow down, I got a little worried. Sure, I was pushing myself, but I always pushed myself. Except after the dissection incident (when I'd been pushing too hard), I had eliminated pushups and burpees from my workout routines.

Wasn't that enough?

I'd also be fooling myself if I believed having a heart rate of 195 wasn't a little scary. I never wanted to do anything to bring on an artery dissection again and trying to keep up with the twenty and thirty-somethings might shove me over the edge.

No matter how much I wanted to forget about FMD, whatever had happened that Saturday at the dojo wasn't natural. And I'd come to realize my visit with Dr. Vaughn in Denver had been an utter waste of time. I discovered that vascular surgeons specialize in different disciplines. I also looked up Dr. Vaughn's practice. His specialty was in angioplasty and arterial stenting, which explained why he only saw elderly patients.

It did not, however, explain why he blew me off as if I were a woman who complained about every trifling ailment. In my opinion, his abject disregard was unforgivable.

I still didn't have a satisfactory answer as to the possible repercussions of what happened to me, and subsequently to Meg. Maybe if I were the only one affected I wouldn't be so bothered, but Meg was too young to have vascular issues. She had so much life yet to live.

I guess I wasn't ready to call it quits, either. After all, who would take my mother milkshakes if I kicked the bucket? Definitely not my brother, Roger. He'd probably leave our mom's care in Meg's hands without an iota of guilt.

Since I was only going to be on Bethany's health insurance for a couple more months, no matter how much I didn't like doctor visits, I wanted answers—*if* I could get someone to take me seriously. So, after arming myself with as much information about FMD as I could find, I decided to resume my quest, no matter how much I had to bite back my pride or put up with doctors who found it their roles in life to belittle their patients and fill them with self-doubt.

My records had already been transferred. I'd go in, tell them about my heart rate issues, then I'd mention the radiology report from Denver and see if I could get a referral to a doc who actually treated FMD patients.

I had carefully researched the physicians online, and made an appointment with Dr. Wahl, a specialist in internal medicine who also had a background in vascular. Once I checked in at the kiosk, I waited less than five minutes before I was called. I was also pleasantly surprised when I overheard the nurse actually relay the information I'd given her to the physician before Dr. Wahl came in, introduced herself, and took a seat on the stool.

"You have FMD," she said, sounding concerned as she scanned through my records, then turned the monitor toward me and pointed to an image of my beaded and twisted carotid arteries, something neither Dr. Panda nor Dr. Vaughn had done.

I gripped my hands together. Here I was for the umpteenth time in my life, needing to explain my weird medical stuff. I had quite a history, including spontaneous hemorrhaging on a plane for no apparent reason as well as the ruptured uterus when Meg was born. I didn't mention any of those things and kept it current. Other doctors had told me those things were ancient history and no longer needed to be addressed, though I did put my heart prolapse on the intake form. "I don't know if I do or not. The radiologist seemed to think so, but the vascular surgeon Dr. Panda sent me to when I was in Denver wasn't sure. He didn't seem to think the dissected carotid artery was a big deal, either."

She readjusted the monitor then peered at me with an expression of utter sincerity. "I assure you, a dissection of *any* artery is serious. FMD isn't a picnic either. Tell me what happened."

Hello? I didn't expect her to be quite so interested. I thought she'd be in a hurry like most docs and pass over the dissection so I could just get to my speedy heart rate issues, which had been what I'd told the nurse was the main reason for my visit.

To my surprise, Dr. Wahl listened thoughtfully while I described the incident at the dojo, including the screaming pain, and going blind. "My daughter thinks I had a TIA, but the CT scan I had a few days later indicated my brain was fine."

The doctor started scrolling again. "You very well might have had a TIA. By definition, a transient ischemic attack happens when blood to the brain is briefly interrupted. If you lost sight in both eyes when you dissected, we certainly cannot rule out a TIA."

I relaxed a bit. Dear God, the woman was actually talking to me like I possessed intelligence. As if I mattered. "The FMD website says I shouldn't do martial arts."

"Oh, no. Definitely not. You shouldn't do anything that might cause sudden jolting of your head and neck."

I gulped, glad that I decided to move to Wisconsin, otherwise I might have been obstinate and gone ahead and tested for my second-degree.

"If you have FMD, it is in all of the mid-sized arteries of your body. They should have done a scan of your abdomen and pelvis as well."

News to me.

Her stool squeaked as she turned. "I also detected a heart murmur. Have your other doctors ever mentioned it?"

I blinked as my mind sifted back through three decades. "When I was pregnant, my obstetrician sent me to a cardiologist for a heart ultrasound." I guess I'd buried this information in a little-used part of my brain because I'm positive that somewhere along the line, someone told me it was ancient history and I didn't need to refer to it again. "He said I have a mitral valve prolapse. Is that something to worry about?"

"It's something that should be listed in your history, certainly." Dr. Wahl's lips thinned. "I'd like to refer you to Moya's vascular center in Rochester—it's an hour's drive. Will that be okay?"

Another vascular doc? "Do you think it's necessary?"

"I believe it would be advisable for you to be seen at one of the best facilities in the country. I personally know Dr. Davis. I'll refer you to her. She's extremely thorough."

"Does she know what FMD is?" I asked.

"She's an expert on the subject—even published."

Dr. Wahl counseled me for a half-hour and though she didn't think the mitral valve prolapse in my heart had anything to do with my high heart rate readings, by the time I left the clinic, I'd given five vials of blood and had been fitted with a heart monitor which I was instructed to wear for a week so they could identify what was going on when I exercised.

Meg and I pushed into my mother's apartment in her new assisted living facility. "Hey, Mama, how're you doing?"

"Jane!" she said as if she hadn't seen me two days ago.

"I brought you a vanilla milkshake." I set the cup on the table beside her recliner. "I also brought along your granddaughter, Meg."

"Hi, Grandma," she said, peeking around me with a brown paper shopping bag in tow.

My mother picked up the milkshake and greedily sucked on the straw. "Mm, this is good. Thank you." Mama loved vanilla milkshakes, though her blood sugar had been borderline diabetic for years. I used to try to keep her on a strict diet, but she got way too thin and Roger told me to pump calories into her and give her whatever she'll be likely to eat.

Meg and I settled on the teal loveseat I purchased to make her room cozy. It coordinated with her lampshade and bedspread.

"How have you been, Grandma?" Meg plastered on one of those doll-like smiles, though she liked to visit about as much as my brother did. At one time my daughter idolized her grandmother, though now had a terrible time accepting her as a doddering old woman. "I'm sorry I haven't been to see you for a while."

Licking her lips, Mama gave her a blank stare, then shifted her gaze to me.

"Meg works at the library." I pointed to her bookshelf which was full of activity paperbacks and some of the novels my mother had read over the years. "She's the granddaughter who gave you all those books."

"Oh. Thank you. I love to read," Mom replied, though she was no longer able to follow story plots.

We sat awkwardly for a moment while Mom sipped again. "This is delicious."

I beamed, now fairly certain my smile looked as plastic as my daughter's. "I'm glad you like it."

"Did you say your name is Meg?" Mama asked.

Dear God, I didn't have to wonder if that question tore Meg's heart out but bless her, the girl's only outward sign of her frustration was her blink. "Sure is."

"Isn't that short for Margaret?"

I nodded. "Yes."

It seemed the old girl was quite in the mood for a chat today. "My mother's name was Margaret, but she didn't go by Meg."

For the past seventeen years we'd had this conversation every time Meg was in the room.

"Isn't that crazy?" My dear daughter played along, though she jabbed my arm with her elbow—hard enough to leave a bruise. "Mom named me after her!"

I scooted away and rubbed the sore spot. "I've been refinishing my floors with a very nice contractor."

"Have you?"

"Yes, he's become a friend."

"I have a friend here, you know," Mama said, moving the conversation right along.

"Oh?" My eyebrows shot up. "What's her name?"

She slurped. "I can't remember."

I sat for a moment. When it came to my mother, conversation was usually one-sided and always challenging. "So, I'm going to Moya in Rochester for some tests."

"Are you?" she asked, sounding interested.

Meg jammed her fists onto her hips. "You didn't tell me about that."

Honestly, I wasn't sure I was going to say anything until afterward because I wanted some concrete results first. But given the fact that Meg was as *neck* deep in this as me, there was no reason to keep it to myself. "Well, now you know."

For the first time since it happened, I told Mama about my dissection incident. Meg also described hers.

As we relayed our stories, my mother gazed off in the distance at something, maybe nothing. "I think I had a stroke once." Yes, this is what Alzheimer's did to people—deprived them of their capacity for empathy.

"You did?" I asked. "When?"

She shrugged. "I don't know."

Meg and I exchanged eye rolls, then I started in on my routine of checking her supplies while the dregs of the milkshake bubbled loudly in the plastic cup.

"Hey..." I picked up a flyer from Mama's counter. "This says school kids are coming here for trick-or-treat."

She tossed her cup into the trash. "Are they?"

"Yes, and you'll be able to pass out candy on Halloween. Would you like that?"

Mom's eyes lit up. "As long as they behave."

"I'll bet they will. And they'll all be dressed up in costumes."

"Really?"

Meg scooted forward and pulled out a pumpkin candy bucket from the shopping bag. "The local kids come to the library and we give them candy. I thought you'd like to have one of these."

Mama stared at the smiling jack-o-lantern, her expression blank. "I don't eat much candy."

Meg set the pumpkin on the counter. "Then give it to the kids when they come around for trick-or-treat."

"Oh, okay."

"Well, Mama, we have to get going." I bent over the recliner and gave her a hug. "I love you."

She didn't hug me back. "Love you, too."

Meg opened the door and waved. "Bye, Grandma." Once we were in the hall she looped her arm through mine. "I don't see how you can take coming here twice a week."

"She's my mother."

"She *was*."

I stopped and shook my finger at her nose. "That woman raised me. No, she isn't all there, but I'm not going to abandon her and pretend she doesn't exist like your Uncle Roger does."

Meg threw out her hands. "I know you feel responsible on some level...even guilty, but she probably has already forgotten that we were just in her room. In fact, I'll bet if you walked in there right now she'd say, 'Jane!' like she hasn't seen you in decades."

I continued out to the car. Meg was right. But I was brought up to carry the responsibility of the family on my shoulders. Besides, someone needed to look after her. Someone needed to take her to doctor appointments and shop for her supplies. Though those tasks did add up, a voice at the back of my head always whispered I ought to be doing more. So what if she didn't remember anything? The woman was still my mother.

Once we were in the Volvo, Meg fastened her seatbelt. "I'm sorry. I just can't bear to see her like that."

"I know." I started the engine. "So, let's go get something to eat and talk about—"

"Sex?"

I snorted out a laugh. "If you really want to." Then I gave her a sideways glance. "I finally figured out what happened with the goose shit debacle."

"Seriously?" she rubbed her hands together. "I love a good sleuth story."

As I drove to the restaurant, I told her everything, including my phone call with the FBI. At last, my inadequacy complex was crumbling. In no way had I been "culpable" as Leon had egregiously claimed.

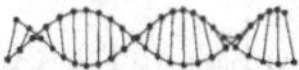

In the library of my Victorian home (aka office), I was playing Bach's Ave Maria on my recently tuned 1905 Sleger & Sons piano. My fingers only hit a few wrong notes as I sang my heart out, drawing in a humongous breath before holding forth with the high G toward the end of the piece, then softening to a decrescendo finale, my fingers finding the notes...more or less.

If I hadn't had the piano tuned, I could have blamed my awful playing on the instrument. But I was no virtuoso.

Maybe I shouldn't try to sing and play at the same time. I was never much of a pianist. I had a few lessons in the second grade, but when my piano teacher was arrested for child abuse I ended up on my own, teaching myself—something I wouldn't recommend. At least I was fortunate not to suffer abuse from the man aside from a ruler across the knuckles once or twice.

As I held the last chord, the Google Nest in the parlor nearly gave me a heart attack, boisterously announcing there was someone at the front door. I was immensely proud of myself for installing a Nest system without having to ask anyone to help, but ever since, people had stopped using my beloved brass knocker.

I darted off the piano bench then wobbled dizzily through the entrance hall, having to stop for a second and put my hands on my knees. "Coming!" I shouted, taking a deep breath to clear my head. Jeez, just this morning, when I was getting dressed upstairs I'd felt like the floor was moving. It was akin to being on a ship in rough seas. I attributed the sensation to the uneven floorboards, but I didn't think the floor in the entrance hall was wonky.

The good news was the results from wearing the heart rate monitor had been useful. Dr. Wahl called me herself and said that though my heart rate went as high as 175, it came back down as soon as I stopped exercising. She told me to keep an eye on it and try not to go over 160.

So, I was still pushing myself too hard.

By the time I opened the door, I figured the caller would be gone, but no. Bob stood there with a goofy grin on his face, his green eyes shining.

My stomach dropped to my toes as I glanced in the direction of my piano. "You didn't hear that fiasco, did you?"

"Of course not," he said with an unfettered snort. He most likely had been there through the entire abysmal concert and hadn't knocked until the concert was over.

"Whew." I sank about two inches as I stood back and ushered him in. "So why are you here?"

"Just came to check on the floors," he replied, reminding me that I loved to hear the bass of his speaking voice and I wondered if he liked to sing—though my piano playing was so bad, I'd have to practice every day for ten years before I was good enough to accompany anyone.

"They're beautiful, thank you." We'd finished varnishing the hardwoods a couple of days ago. I inclined my head to the dining room. "Want a cup of tea? The contractors have finished with the kitchen for the day and about all I can get to is the electric kettle."

"Do you have something herbal?"

I beckoned him. "Sure do."

Bob followed me into the butler's pantry where I made the tea. He stood on the threshold and looked at the disaster that had been my kitchen as of yesterday morning. "At least it will be done in time for Thanksgiving."

"Plenty of time," I put the teabags into cups. "And the floors turned out better than I'd hoped. I couldn't have managed without you."

"Thanks, Jane, but you worked your tail off." He sauntered back into the dining room and sat at the head of the table in one of the chairs with armrests. "I've been thinking...we ought to join forces and start up a partnership."

I breathed in cinnamon wafting from my mug. "Hmm?"

"Well, there are a heck of a lot of older homes in this town and not many contractors who do restoration work."

"Ugh." I took the side chair closest to him. "I don't mind restoring my own house, but I'm not sure about meeting the expectations of the general public. I'd probably refinish their floors and they wouldn't pay me."

Bob's eyebrows pinched together. "Where are you from? This is Wisconsin. You do a job for someone and they'll be happy. Hell, you answer the phone and do the work within a decent timeframe and they'll adore you."

"You mean *us*. You're proposing a partnership, right?" I asked carefully.

"I think we'd make a good team." He gestured toward the hardwoods. "We worked well together on the floors."

The floors are gorgeous.

True, I wasn't ready to retire, but it was a big step to form a partnership with my landscaper who also had been a pharmacist and had subsequently proved to be a jack of all trades. When I put it that way, the idea had its merits. "Let me think about it. After all, I still have work to do here."

"And we're heading into winter."

I blew on my tea then sipped. "You keep saying that."

"Yes, well, it's not the best time to start a new business venture. Though I could always put in a word or two with my contractor buddies. Who knows, we might get a few gigs—nothing too overwhelming."

"If we were to start restoration work, what would happen to your landscaping business?"

His shoulder ticked up as he reached for his mug. "There are a lot more landscapers in La Crosse than there are restorers."

"Interesting."

"Well, mull it over. Maybe make a list of pros and cons." Bob took a drink, then let out a sharp breath as if his tea was a little too hot. "I will, too. After all, the idea only popped into my head when you opened the door."

I chuckled, shaking my head. "You're crazy."

He grinned. "Nah, just spontaneous."

I liked his smile. It triggered something deep as if I'd just swallowed a bite of the creamiest, most delicious chocolate soufflé ever made. "So, what are you doing for Thanksgiving?"

The man looked lost. "I'm coming here, aren't I?"

I wouldn't have asked the question if I didn't want him to come. He'd been such a humongous help over the past weeks, I was more than happy to have him join my little family. "Of course I'd love it if you joined us. What do you normally do for Thanksgiving?"

"I usually serve food at the Salvation Army, but they always have a boat-load of volunteers show up for the holidays."

"All right, then. You're officially invited."

He sipped his tea and licked his lips. And was that a blush I saw peeking above the trim line of his beard? "Thank you, ma'am," he said, his expression familiar and comfortable. "I'd like that very much."

CHAPTER EIGHTEEN

MEG

As I turned the corner, Mike stood a block away in front of the church with his hands clasped behind his back. He hadn't seen me yet and was gazing up at the bell tower, constructed of large stone bricks, not red, but beige in color. He wore a waist-length black jacket with a maroon muffler. From this distance, his long legs made him look even taller than he did up close. I liked how he wore his dark brown hair neatly trimmed, how his fashionably cropped beard suggested a hint of danger, of mystery. And it made me snigger how those black-framed glasses of his screamed geek.

I must admit the dude could be a GQ poster child for nerdy. Or maybe he could pass for Henry Cavill's Clark Kent in *Superman.*

Not that I was attracted in any way. I was not going to let myself be swept off my feet by anyone. The fiasco with Lance had ruined me forever.

As I approached, I watched him, assessed him. Undeniably, I appreciated what I saw.

I glanced to the ominous-looking clouds above. Were they telling me I was a glutton for punishment?

He turned toward my way and I waved like a fellow geek, now standing at the crosswalk on the opposite corner. "Hi."

The man grinned like Clark Kent as well. "You came."

I looked both ways and strolled across. "You thought I wouldn't?"

He kept his hands gripped behind his back. "Broken hearts don't heal easily."

"No, they do not."

"Shall we?" he asked, charming, handsome, nice. He even liked classical music.

And I really need not to like him.

Mike didn't take my hand but led the way inside and dropped a donation into a basket before we slipped into one of the many vacant pews toward the back. The church was enormous, and though there had to be at least fifty people sitting up front, the sanctuary still seemed empty. I'd lived in this town for nine years, yet I'd never been inside Christ Church. It was old, other-worldly, and at the rear of the altar was the largest pipe organ I've ever seen.

Mike rubbed his hands together. "This is going to be fabulous."

"Who's playing?" I asked, whispering.

"A protégé from Viterbo. I'm told over the summer he went on a European tour."

"Oh, my, then we're in for a treat."

His shoulder bumped mine as he leaned closer. "I'm surprised as a librarian in this town you weren't aware."

"I guess I haven't been paying attention."

Mike glanced at me out of the corner of his eye. "Still hurting?"

I nodded. "Stupid."

"I'd like to hear about it."

I studied the stained-glass window on the south side of the sanctuary. It was serene in soft pinks, ivories, and grays, depicting Jesus with his hands outstretched. "I guess there's nothing to say, except I'm gullible and naive and too trusting."

He clasped my hand and squeezed. "Yeah, once trust is broken, it's nearly impossible to get back."

Though Mike's palm was warm and comforting, I slowly slid my fingers away. "It sounds like you're speaking from experience."

Before he replied, a man in a tuxedo moved in front of the altar, right beneath an enormous wooden cross suspended from the domed ceiling. He gave a brief introduction and the music began, opening with a series of sonatas, growing in fervor until the unbelievably transportive finale of the *Toccata and Fugue in D Minor* shook the entire church.

By the time the last chord resounded through the sanctuary, I had been totally swept away with the gripping passion expressed through the music. I'd heard a lot of people play Bach with precision, but this protégé played with heart, as if his life depended on conveying the magnificence and splendor of the composer's genius.

After the applause, we both sat silently. I, for one, was awed. I didn't look at Mike, but I felt his presence and sensed he was in no more of a hurry to move than me.

"Would you like to go to Digger's Sting for a drink?" he whispered only inches from my ear.

Wanting to sustain the sanctity of the moment for a few seconds longer, I nodded. The idea of going home and hiding under the covers with Maya so that I could continue wallowing in misery didn't hold its usual appeal. Maybe I could resume my pity party after imbibing in a libation.

We agreed to walk the eight blocks, which always suited me fine. The streets were wet, flurries of snow melting as they hit the pavement.

"Did you drive to the concert?" I asked.

"Nah." He slipped his hands in the pockets of his black jacket—which might have been a little too light for a cold November evening. I'd already broken out my puffy winter coat—Nordic blue, though my hat and muffler were bright and multicolored which I'd purchased to support the LBGTQ movement.

A brisk breeze made my cheeks cold and whisked away every steamy breath. "Where do you live?"

"Tenth Street. It's only three blocks away from the church."

"Nice."

"How about you?"

"I rent." I threw my thumb over my shoulder. "The house is on Ninth Street, same as the church and the library."

"We're neighbors." His eyes shifted downward as he looked at me, grinning—a pleasing smile. Friendly. Not too sexy, but sexy enough for me to realize I needed to keep my guard up.

"Yes we are. I like living close to town. I can walk to work—walk just about everywhere."

Mike opened the door to the restaurant and led the way to the bar. Digger's always had a more mature crowd, but it was on the pricey end. The college kids tended to go anywhere they could find happy hour and cheap drinks. Digger's wasn't it.

I ordered a margarita and Mike opted for a beer.

He sipped his lager. "So, tell me about your breakup."

I dabbed my finger on the salt, then licked it. "You don't want to know."

"It must have been pretty bad."

My head dropped forward. I guess I did owe Mike some sort of explanation. "He was a douche. I should have been smarter. There were so many signs and I just ignored them all because I wanted the asshole to be Mr. Perfect."

"Nobody's perfect."

"No, but most garbage truck drivers don't set up Facebook profiles that say they're doctors. Then go on cruises and prey on unsuspecting women."

Mike gaped, his gray eyes filling with disbelief—either that or disgust. "Really?"

"I wish it weren't true." I ended up blurting out the whole sordid story, complete with Lance's Octoberfest antics and how Elaine had urged me to wise up and do my research.

"Unbelievable." Mike moved his hand slightly so that our pinkies touched—just a tiny gesture, but the connection expressed his concern, showed me that he'd not only heard, but understood. "I'm so sorry."

"I'm smarter than that. I should have Googled an image of the dude as soon as I got home."

The pinky slipped over the top of mine. "It isn't a crime to trust some-one—especially a person you had a lot of fun with."

"I guess. At least he didn't string me along for years, the bastard." I took a drink, though the margarita did nothing to drag my heart out of the doldrums. "How about you? You said breakups can be hard. Are you reeling from a bad one?"

Mike removed his pinky and pushed his empty glass to the edge of the bar, signaling for another. "It's been a few years—college sweetheart. We were engaged but she decided she wanted more out of life."

The dude was so incredibly nice—a little shy, smart, polished. He was totally different from Lance. Comparing the two actually made me realize I had been too gullible and had ignored far too many warning signs. "Like what?"

"Well." He pushed his fingers over his neatly cropped hair. "She wanted to date other women."

"Ouch." I pulled off the muffler around my neck and rolled it in my lap. I did want to show support for all marginalized people but I also wanted to be sensitive to Mike's feelings.

He rubbed the wool between his fingertips. "I like it. You didn't need to take it off because I had a bad experience. If a person is gay, they're gay."

"Right." I tipped my chin up. "Glad you agree."

"Anyway, it's over." He batted his hand through the air. "And I'm done with feeling sorry for myself."

"Is your breakup why you moved to La Crosse?"

"Not really." The bartender put a fresh beer in front of him. "I guess I initially started looking for a job outside of Madison because there were too many memories there. But once I spent some time here, I realized this place is ideal."

I drew in a reviving breath, filling with a tad of the old hutzpah for the first time since I broke things off with Lance. "It is, isn't it?"

"Too bad, though."

"Why?"

He slid his hand over and laced his fingers through mine. "Here we are, two single people who both love La Crosse, who enjoy classical music, who adore libraries, and…"

My gaze dipped to his lips, shiny and moist. "And?"

"We can't date," he said, kissing me so quickly, my eyes flashed wide.

"I don't think it's a good idea," I replied, my girl parts tingling, telling me they disagreed—*traitors!*

One corner of his mouth ticked up…yup, sexy and dangerous. "Yet."

"Okay, I'll go with *yet*."

Did I really say that out loud?

"So when can I see you again?"

I guess I needed to go home and remind myself that I never wanted another boyfriend in my life.

"What are you doing for Thanksgiving?" I asked. I didn't want to appear too anxious and the holiday was one and a half weeks away, which would give us a decent amount of time to mull things over. Lord knew I needed to, because if Mike tried to kiss me again I might end up on his lap and that was so far off my plan to stay away from men, I could wake up in the morning full of regret and have a meltdown.

"I was planning to go to my sister's in Madison, but if you're offering…"

"My mom's making dinner at her house."

"Her fixer?"

"Yes, and she has a brand-new kitchen." I admonished myself internally, making a mental note to go over there to see it.

He reached for his beer. "It sounds like she's been busy."

"That's my mom. She's the original Energizer Bunny."

CHAPTER NINETEEN

JANE

"**R**ight on time." I stood back and opened the door for Meg. "How was work?"

My daughter carried Maya inside and set her on the floor. The dog was wearing a down coat—hot pink with a ruffle around the edge. "Same as always. You know the exciting life of small-town librarians."

I chuckled and bent down to give Maya a one-fingered scratch under the chin. Now that she saw me on a regular basis, the Chihuahua had decided to tolerate me. "We're having taco shrimp salad for dinner. Want to see the kitchen first?"

"Yes I do." Meg took the lead and headed through the butler's pantry where she stopped, clapping her hands over her mouth. "Wow, this doesn't even look like the same house! It's gorgeous."

It was a masterpiece, though I couldn't take the credit for anything aside from picking out the Mission oak custom cabinets and the white quartz countertops. I suppose I might add the stainless steel sink which I had installed with the pull-down faucet that looked like it belonged in a gourmet kitchen. The extra touches helped the overall aesthetic and made it solely mine. "I'm just grateful they got everything completed before Thanksgiving."

"Speaking of the holiday." Meg brushed her fingers over the island's shiny countertop. "Do you mind if I bring a friend?"

My mommy radar picked up a positive signal. "Not at all—is this someone I know?"

She blushed. Poor Meg, with her fair skin and red hair it was impossible for her to hide anything. "Nope. A new friend."

"Male?" I probed.

"If you must know, yes. But he's not a boyfriend. He's just a nice guy who came into the library to do some research on his house." She shuffled to the sink and tested the faucet, spraying it from side to side. "He stopped by the front desk and we got to chatting. It turns out we're both going through rough breakups, so we drowned our sorrow with Mississippi Mud ice cream."

"Oh?" I arched my eyebrows in hopes of encouraging her to say more about her ice cream social. I hoped this was a sign Meg was recovering from being catfished by Lance. When she ignored me by opening the silverware drawer, I added, "Any friend of yours is welcome. And by the way, we don't need silverware. The table is already set for our salads."

She dropped the forks back in the tray and shut the drawer. "Okay. Can I bring anything—for Thanksgiving dinner, that is?"

"Just you and your friend." I put on some oven mitts and removed the shrimp. "The plates with the salad are in the fridge if you could pull those out, please."

She opened the refrigerator door and poked her head inside. "Should I invite Ripper?"

I laughed as I followed her into the dining room and put the finishing touches on our salads. "Mr. Subwoofer? How is he doing?"

Meg set the plates on the table. "He's been friendly. Says hi whenever I see him."

"Do you think he'd come?" I asked, spooning the shrimp onto each salad.

"I have no idea. I could ask."

I put the pan on the potholder and sat at the head of the table. "Wouldn't that be awkward, inviting the man who lives upstairs and the new boyfriend."

Meg sat in the corner chair. "He's not my boyfriend."

"Okay. So, are you going to ask Ripper?"

"Will Grandma be here?" she asked, taking a sip of iced tea.

I added a dollop of guacamole on the side of my plate. "Of course."

Meg picked up her fork. "Honestly, now that I think about it, you're right. I mean, I don't want to give Ripper any ideas."

I smiled—who didn't like being told they were right?

"You know, Grandma won't remember being here for the holiday."

"You're right," I replied, setting my spoon aside. "The next day she'll probably complain about how much I ignore her."

"So sad. I wish I could fix her brain."

"I know, but she seems to like it there, and that's important." I took a bite. "Oh, I nearly forgot, I had a back door key made for you."

"Good. Someone needs to be able to check on you." Maya jumped up on Meg's leg. "Down. You already had your dinner."

The corners of my lips tightened. I never approved of any dog begging at the table. "Maybe we should have put her outside."

Meg added a small dollop of ranch dressing to her salad. "No way."

"The backyard is fenced."

"Yeah, but some estranged homeless person might kidnap her. Besides, it's too cold."

I snorted. "She's wearing a down coat." Maya was about the cutest Chihuahua I'd ever seen, but if anyone tried to go near her, they'd give up for all the snarling.

"You ought to advertise for a boarder," Meg said, changing the subject. "I'd feel a lot better about your living alone if there were someone else here."

"Oh, really?" I took a drink of water. "I've been by myself since you left for college. And what about you? You live alone."

"Yeah, but I'm thirty years younger."

I speared a shrimp and pointed it at her. "I'll have you know I'm still in my prime."

"Right."

"For Pete's sake, *I am*." I pulled the shrimp off with my teeth. "I'm walking five thousand steps almost every day."

"Okay, Mom, whatever you say."

I gaped at her. Next she'd be telling me I needed to move into my mother's assisted living facility, the insolent millennial. "I'd rather have a dog than a boarder."

"Maya!" Meg shouted, hopping out of her chair. "You naughty girl."

I turned to see the little devil-princess standing beside a puddle. Jeez, these were my newly refinished floors. "What did I say about putting her outside?"

"She can't go outside by herself." Meg headed for the kitchen. "I'll clean it up."

"Maybe I shouldn't get a dog," I hollered after her, smiling to myself. Naughty Chihuahua or not, moving to La Crosse was a great idea. I love being able to have Meg over for dinner on a whim. Maybe Bob, too.

Google maps indicated the drive to Rochester would take an hour and fifteen minutes. I tacked on another half-hour to find parking and locate the fifth floor of the Gonda Building where I was having my appointments. The clinic must have been accustomed to out-of-town patients because they scheduled me for a full body CT scan at ten in the morning and a face-to-face appointment with the specialist at one in the afternoon.

Thus far, I'd been impressed with how the Moya system worked. At least I really liked Dr. Wahl, which was unbelievably refreshing. "Like" wasn't a word I usually used when referring to a medical practitioner. Dr. Panda aside, I was more accustomed to terms such as arrogant, aloof, apathetic, and cocksure.

However, as I crossed the Mississippi into Minnesota, it wasn't doctors or FMD I was thinking about. I appreciated Bob's help refinishing my floors. The man worked exceedingly hard and he refused to take any money. And though there had been several contractors at the house since I moved in, installing everything from air conditioning to kitchen cabinets, Bob had gone out of his way to be helpful. And I did like him. I was comfortable around him—able to be myself. I'd spent so much time in the corporate world acting the way Leon expected me to, the rigid persona I'd affected leaked into my personal life and took over—made me uptight and hard.

But Bob's easygoing attitude often had me laughing. I liked his smile, his affable nature. He was nice to talk to and as far as I could tell, he carried no chips on his shoulder. He was self-confident, smart, and polite—all qualities I admired in a man.

However, like is where it had to end. I was damaged goods—plagued by this whole FMD/dissection/TIA fiasco. Bob surely wouldn't want to get involved with a person who was at risk of having a stroke. Worse, not everyone who had a major stroke died. Some ended up vegetables being hand-fed, bathed, and diapered.

I shuddered.

Who was I fooling? Sure, the man had come around to the house often enough, but he'd never made a pass. He hadn't even asked me out on a date. Bob had seen how I applied myself to painting and floor refinishing...and a gazillion other little things in the house, like putting replica brass drawer pulls on the dining room's built-in china cabinet. He saw a person with a good work ethic. Full stop.

He wasn't looking for a girlfriend and I sure as hell wasn't on the hunt for a boyfriend. I had boyfriends in high school and college. The term seemed adolescent for a middle-aged woman.

However, a *companion* might be nice.

And I'd been adamant from the outset that I was definitely not ready to retire.

Perhaps his proposed partnership might be what I needed. We could pick and choose our jobs. Hell, if someone didn't like my work and refused to pay me, I'd still survive. Though Bob might have to restrain me from taking out their knees with a side kick. Black belt here had gotten pretty good at knee kicks—at least on the punching bags.

By the time I took the exit off Highway Fifty-Two in Rochester, I'd decided that when I got home, I'd call Bob and suggest we sit down and draw up a business plan. Maybe tomorrow if he has the time.

The Google assistant quickly fired explicit directions. Though Rochester had looked small on the map, the downtown area reminded me of a city like Denver or, perhaps Des Moines. I parked on the fifth floor of the garage across from the Gonda Building, then followed the signs to the subway—no train, but a freaking underground city if you ask me.

Talk about going to the hallowed mecca of medicine. The ground floor of the clinic was hewn from white marble and there were more wheelchairs assembled by the doors than I'd ever seen in my life. There were little shops and four elevator banks. It took me a minute to find the right one, but in no time, I was checked in and waited for about ten minutes before I was called for my CT scan.

Everything was carried out with efficiency except I nearly peed my pants when they injected the dye into my veins during the CT. Thank goodness the hot-sweaty sensation only lasted about a minute. In between appointments, I ate a tuna salad in the Skylight Commons on the subway level, browsed through a few of the shops, then rode the elevator back up for my appointment with Dr. Davis.

She was younger than me with a full head of brunette hair. "Tell me what you know about FMD."

Since she was the expert, I considered throwing that one back at her, but answered truthfully, "Only what I've read online."

"I hope you're sticking to credible sites like Moya and Cleveland Clinic."

"Yes, ma'am. And the Fibromuscular Dysplasia Society of America. They have a lot of information."

"Good, good." She scrolled through my information on her computer screen.

"I assume I have a higher-than-average risk for stroke," I added, sounding none too confident. If Bob ever found out there was a chance I might become a vegetable, he'd probably withdraw his partnership offer.

"That would be correct, though we can help prevent potential events with medication. Tell me about your dissection."

I explained what happened at the dojo, and not going to the ER until two days later, which in retrospect was a mistake. I omitted the details about how difficult it had been to get the urgent care doc to approve the scan of my neck the following week.

She took a couple of steps across the exam room to a big computer monitor on the wall and flicked it on. "This is the CT scan we did today and here is the point of dissection." She used her pen to show me exactly where my twisted carotid had been weakened. "I would have thought it might have healed by now, but it appears to be chronic."

"It is?"

"Yes, and there's stenosis forming at the site." She moved her pen. "And a plaque here at the branch."

"Already?" I asked.

"You need to be on a blood thinner and cholesterol medication."

"I take a statin, is that okay?"

"Yes. I'll prescribe a blood thinner."

I didn't like the sound of that. Wasn't I too young? "What about low dose aspirin?"

"I want you to take the prescription for at least six months, then if you'd prefer to go on 81 milligrams of aspirin, that will be your choice." She brought up another image of my vascular system and pointed. "You have pronounced tortuosity in your splenic artery and two fairly small aneurysms."

The word meant death. The room was suddenly too hot. I narrowed my eyes. "What do you consider *fairly* small?"

"One is point-nine millimeters and the other is one centimeter."

"Oh, my God," I mumbled under my breath. "My father died from a burst brain aneurysm."

"Well, the good news is that your brain scan is clear. However, you also have a three-millimeter aneurysm in your right renal artery and a tiny, two-millimeter aneurysm in your left carotid which also is more twisted and torturous than your right. Regardless, that one concerns me because it's new since your Denver scan and we're going to have to keep a close eye on it."

She flicked back to the neck scan and pointed to a bulge that I had missed, mostly because the entire artery was beaded and looped around like a wet noodle. How could they tell beads from little aneurysms? "I don't want you to worry. We won't do surgery until they reach two centimeters."

"Two?" If I had my druthers, they'd all be fixed immediately. "Why is that?"

"Oftentimes we find they're dormant. It's not uncommon for splenic aneurysms to develop during pregnancy. You could have had them for years. You'll need to get another CT scan in six months, then we'll decide how often you should have them after we establish a baseline."

"Oh." I stared at the image of my twisty splenic artery with the two bubbles which indicated the aneurysms. "So, what does all this mean? I just wore a heart monitor for a week because my heart rate gets pretty high in fitness classes."

Dr. Davis flicked off the screen and cleared her throat. "About that, your best exercise is walking. I don't want to ever see your heart rate above one-forty."

"But Dr. Wahl said one-sixty was okay."

"That might be all right for someone else, but with your history of dissection during exercise, one-sixty is too high. You're taking a risk every time you push too hard."

My stomach churned, threatening to throw up my tuna salad. "Just walking?"

"Yes. I reiterate, *don't push*. Be wary of bearing down when you're on the toilet—you know what I mean, when you push so hard your face gets red?"

"No bearing down? No straining and putting pressure on my face?" For Pete's sake, it was a wonder I was still alive. I'd been driving myself athletically since I was a kid.

"Correct. And if you have the time, I'd recommend ten thousand steps a day."

"Ten thousand?" I did a quick calculation. "That will take over an hour."

"It is a time commitment that might save your life—five thousand at the very least."

I mentioned my headaches and dizziness before Dr. Davis used her stethoscope to examine my neck, finding a bruit—which she explained was causing my pulsatile tinnitus (that thundering heartbeat I always heard in my ears, especially when I bent over, or exercised, or at three in the morning when everything was quiet...the one Dr. Vaughn had said was in my imagination).

We discussed my mitral valve prolapse and she gave my heart a good listen, then said she wasn't overly concerned, but would add it to the list of things to monitor.

At the end of the consultation, I told her about Meg's dissections and Dr. Davis definitely wanted to see my daughter as soon as possible. In fact, she had me get together with a scheduler and we called Meg and set up appointments for her before I left the Gonda Building.

God save me, this was one of the first times in my life I felt like the doctors were listening to me, but the experience wasn't gratifying at all. It was terrifying.

I have four aneurysms. I have twisted and torturous arteries, stenosis, and a concerning plaque in my aorta. I need to exercise but not push myself.

The outlook on my longevity just took a nosedive and it scared the bejeezus out of me.

Maybe Meg was right. I am getting old.

When I got to my car I realized I still didn't have an answer for my dizziness or the headaches. I slid behind the wheel trying to recall—I had told her about them. I'd even put them on the pre-appointment questionnaire. Did vascular specialists not treat headaches?

CHAPTER TWENTY

MEG

On my way to Mike's house, my boots crunched over the newly fallen snow. I loved that my footsteps were the first to tarnish the smooth blanket of white on the sidewalk. I may have resented all the winters when I was growing up, but after I chose to settle in La Crosse, I've developed a fondness for snow and winter—as long as I got to enjoy *all* the seasons. With winter came hot chocolate and spiced herbal tea—and lots of cuddling up with Maya under a fluffy comforter while I was reading.

As I turned onto Tenth Street, there were only four residences on the odd-side of the block, and Mike's was the largest—the Victorian wasn't just large, it was gargantuan—as showy as the homes on Cass Street. The house was set back from the road and surrounded by a stone and iron fence. The clapboard siding was beautifully painted in subtle hues of blue with an expansive yard including a half-dozen orchard trees, which I was certain with the squirrel problem in this town, Mike never harvested a single piece of fruit.

The sidewalk in front of his house and pathway to his door had already been shoveled, though snow was still lightly falling. The stone pillar supporting the gate had a brass nameplate inlaid that read "Crosby". I recognized the surname as one of the city's founding families.

All the substantial nineteenth century homes in La Crosse had been built by prominent businessmen and families who had made their fortunes by supplying and shipping commodities up and down the Mississippi. Though the river was still used by barges to ship goods, in the Victorian and Edwardian eras it had served as a thoroughfare that contributed to the expansion and industrialization of the United States.

I turned the iron handle on the gate, making it screech as I opened and closed it. "Here goes," I mumbled under my breath as I climbed the steps to the porch and knocked on Mike's door.

I swear, the man must have been watching me through the front window because he opened immediately.

"You live here by yourself?" I marveled at the stained glass above. "This Victorian is even bigger than my mother's."

"It's nice to see you, too." He took my hand and led me inside. "Would you like a tour?"

I checked my watch. "Mom said the turkey ought to be ready about four."

"Great." Wearing jeans and a navy-blue nautical sweater with one button at the top, he kissed me on the lips—so quickly I might have missed it if I'd blinked, aside from the erratic fluttering of my heart. "We have some time."

I stumbled into this arms, not planning to throw myself at him, though I had made a resolute decision to keep seeing him—as long as we kept it chill. Rather than turn my chin up for another kiss, I pressed my cheek against his warm chest.

He kneaded my shoulders, the gentle touch taking away weeks of pent-up tension, and replacing it with a stirring deep inside—familiar, but different. A feeling I wanted to explore but didn't at the same time. My heartache was still too raw.

I took off my boots, coat, and hat.

Mike gestured to his stockinged feet. "You okay in your socks?"

"Sure, they're wool and warm."

His home was full of beautiful woodwork including oak doors, wood-wrapped windows, and plush wall-to-wall carpet. Mike's furniture was cozy—a couch, an overstuffed chair, a coffee table...then we moved to an empty room that totally needed someone like me to fill it. For the most part, the ground floor was stark as if he'd forgotten to buy artwork for the walls or lamps or anything to give the rooms unique character. Maybe, like Mom, he was still in the process of decorating.

He led me into the kitchen and gestured with an upturned palm. "*La piece de resistance,*" he said in French.

"Wow, this looks like it could be used for the set of a television cooking show." I was exceedingly impressed. The kitchen was enormous, flooded with brilliant light made brighter by white cabinetry. Mike had two ovens, and a long island with a sink in the middle. Even the countertops were white and so spotless I wondered if they'd ever been used.

I ran my fingers over the shiny quartz. "How do you manage to keep this place clean?"

"Housekeeper. One floor a week."

"I guess it's a good thing you don't have kids."

He followed me as I wandered up the oak staircase. "Kids would be nice."

"You want a family, huh?" I said. I'd never asked Lance about kids. Hell, he said he didn't want to leave Ohio, which basically kept me from mentioning anything about the future.

And I will stop thinking about that jerk this very moment.

At the top of the steps, Mike's arm brushed mine as he sidled past, the connection sending fissions of energy tingling up my neck. "Someday."

"What's up here?" I asked, rubbing away the sensation.

"Bedrooms. Lots of them."

Too many inappropriate things came to the tip of my tongue. The worst being, "*Want to have a sleepover?*" Which I definitely did not want to say, should not say, and I ought to admonish myself for even thinking it.

"Where's your office?" I asked instead.

He pointed upward. "Servants' quarters."

"You still have servants' quarters?"

"Technically no, since I've turned the entire third floor into an alpha-geek dreamland including a home theater."

I spotted the staircase to the next level. "Do you mean to say you watch the Badger games on a movie screen?"

He shrugged. "Not quite Megaplex Theater-sized."

I laced my fingers through his and took a step nearer—bold move, I know. But we both were major Wisconsin football fans. Badgers on a big screen? Sexy as hell. *Whoa, I need to chill.* "You know they're playing on Saturday?"

"Sure do." Mike's eyes turned dark as he arched his eyebrows. "Want to come over?"

"Yes. Want me to bring food?"

"Pizza?" he asked, sliding his hands to my waist.

"Oven ready?"

"Mm." His agreement sounded more like a sigh as he slowly dipped his chin and kissed me. This one wasn't a flyby peck, faster than a blink. Nor did he try to devour me like the turd who shall not be named. Mike took his time as if he were asking permission—soft, warm lips. The scent of a forest, woodsy and clean. I think woodsy just became my favorite perfume. Sighing, I turned into a melty candle as I closed my eyes and let him in.

When we finally broke apart, we were both panting. My head was reeling. I glanced aside, straight into a room with a king-sized bed, neatly made with a white comforter and heaps of pillows—one dresser, no wall art. I lowered my forehead to Mike's chest. "Maybe we ought to get going before we miss Thanksgiving altogether."

"Okay. But..."

"Hm?" I took his hand, leading him back down the stairs before I asked if I could test out his mattress.

"Um...how's your heart healing?"

I really didn't want whatever this was with Mike to turn into a rebound fling. But I'd be a damned fool if I tried to discourage him too much. "I'm here, aren't I?"

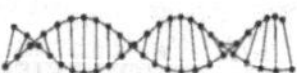

We held hands as we walked to my mother's house, though we didn't talk much because I was thinking about what I'd say to her when we got there. Generally, I avoided confrontation which is why I never got around to asking Ripper to turn down his music—go figure, the hairy beast turned out to be kinda friendly. Anyway, the problem was when I decided to confront someone, I would stew for so long, I usually blew everything out of proportion and exploded. But I was a little peeved with Mom at the moment. She still hadn't called me to give me the details about her appointment at the Moya Clinic in Rochester.

Yes, I was glad to be seeing a specialist who might be able to explain what happened to me in Elaine's car, but Mom hadn't shared anything aside from insisting I set up appointments with a vascular specialist named Dr. Davis. Since she'd moved here, it wasn't terribly unusual not to see her for a couple of weeks here and there. We were both busy. Mom by her nature was busy and I had a *real* job.

Nonetheless, I expected her to call me and tell me how her appointment went. When she didn't, I'd phoned her and she merely said it was fine, that I needed to be checked out, then continued to cut me off by telling me about Grandma's disgusting podiatry appointment. It infuriated me to have my mother so reluctant to open up. I was her next of kin. She should have at least explained the details about Dr. Davis. But what frightened me the most was I didn't know if my mom was okay or on the verge of having another TIA. Though I assumed she would have informed me if she needed surgery or if her scans found something serious.

After all, she had talked to me about her dissection—probably because it had been misdiagnosed with a migraine. I don't know. I'll never figure her out.

At least she hadn't brushed aside our dissection incidents as if they'd never happened. I swear, the woman was the queen of downplaying anything that related to health. When I was a kid, she told me time and time again my headaches weren't worth complaining about—after all, she lived with them, too.

The problem? Mom was usually right and I hated that. I wanted answers. I was too young for debilitating migraines or arterial dissections. Who had those at the age of twenty-nine?

I'd gone to see the neurologist who visited me in the hospital without much success—at least no explanation as to why the arteries in my neck had dissected just because Elaine had braked too hard. Hell, I didn't even have whiplash. The neurologist ended up giving me a prescription for a new migraine medicine which definitely helped—so far.

Anyway, today was Thanksgiving and Mike lived only four blocks from Mom's, so it took us less than five minutes to walk. I used my back door key and was surprised not to see Mom in the kitchen, even though it smelled incredible.

Mike and I followed the laughter through Mom's empty drawing room to the parlor.

My gaze homed in on the man standing in front of the bay window while my blood pressure rocketed skyward. "Bob?" My question didn't sound polite or welcoming or friendly. No, no. In fact, I don't think I'd used that tone since I was in high school.

"Meg!" He buried me in a hug like we'd known each other forever and I hadn't just spat out his name as if he were shower scum. "It's good to see you without tears in your eyes. Can I get you two something to drink?"

Mom was sitting on the little settee beside Grandma and I gave her a questioning eyebrow slant. What the hell was the yard guy doing crashing Thanksgiving and then offering to pour the drinks? The man sure was making himself at home.

Mom smiled as if there were nothing amiss, then she hopped up, made the introductions, and gave me a kiss on the cheek. "We just opened a bottle of chardonnay, or would you prefer something else?" she asked as Bob stood by expectantly with a stupid smile stretching his gray beard.

Yes, stupid.

I refused to acknowledge the fact that the man was handsome. Attractive older men had no place in my mother's parlor unless they were vetted by me.

Mike and I agreed to wine, then we sat on the floor beside my grandmother because my mom hadn't bought enough furniture yet. At least she'd found lovely Persian carpets—blue for the parlor and burgundy for the drawing room. "Are you ready for the snow?" I asked.

Grandma cringed and shivered even though she had a fleece throw covering her lap. "If it snows, send me to the Bahamas."

I glanced at the winter wonderland outside—the snow-kissed tree branches and the blanket of pristine white covering the grass. Then I leaned forward and tugged Grandma's throw a bit higher. "Okay, the Bahamas it is."

"The best thing about modern conveniences is that it's warm inside," Mike added as Bob set two glasses of wine on Mom's new Louis XIV coffee table as if he lived here.

Grandma tugged the throw up to her shoulders. "I'm never warm."

Without a fast comeback, I looked to Mom. "How are the renovations coming?"

"Most of the big things are done, the painters will start the exterior in June."

"We finished the floors a couple of weeks ago," said Bob.

My hackles rose as I mouthed *"We?"* to my mother.

And then she patted the yard guy's shoulder—a very telling pat, mind you. "I haven't had a chance to tell you, but Bob and I have decided to start a renovation partnership and I've been busy developing our business plan."

"Really?" asked Mike before I could erupt. "I'll be your first customer. I have a number of projects for you."

I glared at Bob. "I didn't realize you did more than yard work."

"He's a retired pharmacist," Mom said as if that explained everything.

I clamped my mouth shut. I don't remember my mother ever going on a date after she divorced my dad. And once I left home, she never mentioned anything about dating. But she hadn't said she was dating Bob, she'd just said they were forming a partnership. Mom's decision to start some sort of business didn't surprise me, but her choice of partner did.

I hated being surprised by shit out of left field. And on a holiday of all things. "Why does a retired pharmacist need to mow lawns for a living?"

Bob shrugged. "Something to do."

Fortunately, my interrogation was interrupted by the oven timer. But I was bamboozled when Bob and Mom disappeared into the kitchen to slice the turkey, leaving me and Mike with Grandma. "Do you need me to set the table?" I called after them.

Why was I was so piqued? Because everything was happening too fast?

"If you haven't noticed, it's already set," came my mother's disembodied voice.

I wasn't usually irritable, but I felt like marching into the kitchen, facing the pair, and demanding an explanation. Why didn't Mom tell me Bob was coming? Why didn't she discuss her decision to start up a renovation business with me? And most of all, why was a former pharmacist-turned-landscaper making himself at home in my mother's house?

By the time dinner was on the table, the glass of wine I'd consumed had done a decent job of helping me relax—or had it been the soothing way Mike had rubbed my shoulders while I was drinking the wine? Anyway, I was relieved to have Mike sit beside me. Not only did his presence provide generational support, his easygoing demeanor helped to tamp down my anger. Mom seemed more chill than I'd seen her in ages—Bob aside, maybe it was good for her to move to La Crosse. After all, for years I'd been asking her to quit her job.

"You didn't tell me about your appointment at Moya," I said, leaning forward, eyebrows arched, ready to stand on my chair and scream.

"Let's talk about it later." Mom cut me off like I was some bratty twelve-year-old. I hated to be cut off. She reached over and squeezed my hand. "How about after we take Grandma home?"

My grandmother waved her fork, sending a bite of green bean casserole flying across the table. "You don't have to share secrets behind my back."

"I told you about my appointment." Mom used her damask napkin to clean the mess. "In fact, you were the first person I went to see because I knew how concerned you'd be."

Grandma stared at my mother with a lost expression, her lips twisted as if she wanted to argue, but couldn't because she didn't remember her last conversation let alone one weeks ago. She didn't even remember that it had snowed today or that we drank wine in the drawing room before we sat down to eat.

"So, Bob." I gave the yard guy a half-smile and changed the subject. "What do you usually do for Thanksgiving?"

After we ate pie and ice cream, Mike and I did the washing up while Mom and Bob left to take Grandma home. "I need to tell you something," I said, standing at the sink, wearing pink rubber gloves with tulips, and looking at him through the fan of my eyelashes.

He pulled the drying cloth off the rack. "Oh?"

Well, it was probably too early to give him a full billet of health, but the dude ought to know I've had a few weird issues of late. I needed to tell him about my medical stuff now, before things got out of hand—or before things turned romantic which I still wasn't sure I was ready for...aside from the kisses, the flirting, the hand holding.

We'd already filled the dishwasher, so I doused the turkey roaster in sudsy water. "This summer I was in a car accident—actually, it wasn't a collision, the car just braked hard and I ended up in the hospital with dissected carotid and vertebral arteries."

There. I'd said it. Now he could put on his coat and head for home, never to enter the library again.

Mike twisted the dish towel between his hands. "That sounds awful."

Why doesn't he just make his excuses and leave?

I scrubbed ferociously. "It was scary and excruciatingly painful. It's the main reason why I'd rather walk than drive."

He placed a hand on my shoulder and squeezed gently. "God, I don't blame you. I'd be scared if something like that happened to me."

I wanted to close my eyes and melt against him, but I reminded myself not to dive in and crush hard on a dude for once in my life. Fortunately, I found a spot of baked-on grease and attacked it. "I guess you should also know that a week before my accident, my mother was doing pushups and basically had the same thing happen, except her carotid dissection was a result of strenuous exercise."

Mike leaned his hip against the counter. "Seriously? Back-to-back dissected arteries? What does that even mean?"

"We're trying to find out." I rinsed the turkey roaster and put it on the rack to dry. "So far, we've been given a lot of contradictory explanations. That's why my mom went to Moya in Rochester."

Mike dried a water glass. "Oh...didn't you ask her about that at dinner?"

"Yes—and she hasn't told me *anything*. I'm pissed because she called from the clinic and scheduled an appointment for me with her vascular doctor. They're going to do CT scans and the whole business."

He put the glass in the cupboard. "That's a good thing, right?"

"I think so. I wanted to talk to Mom about it today, but Bob was here and he..."

"You didn't know Bob was coming for Thanksgiving?"

"No!" I grabbed the cutting board and started to scrub off the greasy turkey residue. "Can you believe it? The dude does her yard. I had no idea he'd be here, let alone join forces with her restoring old houses."

"Help me understand," Mike said calmly, slipping the board from my fingers and rinsing it. "Are you worried that he'll take advantage of her?"

I had to think about that for a moment. "Mom doesn't let anyone take advantage. She's a badass. The woman even has a black belt in karate." I told him about her former job as VP of Operations. I also told him about the fact that my mother never dated. At least not that I was aware of.

How many other things was Mom keeping from me?

Mike folded the dish towel and hung it on the rack. "Look, it sounds like you need some time alone with her. Why don't I go?"

"Go?" I asked, sounding a little outraged. This was not how I'd expected the evening to play out. We were supposed to walk home together and kiss...maybe make out. "It's still early."

"Yeah, but she'll be back soon." He leaned against the island. "And didn't Bob say something about going home and calling his daughter in Florida?"

"He did."

"Well, then I should slip out. It'll be easier for you to talk to her if I'm not here."

"I could walk home with you and come back," I offered.

"I'd love for you to walk me home, but I'd have to follow you back here because it's dark outside." He clasped my cheeks between his warm palms and kissed my forehead. "See you Saturday?"

"I'll bring the pizza."

Heaven help me, I was falling for another man only weeks after I'd sworn off the opposite sex forever. Perhaps karma had intervened in my musings of a steamy make out session. After all, I'd tried to convince myself to proceed with caution. Now I had no choice but to take my own advice.

But what had just happened? I started out trying to tell Mike about my weird health stuff and ended up holding forth about my mother...who happened to come in the back door just as Mike closed the front.

Mom smiled as she took off her hat and coat, hanging them on the peg by the door. "Where did your date go?"

"Home."

"That's a shame, he seems like a really nice guy—far more your type than Lance."

I thrust my fists onto my hips. "Exactly what do you mean by that?"

The woman gave me a knowing mom-stare. "Mike's educated, polite, he combs his hair."

"Seriously?" What gave *her* the right to judge? "And because Lance looked like a bum, Mike is a better person?"

Mom crossed her arms, her expression turning from patronizing to annoyed. "What is this about? Lance chose to lie about his name and his marital status. He's a scumbag. Don't tell me you're back in touch with him?"

My shoulders fell. "No. And I like Mike. I just don't like you telling me what my type is."

"Right. Sorry." Mom tucked a string of gray hair that had escaped her bun behind her ear. She'd complained about thinning and under the new, brighter kitchen lights, her scalp shone through more than I'd noticed before. "Is this about me cancelling Bermuda?"

"No!" I shouted. "I don't give a flying fig about Bermuda. I thought I was having a good time and it turned out to be a sham!"

Mom took a glass out of the cupboard and pointed to the half-full wine bottle. "Want one?"

"No, no, no!" I was on the verge of erupting, and she was drinking a glass of wine?

She poured one for herself. "I'm not going to try to guess what has you so upset."

How she could pretend that she didn't understand what had pissed me off and speak to me without an iota of hysteria as if she were on Grandma's beach in the Bahamas.

I took her glass and downed half. "*You*, that's what."

"Me? What the hell, Meg? You sound like an adolescent."

It was like her to be condescending, but I wasn't going to back down even if I sounded like a teenager to myself. Not after the yard guy crashed Thanksgiving. "You didn't tell me you were going to Moya. Then you called me from

Rochester and had them schedule an appointment with some doctor who's going to do CT scans, then meet with me afterward. What happened? Why didn't you tell me? You never open up to me!"

Mom looked at the glass, her nostril's flaring. "Sure I do."

"When?" I clenched my fists, my nails digging into my palms. "When, Mom? You didn't say one single word to me when you left Dad. You already had my bags packed and took me on an airplane thousands of miles away from him."

"But you were just seven years old."

"I was a human being capable of cognition! I had no say in what happened to me. Do you have any idea how much I hated spending winter in America followed by winter in Australia?"

She rubbed her temples. "You've mentioned it many times."

"Well I'm mentioning it again because you *ruined* my childhood and I'll never forgive you for it!"

Mom closed her eyes and blew out a long breath. "And for that, I am eternally sorry. Ever since, I've done my best to try to make it up to you, but it's never enough."

Oh, my God, she always tried to make herself out to be the martyr. "Make it up to me by not going on cruises to Bermuda?"

"I'm sorry!" My mother appeared to shrink before my eyes, the corners of her lips drawn downward, her shoulders tensing. "I should have gone. I should have told Leon to eat the goose shit. Especially now that I know he's the twisted freak who planted the damned botte."

I pounded the counter making the wine in the glass slosh. "But you didn't!"

"No, and now I don't have a do-over."

"No, you don't." I grabbed the dish towel and dried the turkey roaster. "And what about this Bob guy? Why didn't you tell me about *him*? What else are you hiding from me? I hate it that you still treat me like a child as if telling me the truth about your life will wound me."

"What do you want to know?" Mom asked, taking the roaster and stowing it in the cupboard above the microwave.

"Why the hell was Bob at Thanksgiving?"

She brushed off her hands. "Because I invited him."

I crossed my arms and tipped up my chin. "And didn't tell me."

Mom might have appeared to be a tad meek before, but now that I was challenging her about Bob, she jammed her fists into her hips. "Excuse me, but I didn't realize you needed to approve the guest list."

Grr, my mother could be so infuriating. "What is he to you?"

She headed for the dining room and started collecting the damask napkins from the table. "He's a friend—he's been incredibly helpful ever since I moved here. He helped me with my floors. He did a good job on the yard. He's knowledgeable about older home renovations—starting up a partnership was his idea."

I pulled off the tablecloth. "I'll bet it was."

Mom shook her wad of dirty napkins. "He's a nice man."

"Are you sleeping with him?"

Those vice-president shoulders squared while her blue eyes sparked. "What the hell kind of question is that?"

"Are you?"

"No!"

A weight lifted from my shoulders as if our roles had just reversed and I was the parent worried about my kid having premarital sex.

Mom grabbed the tablecloth from me and headed toward the front staircase. "One thing is for sure, I'm not going to ask permission if I decide to start."

I gasped. Maybe our roles were solidly established. Mom had never shared anything about sex—at least sex as it pertained to her.

She stopped on the landing. "I thought you wanted to be treated like an adult!"

Damn, she could push my buttons. But rather than storm out, I followed her. I was damned-well going to get some answers. "Will you please just tell me about your appointment with Dr. Davis? Why in God's name is she so anxious to see me?"

Mom huffed out another sigh. By all her deep breaths, she was way more stressed out than she tried to let on. "I didn't give you a lot of details because I wanted you to go into your appointment without any preconceived ideas. I wanted you to tell Dr. Davis what happened to you without knowing my results. I wanted you to have the scans—to see if you have FMD or what."

"Did the doctor talk to you about your CT scan?"

"Yes." She continued into the laundry room and tossed the soiled linens in the washing machine. For the first time in my life I saw fear haunting my mother's blue eyes. By God, a tear dribbled onto her cheek—one she quickly swiped away. She added detergent, her hand trembling. "I have four aneurysms and my splenic artery is as messed up as my carotids. The good news is that the aneurysms are small. They clip them after two centimeters. For the time being Dr. Davis is going to monitor them closely."

Good Lord, my knees buckled. My grandfather *died* of a burst aneurysm. "Are you okay?" I asked, kicking myself for being so pushy—dammit, if she had just opened up to me in the first place, I never would have lost my temper.

"Yes, I'm just terrified that I've passed this FMD thing on to you." She drew in a ragged breath. "And I could barely admit the aneurysms to myself, let alone to you."

"Oh, God, you're afraid," I whispered, the back of my neck tingling.

Mom wiped away another tear. "Yes."

I stared, my lungs starting to burn. "This sucks."

"It does. There's another thing."

"Okaaay." I braced myself, wanting and desperate to hear all of it.

"I'm not allowed to push—no tough workouts, no bearing down when constipated. I'm supposed to walk every day—ten thousand steps."

"Ten thousand?"

"That's what Dr. Davis recommended." Mom pulled me into her arms. "Oh, Baby, I wish I had been a better mother. You know I'll do anything for you."

Why did Mom's hugs always make me want to break down and bawl my head off? "I know," I squeaked, my throat closing.

"Do you want me to go with you to your appointment in Rochester?"

"No." I twisted away from her embrace and tipped up my chin. There would be no crying tonight. "I think I'd rather go alone."

"You're still mad at me, aren't you?"

"Yeah." Regardless of my resolve, a gamut of emotions still flooded through me, wringing me out. "Your feelings are like a spigot, but mine can't be turned on and off quite so easily."

Mom snorted with an ugly sounding sob. "I'm kind of an insensitive witch."

"You are."

We stared at each other for a beat before she reached out her arms. But she didn't hug me. It was a peace offering, giving me the choice of whether or not to impart affection. I liked being giving the choice, but my right brain told me I wanted my mommy to hold me—to not present an option. In concert with my warring emotions, I raised my arms a fraction.

With a sob, the woman pulled me into a bear hug so tight, she stole my breath. "I love you more than anyone in the world. You do know that, don't you?"

I couldn't talk because my throat closed. Nope, wasn't going to avoid crying this time. "Mm hmm."

"Know what?"

Gulping through my tears, I shook my head against her shoulder.

"We're going to face this thing. You and me. We're going to face it together."

CHAPTER TWENTY-ONE

JANE

Bob opened the aluminum ladder and placed it beside the wall. "You okay to start with the crown molding?"

I turned full circle in the drawing room of a Victorian where we'd been contracted to restore the wood, including the window frames, the molding, and doors. Thanks to Bob, all it had taken was a few phone calls to his contractor buddies and we booked two restoration jobs. Maybe word of mouth wasn't dead in advertising, at least in small towns.

"Sure thing," I replied, opening the container of paint stripper and pouring a dollop into a pint-sized plastic bucket.

Bob plugged in the sander. "I'm going to hit these window ledges—see if I can smooth out the water damage."

The molding had been painted white, but it was made of walnut and the homeowner wanted it restored to the natural wood. I used a small brush, doing my best not to touch the plaster, even though we were going to paint the entire room after we stripped the wood. I let it sit for the requisite ten minutes, then used a scraper to remove the paint. It was tedious work because of the grooves, but it would be worth it because I could already tell the wood underneath was pristine—vibrant and dark which was very important to the Victorians as a show of wealth.

The noise from Bob's sander made my brain rattle. It wasn't just the noise, but the frequency was barely tolerable. After trying to ignore it, I climbed down the ladder and headed for my toolbox, except the toe of my tennis shoe caught on the tarp, sending me stumbling face-first into the metal box.

"Ow!" I shouted, clapping my hands over my chin. In seconds, blood streamed through my fingers and dripped down my shirt and onto the tarp.

"Oh, my God!" Bob turned off the sander and kneeled beside me, grabbing a clean white rag. "Are you okay?"

I took the rag, wincing at the searing pain made worse by the thundering heartbeat at the back of my head. "I'm a klutz."

"Could have happened to anyone."

I'd been having the odd dizzy spell now and again, but I wasn't going to tell Bob or else he'd ban me from climbing ladders. I'd never been klutzy in my life. I had taken twenty years of ballet lessons. That combined with my martial arts training gave me a good center—I was balanced.

Usually.

But at the moment, nothing was going according to plan. I moved to La Crosse to be closer to Meg, not to be an invalid. All this FMD crap could stop right now. I was healthy, vivacious, and fit.

"Let me have a look at your chin." Bob tipped the cloth down slightly and hissed. "You're going to need stitches."

I leaned away. "Oh, please. It will stop bleeding in a few minutes."

"Not likely." He grabbed another cloth out of the bag and handed it to me. "You've already bled through that one. Come on, I'll drive you."

I gave him a dour frown. "I don't want to go to the emergency room."

"Okay. There's an urgent care clinic on Losey Boulevard that's close."

After he twisted my arm, Bob marshalled me into his truck, pointing out that my knee had bled through my jeans. Great. First day on the job and I was already an OSHA statistic. Good thing I didn't still work for Bethany Plastics or else they'd make me take a course on safety in the workplace.

How did I trip? Was there something sticking up under the tarp? Was there something wrong with my ears? I'll admit to being unusually tired and possibly overwhelmed after Thanksgiving. I had no idea that Meg would get so upset about Bob. I suppose I should have told her about the aneurysms, too. Except I had been in a state of denial. Or maybe it was a state of shock. But I needed to face reality. I had been insensitive by not telling her. I needed to work on opening up, on putting myself in her shoes. My idea to have her go into the appointment without preconceived notions was flawed. Meg deserved a mom who was candid. I wanted her to trust me. I wanted to be there for her. More than anything, I wanted us to be close, not just now but always.

Dr. Davis had spoken to me as if having FMD along with four aneurysms was perfectly normal. But upon reflection, I wonder if she was trained to act that way—or she just saw a lot of devastating vascular stuff on a daily basis. After all, how would any patient feel if their doctor freaked out? Thinking back, in Denver Dr. Panda had been alarmed while, conversely, Dr. Vaughn behaved as if my CT scan was superfluous.

Rare diseases obviously weren't studied by the average doc. I guess that's why there were so many tales of woe in the FMD Facebook group. I'd seen post after post from people who had been diagnosed with FMD and couldn't find a local doctor to take them seriously about a litany of issues, including dizziness and migraines.

I wanted to ignore my results and hide them away in my attic, but they kept rearing their ugly heads. I owed it to Meg to be truthful with her. I had intended to compare notes after her appointment, which wasn't until January second, but she was impatient just like me. Really, what did it matter? She was my beloved daughter. I hated to admit that it appeared as though she inherited my vascular stuff, which I suppose I inherited from my dad.

"Why did you climb down from the ladder?" Bob jolted me from my thoughts as he put on his blinker and turned a corner. "Hadn't you just moved it?"

For better absorption, I folded the rag I was holding against my chin. "Yeah, but I couldn't bear the sander noise any longer. I was going to get some earplugs out of my toolbox."

"An orbital sander was too loud?"

"It was the frequency more than anything. Sometimes I get migraines and I never know what's going to set them off—a noise, light, thinking too hard."

"Thinking too hard?" he asked, chuckling.

I rubbed the back of my neck. "Maybe I should have said trying too hard."

"Now that I can believe."

He pulled into the parking lot at Festival Foods of all places, but sure enough, on the south end was an urgent care clinic. I unfastened my seatbelt. "I can take an Uber if you want to go back to work."

"Hell no. You've already gone through three rags. I'm not leaving you to bleed to death."

"Believe me, this is nothing."

"Huh?" he asked, but I wasn't about to explain my ancient history of bleeding profusely. I also didn't let him go into the exam room with me.

Four stiches later, I sat in the recliner in my TV room with an ice pack on my chin and another on my knee which had a bruise the size of a ribeye steak. The urgent care doc consulted with Dr. Wahl and then referred me to a vascular neurologist for my headaches and dizziness, but my appointment wasn't until May.

Ugh...yet another doctor appointment. When would it end?

Bob came in, carrying a tray with herbal tea and slice-and-bake chocolate chip cookies still warm from the oven. "Here we are."

I took one, my eyes rolling when I bit into it. "These are delicious."

He set the tray on the coffee table. "I've already had four—couldn't help myself."

I snorted. "Four?"

He slid onto the couch. "We skipped lunch."

"Sorry," I hissed through my teeth. "What are the homeowners going to think when they see blood all over the tarp?"

"They're going to think it's paint. Good thing the tarp is old. There have to be at least seven different colors of latex on it." He handed me a mug of steaming tea, the scent of cinnamon making me sigh. "By the way you were bleeding I'm surprised you only ended up with four stitches."

After blowing on the hot tea, I took a slow sip. "I'm more mortified with the fact that it was my first day on the job."

"First day of a paid job. You did well on your floors. The sander didn't seem to bother you then."

"Yeah, but I was wearing earplugs."

"Note to self, make sure Jane has hearing protection any time we use power tools."

"So, you're not going to fire me?" I asked, trying to be funny, but posing the question hit a raw nerve. Before I could cover up the raw wounds made by my former boss, I groaned and hunched forward.

"Hey." He reached over from the couch and rubbed my back, his touch way too soothing. "You okay?"

"Maybe I'm pushing myself too hard," I said, clenching my teeth. I've always been tough—fought my way through every problem. But of late, circumstances have left me vulnerable and weak, like my body was failing me. And I didn't want to look as if I couldn't cut it to Bob. I liked him a lot. At last, I had a friend and it felt amazing to be close to somebody my age. To have someone actually care (besides Meg, of course).

"Probably, but I've been around you long enough to know you've been through something bad. What happened at that high-flying job of yours, anyway?"

Leon's heartless laser eyes drilled through my mind as if they'd addled my brain permanently. "You don't want to know."

Bob took my hand and clasped it between his warm palms. "Look at me."

I didn't turn my head but regarded him out of the corners of my eyes.

"Come on, look at me," he said, his tone caring, but commanding at the same time.

I heaved a deep sigh and lowered my ice bag so I could stare at those kind, concerned, green eyes.

"I know you were VP of Operations. And a woman with your kind of moxie is too young to retire. You moved to La Crosse and bought a fixer where you worked like a fiend. Hell, woman, you haven't taken a break. You run around like your hair's on fire from dawn till well after dark, and I'll bet you fall into bed in a comatose sleep because you're exhausted. Am I wrong?"

I set the mug on the tray. "If I don't push myself, I think about it."

"Think about what?"

Oh, God, here goes.

"About getting fired," I blurted, the words like acid on my tongue.

"What?" Bob sat back and coughed out an expression of utter bewilderment. "That's unbelievable. Horrible. Man, I'm sorry."

"Don't be. The responsibility came with the territory."

"What happened?"

"I'd like to say it wasn't my fault, but when you're the vice president, everything is your fault even though there are some things you can't possibly prevent."

Bob urged me to move from the recliner onto the couch beside him. "I know how that can turn out. I've seen pharmacists lose their jobs because they didn't question a doctor after over-prescribing opioids. Look, I'm not going to beat around the bush here. Sure, I suggested forming a partnership because you work hard and you don't leave things half-done. But when I dig right down to it, I like you. I like being with you. Doing things like holding your hand, baking you cookies makes me happy."

"Slice-and-bake cookies," I said, even though they were my go-to, not necessarily Bob's.

He kissed the back of my hand. "If you want me to go downstairs and make a batch from scratch, I'll do it right now."

"No, no."

"I'm not going to judge you, Jane. Just open up a little and tell me what happened." He kissed my cheek this time. Even though it was just meant to be nothing more than a kind gesture, my resolve melted a little along with the ice encasing my heart. "But only if you want to."

I glanced to our joined hands and realized how much I had been aching for his touch. Sitting beside Bob was comforting. It felt like we had been together for years, as if the two of us were destined to be in this place at this time.

"My company had a contamination issue with a high-profile customer..." Once I began, it was hard to stop. As I relayed the events leading to the loss of my job, Bob stroked my hair, rubbed my shoulders, as if I were worth something to him. His human touch reminded me how good it was to be loved and cared for, something I'd been missing for so long, I'd forgotten what it was like to have a man's affection. But the words tumbling from my lips were anything other than romantic. I have to admit I sat taller when I told him about sticking to my guns and watching the warehouse film for mindless hours on end. It also felt good to tell him about contacting the FBI.

"So." I drew in a deep breath. "After Leon gave me the axe, I moved to La Crosse and bought this house to have a project while I figured out what I was going to do."

Bob brushed my cheek with his knuckle. "Have you decided yet?"

"Before today, I believed our little renovation business might pose the perfect challenge—as long as we don't take on too much work and overextend ourselves."

"Agreed. But..." He looked down.

"But?" I grazed my teeth over my bottom lip. Maybe I shouldn't have exposed my past. What if he had second thoughts?

"I wasn't exaggerating before when I said I like you. I'm not great at being romantic—obviously, because instead of asking you on a date, I came up with the partnership idea."

The stitches on my chin seared with my grin. "You mean you weren't serious about starting up a renovation business?"

"No, no. I was very serious about that. Your detail work is top shelf. I just...um...well...um..."

I kissed Bob's cheek. "Do you want to go out to dinner sometime—just the two of us?"

You know the serene smile a man gets on his face when he slides into a hot tub and all his tension whisks away? When he's completely content? When he receives the very thing for which he has been yearning? Well, Bob's expression pushed those buttons. It even made me forget about my stitches. "I never thought you'd ask."

Chapter Twenty-Two

Meg

Pizza, beer, and the UW Badgers on a big-screen TV was my idea of a fantastic way to spend a Saturday afternoon. Mike and I did the wave, we sang all the game-time songs, like *Fireflies* and *Sweet Caroline*. Both of us knew the words to the fight song, and by the nail-biting end of the fourth quarter, we were on our feet, jumping up and down, shouting at the tops of our lungs.

The game was tied, we had the ball on the opponent's thirty-eight yard line, there were three seconds left, and our kicker was jogging out onto the field.

I covered my face in my hands. "I can't bear to watch."

"Come on," Mike urged. "At least if he misses, we'll go into overtime."

"But I don't want to go into overtime. It's Ohio State. They always pull something out of their asses at the last minute, and I want to annihilate them!"

He put his arm around my shoulders. "We'll watch together, okay?"

I opened my fingers. "Okay."

I held my breath as the ball snapped. The place kicker moved forward and gave it a cannon of a kick. Cringing, I leaned into Mike as it looked like the ball was going wide.

"He made it!" shouted the announcer.

"Woooooo!" Mike and I faced each other, our eyes round, jumping up and down, grabbing hands and going utterly insane!

"We did it!" I shouted, throwing my arms around him.

He spun me in a circle. "We sure did!"

Setting me down, we both shimmied with a little dance and fell into each other's arms. "That was amazing."

"My God, it had to be the most exciting game of the year."

I rose up onto my toes and kissed him. "So exciting."

He cupped my cheek, his eyes suddenly serious, and damned sexy. Slowly, he lowered his lips to mine and kissed me. Kissed me like we were the only two people left on the planet, starving for affection.

My ovaries went on hyperdrive while I slid my hands around him. Up and down his back. To his butt.

Oh, my God, he had a tight ass. I pulled his hips closer and rubbed against his erection.

Mike rested his forehead against mine. "Are you okay?"

I tugged his red sweatshirt over his head and dropped it on the floor. "More than okay."

He kissed me again. "That was epic."

I took his hand and led him downstairs—straight to the king-sized bed I wanted to test. "Know what else will be epic?"

Clothes flew off. On went a condom and away went every memory of Lance. Mike took his time, paid more attention getting me to climax than Lance ever did. Mike was a better lover, a better man. By the next morning, I was so glad I didn't try to resist the call of my ovaries. I totally felt like Andy in the scene at the end of *The Forty-Year-Old Virgin* where he's singing *Aquarius* because he's so blown away after losing his virginity. Sure, I was only twenty-nine, and I wasn't a virgin, but I could have run through Riverside Park with flowers in my hair and belted *Let the Sunshine In* at the top of my lungs. Even with two feet of snow on the ground.

Because everything about Mike was *epic*. He was the nicest guy I'd ever met. He made Lance (before I found out he was a douche) look like a narcissistic, insensitive slob.

We spent every night together for a week, then we drove down to Madison for the Badgers' last football game of the regular season. And after our team won, we partied on State Street like a pair of coeds. Mike rented a hotel room so we could enjoy a couple of drinks and not have to drive two hours back to La Crosse.

Since then, we've been swapping houses—his one night, my apartment the next. We even read *The Best Christmas Pageant Ever* aloud, curled up in my bed while Maya slept on Mike's lap the entire time. My dog was an enigma. The first time Mike came to my apartment, she ripped a hole in the bottom of his jeans. He'd just laughed, swept her into his arms, and kissed her.

And rather than biting his nose off, she licked him. From that day on, my dog was as infatuated with the man as I was.

While my mom was working at her new home restoration job, she smacked her chin on her toolbox. Even though she had four stitches, the wound was healing slowly. At least it was on the underside of her chin so the scar wasn't too noticeable. She said Bob had rushed her to urgent care, which elevated him a few notches out of the dungeon. Also, my mother mentioned they'd enjoyed a couple of dinners together. The weird thing was that when she shared the news that she'd seen Bob outside of the realm of their partnership, I was totally cool with it—happy for her.

I don't know what came over me on Thanksgiving, but I was way out of line. I always let things stew and then would blow up for one teeny weensy thing, making everyone think I'd turned into Godzilla. I admit, at the time, I'd stewed for too long. I was furious that Mom hadn't told me about her appointment with the FMD doc, especially since she'd all but scheduled my appointment. Regrettably, I focused my fury on Bob at Thanksgiving.

I shouldn't have.

Everybody deserved to be happy, especially my mother who had single-handedly paid for my bachelor's and master's degrees without a word of complaint. I didn't want Mom to be lonely. I didn't want her meddling in my life, either. And Bob seemed to keep her busy enough to prevent her from micromanaging me. Mom seemed to really like him, too.

Mike in his Chevy Volt rolled to a stop outside my apartment. If I hadn't been watching for him, I never would have heard his car. It made me wonder if the new electric motors were hazardous to pedestrians. There has been more than one time where I've stepped off a curb and stopped because I heard a car coming but was unable to see it because of a tree or a truck parked in the way.

Wearing a pair of purple-paisley ski pants, I gave Maya a kiss and grabbed my coat, hat, and gloves then slipped out the door.

Mike stepped onto the sidewalk. "Let me be a gentleman for once."

I fell into his arms and gave him a kiss. "Thank you. It's wonderful to know chivalry is not dead."

"You ready for this?"

I glanced back to the house. "I suppose we could stay here and find a YouTube video about learning to ski."

"Nah." He opened the car door for me. "I've already paid for the lessons."

"All right, but don't expect me to be graceful. I tried ice skating when I was ten and broke my leg."

Mike hopped into his seat, then drove away from the curb. "Don't break a leg."

"Okay," I said, grabbing the side handle and watching for speeding cars running stop signs.

Mike's driving was pretty chill, but I sucked air through my teeth every time a car cut in front of us, or whenever he stared to slow down for a stop light.

He glanced at me with a quirky grin. "Are the brakes working on your side?"

I shifted my gaze down to my feet, my toes pressed against the floor as if I were bracing for impact. "Sorry." As I chuckled, the humor helped take away some of my tension.

He patted my knee. "I'm not going to let anything happen to you, okay?"

I nodded. "Thank you."

I covered my mouth with my palm to stop myself from hissing while we drove to the south side of town, and out the Old Town Hall Road to the Mount La Crosse Ski Area. I'd been to Seattle to visit my Uncle Roger several times, and after seeing Mount Rainier, the Midwest ski slopes looked like kiddy hills. But if I was going to actually put on a pair of skis, I'd take these hills over the mountains in Washington any day.

We checked into the desk at the chalet, and I salivated as I passed a kid drinking hot chocolate. "We could skip the slopes and go to the café," I said, almost serious.

Mike just pulled me along.

They outfitted us with gear including a helmet and goggles. I doubted I'd be going fast enough to need the eyewear, but I was definitely a candidate for a helmet—maybe a neck brace.

Our ski instructor, Deb, met us outside. She took one look at me and decided to start with the basics. I so did not look like a skier. I was more of an abominable snow woman in a puffy purple suit with flaming red hair poking out from under the back of my helmet.

The basics were way easier than I'd imagined. Putting skis on and taking them off, how to use the poles, sidestepping, how to feel your foot and ankles and how they moved inside a boot as rigid as a plaster cast. We started wearing one ski and learned to step sideways and in circles before we were asked to propel ourselves forward with just the single ski and poles.

By the time we put both skis on, I was definitely ready for hot chocolate. I think Mike was, too. He even yawned. But two skis proved a bit more interesting because after we learned how to make a wedge and stop without crossing the tips of our skis, we actually got to ride up the conveyor of a miniscule slope.

"You're a natural, Meg!" Deb hollered as I glided downward and executed a perfect wedge, stopped and started again. Who knew? My sport was skiing.

On the kiddie slopes.

I glanced past the chairlift at the insane humans flying down Mt. La Crosse way faster than Mike drove through town.

"To the left, Mike," Deb hollered, her voice ratcheting up in pitch. "Mike! Left!"

I glanced over my shoulder just as my boyfriend plowed into me, his wedge never quite materializing. Together we crashed into the snow, which was nearly as hard as the ice had been during my one and only skating lesson.

"Ow," I said, flat on my back with Mike sprawled on top of me.

"Are you okay?" He sounded concerned, wriggling, and awkwardly trying to move off of me while tangling our skis. "Did I hurt you?"

Deb released his heel levers then mine. "You guys all right?"

Mike stood and pulled me up. "Fine."

I bent my knees and rubbed the back of my neck. "I think I survived this one." Thank God. I'd had dissected arteries for less. Maybe I was wrong, skiing wasn't my sport.

Mike tried the hill one more time while I watched from a safe distance. This time, he executed two decent wedges and met me at the bottom of the hill, a triumphant grin across his face like he'd just tamed his dragon. "How'd I look, Lady Rose?"

"Like an ace," I replied. "But why did you call me Lady Rose?"

"Because you have the most gorgeous red hair I've ever seen, and you're a..."

"Hm?"

"Goddess—there's no way anyone could possibly look at you and not be mesmerized."

"Yeah, right. In my dreams."

"Then dream it, woman. Haven't you ever seen Christina Hendricks in *Mad Men*? You remind me of her, except you're sexier."

I gulped at the compliment. "But she's *gorgeous*."

"See what I mean?" He blew me a kiss and grabbed my hand. "Come on, let's return our gear and get some hot chocolate. We've earned it."

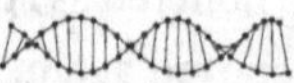

Throughout the rest of the month of December, I was happier than I'd ever been in my life.

The only free time Mike and I didn't spend together was Christmas. He went to his sister's house in Madison and I celebrated the holiday with Mom and Grandma. Bob had flown to Florida to see his daughter, so Christmas was quiet aside from my grandmother loudly singing carols even at the dinner table.

Mike didn't end up bringing his niece to La Crosse as he'd planned weeks ago, but he did come back to celebrate New Year's with me. He made a reservation for a late dinner at La Charmant, one of La Crosse's higher end restaurants and though it was only eleven degrees outside, we donned our boots and winter gear and did the responsible thing—we walked.

A brightly-lit Christmas tree in the window welcomed us, as did the maître de who opened the door and took our coats. "Are you staying for the celebration on the rooftop terrace?" he asked.

Mike gave me a squeeze. "Our reservation is all encompassing."

"Ah yes, I see right here."

We were shown to a table for two that overlooked Riverside Park which the Rotary decorated with a holiday light show every year. A candle flickered on the table as if in harmony with the Christmas lights outside reflecting on the unfrozen part of the Mississippi.

"Does the river ever completely freeze over?" Mike asked.

"Not usually. Whenever I've been down here in subzero temperatures, there's almost always a channel in the middle where the river is moving too fast to freeze—like now. Just wait until things start to thaw. Bald eagles ride the icebergs down the Mississippi and catch fish."

"Whoa, I definitely want to see that."

"It's amazing. I drove down the river highway in March a couple of years ago and literally saw hundreds of them."

We ordered our food, the band from the bar serenading us with original light rock tunes. The musicians all looked to be about Mom's age, but they had talent.

"What's this?" Mike picked up a stack of cards and read the top one. "Huh."

I leaned in. "Conversation starters?"

"Want to give it a go?" he asked, waggling his eyebrows as if issuing a challenge.

"Can I plead the fifth?"

Not answering, he laughed and picked a card. "*Do you have a secret talent? If so, can you do it right now?*"

"I can whistle really loud with my fingers in my mouth. Does that qualify?"

"Definitely, but I think maybe we ought to save the demonstration for the fireworks up on the terrace."

"Agreed. You definitely would split an eardrum if I tried it in here. We might be asked to leave as well."

"Before they feed us?"

I winked. "Best to wait, as you suggested." I reached for the next card. "*If you had a parrot, what would you teach it to say?*"

Mike drummed his fingers on his chin. "Well, it certainly wouldn't be 'Alexa, turn on the lights.'" He shook his head as I imagined his electricity bill. "Maybe, 'I love you.'"

My breath hitched as those gray eyes homed in on me, suddenly blocking out everything, turning us into the only two people in the restaurant. Possibly the only two people in La Crosse. But that's what he'd teach a parrot to say to him, right? Of course he didn't love *me*. How could he? It was way too soon.

My fingers trembled as I slid the card to the bottom of the pile while Mike picked one off the top.

"Oh, this one's good. *What's the best pick-up line you know?*"

"You're the one who said it, dude." When he knit his brows, I shimmied my shoulders and affected my best Mike Reynolds impression. "My niece is coming to visit for a few days and I was wondering if the library might have a copy of the complete set of *Harry Potter* movies." I laughed so hard, my side cramped.

Mike did, too. "What must you think of me, now that she didn't even end up coming?"

The food arrived along with a bottle of red wine. We ate and asked a few more conversation questions. I learned Mike's favorite childhood stuffed animal had been named Bear. It was a beaver and huge. Oh, if only I could have seen him dragging it by the tail and insisting emphatically it was (a) Bear.

Before midnight, we donned our coats, gloves, hats, and mufflers and followed the crowd to the rooftop terrace where we had the choice of drinking champagne or hot toddies. Since there was ice floating in Mike's champagne, I opted for the toddy which cooled down in about two seconds.

Music from the eighties was piped through the speakers, and we joined the crowd on the dance floor, lighting it up in winter gear, our snow boots clomping gracelessly. At midnight Mike wrapped me in his arms as we watched the fireworks explode over the city, set off from Grandad's Bluff. I gave a very short demonstration of my whistle before we kissed, bringing in the New Year with gloved hands, so cold our fingers were numb. It was romantic and fun. I'd never felt so alive.

We spent New Year's Day watching the Badgers beat UCLA in their bowl game, making love on the foldout couch in front of Mike's TV. Oh, my God. There's nothing better than reaching climax just as my team scored. Scores for everyone. Boo ya, baby!

On January second, Mike was still on winter break. However, I'd convinced him to stay at home while I drove myself to the Moya Clinic in Rochester. I probably should have invited Mom to come along, but I'd already told her I wanted to go alone, and I stood by my decision.

Five months had passed since the accident and driving had gotten a little easier, but I didn't ever go over the speed limit and made sure I kept plenty of distance between me and the car in front.

Dr. Davis had ordered a preliminary blood test which I was able to take a couple of days ago at the Moya Clinic in La Crosse. Of course, Moya in Rochester made the La Crosse facility look miniscule. I was both shocked and awed by all the marble used on the first floor of the Gonda Building. Shocked because as a frugal librarian, I instantly came up with a gazillion better uses for the financial outlay for such lavishness. Awed, because the expansive foyer made a statement that boomed, "This is the temple of healthcare, be respectful and reverent."

After check-in, it didn't take long for the technician to call my name and lead me to a dressing room. "Dr. Davis has changed your scan from a CTA to an MRA."

"Really?" That was odd because I was sure Mom had a CTA. "Do you know why?"

"I'm just a technician. You'll have to ask the doctor. You still have your appointment with her this afternoon, right?"

"Yes."

The MRA procedure used contrast dye but the technicians said it was a lot more comfortable than the CT contrast dye. At first I wondered why they didn't just do magnetic resonance angiograms on all vascular patients rather than CTAs. I got my answer when my scan took a whole lot longer. Afterward, I barely had time to grab a sandwich before I headed back up the elevators for my face-to-face with the doctor.

I was surprised at how young Dr. Davis was when she came in. I'd assumed if my mother saw her, she'd be at least in her fifties, but this woman was mid-forties at the oldest. She carried an air of professionalism, yet there was something very human in her smile.

We exchanged pleasantries before she sat down in front of the computer screen and faced me, her hands folded. "Were you aware that you're pregnant?"

In a nanosecond, my skin flushed hot, my face burned, pits stung, and I couldn't breathe. "W-what?" was all I managed to say, given the room had started spinning.

"Your blood test. Of course, it shouldn't come as a surprise that it's common practice to give all women between the ages of twelve and fifty pregnancy tests before they have a CTA."

Had I been given a quick pregnancy test in the ER? *Maybe?* I was pretty freaked out at the time and they'd drawn a lot of blood for a myriad of reasons. I pressed the tips of my fingers against my stomach. "I-I guess I must have forgotten about that."

Pregnant? I couldn't be pregnant. Not now!

"Well, it's a good thing we did." Dr. Davis' eyes smiled, crinkling a little in the corners. "I hope this is good news."

Good? Better descriptors might be shocking, terrifying, and frantic. "Ah..." Who was the father? God! This couldn't be happening! "You wouldn't know how far along I am, would you?"

"No, but I recommend you make an appointment with your PCP as soon as possible."

Fuuuuuuuck, no! I just met the man of my dreams and now I'm going to lose him because I'm probably pregnant with a douchebag's baby. *Fuck no! No, no, no!*

I must have looked like I was about to faint because the doctor put her hand on my shoulder, patting gently. "Are you okay? Do you need a minute?"

If there was one thing I knew about doctors, they had very few extra minutes in their days. "I'm a little taken aback is all. This was unexpected news. Quite unexpected."

Dr. Davis' eyes crinkled again. "Sometimes surprises are the best gifts."

I rubbed my stomach which was never flat, but always a little round. How had this happened? I didn't take the pill because they all had side effects, but both Mike and Lance had used condoms.

Ugh, it felt disgusting and filthy to think about Lance.

"Shall we talk about today's scans or would you prefer to reschedule our appointment?"

I took a breath and fanned my face. "Since I'm here, I'd like to know what you found."

"Excellent. But first, in your own words, please tell me how you ended up with carotid *and* vertebral dissections."

I described the braking incident, the excruciating pain, the loss of sight in one eye, and Elaine rushing me to Gustafsson Hospital. "The problem is the radiologist said I had dissections, the ER doc concurred and told me I'd had a TIA—he's the one who admitted me. But in the hospital, the vascular doc questioned everything."

"Interesting," she replied, examining the MRA scans that had been done today. "I see dissections and aneurysms every day, and looking back at the images taken at Gustafsson, you definitely had two dissections. Reviewing today's results, it appears your vertebral artery is healing but I'm concerned because your carotid hasn't. It looks to have a chronic dissection—similar to your mother's, though there's no visible stenosis."

"Mom has stenosis?"

"Yes, but she is a lot older than you are."

I leaned in and looked at the screen where Dr. Davis was pointing. Sure enough, there was a break in the artery wall that reminded me of a hemp rope just beginning to fray. "Do I have FMD like my mom?"

"Honestly, that's what has me baffled. You're not showing the tortuosity that your mother has. You don't have any aneurysms either. By the way, she gave us permission to talk to you about her health history, otherwise, I wouldn't have been able to mention it."

"She did?" Wow, Mom actually trusted me with such personal information? Maybe she was finally realizing I'd grown up. "I'm worried about her aneurysms. You are aware her father died from one?"

"I am, and we're going to watch her carefully, okay?"

I nodded.

"Because I don't see classic FMD on your scans, I'd like to send a blood sample to a genetics lab. Would that be all right?"

"Sure. Do you think they'll find anything?"

"Possibly. The field of genetics is changing every day. They've been working on identifying a gene mutation for FMD, but the studies have been inconclusive."

"Working on? So, are you testing my mom?"

"Let's start with you and see where it goes. If we find anything, we can talk about whether or not it makes sense to test your mother."

I drove home from Rochester in a state of shock. Of course, I still wasn't super cool with driving. I set the cruise control at the speed limit and had a mini panic attack every time I had to change lanes to pass someone going slower than me.

But that's not why I was in a state of shock.

I was pregnant.

There was a tiny human growing inside me.

Yes, I'd always wanted kids, but I'd expected to be married first. And I wasn't the type of girl who slept around. In the past year I'd had sex with two men. The first time with Mike had been the Saturday after Thanksgiving, I needed to consult a calendar but it must have been about six weeks ago...five, maybe?

God save me, either one might be the father!

Chapter Twenty-Three

Jane

"Where are you?" Meg asked, her voice tinny, sounding like she had me on speaker.

I balanced the phone between my cheek and shoulder while I used a screwdriver. "We're installing a mini-split air conditioning system."

"You know how to do that?"

"YouTube, Sweetie. Everyone can learn to do anything online. Except we called in electricians for the power connection."

"I thought you were restoring old houses, not installing air conditioning."

"That was our plan, but this homeowner wanted an AC system for her Victorian and didn't want to have to install a lot of duct work or rip out walls. It's the same system I put in my house."

"Oh, right—the one you got to use for about a week before fall hit. Why the heck are you installing AC in January?"

"Because the units arrived." I put down the screwdriver and wrapped my fingers around the phone before I ended up with a crick in my neck. "How did it go in Rochester?"

The line went silent.

"Meg? Can you hear me?"

"Yeah. Sorry—got distracted."

"So, how was your appointment with Dr. Davis?"

"Okay I guess. Um…"

I grabbed another screw while I waited.

"Um…she says I don't present with typical FMD so she's sending a blood sample for genetic testing."

"Really?" I balanced the phone again and started on the next hole. "Does she think they'll find anything?"

"She doesn't know if they will or not."

Why didn't Dr. Davis send me for genetic testing? Because she could tell I had FMD without it? "How do you feel about that?"

"Not sure. They could be grasping."

"Yeah, genetics is such new field." I twisted in the screw. "Hey, you want to come over for dinner Friday night?"

"Um...maybe?"

"You can bring Mike—I like him."

"Can I let you know? I have a few things going on at the moment."

I snatched my phone from my chin and shoulder and looked at it. Meg had things going on? She was a librarian in La Crosse which meant she was all but hibernating in January. "Anything I ought to be aware of?"

"Too soon to tell."

My eyebrows pinched together. "That sounds cryptic."

"I just need a little time, okay?"

I went silent while Bob took over for me and finished putting in the rest of the screws.

The needle of my mommy meter pointed to overload, warning me it was time to back off. I had to be careful how I chose my words, especially when Meg decided not to tell me about things that were obviously weighing on her. I was the type of person who wanted answers and, as a former VP of Operations, I was used to getting them. But when it came to my daughter, I couldn't fire on all cylinders or else she'd combust. "Is this about your CT scan?" I asked carefully, sliding my fingers over my tender chin.

"Nope."

I inhaled, drawing out a pause before I responded, "All right, then, don't tell me, but I'll plan on seeing you and Mike on Friday unless I hear differently."

Bob holstered his screwdriver as I hung up the phone. "Is everything okay on the daughter front?"

I gave him a wide-eyed guffaw. "Is it ever?"

"Not with my Sophie, that's for sure." He looked at the ceiling and groaned. "She needs to get married. Then she'll be someone else's problem."

"Surely you don't mean that."

"No?" Bob took off his hat and scratched his shiny head. "In the past year, I've helped her buy a condo, been strapped with her mortgage payments for three months because her car broke down, flew to Florida to console her after she broke up with a guy she'd been dating for a year and a half, and those are just the big things. She's a great girl—smart—beautiful as a winter sunset. But she's going to send me into bankruptcy."

I slid my arm around his waist and gave him a sideways hug. We'd gone out to dinner three times now, but Bob hadn't kissed me goodbye, which I decided was a good thing. A companion is what I needed, not a lover. "I know we haven't talked much about money, but in the time I've come to know you, I doubt you'll be penniless anytime soon."

"Doesn't matter. I love her more than anything, but I'm the first to admit that daughters are a challenge."

"Mine's not."

He put his hat back on and pulled down the brim. "No? Have you forgotten about Lance already?"

"Of course not, but anyone can wind up in a bad relationship—after all, it happened to me when I married her father. At least Meg ended it before the asshole tried to string her along for years, popping in and out of her life every time his wife left town." I wadded up the plastic film we'd taken off the AC unit. "Sure, she likes her privacy. She'll tell me what's going on when she's ready."

"As long as she doesn't wait until she's completely desperate like Sophie does."

"I'm sure whatever is bothering Meg, she'll handle it. Hormones aside, she's the most levelheaded twenty-nine-year-old I know."

Bob's eyes bugged wide. "You know a lot of twenty-nine-year-olds?"

"Stop." I tucked the plastic under my arm and grabbed the mini-split remote control. "Let's see if this baby works."

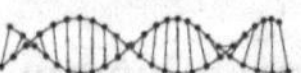

At least Meg texted me to say she wouldn't be able to make it for dinner this evening, but that only caused me to worry. I was ready to march over to her apartment and demand to know what was going on. But getting in my daughter's face had never been an effective method for making her open up. Still, something was bothering Meg and I couldn't help her unless I knew what.

Even then I probably wouldn't be able to help. No one ever told me parenting was much harder once your kids became adults. Grown-up problems were always a gazillion times worse than they were at the age of nine.

I'd already walked my ten thousand steps for the day and now I was on the verge of driving myself out of my mind, pacing my huge house, looking at my phone, willing Meg to call. I should have taken Bob up on his offer to go to the Recovery Watering Hole for a drink after we finished restoring the tile on an Edwardian fireplace, but I told him I needed some time to myself, which earned me a harrumph.

Aside from Bob, I hadn't made many friends yet, especially since Dr. Davis told me to keep my heart rate steady and I had quit my exercise classes at the Y. Honestly, I was kind of out of practice at acquiring friends. VPs and even plant managers needed to be careful about not getting too close to employees, which meant a lonely existence for a single person who worked every waking hour.

But Bob was unique. He was a good man—a good friend—maybe a little more than a friend.

I ended up in my office, staring at my computer screen. As I clicked to the news, my breath caught. The headline read: *Bethany Board Members Charged with Fraud.*

I clapped a hand over my mouth, reading about how the FBI received an anonymous tip which led them to the arrest of CEO Leon Worthington. The story went on to name the CEO of Hydroade as well. He was also arrested for colluding with Worthington by staging a tampering incident designed to force Bethany into bankruptcy while the guilty parties laundered the insurance payout through an offshore account in their attempt to make it appear as if the company was insolvent. Had the plan worked, every member of the board would have received five million in protected preferred shares with the two CEOs plotting to split the fifty-million-dollar insurance windfall.

It was no secret Leon had gone through three nasty divorces that had cost him dearly, but I never suspected him capable of fraud.

Out of the blue, an email from Curt Hastings, the plant manager in Philly, appeared. As I opened it, I realized I hadn't heard from anyone at Bethany Plastics since I moved to La Crosse. I'd dedicated my life to that company, putting in ungodly hours (sometimes at the expense of my own family), yet it had been incredibly easy for all of them to write me off.

Hello, Jane,

I hope this finds you well. If you haven't seen the headlines, I would assume you are living in a cave without internet. But a little bird tells me you had something to do with the anonymous tip. You're the only person I know with enough savvy to nail Worthington. I'd like to buy you a drink, Boss.

We also just got word that Bethany will not be proceeding with bankruptcy. Even better, sales negotiated a new contract with Hydroade. I hope you're considering coming back. I heard you're on the short list for the next CEO (nudge, wink). We miss you!

Best,

Curt

Salivating, I sat and stared at the words "next CEO". If I'd been faced with such an opportunity a few months ago I would have jumped at it immediately. And right now, I couldn't say it wasn't tempting, but I'd changed since I moved. I'd started a new life. I bought an amazing home that I still had dozens of plans for. I moved my mother and lived within walking distance from my daughter. I needed time to think before I jumped on the executive treadmill again. Besides, no one had reached out to me yet, possibly because the FBI made their arrests less than twenty-four hours ago?

I decided to reply to Curt without mentioning anything about the open CEO job.

Hey, Stranger,

Glad to hear they caught the culprit. Sad to hear it was a man who should have been a paragon of honesty and integrity. Congratulations on getting the Hydroade business back!

Best,

Jane

As I clicked send, I had a twenty-pound weight lifted from my shoulders. So, my old boss turned out to be more of a son-of-a-bitch than I'd realized. I slid onto my piano bench and played *Beethoven's Fifth*—pounding the keys as hard as I could, ready to dance all night not giving a rip if anyone watched.

My moment of triumph was interrupted when the knocker on the door resounded, followed by the Google doorbell. I checked the app on my phone, expecting to see Meg on the doorbell's feed, but it was my partner in crime.

"What the hell are you doing here?" I asked, opening the door, trying to sound stern but utterly failing.

Bob's easy grin was just what I needed after learning the man who fired me had been arrested for white-collar crime. The man pulled a bottle of merlot out of a brown paper bag. "Since the Recovery Watering Hole wasn't your idea of fun, I thought you might feel like a drink about now."

I stood back and gestured inside. "Come on. It's freezing out there."

He took off his boots in the vestibule. "It's a balmy twenty-two degrees."

"Now I know you've been drinking," I said, shivering and leading him to the kitchen. Heck, this weather was what I signed up for. "I need to embrace Wisconsin winters. Come on snow!"

"That's my girl. If you're going to live in the Badger State, you need to take the frigid winters along with the humid summers." Bob found the corkscrew in the drawer by the sink. "By the way, I never drink alone. In fact, I never have more than two drinks in one sitting."

Bob didn't bear the signs of a heavy drinker, but it was reassuring to hear him say so. He opened the bottle while I pulled a couple of glasses out of the cupboard. "What is it?"

I grinned and did a little shimmy. I think I'd been smiling since I read the news article. "What do you mean?"

He poured the wine. "You look very happy."

I took one and downed a healthy sip. "That's because my ex-boss was just arrested and charged with fraud."

"Seriously?" Bob's eyes lit up as he rubbed his hands together. "This has to be good."

I relayed what I knew, omitting the email from Curt because I needed time to think.

When I finished, we toasted to my success as an anonymous tipster.

"Want to watch a movie?" I asked.

"One with lots of action?"

"Sure." We headed upstairs to the TV room. "We ought to find plenty of those on Netflix."

The wine was delicious and the first sip went straight to my head.

We'd both opted for the couch and Bob moved a little closer, his shoulder brushing mine. "How are you doing?"

"I'm great." I savored another sip of wine. "Why wouldn't anyone be after finding out the man who fired them was covering his own backside?"

"Um...you still okay with our partnership?" he asked.

"Yes. I think we're a good team." Was he having doubts? "Don't you?"

The lines on his forehead creased. "I do...but..."

Any buzz I might have been enjoying from the wine disappeared. "What?"

"This contracting stuff doesn't pay much. Are you okay financially? Do you have health insurance?"

"First of all, I could have retired if I'd wanted to, even without the golden handshake. Secondly, this month I went off Bethany's COBRA and started a medical plan through The Affordable Care Act. How about you?"

"I'm fine. I don't need to work, either."

"And health care?"

"Got that covered, too." As I turned on the TV, he took my hand. "Hey, you're like a magnet who attracts people without even trying. You're witty, vivacious, a splendid hostess, generous, kind and you bend over backward for the people you love. How did you end up divorced?"

I savored Bob's words for a moment. I don't think anyone has ever used so many lovely adjectives to describe me. But he'd also asked me a pretty pointed question that needed a reply. I patted my chest and cleared my throat. "Well, when I married my ex, he was a sailor in the Royal Australian Navy—you know how sailors are renowned drinkers?"

Bob nodded.

"Jack was one of the best."

"Royal Australian Navy? How did you end up in Australia?"

"It was kind of the other way around. He was on the commissioning crew of a ship that was built in Seattle. I met him right before I graduated from college—we had a whirlwind romance and in order for us to be together because of immigration laws, we had to get married. Meg was born in Australia."

"She was? Whoa, Jane, you're like peeling an onion. Every time we're together I find out something about you I'd never expected. So was it the drinking that made you come back to the U.S.?"

"Yes, to say it got out of hand was an understatement." I clicked on the Netflix icon while I told Bob about Jack's seven-year bender. "How about you? What happened with your ex?"

"I don't know. Stress I guess. She was in med school when Sophie was born—had an affair with one of her study partners."

"That sucks. I'm sorry."

"It was a long time ago." He kissed my cheek. "You haven't seen my house yet."

"No I haven't." I looked at him, touching the place where his lips had been. The kiss had been quick, yet in that second, I knew without a doubt we were no longer just friends. "What's it like?"

"Just a cottage—over by the golf course. Want to come to dinner tomorrow?"

"Yes. Yes I do."

He kissed my mouth and a few minutes later, the remote control dropped from my fingertips.

Chapter Twenty-Four

Meg

After finding out I was pregnant, my primary care doctor got me in for an appointment right away, but the earliest I could schedule an ultrasound was January 25th. How the hell was I going to hold it together for two weeks and six days?

I examined my profile in my full-length mirror and rubbed my hands up and down my belly. I didn't look any bigger than I did three months ago—three months since Lance darkened my door. If I ever saw that imposter's face again, I'd explode.

I should have paid more attention to my cycles. But my periods have never been reliable. Sometimes I'd skip a month and then I'd have a heavy flow the next. Because they were so erratic, I've never been good about keeping track of them which worked because I wasn't one to sleep around. I didn't even lose my virginity until I was in college.

Now I was so freaked out, I didn't know if the sudden onslaught of nausea was because of stress or because of the pregnancy. I'd been so close to telling my mom about it more than once, but every time, I stopped myself. I wanted the damned ultrasound first. Of course, I was going to tell her and everyone else. I just really, really wanted to know the due date before I went public...or told my mother she was going to be a grandma.

The doorbell rang and Maya darted out of my bedroom, yapping like a demon.

"Meg!" Mike shouted from the porch. "Open the door!"

I stood frozen, my miniscule dog jumping, barking, and running in circles.

"Are you okay? Please. I just need to know that you're all right!"

The poor guy was worried.

About me.

And once I told him the truth, he was going to throw up in my face.

"No, Maya," I said, my voice calm, unlike the tempest churning inside me. I might have been able to hide from Mike for a few days, but obviously I couldn't avoid him for two weeks and six days. Hell, I'm surprised my mother hasn't beaten down my door and demanded to know what's going on. But at least I'd told her about the genetic testing.

I swept the Chihuahua into my arms and opened the door, only to end up with a flurry of snowflakes in my face. "Sorry."

"Sorry?" Mike's dark eyebrows pinched together beneath his snow-covered black hat. "You haven't answered a text or a phone call since you went to see the doctor in Rochester. That was *four* days ago, Meg! And when I called the library they said you were out for the day."

I ran my hands down my face. I'd gone in the previous two days that I'd been scheduled, but I happened to be off today and desperately needed time for zoning out on the couch. "Sorry," I repeated, taking in a deep breath while snow continued to blow in and melt as it struck the hardwood. "The news isn't what you expect."

"Not what *I* expect?" he said, almost shouting, but his voice was more intense than loud. "How about what *you* expect? Are you going to have another dissection or something? Do you have a brain aneurysm?"

Oh, shit. After Dr. Davis gave me the baby news I didn't think about how going to a vascular surgeon would worry him—worry anybody. I tucked Maya under my arm, pulled him inside, and shut out the blizzard. "There's something I need to tell you."

Mike pulled off his hat and gloves. "Oh, God, you don't have cancer do you?"

I urged him onto the couch, setting Maya on my lap. "No, it's not cancer."

"Then what is wrong?"

The room spun. "You don't want to know."

"I assure you my present state of ignorance is definitely *not* blissful."

That's what he thinks. I gulped, glanced at his beautiful gray eyes, then my gaze darted to the floor. I did not deserve him. "Well, before a CT scan, they test all women of childbearing age for pregnancy."

"Pregnancy?" he asked as if he'd never heard the word before.

"Mm hmm. And instead of having a CTA, they gave me an MRA, but I didn't find out why until I met with Dr. Davis."

"Wait." The tension creasing his brow went slack as his mouth dropped open. "You're not pregnant are you?"

I tried to breathe but only managed a strangled cry.

"You are?"

Whoa, did he just sound hopeful?

I'd better set him straight before he dashed out to his car and sped through a blizzard to set up a baby registry at Target. "That's what Dr. Davis told me, but I can't get in for an ultrasound for nearly three weeks."

He cupped my cheek with the cool palm of his hand. "You don't sound excited. I thought you wanted kids."

"I do, it's just—"

"You wanted to be married first?"

"Yes, but—"

"Then let's do it." He dropped to his knee. "Marry me, Meg. Anywhere you want. We can go big or go to Vegas."

Holy mother, he needs to slow the fuck down!

"Wait." Groaning, I put Maya on the floor and started to pace. I clapped the heels of my hands to my temples. Fuck, fuck, fuckety, fuck, there was no skirting around this. No making him wait two weeks and six days.

"You don't understand!" I shook my fists. "I need to get the ultrasound to find out how far along I am."

He stood and threw out his hands. "Of course you do."

With a strangled cry, I slid my hands down my face, pulling my lips into a frown. "Because the baby might not be yours!"

Mike stared at me as if I'd just stabbed him in the gut. He took a couple of steps away and fell onto the couch, his head dropping forward. "Oh." His body language expressed deflation with a capital D.

"Remember when we first started not dating?" I asked, my head swimming like I was going to faint and puke at the same time.

"You were reeling from a bad relationship." His lips formed a thin line as he glanced away. "The douche."

Maya jumped against my leg, asking to be picked up again. But I couldn't draw my focus away from Mike. With every fiber in my body I wanted this baby to be his, but there was no way in hell I was going to assume anything. This was a major life event. This honest, wonderful, caring man deserved nothing but the truth, no matter how much it killed me.

Mike squinted. "Wasn't the last time you saw him during Octoberfest?"

I nodded, relenting and picking up my dog. She was warm and furry and she loved me no matter how bad my dating decisions had been.

For once in my life I started going out with a nice man, and this happens. Mike's going to ditch me and I will end up being one of those single moms who bakes the cookies for the PTA meetings because everyone else is too busy making dinner for their husbands.

He drummed his fingers on his knees. "But that was three months ago. Haven't you had a sign—nausea, missed your period or *something*?"

I clutched Maya beneath my chin. "I've never been regular. And I didn't get morning sickness. At least not until Dr. Davis told me I was pregnant."

The finger drumming morphed into rubbing his hands back and forth along his thighs. "Wow."

"I know. It's a shock—and you don't need to hang around just because—"

"What?" Mike shot to his feet. "The baby could be mine, right?"

"What if it's not?"

"We can't know that until we get the ultrasound."

"We?" I gulped. "Are you planning on going with me?"

"Absolutely, I'm going with you."

"Right, and what if they say I'm three months preggers? What will you do then?" I reached for his hand and he snapped it away. I stood stunned. Dear God, if only he would hug me and tell me everything was going to be all right. But there was no way I could let him go to the ultrasound with me. "I think I ought to go alone—to the first one, anyway."

Mike paced, running his fingers over his hair, then he faced me. "If it is his, he's married, right? Are you going to tell him?"

Lance was the last person I wanted to talk to ever again in my life. "Do you think I should?"

I'd never seen Mike look grim, an edge to his jaw, his gray eyes almost black. "I can't answer that."

"Would you want to know you knocked up a librarian if you ran around with a fake name, telling people you were a single doctor, when you really were a married garbage man?"

"I...ah..." Mike grabbed a throw pillow off the couch and punched it. "*Fuck!*"

My fingers riffled through Maya's fur as if doing so would calm me. It did not. "I don't think scumbags want to know about their illegitimate children."

He tossed the pillow and squared his shoulders. "Does your mom know?"

"Not yet."

"When are you going to tell her?"

Maya wriggled so I reluctantly set her down. "I wanted to wait until after the ultrasound. I didn't want to face it myself until then. For the love of God, I've hardly been able to think for the past four days."

Mike dropped his head back and groaned. "Jesus, Meg."

I twisted a lock of hair around my finger and suddenly started sobbing. I mean, I didn't even feel the tears coming on but within a snap I was bawling my head off.

He pulled me into his arms. "We were careful."

"I'm so-o-orry," I cried, starting to hiccup. "I-I guess it's the hormones."

He kissed my forehead and took a step back. "I get it. If you don't want me to go to your ultrasound, fine. But I'm not turning my back on you, okay?"

"K," I managed through my sobs.

"We'll get through this."

I nodded, hopeful. "Y-you're not m-mad?"

"No." Mike surrounded me in his arms again. "Maybe a little peeved with the douche, but I really care about you. God, the first time I saw you, I said to myself, 'that redhead is gorgeous.' And know what?"

I shook my head against his warm chest.

"You're smart and funny and creative, so much more than a pretty face." With the crook of his finger, he raised my chin. "Are you going to be okay?"

"Yeah."

"Good." He gently kissed my lips. "Hey, I'm kinda dazed at the moment. I just need a little time to think this through, all right?"

"K."

He hugged me tight, gave me another kiss, and slipped out the door.

Chapter Twenty-Five

Jane

Meg finally broke her cryptic silence and asked me to meet her for lunch at Buzzard Billy's. Though the mighty Mississippi ran through La Crosse, the town wasn't anywhere near New Orleans, but this iconic restaurant offered things like gator fingers and shrimp creole. I opted for the Bayou platter which included hushpuppies while my daughter ordered blackened salmon. I couldn't resist greasy corn hushpuppies and probably should have just ordered a side of those.

As soon as the waitress left us, I squeezed my daughter's hand. Something was off. Though she was wearing makeup, her eyes were puffy, her posture rigid, and she was wearing a beige sweater. I didn't realize Miss Colorful owned anything in beige. "What's wrong?"

"Why do you always assume something is wrong?" she asked, challenging me like she did whenever she wanted to take control of a conversation—or she'd worked herself into a frenzy over something else entirely.

Well, she invited me to meet her here, so I merely folded my hands. "Forgive me. I shouldn't have assumed."

Her shoulders relaxed a little as she took a sip of herbal tea. "How is the restoration business?"

"Slow, but that's a good thing. I still have a long list of projects for my house. And now I have to get in my ten thousand steps per day."

"How can you walk that much?"

I had walked here, trying to avoid slipping on patches of ice, bundled up with a full-length winter coat, a trapper hat with lined earflaps, and ski gloves. "In this weather?" I blew a raspberry. "My treadmill is getting plenty of use. I also read an article that said ten thousand steps doesn't give you a lot more benefit than five thousand. The bottom line is keep moving."

"I hear you. That's why I rented an apartment close to downtown so I could walk more. Even when it's ten below." Meg studied the ingredients on a pack of Splenda and tossed it back into the bowl. "How's Bob?"

Before I had a chance to check myself, my face burned. I fanned myself with the cocktail menu, pretending I'd had a hot flash even though those had stopped years ago. "He's fine. We've had a few...ah...dates."

Meg grinned—almost. Though I could tell she wasn't herself, she might bite my head off if I pushed her. "So you *do* like him."

I replaced the menu. "I never said I didn't like him."

"No, but you told me to butt out of your business when I asked if you were sleeping with him."

For Pete's sake, kids these days were so forward. "Because it *is* none of your business. Bob is smart and fun and full of energy—a good man for the likes of me."

"Likes of you? In my book, no man is good enough to date my mother even if he is kinda nice." Meg picked up the packet of Splenda again, tore it open and sprinkled about two grains into her tea. "Um, I need to tell you something."

My breath hitched. Oh, God, I knew it. They found something at Moya in Rochester. *Please don't be an aneurysm, please, please, please!* "Have you received your results from the genetic testing?"

"Not yet. I guess I'll hear from them in a few months. I got a sign-on from the genetics lab, but their website says they're experiencing delays." Meg scooted her chair back a tad. "But I asked you out to lunch today because I wanted you to know that I'm *pregnant.*"

I blinked, wanting to ask her to repeat herself, but very sure of what I'd heard even though the word had been whispered. I glanced over both shoulders to make sure we didn't have any eavesdroppers. "Oh, my goodness!" I whisper-shouted, squeezing her hand. "Is this what you wanted?"

Her lips quivered. "Eventually, but it certainly wasn't planned."

My mind whirred. "Did they find it on the CT?"

"No, Mom, after my blood test came back positive, they did an MRA. CTs have too much radiation for pregnant ladies."

"Oh. Things sure are a lot easier after menopause." I guzzled my water, only to bring on a coughing fit. Meg was pregnant? I needed to show more support and enthusiasm!

Cough, cough.

My eyes teared up as I pounded my chest. Lots of single women had babies these days. But why now? Why now when we were trying to figure out this weird FMD stuff?

"Sorry," I said, sipping my water again and clearing my throat.

"I know. It's a shock." Meg sat back as the server set the blackened salmon in front of her.

After she set down my plate, I took a hushpuppy and bit into it, the hot pastry nearly burning my tongue. "Does Mike know?"

"He does." Meg curled forward covering her face with her hands. "But I have to be the stupidest, most abhorrent woman alive."

I glanced at her stomach. She didn't look pregnant, but Meg always had a little bit of a tummy just like my mother did. My appetite vanished. "He doesn't want children?"

"Yes, he wants children," she whisper-shouted, looking over her shoulder. "I never should have asked to meet you in a public place."

"Do you want to go somewhere else?"

"No!" She picked up her fork and stabbed her salmon. "I'm starving."

I took a drink of water while she ate a few bites.

"When are you due?" I asked as gently as possible.

Her hands stilled as she looked at me with haunted blue eyes. "I won't find out until I have an ultrasound. You know me, I'm about as predictable as snow in July."

Oh, shit. Lance was here in October. If the baby is his she might not be showing yet. "Does Mike know about Virgil?"

Meg swallowed her bite. "I hate that name."

I nudged a steaming hushpuppy. "Lance."

"Yes, yes, of course I told Mike everything." Her fork clattered to the table as she sobbed. "But I'm going to be dangling in purgatory until I get the stupid ultrasound and it's not for another two weeks. Meanwhile, my entire world is imploding around me!"

"Of course, it is." I pushed my plate away and pulled her into my arms. "Being pregnant is the most emotional time in any woman's life. But really, two weeks will go by faster than you think."

She pulled away and dabbed her eyes with a napkin. "I told Mike I didn't want him to go to the ultrasound. I don't want him there when they tell me the due date."

I suppose that would be for the best. "Would you like *me* to go with you?"

"Yes, please." She nodded, brushing away more tears. "I promised myself I wouldn't cry, but it seems I can't control *anything*.

"Oh, Baby." I slid my hand over her shoulders and squeezed. "Everything's going to be okay. You're going to be a great mom. And your baby is going to have its nana nearby."

The tortured expression on my daughter's face took my heart and twisted it into knots. "But what if it's Lance's?"

I tugged my daughter into another hug. "Whatever happens, you're going to get through this. I didn't move to La Crosse for the hell of it, either. I'm here for you, Margaret Lehn. No matter what."

As I bit into a hushpuppy, I decided there was no job in America more important than the one I had right now—not refurbishment, but being a mother and a grandmother, not to mention a daughter...yes and a *girlfriend*, too. I needed to be here for the people I cared about. Yesterday I received a phone call from Bethany's VP of Human Resources asking me to step in as an interim CEO and they agreed to give me a few days to think about it. But I've had enough time. As soon as I get home, I'm going to respectfully decline.

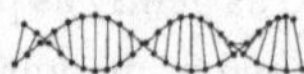

Bob followed me up the stairs of an old warehouse that had been turned into an antique shop. "These days, no one cares if an expecting mother is married or not."

"I know." I exited the stairs and strolled toward a bay of shelves with China on display. "But Meg has always been so frail."

"She doesn't seem frail to me."

I gawked at him, but then remembered that I hadn't told him about FMD and arterial dissections. Damn, I'd gone from being super fit and healthy to being a decrepit old lady and I certainly didn't want Bob to see me that way.

"Meg has asthma and high blood pressure. She gets headaches."

"Like you?"

I picked up a teapot and examined it. "Sure, I get headaches, but I don't have the complications she does because of her hypertension."

Bob moved away from my line of sight. "Well, even if Mike isn't Mr. Right, at least she has you to look after her. She's in good hands."

"Thank you," I replied, replacing the teapot. "I appreciate your vote of confidence." I worried about Mike. Honestly, if I were in his shoes, I don't know what I would do if I had to face the fact that the baby might not be mine—and they hadn't been dating all that long. Maybe he wasn't Mr. Right. Maybe Meg would be better off being a single mom. I know I was.

"Hey, Jane, come here once."

I stepped into the aisle. Where had Bob picked up the "once." He'd beckoned me before using "once." Who said that? If I joined him, it would naturally be only once. Right? Or was I overthinking? I peered across the cluttered store. "Where are you?"

"Over here."

A hand flashed above the shelves and I headed for it, finding Bob standing between two red velvet chairs and a matching settee that looked new, but very old at the same time. I bent down to examine the woodwork. "Wow, are these replicas?"

"I don't think so. Look at the wheels. My guess is they've been recently reupholstered." He smoothed his fingers over the velvet. "These would look fantastic in your drawing room."

He wasn't wrong. And it was about time I put some furniture in that great big room. "They'd be perfect."

"Pricey, though."

I looked at the tag and didn't even blink. "Hey, have you checked the auction sites online? These are an amazing buy."

"Don't you need to think about it for a while?"

"We both agreed they're perfect, didn't we?" I headed for the sales desk. "I'm buying these babies before anyone else has a chance."

Chapter Twenty-Six

Meg

Bundled up, I locked the door to the library on my way out. Though the entry was always well-lit, I sensed someone behind me and I jolted. "Ack!" I cried, turning and brandishing my keys.

Mike stopped a few feet away and held up his hands. "Meg, sorry. Did I scare you?"

My breath whooshed through my lips while I dropped the keys into my purse. "I was just closing up."

"Yeah, I knew you would be." He gestured toward the sidewalk. "Can I walk you home?"

Since he left my apartment, we had texted, but this was the first time I'd seen him. It didn't take a mind reader to know he was upset about the ultrasound thing, even though he said he understood why I didn't want him in the room. Still, looking at him twisted my gut into knots. "Okay."

He reached for my hand. "I haven't been able to sleep."

I started to pull my fingers away but tightened my grip instead. "Me neither."

"How are you feeling?"

Aside from being wrung out like I'd been crushed between the rollers of a 1930s washing machine? "I'm all right."

"Um...well...I've missed you."

I missed him, too. But I just kept walking.

"And I've been thinking." He moved in front of me and grasped my shoulders. "I know we haven't been 'officially' dating for very long, but I think I'm in love with you."

I gulped, staring up into those gray eyes expressing so much emotion from worry, to fear, to... "You love me?"

"Yes, I love you, Margaret Lehn Corley. And regardless of whether or not you want me to go to the ultrasound, I'm all-in."

I was so confused, my brain was in a fog. But before I completely gave in, I had to ask one more time, "Even if the baby isn't—"

"The child is mine."

"How can you be sure?" I pressed because I'd never be able to handle it if he got on board then ditched me when I was eight months pregnant.

"Because children are beautiful and innocent." Mike pulled me into his arms. "She'll be half you, and a child who is half you will be amazing, and smart, and *perfect.*"

I was so sick of crying, I did my best to blink away my tears as I buried my head in his shoulder. "I don't deserve you."

"You deserve to be loved. You deserve to be worshiped and cared for." He kissed my temple. "You're going to marry me, right?"

God save me, I wanted to marry him more than anything. "W-what if you change your mind after...you know..."

"I'm not going to change my mind." Mike took my cheeks between his gloved palms and kissed me. "The first time I saw you in the library this summer, I wanted to go out with you. You were so beautiful and confident when you took me up to the Archives. I never told you how disappointed I was that you weren't the one I'd be working with. I never told you how many times I walked past the library wondering if you would go out with me, but too afraid a woman as amazing as you would want to date a guy like me."

"What do you mean?" I brushed his beard with the tip of my glove. "You have the whole swanky geek thing going on."

"Swanky?"

"Well, you're like Clark Kent on steroids." I slid my arms around his waist and hugged him. "There isn't a single librarian in La Crosse who doesn't drool every time you walk through the door."

He grinned—sexily, irresistibly. "So, I'm a librarian magnet?"

"Yes."

"Are you ever going to answer my question?"

Oh, my God, in the past few days the man of my dreams has asked me to marry him twice and this time, I had no doubt about his sincerity. "I absolutely want to marry you, but would it be okay if we waited until after the baby is born?"

"Why?"

"Aside from walking down the aisle looking like a blimp, we've only been dating for a couple of months. You need time to process."

"Me?"

"I'd be lying if I didn't tell you I want to get married tomorrow. But the cautious side of my brain, which doesn't always get a lot of airplay, is reminding me that we need to be together for a whole year. I've always felt any woman serious enough to take marriage vows ought to have known her husband for a least a year."

Mike kissed me. "All right, but just remember it was July eighteenth when I came into the library to get information about my house. That's officially the day we met."

"The eighteenth? Did you just pull that out of your computer brain?"

"Not exactly. It was a week after I moved in—not so hard to add seven to eleven." He kissed my cheek, his lips trailing to my ear as he whispered. "Marry me?"

"Yes," I whispered back.

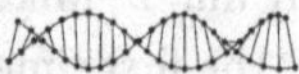

I stood by my decision and didn't have Mike go to the ultrasound with me. At least not the first one. Of course I was going to tell him the truth no matter what, but I couldn't imagine having him there holding my hand and finding out the baby wasn't his. That would be too cruel. If the baby was Lance's, Mike needed to find out in the privacy of his home.

Honestly, I almost told Mom not to come as well so I could be alone when *I* got the news. But I'd broken down in sobs when I'd told her I was pregnant at Buzzard Billy's and she was worried. And I guess I needed support. This was terrifying and exciting. Moreover, I hadn't told anyone at work I was expecting, not even Elaine.

Mom met me at the library all bundled up. Together we walked to the Moya Clinic in La Crosse and waited for about five minutes before we were called.

"So, is this your first ultrasound?" asked the technician.

"Sure is." I tried to sound chirpy but my voice still trembled. "I'm hoping we can establish the due date."

Mom squeezed my upper arm, her excitement almost palpable.

"Do you have any idea how far along you might be?" asked the technician.

"Nope." I was either three-and-a-half months or seven weeks or maybe a little over a month, but if I told her that she'd think I'd lost my mind.

"Well, if we can't detect the heartbeat, we might have to do a vaginal ultrasound."

I cringed—I totally should have come alone. "Seriously?"

"I promise it won't hurt and I'll be discreet." The technician opened the door to a room with dimmed lighting. "We'll be in here."

After donning a gown, I climbed onto the bed while Mom sat on the opposite side of the technician. She covered my belly with warm gel, then made a few passes with a probe. After a series of clicks, she turned the monitor and pointed to a little tiny white glob that looked like it might be the start of a human with a really big head and an appendage that might have been an arm. "This is your baby."

"Oh, wow! Is that an arm?" My breath stopped as the little image moved. At least I think it moved.

"Actually, it's a leg." The technician pulled the probe away from my belly. "I'll need to do a vaginal to get the heartbeat. Okay?"

What was I going to say, no?

As she'd promised, the technician draped a blanket over my lap and re-spected my modesty. Using a serene voice, she explained everything she was doing while she found the heartbeat, the sound filling the room with life and, to me, it was nothing short of a miracle.

"Can you tell me the baby's age?" I asked.

The technician rolled her fingers over a huge ball and made a few clicks. "Sorry, but only the doctor can do that."

Seriously? I have to wait? But I'd made such a big deal about not having Mike here! "The results will be in my portal, right?"

"Should be. It usually takes a couple of hours for the radiologist's report to appear, otherwise someone from Moya will call you."

"Today, right?" Couldn't she tell I was on the verge of exploding? Espe-cially given my medical file. I needed to know, goddammit!

She removed the probe. "Should be."

I squeezed my knees together. "How old does the fetus need to be to determine the sex?" I asked.

"Not until about eighteen to twenty-one weeks."

My stomach roiled. If this was Lance's baby, I ought to be about sixteen weeks—still too early to determine if I was having a boy or a girl. But wouldn't the fetus be more developed? Why didn't I look that up? Gah, I needed to get rid of the fog and engage my brain.

After I dressed, Mom met me in the waiting room. "Want to go over to my house for a latte?"

I looked at my phone, then refreshed it. Of course, there wasn't a message from the portal yet. "Can you add valium?" I asked, joking.

"Not in your condition." She chuckled and put on her winter gloves. "Maybe we ought to have decaf."

By the time we finished our coffee and ate two of Mom's efficacious slice-and-bake cookies, Mike had texted me five times. On the sixth ding, I was so sick of having my heart nearly fly out of my chest with excitement, I didn't even look at my phone.

Mom picked it up. "Ahem, this says you have new test results in the portal."

I snatched it from her. "Finally!"

Of course, my fingerprint reader decided to go on the fritz and I had to type in my password, which I fat-fingered the first time and had to do it again. After what seemed like an eternity, I read the report, which was prefaced with a whole bunch of technical jargon. It wasn't until the end where it stated the measurement calculated the fetus to be seven weeks gestation and was due to be born on August twenty-third. There was also a tab with the ultrasound images of my baby—OMG, I couldn't believe there was a living being inside me.

Mom leaned in. "What does it say?"

I tapped back to the report and showed her the sentence at the bottom while a weight the size of Gibraltar lifted from my shoulders. Mom steadied my hand...I didn't even realize I was shaking. Usually I had no trouble doing sums in my head, but I couldn't think straight.

"Mike is the father," I whispered, pulling up my calendar and counting backward by weeks. If our baby was only seven weeks gestation, she (or he) ought to have been conceived around December first. My God, that was the first time we had sex.

I clapped a hand over my mouth. *Unbelievable.*

"What?" asked Mom.

"I need to go see Mike—he's at work." In this weather, the university was too far away to walk.

"You want me to drive you?"

I laced my fingers around the back of my neck. "You promise not to brake hard?"

"Are you kidding? I drive the safest car on the planet. There's no way in hell I'll take any chances with you or my grandbaby!"

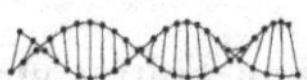

I'd never been in Mike's office before, but as a former student at UW La Crosse, I knew where the technology center was. In no time, I stood outside his open door, impatiently waiting for him to finish talking to somebody.

Mike hadn't seen me yet, but as soon as he glanced toward the open door I grinned so wide I could have split my face in two.

He hopped up and grabbed my hands. "Why didn't you text me back? I've been worried out of my mind."

I fell into his arms and kissed him. "First, I had to wait for the results to come in and then my mom drove me straight here so I could give you the news in person."

He held me at arm's length. "So...?"

I was so excited, I almost peed my pregnant panties. "Remember when I brought over oven-ready pizza and you let me test out the mattress on your king-sized bed?"

His eyes brightened as he gaped wide and laughed. "Are you referring to the night you decided to come out of mourning?"

"Uh huh!" I bobbed my head emphatically. "That was seven weeks ago, and the report said I'm seven weeks pregnant!"

He grabbed my hands and jumped up and down like a little kid, and I jumped right along with him. "Oh, my God! Our first time."

"Can you believe it?"

"I sure can." He swept me into his arms and twirled me in a circle. "This dude doesn't fire blanks."

I howled with laughter. "Obviously not."

"A little condom isn't going to get in my way." He set me down and steadied me with his hands on my shoulders. "Are you okay? Should I be swinging you around like that? When is our baby due?"

"August twenty-third...and I'm fine." I fumbled for my phone and brought up an image from the ultrasound, then shoved the screen under Mike's nose. "This is the first official picture of our baby."

He took the phone and a tear splashed from his eye. "There you are, precious."

I pointed. "The wee one moved her leg for us."

"Her? It's a girl?"

"We won't find out until the next ultrasound," I said, dropping the phone into my purse.

"Whoa, I didn't dare allow myself to hope that our little fetus actually had my DNA! Let's do something to celebrate." Mike looked toward the hallway. "Is your mom still here?"

"Nope." I bounced up and down, trying not to pee my pants. In this exact moment, I had no doubt that I'd found the right man and thanked God he was the father of my child. "She dropped me off. I told her you'd give me a ride home."

He kissed my lips. "Ice Cream? Hot chocolate?"

"I'm craving a Milwaukee Burger."

"Mm—with blue cheese potato salad?"

"And a vanilla milkshake."

He grabbed my hand. "Let's go!"

CHAPTER TWENTY-SEVEN

MEG

Nine weeks later ~ March 31st

When my blood pressure cuff released, I stared at the reading. One-forty over ninety-two. Dammit, I was already taking two blood pressure medications and was only sixteen weeks pregnant. And it wasn't as if I had a stressful job. After I'd shared the news with my fellow librarians, the director told me to take as many breaks as I needed. Sitting at my desk in my little office, I closed my eyes and drew in a deep breath, focusing on the little life inside me. Breathe in, two, three, four, breathe out, two, three, four.

Moya's website said pre-eclampsia wasn't even a thing until twenty weeks. I couldn't deal with blood pressure this high this early, but worrying only made it worse.

The tension in my shoulders began to ebb but my moment of relaxation was interrupted when my phone dinged with a text. I let out a long exhale before I looked down. It was from the genetics laboratory where Moya had sent my blood test.

With all the crazy stuff happening over the past few months, I'd completely forgotten that Dr. Davis had ordered genetic testing. I logged on to my account and opened a document entitled *Diagnostic Testing Results*.

It had my data listed at the top followed by a subtitle: *Variants*.

Beneath it, they listed the gene COL3A1 with the following data: *Variant c.2096_2098delinsTT (p.Gly699Valfs*92), Heterozygous/Pathogenic/Detected.*

Hmm. So they found something. Doesn't everybody have something?

Gone were the days when people studied the stars in search of answers. Though I have to admit I'm glad I live in the twenty-first century and not the second.

I paged down to a section outlined in bold:

RESULT: POSITIVE

One pathogenic variant identified in COL3A1. COL3A1 is associated with autosomal dominant vascular Ehlers-Danlos syndrome and autosomal recessive brain malformation.

The report went on to say that this was a medically important result and should be discussed with my doctor to determine the next steps. It also said that my relatives might be at risk.

Something wasn't right.

I swear, I felt the baby kick—or flutter. Anyway, the baby that I was creating just moved. Had I passed this variant on to him...or her?

I read further and sweat broke out across my forehead. I couldn't breathe. Yes, my child might or might not have it. *A COL3A1 variant affects everyone differently and can vary widely in the same family.*

Shit!

"vEDS is a connective tissue disease characterized by increased risk for rupture of the blood vessels and/or visceral organs (like the uterus and colon). Rupture of an artery can cause rapid blood loss and is a life-threatening medical emergency. Arterial dissection and/or rupture most commonly occurs in the aorta, renal, mesenteric, iliac, femoral, vertebral, and carotid arteries..."

Oh. My. God.

Oh!

My!

God!

I wasn't about to take my blood pressure now because my heart was pounding so fast I had no doubt I was pushing the limits of hypertension. *For the love of Moses, by the way this reads, it's a miracle I'm still alive!*

Now what? Do I call Dr. Davis?

The thought no sooner passed through my mind when my phone rang, the number from a Rochester area code.

"Hello?" I answered, so frantic I had to rest my forehead in my hand.

The woman on the phone introduced herself as being from the genetics department at Moya and went through all the HIPPA protocols to ensure I was Margaret Lehn Corley. "We've received a diagnostic test and we need you to meet with our geneticist."

"Tomorrow?" I shrieked. "I need an appointment tomorrow!"

"Well, we're scheduling out a few months at the moment—"

"You don't understand." I slapped my hand on the desk. "I'm pregnant and I've just read the report. It says I can have ruptured organs—like my uterus! I need to know what's going on. Today! Three months from now I could be dead!"

Silence hissed over the line.

"Dead!" I shouted for emphasis.

"Um...I'll need to check with the doctor's nurse and call you back. I take it you are open to an appointment at any time?"

"Yes." I leaned forward, trying to breathe, trying to keep myself from fainting. "Any time you can fit me in. If I'm still alive, I'll be there."

After the phone call, deep breathing was no help whatsoever. I grabbed my coat and hat. It took me fifteen minutes to walk to Mike's office, tears icy on my cheeks with a cold March wind blowing on my face.

As soon as he saw me, he darted from his desk and pulled me into his arms. "What's wrong?"

His voice was so calm and soothing, all I could do was bury my face in the warmth of his sweater while I broke down into uncontrollable sobs.

"Is it the baby?" he asked.

I managed to shake my head.

"There, there," he soothed, tugging me into his office and closing the door. "Whatever it is, everything is going to be okay."

"Nooooo!" I cried shaking my head and beating against his chest, unable to explain, hardly able to breathe. I'd already had carotid and vertebral dissections. And now I was in danger of having a ruptured uterus? My wails grew louder, my gasps for air more frantic but all the while Mike just held me, spoke softly, smoothed his hand over my hair, and kissed my forehead as if I were the most precious person on earth.

"It's okay, Meg. I love you. I'll always love you no matter what," he repeated over and over, his lips kissing my hair, my forehead, my ear.

I had no idea how much time passed until I was able to talk, but it had turned dark outside.

Mike brushed away my tears. "Now, tell me, what has you so upset?"

If I tried to explain, I'd erupt all over again, so I pulled the phone out of my purse and brought up the lab report, handing it to him. "Read it all."

Mike slid into his chair while I sat across from him and watched in a state of shock as he paged through the report, his jaw tensing, his lips thinning and growing white.

When he stopped scrolling, he set my phone down and folded his hands, staring at them for a time.

This was it. The end. How could a guy as awesome as Michael Reynolds want to hang around with a genetically flawed person like me? *I should take my phone and tell him to find somebody who has normal genes as I boldly march out of his office.*

Except I sat there frozen. Terrified. What the hell was I going to do if I just up and walked out? Would I be able to make it to the foyer without collapsing in a desolate heap? I loved him. I was carrying his baby. We were supposed to start a family.

"I can't even begin to understand what this means," he finally said, making me startle out of my reverie even though his voice was barely above a whisper.

"They called and are going to make an appointment." I sounded raspy from crying.

"When?"

"Well, they initially said three months, but when I told the scheduler I couldn't wait that long because I was pregnant, she said she'd have to call me back."

Mike looked at my phone. "Has she?"

I bit down hard on my bottom lip as I shook my head. "Not yet."

"Well then, we wait."

"*We* do?" I emphasized the "we" because any other man on the planet would be double-timing it backward as fast as he could to get away from me.

"Who have you talked to so far?" he asked, coming around his desk and sitting in the guest chair beside me.

"Only the scheduler in Rochester."

"Well, we need answers. Your life is at risk. So is the baby's." He rapped his knuckles on the desk. "God dammit, why did the genetics lab take so long in the first place? You're already into your second trimester."

I nodded as he took my hand. "Look," he said. "I know you wanted to go slow, but you need someone to look after you. My house is huge. Move in with me. I don't want you to be alone. Not ever. I want to take care of you."

Take care of me?

This was one question I didn't have to think about for long. After all, I was already spending a lot of time at his house. "Maya, too?"

"Of course." He winked. "We can give your little princess her own room."

When my phone rang, I answered it without even glancing at the caller ID.

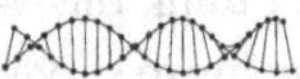

They didn't get me in to see the geneticist the next day but did by the following week. Also, within that period of time my pregnancy had been classified as high-risk. My case had already been transferred to the obstetrics and gynecology department at the Moya Clinic in Rochester where I would have to see a doctor weekly—driving an hour and fifteen minutes each way. And I hated driving!

Today I had a genetics appointment in the morning, followed by an ultrasound and an appointment with my new obstetrician in the afternoon. Both Mom and Mike were with me as we met with the geneticist who now knew about the pregnancy, which is why they asked for my mother to come. The geneticist had a concise PowerPoint presentation that explained vascular Ehlers-Danlos in a great deal more detail than the report I'd received from the genetics lab.

The chilling slide was the one in bold letters, saying the life expectancy was fifty-one. Holy hell, my mother had just turned sixty.

Another thing I found particularly sobering was that there are actually two mutations. Both were caused by the lack of type III collagen, but my variant was the best of the two in that people with it lacked type III collagen by about half. The collagen we produced was good, whereas the other mutation caused type III collagen to be mixed up and ineffective. Those poor souls were the ones who died super young, sometimes not making it into adulthood.

The doctor shifted his gaze to Mom. "Of course, we won't know that Margaret inherited the vEDS gene mutation from you until we get your test results back, but since your father died from an aneurysm, we're opting to test you before we test her father."

I smirked. As if my dad would get genetic testing.

Mom nodded. "I would think the odds point to me considering my father's death combined and the fact that I have FMD, four known aneurysms, and a dissected carotid artery."

"Exactly."

"But that's not what has me worried." She glanced at me with terror in her blue eyes. "When Meg was born I had to have an emergency C-section because my uterus ruptured."

Oh. God. A wave of nausea hit as the room spun. Of course, I knew about the emergency C-section, but I think this was the first time she used the words ruptured uterus. Was I going to survive this? Was my baby?

Mike squeezed my hand.

The doctor cut her a look as if to say this appointment was about me and not my mother. "Well, we can't assume anything until your genetic results are back."

Mom gave the man a sharp nod, her lips pursed together in a straight line.

The geneticist regarded me with a stern expression. "So you've had your appendix out?"

"Yes—appendicitis when I was in college."

"That's a good sign if you tolerated abdominal surgery."

"A good sign?" asked Mike while I sat there and cogitated the meaning of producing half as much but nonetheless "good" type III collagen. Maybe it took me longer to heal from a wound, but I did heal eventually.

The doctor nodded. "You'll have to discuss your options for this pregnancy with your obstetrician, of course, but the fact that you lived through an appendectomy increases your odds of surviving the delivery."

Mike's back was as erect as a horizontal board. "By how much?"

"Well, let's just say that there are many women with Margaret's COL3A1 mutation who have survived not only one pregnancy but multiple births. Some women with this mutation don't know they have it—they don't know until they have a dissection or ruptured aneurysm."

Or a ruptured uterus.

I exchanged glances with my mother while my heart felt like it was crushing against my rib cage. We both had dissections and Mom had aneurysms. A year ago, either one of us could have passed as poster women for the epitomes of health. Now we were sitting in a geneticist's office talking about inherited faulty gene mutations.

I wanted my baby to be healthy and live. I wanted to be able to hold the newborn in my arms and be a mom. Couldn't I have both?

Chapter Twenty-Eight

Jane

We had enough time between Meg's appointments to grab some lunch. If the kids were half as gobsmacked as me, they had to be operating on auto pilot.

I'd wanted to take the geneticist by the collar and shake him—give him the details about my disaster of a cesarean, waking up in so much pain I thought I was being ripped in half, bleeding like someone opened a spigot. I wanted to tell him about the time I'd spontaneously started bleeding on an airplane and had to be rushed to a hospital when we landed in New York City. My mind whirred with dozens of other unexplained events in my life that pointed to vEDS now that I knew Meg had inherited it.

I had a ruptured uterus, God dammit. In my opinion, the doctor should have shown a hell of a lot more concern for my pregnant daughter!

As soon as she told me about her genetics results, I Googled vascular Ehlers-Danlos. With sinking dread, I read through the exhaustive list of symptoms, some of which I had and some of which I did not. I'd always thought Ehlers-Danlos syndrome meant hypermobility of joints, but that was not the case with me or Meg and was not necessarily the case with vEDS patients. Aside from the rupture, red flags for me were dissections and aneurysms, of course. But there were others: the mitral valve prolapse that had been found when I was twenty, thin skin, easy bruising, excessive bleeding, wounds took longer to heal, the appearance of old hands. If anyone tried to guess my age by looking at my hands, they'd probably think I was ninety.

But to me, the absolute most hideous red flag was alopecia. I'd taken every supplement known to man to combat my hair loss, yet it seemed to get thinner by the day. For the past several years I hadn't needed to cut it because the strands broke so easily. It was humiliating to look at my ponytail, its diameter no more than a centimeter. Type III collagen was essential for hair growth. Not only was mine thin, it was so fine, I had difficulty seeing individual strands.

At least the genetics lab was going to put a rush on my results so that Meg's doctors might be able to give her appropriate guidance.

Damn!

This was all my fault!

When Meg was born, the world of genetics was in its infancy—was basically nonexistent. Throughout my life, I'd been having vEDS events and no one even knew what they were—just told me I was imagining things, or I was having a migraine—or one of my favorites—it was ancient history and never needed to be referred to again.

Damn, damn, damn!

I excused myself and headed for the bathroom where I locked myself in the privacy of a stall and did my best not to scream. If only someone had told me about vEDS at some stage during the course of my life, Meg might not be in this situation right now.

Of course my daughter had inherited it from me. I didn't need a genetics report to prove it. And because of me, my baby was in an untenable situation. Over the years, I've watched her go out with one deadbeat guy after another. She finally meets a man who is charming, respectable, who has similar interests, and who has a great career, and she's broadsided by this crap.

It's not fair.

Why in God's name did we draw the short end of the stick?

Why the hell am I still alive? I've already beaten the odds by nearly a decade. But if I can beat the odds, my daughter surely can!

My father was fifty-one when he died—he hit the average life span right on target.

But he was a drinker.

Meg's not.

I'm not.

Meg will be fine.

I slammed my fist against the side of the stall. *God dammit, Meg will be fine!*

I closed my eyes and clasped my hands in prayer. *Dear God, you blessed me with a miracle when Meg came into my life. Now I ask you to bless her as you did me. Hold her in your hands and keep her and her baby safe from this awful disease. Amen.*

p.s. God, if you need somebody. Take me. Please, please, please take me.

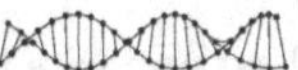

They allowed both Mike and me to attend Meg's second ultrasound—though this one was at Moya's world-renowned birthing center. Mike sat in a chair beside my daughter and I was directed to a seat across the room, but at least I had a great view of a large monitor mounted on the wall.

As she worked, the technician explained every angle of the baby and I marveled at how far things had progressed in the past thirty years. The images were so clear, I could make out the baby's nose, and count its fingers.

"Baby's heartbeat is strong," said the technician, turning up the volume so we could all hear the rhythmic beat of life. "Do you want to know the sex?"

"Yes," Meg said while she and Mike nodded excitedly. The man must be a saint because he seemed to be taking all of Meg's high-risk complications in stride like a cheerleader on happy pills. My daughter needed that kind of positivity in her life and I had no doubt Mike was a gift from God just like the baby.

Even before he knew the child was his, he'd asked her to marry him, which in itself made him a hero. They'd decided to delay the wedding until after Meg gave birth but I didn't care. They were together and he was incredibly supportive and that's what mattered.

The technician moved the probe giving us a clear shot of a penis. "Your son is cooperating with us today."

Meg grasped Mike's hand, her smile radiant. "It's a boy!"

"Do you have a name picked out?" asked the technician.

"Zachary after my grandfather," said Mike.

"Zachary James," Meg added, "After *both* of our grandfathers."

James wasn't my father's name but was Jack's. I guess they must have opted to take names from their paternal side?

Once the technician got all the images she needed, we waited in the ultrasound room for Meg's new obstetrician to come in—this would be the person who would manage her high-risk pregnancy from here on out.

I was surprised when a woman who looked as if she might still be in her thirties came through the door. She was hardly older than Meg. I expected someone a bit more senior—someone who had seen every crises known to man and nothing daunted her.

"I'm Dr. Sandy."

She pulled over a stool and sat opposite Meg, her expression filled with concern. "I just read the report from the geneticist."

"Is my baby going to be all right?" asked Meg.

"He's doing well." She folded her hands and looked my daughter in the eyes. "But we need to have a conversation."

My heart squeezed and I swear I sank in my chair, preparing for the worst.

Mike slid his arm across Meg's shoulders and pulled her close. "Okay."

"You know why you've been sent here to Rochester, right?" asked the doctor.

"Because I'm high-risk?" Meg sounded so confident even though I knew she was terrified.

"Yes, you are. vascular Ehlers-Danlos syndrome is particularly nasty. And I need to say up front that even though you have inherited the less life-threatening mutation, you can still die from a ruptured uterus. That combined with your history of high blood pressure concerns me...a lot."

We all stared at Dr. Sandy. I, for one, was afraid to inhale.

"So," the doctor said after a long pause, shifting her gaze between Mike and Meg. "I urge the two of you to discuss how you wish to proceed. If you decide to terminate the pregnancy, we will support you."

"What if I want to keep the baby?" Meg whispered while a tear dribbled from the corner of her eye.

"Then we will do everything possible to guide you through the process. The delivery will have to be a caesarean. And because of your blood pressure, there is a higher risk of pre-eclampsia, which means a premature birth. We have an outstanding NICU unit here, but preemie babies are subject to a number of possible complications."

Meg nodded, her shoulders shaking.

Mike kissed her temple.

Dr. Sandy gripped my daughter's hands. "You don't have to make the decision now, but you're already into your second trimester. We'll need to—"

"I want to keep the baby." Meg's back straightened, her voice sure and determined. "Whatever it takes, I want this. *We* want this."

The air whooshed from my lungs as my eyes welled with tears. By God, somehow I'd raised a warrior princess.

Chapter Twenty-Nine

Jane

On the second of May I received an email from the genetics lab confirming that I was the parent who passed on vascular Ehlers-Danlos syndrome to my daughter. I stared at my computer screen, my mouth dry, my heart in my throat.

True, I had assumed I was the guilty party, but reading the words *"Result: Positive"* took all the guilt roiling in my gut and strangled me with it.

I never should have married Meg's father.

And having made such an egregious error, I should have realized my choice of spouse had been a gross lapse in judgment years before I actually got pregnant.

I should have realized something was extremely wrong with me. I'd had enough signs—the bleeding incident on the plane, the easy bruising, the thin hair, the narrow bridge of nose, the tiny earlobes, translucent skin through which I could see my entire vascular structure, sinew and bone, wounds that took weeks, sometimes months to heal—these were all signs of vEDS that were overlooked by every medical practitioner I'd ever seen prior to visiting the Moya Clinic.

After my second miscarriage, I'd had some blood tests and subsequently was told I *might* develop a disease of the connective tissue. The insane thing was, I'd already developed a connective tissue disease. I had been born with it.

Thirty-odd years ago, after a stillbirth, they'd tested my chromosomes, but those results had revealed nothing abnormal.

Why didn't someone suspect vEDS? I read somewhere in all the literature that it had been a known disease since the 1930s.

Why?

Because I didn't have issues with hypermobility as with cases in *Classic EDS?*

Because vEDS is rare? Because a mere one in fifty thousand people are affected? Because there are too many rare diseases out there for doctors to ever be expected to know about them all?

It was just not fair to bring Meg into this disaster—for her to find out that not only her life was in danger, but my grandson's life was hanging in the balance as well.

No, I wouldn't give back Meg's childhood for a million bucks. My every breathing moment has been enriched by having my daughter in it. She is smart and vibrant, and over the years she has opened my eyes to so many of my flaws, making me work harder to be a better person, a better mom.

And how have I rewarded her for being an exemplary daughter? Guilt is an illogical emotion. I know I had no power to prevent Meg from inheriting the gene mutation, but I still felt responsible.

By God, she got this from me and I am going to do everything in my power to support her.

At least she didn't have FMD. The genetics counselor I spoke to on the phone told me they had not found a gene connected to FMD, and though I definitely had both vascular diseases, it was clear that my daughter did not.

It was raining outside, so I grabbed my umbrella, a light jacket, and walked to the library.

I found Meg in the beautiful children's section that she had designed and painted. She took one look at my face and led me to her tiny office where there was barely enough room for the both of us to sit, our knees touching.

I was grateful for the privacy.

I showed her my genetics report and she read it with a face of stone, not revealing an iota of emotion, which was very unlike her. On the opposite end of the spectrum, my heart was shredding. Every inch of my body felt weighed down and ached as if I were eighty-five years of age.

"I told Dr. Sandy about your ruptured uterus." Meg handed the report back to me, a long sigh slipping through her lips. "She's already decided to have a team of people on hand during the cesarean to sew me up."

I clasped her hands and squeezed. "At least they have forewarning. That's a very good thing."

Her resolve cracked as tears dribbled from her eyes. "W-what if I die?" she asked, her voice haunted.

"Oh, Baby." I pulled her into my arms and held her tight, rocking slowly. "You are not going to die. You and your son are both going to live."

Meg's inhalation stuttered. "What about your miscarriage, your still-birth? That could happen to me."

My heart twisted as a statue of Gandalf wielding his wand caught my eye. If only I could wave a stick through the air and change reality. "I never talk about it, but the stillborn babe had Down syndrome so I don't think you need to worry about that." I rubbed my hand around her back. "I know you'll take super good care of yourself, and that is the most important thing you can do for your baby. Focus on what you can control. That will keep you sane."

"B-but they already have me on three blood pressure medications. They're telling me I might spend the whole third trimester in the hospital. That I might develop pre-eclampsia."

I needed to face the cold truth that a critical difference between Meg's pregnancy and mine was her hypertension. She might be receiving the best medical care in the world, but her life was still in danger. "Well then, you're going to do whatever they say." As her mother, my job was to help my daughter through this in any way I could. "A trimester in bed will be worth every second once you hold your son in your arms."

"I—I'm so scaaaaared!"

I choked back my tears, steeling myself—at least enough to keep my voice steady. "Of course you're scared. I'm scared, too. But you are one of the strongest women I know. You survived eleven years of straight winters going back and forth between the US and Australia. You have what it takes to pull yourself through any adversity." I held her at arm's length and gazed into those red-rimmed, tear-filled eyes. "You have been blessed with a miracle, and you will hold your baby. You will be an amazing mother and will be there to watch as your son grows into a man. I know you will."

Bob's yard was picture perfect, though it was not quite as gorgeous as mine. He'd filled my flowerbeds with splashes of vibrant colors—in a varied assortment of flowers that would bloom all summer long. After the snow melted, the grass grew in green and healthy, and my lilacs filled the house with fragrance.

When I showed up on Bob's doorstep for dinner that evening, I thought I'd painted on a pretty solid poker face. But as soon as he opened the door, he asked me what was wrong.

"We need to talk," I said as he ushered me inside his quaint brick cottage located just below Grandad's Bluff.

"Okay...of course." He led me to a worn loveseat in a cozy living room with a big brick fireplace and a good-sized television in the corner. "Can I get you something? A glass of wine? Water?"

I shook my head, my gaze captured by a wall festooned with pictures of his daughter. "Maybe with dinner?"

"What's happened? Is it Meg?"

I tugged him down beside me. He needed to know the truth about everything. Sure, he knew a little, like Meg was having issues with her pregnancy which I'd mostly attributed to hypertension. "I've been keeping something from you."

He grinned. "You're married?"

"I wish it were that simple."

Bob's face fell. "Seriously? It's bad? Are you dying?"

Who knew that question would hit such a chord? After all, I was already nine years past the average vEDS life expectancy. "We're all dying." I pulled the genetics report out of my purse and handed it to him. "I received this today."

He read the first page and stroked his beard. Actually, it wasn't until page three where it got really interesting and talked about ruptures and dissections. But I didn't wait for him to wade through all the medical jargon even though he had been a pharmacist.

Instead, I slipped it from his fingers and told him about my cesarean disaster, then fast forwarded to our dissection events and the fact that I was diagnosed with fibromuscular dysplasia because my arteries were twisted and torturous with a beaded appearance. "Meg doesn't have FMD and so the doctor at Moya in Rochester sent her for genetic testing."

He tapped my report. "And they found this mutation?"

I nodded. "Vascular Ehlers-Danlos syndrome." I opened the report to page three and pointing out that Meg and I can have arterial ruptures at any time, that I had four aneurysms that they're currently watching, and because of Meg's pregnancy, she was in danger of having a ruptured uterus.

Bob ran a hand over his head, the corners of his mouth tight. "God, Jane, this is awful."

"I should have told you earlier."

"Why didn't you? I'm a healthcare professional."

"I know, but—"

"What?"

"I didn't want to burden you."

"You're never a burden to me, Sweetheart." Bob pulled me into his arms and kissed my forehead. "You do know that you're the best and brightest thing that's happened to this old guy in decades?"

"Really?" I asked, sounding a little juvenile. But I didn't care. "I'm so afraid of losing you. You're my best friend and I haven't had a solid friendship in years."

"You can stop worrying. I knew you were an amazing catch the first day you opened your door, then my mind was made up when you smiled at me with pink paint on your face."

I snorted out a laugh. "Even though I'm damaged beyond repair?"

"Who says?"

I took the genetics report and folded it. "These assholes, that's who. If you read the data on vEDS, I should have died years ago."

"But you didn't, did you?"

I shook my head.

"That's because you take fantastic care of yourself. Because you're as ornery as a tomcat, and you have the intestinal fortitude of a dragon."

I laughed. "I think Meg's the dragon. She has shown more strength through all this than I ever dreamed she had in her."

"Well, there's no doubt you've been an excellent role model."

I wish I hadn't been so hell-bent on climbing the corporate ladder. What kind of role model was I, always working? Even when I took Meg to her lessons, I was usually on my phone or on my computer analyzing numbers. "I don't know. I'm just glad she moved in with Mike. At least if she has something happen in the middle of the night, he'll be there to help her."

"He's a good man."

"So much better than the yahoo she met on her cruise to Bermuda."

A buzzer sounded in the kitchen. Bob kissed my cheek. "The roast is ready. Are you hungry?"

"Absolutely."

"Good." He stood, but before he shifted his attention to the oven, he crossed his arms and gave me a pointed look. "In the future, I don't want you to keep this kind of stuff from me, okay? It's too important."

I nodded. "Okay. Sorry. I'm not used to having a partner, I guess."

"We're a team, aren't we?"

"Yes." I followed him into the kitchen and nabbed a piece of lettuce out of the salad bowl. "Thank you."

"For what?"

"For being understanding. For not kicking me out."

Bob used two big forks to move the roast to a cutting board. "Why would I do that?"

"Because my arteries are twisted and I have four aneurysms? Because I passed on bad genes to my daughter? Because she's facing a high-risk pregnancy?"

He brandished a carving knife. "All families have problems, but that's not why I haven't asked you to leave."

"Why then?" I slipped the knife from his fingertips and started slicing the juicy roast to avoid staring into those penetrating eyes. "Why when things are so bleak on my side of the street?"

"Because I'm in love with you."

Chapter Thirty

Meg

M *ay 10th*

"Surprise!"

Standing in Mom's entrance hall, I clapped my hands over my mouth. "What is this?" I asked, laughing. My mother had invited me and Mike over for a barbeque. At least that's what I thought was going to happen, but no, all my co-workers from the library were here. So was Ripper. Can you believe it? The man was so nice he helped me move into Mike's house.

"My daughter needs a baby shower!" Mom took my hand and led me toward her new, antique settee in the drawing room, which had been decorated with streamers and balloons including a pyramid of cookies on the coffee table.

I glanced over my shoulder at Mike. "Did you know about this?"

He held up his palms. "I neither can nor cannot deny culpability."

"Just sit down and enjoy." Elaine handed me a plate. "The sugar cookies melt in your mouth."

Monique picked up a teapot and gestured to an empty cup and saucer. "Herbal tea?"

"Thank you." I glanced across all the smiling faces. Mike and Ripper were the only males in the room. "Where is Bob?"

Mom turned from the side table with a stack of photos in her hands. "He's outside manning the grill. I asked you to come over for a barbeque, didn't I?"

"She just left out the part about the baby shower," Mike said. Oh, yeah, he was culpable all right.

"Do you guys want to go out there with him?" I asked. "Have a beer or something?"

My fiancé grinned at my mother. "Oh, no. This is going to be way too much fun."

Ripper, however, sidled toward the butler's pantry. "Beer sounds awesome."

Once the big dude left, I shifted my attention to Mike. "What's going to be fun?"

His gaze homed in on the photos in Mom's hands. The baby in my stomach must have done a somersault. Either that or he dropped to my toes. "What are those pictures?"

Mom gave me a salacious grin. "We're going to play a little game called 'How old was she?'"

I reached for the photos, but Mom twisted away before I could grab them. "No!"

"Yes," she said to applause.

The first was a picture of me in a ballet tutu. I think I turned green. Heck, I didn't look good in a tutu at the age of five.

"Seven!" Elaine shouted, followed by shouts of five, six, and nine and a half.

I scowled. "Come on. Nine?"

Everyone guessed the baby picture ages—at least within a couple of months.

"Where did you get that?" I asked when Mom passed around a photo of me on the back of a horse in the parched outback of Australia. I was wearing Dad's hat which he'd tied on my head with a bandanna.

Mom waved the picture. "I have my ways. If you look closely, Meg's front teeth are enormous."

Then there was the freshman prom. I had a pimple in the center of my forehead and braces. My dress was orange. I glared at my mother. "Who picked out that godawful color?"

Mom had the audacity to snort. "You did."

"I would never pick *neon* orange. That gown made me look like a flashing sign on the Las Vegas strip."

"You liked it when you were...um." Mom turned to the crowd. "How old was she?"

"Fifteen!" shouted one of the newer librarians.

I made a mental note to schedule her for a month of weekends straight.

"But you wear orange." Elaine wouldn't let it rest. "Just last week you wore that frilly orange skirt."

"Yeah, but it's cute, and not *orange, orange*. It's more of an apricot and has pinstripes," I said. And it was just a skirt. On top I wore a pastel yellow sweater with a sunflower scarf. It had become one of my favorite outfits since my waistline had started increasing.

But the games aside, the baby shower was fun. I'd thought about organizing one, but since I had to drive to Rochester once a week for appointments, I just hadn't gotten around to it. And Elaine never mentioned anything about a shower, the minx.

I tugged her sleeve. "Was this your idea?"

"It was your mom's, silly. Though she did wrangle me in to help."

"I'll bet she did. Mom is an ace at delegation."

"Oh, really?" asked my boss. "Do you think she'd like to come work at the library?"

I laughed while Monique pushed a laptop in front of me. "My job was to set up a baby registry for you. Mike texted me a few things, and I've added some of the basics. We're just waiting for you to choose anything else you think you might need."

I paged through the work Monique had done. "This is really thorough. You've even added a car seat and a bassinet."

Mike leaned over my shoulder and pointed. "There's a stroller, a crib, and lots of boy clothes and diapers."

"I love it. Thank you!" I said, deciding to go through it in more detail later.

"How far along are you now?" asked the new girl.

"In two days I'll be twenty-five weeks."

"Getting close to third trimester." Mike rubbed my baby bump. I was so grateful to finally be showing. I didn't look pudgy anymore, I looked pregnant.

Woo hoo!

Bob came in with a steaming plate piled with hamburgers and bratwurst. "Get it while it's hot."

Of course, Ripper followed the food with a beer in his fist.

Mom and Elaine set out salads, chips, buns, and condiments.

I pushed up from my seat and waddled across the floor, patting my best friend's shoulder. "My mother really did put you to work."

"Anything for you, Meg." Elaine tugged me aside and inclined her head toward Mike who was deep in a conversation about barbeque grills with the other two men. "I told you he was a catch."

"Are you referring to the time when Mike came into the library last summer?"

"Duh! If you hadn't nabbed him I would have been next in line."

I slung my arm across her shoulders. "You've had a bit of a dry spell of late, haven't you?"

Groaning, she dropped her head forward. "Tell me about it."

"Would you like me to ask Mike if he has any techie friends at the U?"

Elaine's green eyes nearly popped through the lenses of her Coke-bottle-bottom glasses. "Hell yeah!"

Mom's cell phone rang and I was a little surprised when she took it to the kitchen to answer. After all, she wasn't getting calls at all hours anymore. I swear, the only smart thing Leon Worthington ever did was fire her, especially since the jerk got nabbed for fraud.

Mike stepped beside me. "You ready to eat?"

"As usual, the answer is yes. I think this baby is going to come out looking like a linebacker."

He gave me a plate and then picked up one for himself. "As long as Zachary plays for the Badgers."

Laughter filled Mom's house as if it were built for the sole purpose of hosting parties and making people happy.

We went through the assembly line and piled our plates with food. Everyone was talking, laughing, and eating.

My mother returned from the kitchen, her face ashen, her purse draped over her arm, keys in her hand. She whispered something to Bob, whose face immediately fell.

I set my plate on the table and butted into the conversation. "Is everything all right?"

A strangled cry escaped Mom's throat as she drew her a hand over her mouth. "That was Brookdale—Grandma collapsed and the ambulance is taking her to the hospital."

CHAPTER THIRTY-ONE

JANE

As soon as the ER doctor allowed me into my mother's room, I dashed to her bedside and clasped her hand between my palms. Her icy fingers chilled me down to my toes. "Mama!" I cried, blinking to better see her through my tears. Her eyes were closed, her mouth partially open, her face pallid as she lay atop the hospital bed. A white sheet covered her skeletal form, folded at her waist, and tucked in at the sides.

Oh, God.

"Can you hear me? It's Jane!"

Mama's lips quivered as if she did hear, as if she wanted to reply. A faint beep came from the heart monitor, the blue line indicating she was still here.

My mind raced with all the things I wanted to tell her—what a great mother she'd been, how much I loved her, how I admired her strength, her sense of humor, the solid foundation she'd established for me and my brother. "I called Roger and he's making arrangements to fly out here," I rattled as if there weren't enough time.

Again, Mama's lips quivered.

"The priest should be here any minute. I know that will make you happy."

My mother drew in a long, hollow breath.

"You know I love you. You have always been my strength." My body shook with the power of the emotions flooding through me. Yes, this day was inevitable, but it didn't make it any easier to see her lying here, unable to answer me, unable to open her eyes and look at me. "You were the best teacher I ever had. Without you, I never would have survived all the trials of this life. I love you, I love you, I love you."

Gripped by sobs, all I could do was bow my head and clutch her freezing hands, kissing them. I didn't even hear the curtain shift when the vicar came in and opened his prayer book. *"Almighty God, look upon your servant, lying in great weakness..."*

After years of battling Alzheimer's, it was time to let her go. But I wanted my mom. I wanted the woman who was always there with a reassuring word and a loving hug. My mind filled with the happy memories—the best ones. When at the age of four she'd praise me for drawing her picture even though it was a stick figure. Driving me to every lesson imaginable, the two of us animatedly singing show tunes. My God, she loved to sing.

This woman nurtured me. Loved me. Gave birth to me.

And now she was leaving me.

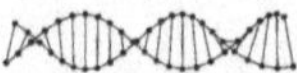

By the time Mom's funeral came, I realized that I'd been grieving for seventeen years. Her form of Alzheimer's lasted so long, taking her away from me far sooner than it should have. Now, it brought me peace to know she was in a better place—happy and singing with the angels.

"Your eulogy was top notch, sis," said my brother Roger, giving me a hug at the funeral reception. He and his wife Peggy had arrived yesterday. It had taken him over a week to clear his schedule, but at least he was here.

Finally.

I decided to push my resentment aside and welcome him with open arms. After all, I wasn't the only one who'd just lost a mother. I hugged him back. It was hard to believe that only nine days ago I had the house decorated for Meg's baby shower, and now we were all gathered in the drawing room, wearing black. The balloons were gone, the baby-blue streamers were gone, the banner bearing the word "congratulations" had been stowed away in the attic.

"So was yours," I replied. "I liked that you added humor. Mom loved to laugh, and your trip down memory lane was priceless."

Roger sidled to the table and took a tea cake between his pincers. "Well, I had to do something to top yours. I shouldn't have let you go first. You hit all the most important parts."

My brief tribute had centered on a celebration of our mother's exemplary life. Most of her years had been amazing, why talk the seventeen that hadn't? "I think we made a pretty good team—and we *both* cried."

"Of course we did. Mom would have wanted us to."

"Do you remember all the times you socked me if I dared to shed a tear?"

"Me?" My brother snorted. "Why would I care if you cried?"

I stared at him, drop-mouthed for a moment before I shook my head. Roger had uncanny amnesia whenever it suited him. Why try to argue about how much he tortured me if I cried when we were kids? I turned out okay. Maybe I ended up being stronger because he was so hard on me.

Like all children, we had our good times, our not so good as well. Last night I'd told him about vEDS and gave him Moya's number so that he could get his genes tested. Interestingly, he knew a little about the disease and expressed his concern for Meg—especially because of her high blood pressure.

Bob came around with a plate of finger sandwiches while Mike followed with cocktail sausages. I took a crust-less sandwich. "You guys don't have to wait on us. Just put the food on the table."

After a sardonic look from Bob, he nudged me with his elbow. "You kidding? We need something to do."

As the guys headed toward the group of caregivers from Mom's assisted living facility, Roger nabbed a sausage and pulled it off the toothpick with his teeth. "Have I told you how much I like Bob?"

I couldn't help but smile as I watched him chatting with the ladies—charming them, of course. "If only I'd met him thirty years ago."

Carrying a cup and saucer, Peggy slipped between us and looped her arm through the crook in my elbow. "Hey, you never showed me your office. You have a gorgeous piano in there."

"I sure do—came with the house. It sounded like a rooster learning to crow when I moved in."

Bob finally set the finger sandwiches on the table. "And you should hear her play it," he said as if he'd actually been impressed with my fat-fingering.

I snorted. "Yeah, bad notes and all."

Roger slung his arm across my shoulders and leaned on me. "Mom would have loved to hear you play."

"Come on." Peggy pulled my arm. "You have to play for us now."

"No, no, no." I didn't budge. "I'm a closet pianist. I'm terribly shy. Terribly awful as well."

"Come on, Mom." Meg pushed me from behind. "You don't have a shy bone in your body."

"That may well be, but no one wants to hear me play."

"I do," said Bob, earning a scowl from me.

They all but harangued me until I had no choice but to slide onto the piano bench and fumble for the music to Pachelbel's *Canon in D*, the only piece I actually knew by heart and hopefully wouldn't butcher too badly.

The entire crowd stood around the piano. Roger leafed through my music books while I managed not to make an utter fool of myself.

As I held the last chord, I smiled at Peggy, relieved to have made it through the piece without too many sour notes. "See?" I asked, driving the attention away from my awful playing. "The tone is so mellow. They just don't make them like this anymore."

"We need to have a singalong." Roger set a music book of tunes from the seventies in front of me. "For Mom's sake."

I cringed—I'd played about two songs in this book. My mother was a decent pianist, and always accompanied family singalongs, especially during the holidays. "How about Christmas carols?" I schooled my features into a pleading grimace. "I've practiced those."

"In May?" asked Mike.

"Grandma would have approved," Meg replied, God bless her. "She loved Christmas."

I grabbed the book of easy carols from inside the bench, then launched into *Hark the Herald Angels Sing* and everyone held forth while I managed to only hit a few bad notes. Honestly, they were all singing so loudly, no one noticed.

As I turned the page to *Joy to the World*, I looked at Roger and we exchanged grins. I'm glad he twisted my arm because everyone in the house knew the words and with our numbers, no one was bashful. What we lacked in talent, we made up for in exuberance. We laughed and a few tried to harmonize, and if you ask me, this was the absolute best sendoff for our mother. I had no doubt she was in heaven singing right along.

We sang *Jingle Bells* and *Away in a Manger* but halfway through *O Come All Ye Faithful*, the singing abruptly stopped as Meg dropped into my desk chair. Her face was scarlet, and I swear the skin on her arms swelled before my eyes.

"Do you have a blood pressure cuff?" Roger asked, his words crisp and urgent.

"I'll get it." I flew off the bench and raced to the bathroom.

By the time I returned, Roger had my daughter lying on the floor with her feet up on the piano bench, doing breathing exercises. He grabbed the blood pressure monitor from me and wrapped the cuff around her arm. "Do you have the number for your doctor?" he asked.

Mike held up his phone. "We both have it."

"Call now," said Roger.

The BP reading popped onto the screen: 145/75, which might be passable for an old lady like me, but it was a medical emergency for a pregnant woman who had vEDS.

After Mike got a hold of the triage nurse, my brother took the phone. "I'm a medical doctor. I'm here with my niece, Margaret Corley, who is a patient of Dr…"

"Sandy," Mike and Meg said in unison.

Roger efficiently took my daughter's pulse and relayed all the information as if he hadn't retired from practicing medicine years ago. He returned Mike's phone and looked at Meg. "Do you have a bag packed?"

"It's at the house in my closet," she replied.

Mike pulled a set of keys out of his pocket. "I'll get it."

"Good. Meanwhile, we're going to take Meg to the hospital. How far is Rochester?"

I wrung my hands. "It's a little over an hour."

"An hour?" Roger scoffed.

Meg pressed her hands to her cheeks. "Because my pregnancy is high-risk."

"I'll drive." I grabbed my purse as I followed Mike to the door. "Meet you there?"

"Can you wait?" he asked.

"No," Roger boomed in an ominous voice, making goosebumps rise across my skin.

CHAPTER THIRTY-TWO

MEG

"Now they have me on five blood pressure medications. Five! And that's it, there aren't any more," I shouted into the phone, frustrated and going crazy from being stuck in the hospital for the past two weeks.

"I know that seems like a lot," Mom replied. I could tell she was trying to keep her voice calm and it wasn't working. "But you're doing great. You knew you might end up in the hospital for your last trimester." Maya was barking in the background on the other end of the line. My mother was taking care of the dog because Mike was spending every free moment at the hospital in Rochester.

"So, you'll be twenty-seven weeks tomorrow—when is the doctor planning the cesarean?" Mom asked because the date seemed to change every other day.

"Dr. Sandy is now saying I'm definitely having a preemie. She's hoping I make it to thirty-two weeks. But I don't think I can take four more weeks of bed rest."

"You can and you will," Mom said in her executive voice.

I rolled my eyes at Mike who was sitting in the visitor's chair. "What if I have pre-eclampsia?"

"Then you'll have to deal with that as it comes. I'm sure your worrying doesn't help your blood pressure. Do you want me to bring you some books? Maybe an adult coloring book?"

"Please." The nurse came in. "I've got to go. Call you later."

The nurse held up a syringe. "Time for your insulin injection."

Wonderful. I not only was on the verge of being pre-eclamptic, I'd developed gestational diabetes. And it drove me insane to have Mom tell me that worrying wasn't helping my blood pressure. Didn't she think I knew that? How the hell was I supposed to not worry when so much was at stake?

Mike smoothed his hand over my hair as the nurse jabbed me. "You're amazing."

Though it was nice to hear, I certainly didn't feel amazing. I better resembled a blimpy ball of lard who hadn't been for a walk in two weeks. Mike was the amazing one. He'd been sleeping in my room, getting up, going to work, stopping by his house for a shower, then driving to Rochester to do it all again.

"Know what I got?" he asked.

I squeezed his hand. "A miracle?"

"Well, you and Zachary are the miracles, but I did get a subscription to Peacock so we can binge watch all the *Harry Potter* movies."

"Aww, you did?" I tugged him down and kissed his lips. "You are the nicest, most thoughtful man on the planet."

"Thank you."

⚭

Mike had left for work when a nurse came in and sat in the chair beside me. She had notecards and envelopes in her hand and looked at me with a serene, yet serious expression. "I understand you are aware that we ask all patients undergoing surgery to fill out their advance directives."

"Yes," I said, though my heart squeezed. It hadn't been easy to check the box beside the words *I do not want to be kept on life support.*

"And you are aware that your situation is high-risk?"

Tears welled in my eyes and I brushed them away. "I know. I chose to keep the baby months ago, and I stand by my decision to live with the consequences." Or die for that matter, but there was no way I'd ever say that out loud.

"You are remarkably brave." She sighed, placing a hand on my arm. "One thing we recommend for our high-risk patients is for them to write letters to their loved ones. I can't stress enough that we will do everything possible to get you and your baby through your delivery. And we're not expecting the worst to happen, but if it does, you will have had the opportunity to…"

"Say goodbye?" I asked, suddenly ice cold and straining to breathe.

Oh, God.

"Yes." She opened her hand, the notecards were lovely with watercolors of wildflowers. "Of course, it is entirely up to you, but if you'd like to write a few cards, I thought you might like these, especially since you'll be on bed rest for the duration of your pregnancy."

"Thank you." I slid the notes from her fingers, my hand shaking. "But I don't want to give them to anybody until I have to."

"What we recommend is for you to give them to your nurse, or someone you trust before you go in for your cesarean."

"Okay." My every breath stuttered as I looked at the pretty design. Would I ever see a field of wildflowers again? Dr. Sandy had already told me my C-section would be done under a general anesthetic because they had deemed it too dangerous to give me a spinal tap. But God save me, if I did have to die, I wanted to hold my son in my arms. *Just once, please?*

"Did I give you enough cards?" asked the nurse.

Not trusting myself to speak, I nodded. I'd have to write to Mike and tell him what a great dad he was going to be, and that I will need him to take care of our baby because I won't be around to help—to breast feed—to rock Zachary to sleep. I'd write to Mom and to my dad...and Elaine. She has always been such a great friend.

Tears spilled from my eyes as the baby moved. I wanted to hold him. I wanted to give him kisses. I wanted to be his mom and watch him grow up.

The nurse gently smoothed a hand over my hair. "Please know this is only a precaution to give you peace of mind. I fully expect you to come through surgery and see a beautiful boy swaddled and warm."

I clutched my arms across my belly. "I need to wake up. I have to!"

"We're going to do everything in our power to see to it you do. And know what?"

Tears blurred my vision as I shook my head.

"Ever since you came into my ward, I've been impressed at your strength. You are not a woman who's going to let anything stand in the way of what you want."

An ugly sob ripped from my throat. I wasn't strong. Not when my body was falling apart. "Really?"

"Absolutely. And in my experience, the key to overcoming any adversity lies in your heart and in your soul."

Was she right? I never considered myself tough in the face of adversity akin to my mother, but maybe I was. Perhaps becoming a mother awakened my inner strength, my need for survival.

"Write the letters. Tell everyone how much you love them, then after you wake up, maybe you and Mike can toss them into the fireplace and celebrate your little man."

Before my fiancé came for the evening, I put on my brave girl panties and started writing.

I told my mom there was a reason for her to leave the corporate world because I knew my son was going to survive and he needed his grandmother to love and care for him. I told her how much I loved her, how much I appreciated her, and emphasized what a great mother she had been to me.

Mike's letter was completely different. I hadn't known him a whole year yet, but I was absolutely positive that he was my soulmate. In our short time together, I'd learned what it really meant to love a man. As I wrote, I prayed that he wouldn't ever read this, but if he did, he needed to know that I put one hundred percent of my trust in him. I knew he'd be not just a good father to Zachary, but a world-class dad. I asked him to lean on my mother and always include her in our son's life.

Droplets of tears peppered the cards, but they were real. They were the evidence that I had written them from my heart. I prayed my words would be treasured forever. Writing these letters completely drained me, wrung me out like a dishrag. Yet for some reason, putting my emotions into words gave me a sense of inner peace.

The final letter I wrote was to Zachary for him to read once he reached the age of twelve. I told him about my dreams of him becoming a man and how much I dearly wanted to be a part of his life, but that my body wasn't strong enough. I told him I'd always be watching from heaven. I described the overpowering love that filled my heart whenever he moved within me. I treasured every kick, my growing belly, every ultrasound where I could see his strong heart beating. I wanted him to know how deeply I loved him even before he took his first breath and I prayed that my letter would one day give him a sense of connection with me.

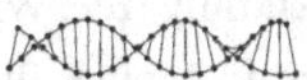

This evening the door to my hospital room opened, bringing with it warmth as soothing as sunshine. Mike greeted me with the most amazing smile—white teeth contrasted with is dark, neatly cropped beard, and his eyes gleamed as if he personally held the key to happiness.

He held up a vase filled with red roses. He'd brought me flowers every day, but this was the first time he'd given me red roses—the flower of romantic love. Maybe because the man was incredibly romantic. "Do you know what today is?" he asked.

"Twenty-eight weeks gestation?"

He put the flowers on my table and kissed me. "No. It's ten months since the first day I set eyes on you and fell deeply and irrevocably in love."

He always made me giggle when he told me about his insta-crush, especially since I tried so hard not to notice him at first. "Of course, it then took you three months to work up the nerve to even come inside the library again."

"Yeah, well, some things can't be rushed." He took a rosebud by the stem and brushed my cheek with the petals. "There are ten of these—one for every month."

I stilled his hand and kissed it. "They're beautiful. Thank you."

"Shall I put them in the window with the others?"

"Please. The hospital table is so small, they're likely to fall and that lovely vase will end up shattered." I scooted over and patted the bed beside me. "Want to cuddle?"

He winked. "Why do you think I've brought all these flowers?"

"I would have given you cuddling privileges regardless."

Mike slid onto the bed, his nearness warm and soothing and I wanted him to stay there forever. "Um...remember when we were looking at pictures of baby rooms online and you fell in love with the image featuring the world map?"

"Oh, that was so perfect. And it had hot air balloons we could place wherever we wanted—like one in Sydney, Australia where I was born and Yelarben in Queensland where my dad has his horse ranch."

Mike pressed his forehead against my temple. "That makes Madison where I grew up look pretty dull."

"No, I love Madison. And we both went to school there. We should add our parents. Maybe our whole family tree. Where were your parents born?"

"Well, my mother was born in Maine. But Dad?" Mike threw back his head and laughed. "Madison."

"I love it. Zachary will love it, too, because he'll be able to visit Madison all the time. Trips down under are expensive and take forever."

"Oh...but I didn't finish..." Mike pulled his phone out of his pocket. "Since you're stuck in the hospital for the duration, I hired your mom and Bob to decorate the nursery—even though they refused to accept payment."

My breath hitched. I so wanted to be the one to decorate Zachary's room, but we didn't even have time to buy furniture. And here I was stuck in the hospital, terrified that I'd never even see the nursery, let alone my son's face.

Mike showed me a picture that looked exactly like the world map I'd chosen, complete with hot air balloons, and early twentieth century airplanes. "So, they've been working like fiends."

I took the phone and paged through the pictures—aside from the wall with the map, the room had been painted a very light shade of blue. It was furnished with a white antique tallboy and a cozy rocking chair I'd added to the gift registry. There was a rocking bassinet and a white crib that matched the tallboy. I touched the screen. If only I could be there to make sure everything was perfect.

"Look." Mike swiped to the next picture. "The crib is full of stuffed animals and—"

"Books!" Tears stung my eyes, but I'd been doing too much crying lately. I grabbed a tissue and wiped them.

"If you don't like it, we can totally start over. I just wanted Zach's room to be one less thing for you to worry about."

"It's perfect." I didn't want it to be. I wanted to scream and shout—to complain about how stifling it was to be stuck in a hospital room while everybody else got to do happy things like decorating my son's nursery. Blast the damned tears, they spilled down my face regardless. "Thank you."

"Thanks to your mom and Bob. They're incredibly fast and efficient."

I tried to laugh. "It sounds like my mother may have met her match."

"They're a good team."

There were so many things I wanted to say, but the words wouldn't form. Mike knew the risks. He'd gone with me to most of my appointments. And he was so darned happy about this baby, I didn't want to keep bringing him down because I was worried.

In his way, Mike eased my anxiety and made me almost believe that everything was going to be okay. God, I loved him—loved the way he could take any bad situation and find the good in it.

We sat and cuddled on my cramped hospital bed and talked about our dreams for Zachary. Well past the dinner hour, we found *The Lost City* on the hospital's movie list.

As we laughed at Channing Tatum wearing a long blonde wig, trying to portray a male model for a romance novel cover, the back of my head started pounding. Just like the braking incident with Elaine, the sensation of a spike jamming into my brain made me curl forward and gasp.

"Meg! What's wrong?" Mike asked as the blood pressure cuff on my arm began to inflate in tandem with my ankles which were blowing up before my eyes.

"I can't breathe. Everything is blurry!"

He punched the call button and flew off the bed. "Nurse! Nurse! We need help in here!"

"Call my mom," I gasped, doubled over and freaking out at the ridiculously high blood pressure reading.

The nurse came in, took one look at my stats, and sounded the alarm.

"I'm going to have another dissection!" I cried, pressing against the back of my neck, trying to stop the screaming pain.

"Not on my watch." She injected something into my IV while an entire team filled my room. "Notify surgery to prepare for an emergency C-section."

Chapter Thirty-Three

Jane

I jolted awake when the phone rang. Noting the caller was Mike and it was after midnight, my heart took a flying leap as I swiped up the green phone icon. "Hello?" I asked with panic in my voice.

"They're taking Meg in for an emergency cesarean."

"I'm on my way." I put the phone on speaker and sprang out of bed while tugging my nightgown over my head. "Is she in the OR now?"

"No, they're trying to get her blood pressure to come down first…and Meg wants Dr. Sandy to be here."

I pulled on a pair of sweatpants and a sweatshirt. "Okay." I'd rehearsed this a dozen times in my head. "I'll just take Maya out to go potty, then I'll be in the car. See you in an hour and fifteen."

"Thanks," he said, hanging up.

Shit, shit, shit! Zachary needs to stay in his mama's belly for at least two more weeks!

I don't remember my feet hitting the stairs as I dashed down to take care of the little dog. I think maybe two minutes had passed by the time I put her in the pen I'd set up with wee-wee pads. Bob was on call to come over and feed her, but I wouldn't bother him until morning.

I drove across the Mississippi River traveling ten miles per hour over the speed limit, but I'd only seen two other cars on the road and I was pretty sure no one was adhering to thirty-five. After crossing into Minnesota, I sped onto the Interstate watching the signs to Rochester, but no matter how much I put my foot down, I wasn't going fast enough.

When I saw police lights on the east-bound side of the road, I looked at my speedometer—ninety-five miles per hour. I forced myself to slow down and set the cruise control to seventy-five, white-knuckling it and leaning forward as if doing so would make the car go faster.

The worst part was my emotions took over and I nearly hyperventilated with worry. Why had our entire world started to crumble around us? Why couldn't the doctors control Meg's blood pressure? I prayed for a miracle, hoping that Zachary could stay inside his mom for a few weeks longer. Even one more week would help!

As soon as I reached Moya's birthing center, I zipped into rockstar parking. I grabbed my purse and ran straight to the desk, my ridiculous head deciding this was a good time to be dizzy. "My daughter is having an emergency cesarean!"

Obviously, they dealt with hysterical grandmothers-to-be all the time because the receptionist was not only very professional, she gave me a name tag and explicit instructions on where to go. "They're waiting for you," she added as I hastened away.

Waiting? Why were they waiting?

As soon as I pushed into the hospital room, I was shocked to see both Meg and Mike there. "What's going on?" I asked, planting my palm on the counter to steady myself and catch my breath.

"The orderlies are coming to get me now." Meg opened her arms and I fell into her embrace. "My blood pressure has come down a little and I wanted to wait until Dr. Sandy arrived."

"She's here?" I asked.

"They said she's on her way and it's time for me to be prepped. God, Mom, I thought I was going to have another dissection." Meg's eyes filled with fear. "They're going to put me under a general."

"Why?" I asked.

"My blood pressure is out of control, I have all the signs of pre-eclampsia, add gestational diabetes, and Dr. Sandy thinks it's the safest option."

"Knock, knock," said an orderly from the doorway.

"Just one minute." Meg gave me her purse. "In here are letters I've written in case I don't—" She couldn't finish her sentence, but by the way my blood turned cold, I knew exactly why she'd written them.

I cleared my throat and steeled my nerves. "I will take care of your purse, but you are going to come through this like a champion. Remember your appendicitis?"

Meg nodded, her eyes filled with fear. "Yeah."

"You got through that without a single problem, and you're going to be fine. You're going to hold your baby in your arms, and you'll be the best mother on the planet." I squeezed her tight. She was alive and vibrant and I could not imagine this world without her. I refused to accept anything else.

Could *not* for one second allow myself to think about the worst.

"Hey, you're fifty percent me." I did my best not to choke up. "I've beaten the odds and have lived a great life. I'm nearly thirty years older than you and there's absolutely nothing that says you can't raise your son to become a good man and live to see your grandchildren."

She hugged me back, her face radiantly beautiful and filled with as much courage as a Spartan facing Xerxes in the Battle of Thermopylae. "Thanks, Mom."

"Are you ready?" asked the orderly.

Meg squeezed my hand. "They're going to let Mike wait just outside the OR so he can take care of the baby while Dr. Sandy is sewing me up."

This scene reminded me so much of the day I gave birth to Margaret, yet it was incredibly different as well. Back then, they had no idea that I would rupture my uterus and nearly bleed out. With Meg they were acting with utmost care. They had a solid plan. There would be a team of doctors and nurses on hand to make sure she didn't bleed excessively.

God dammit, my daughter was going to survive!

No matter how strong my confidence, I could not deny the dread gripping my chest. Meg was only twenty-eight weeks pregnant. *Oh, God!*

All I could do was sit and pray as the clock on the wall loudly ticked away the minutes. I was completely alone in a huge waiting room. One corner contained a child-sized table and chairs and toys. There was a reception desk, but the lights were out and the seats empty. It was strange how in the middle of the night, a facility as large as this seemed to be utterly abandoned. Sure, occasionally the big double doors leading to the operating rooms opened and a person wearing scrubs would glance my way before vanishing again.

There was a monitor on the wall that indicated a surgery was in progress. Only one, but I could tell there usually were multiple procedures going on at once.

Occasionally, the elevators down the hall would ding. From where I sat I couldn't see the doors.

They had told me the baby would be sent to the NICU, but that only the parents were allowed up there. When the big doors to the OR whooshed open, I looked up in time to see Mike following two nurses pushing an incubator. They weren't exactly running, but they were moving quickly.

Mike waved—I think happily, but he was wearing a mask and I couldn't see his smile. I hopped to my feet and followed, but the elevator dinged and they all disappeared behind the shiny silver doors. The numbers above rose until they stopped on the seventh floor, the intensive care unit for infants, a place off limits to grandmothers.

I felt so helpless—like I was stranded in a glass bubble without being able to hear or ask anything. My breathing sped as I turned in a circle and walked to the doors leading to the OR, looking through the glass pane for another human being—anyone who could tell me what was going on. Was my daughter still in surgery?

I hadn't realized the elevator numbers had descended when it dinged again and a nurse stepped out. "Are you here for Margaret Corely?"

Someone was actually acknowledging my presence? I nodded emphatically. "I'm her mother. Is she okay? Is the baby okay?"

"She's doing great and your grandson is on his way up to the NICU. I'm the recovery nurse. They just called me. Would you like to come in once she's awake?"

I gripped my hands against my stomach. Thank God, Meg was heading to recovery! "Please, thank you."

"I'll send someone to get you when she's ready."

My phone buzzed with a text from Mike: *2lbs 8oz, airways clear!*

Now I knew I was blessed. Zachary was breathing and in excellent hands. Meg had been moved to the recovery room.

Thank you, God!

My little girl and her awesome fiancé were starting a family. They might be doing things a little backward, but my daughter sure got this one right.

CHAPTER THIRTY-FOUR

MEG

Gripped in the churning hell of drug-induced exhaustion and nausea, I forced myself to open my eyes. Mom's face was the first I saw. "Where's my baby?" I garbled as if my mouth were full of cotton, wishing I had the strength to grab her shoulders and shake them.

"He's with Mike up in the NICU." Mom brushed her hand over my forehead. "Mike texted that Zachary is two pounds eight ounces and his airways are clear. Congratulations, you are the mama of a tiny baby boy!"

Oh, God, if only I could leap from this bed and celebrate but the nausea was overwhelming. I tried to nod, but only managed to dry heave. I needed to see my baby. I needed to see him now. "W-w-when can I see him?"

"Soon," said a nurse. "How do you feel?"

"Like I'm going to puke." I tried to push myself up, but I only managed to roll to my side and vomit into a plastic pan held by my mother.

"I'll give you some anti-nausea medicine and that should help."

Unable to keep my eyes open any longer, I gave in and let them drift closed. I might be wallowing in the bowels of hell at the moment, but the dregs of the anesthesia would pass and then I'd get to see little Zachary. Two pounds eight ounces? He was as tiny as Maya.

I don't know how long I was in the recovery room, but every time I opened my eyes Mom was there, wearing a mask, giving me little pep talks. Mike came down and told me how great Zachery was doing—that the NICU nurses were impressed with his strength. He even showed me a picture of a strawberry-red-faced alien, who happened to be the most beautiful thing I'd ever seen.

"He has red hair," I said, trying not to puke, wanting more than anything to experience the joy and wonder of a mother who'd just given birth. I needed to see him. I wanted him in my arms right now. As I rolled to my side, my blessed mother caught my vomit in another tray. My entire body shook.

"Argh!" I cried, trying to will the sickness away and only managing to heave again.

"Red hair like his mother," Mike replied as a nurse handed me a cloth to wipe my mouth.

Time ticked by while I went in and out of consciousness. Every time I awoke I tried to sit up, but I was too nauseated. And then it hit me. I was alive. I wasn't even in the ICU. "Did my uterus rupture?" I asked.

"No, thank God," Mom said, "but you were a long way off being full-term."

It must have been hours later when they finally took me up to a postnatal hospital room. "When can I see my baby?" I asked the nurse for what seemed like the hundredth time. Dammit, most women got to hold their babies as soon as they were born.

"When you're able to move into a wheelchair, we'll take you up there."

"I can do it now." I reached out to Mike. "Help me."

The stuff they'd knocked me out with was wearing off, because it felt like someone had taken a butcher knife and sliced open my abdomen, but after my initial bellow of agony, I wasn't about to complain. Someone might tell me I had to wait for the pain meds to kick in before I could see Zachary and that wasn't going to happen. I'd waited long enough.

When I tried to take my weight, my knees buckled, but Mike held me up.

"Easy, Sweetheart." He swiveled the chair so all I had to do was turn ninety degrees and gingerly lower my butt into the seat.

Oof, I was gutted, glad I didn't need to move again for a while.

After an elevator ride and checking in at the desk, the nurse pressed a button which opened the doors to the NICU. Mike wheeled me to Room Four. There was an elephant bearing the name "Zachary Reynolds" on the sliding glass door. We'd decided to give the baby Mike's last name because I was planning to change mine when we got married.

Inside, the incubator was covered with a quilted shroud with little monkeys on it. The light was dim, not nearly as bright as it was in my room.

"They said the baby needs limited light in order for his eyes to develop," Mike whispered. "We need to speak softly as well."

"Can we see him?" I asked.

"Yes."

Mike lifted up the cover on one side. My heart squeezed at the sight of the tiniest human I'd ever seen. His skin was red and wrinkled and his eyes were covered by a sleep mask screen printed with a pair of sunglasses. Over his nose was a CPAP and, though they had told me to expect there to be one, it was a shock to see the breathing apparatus take up so much of Zachary's itty-bitty face. Taped to his chest were probes measuring his vitals. A feeding tube had already been inserted through his mouth and on one ankle a blood pressure cuff was attached with Velcro. A tuft of red hair peeked out from beneath a white cotton cap.

I had given birth to this tiny, tiny boy, yet my insides shredded with despair. My baby should still be protected inside the cocoon of my womb. He was too little to be lying alone, fighting for life.

Mike washed his hands, then slid them into the incubator's arm holes. "For the time being, all we are allowed to do is cradle his head and feet like this," he said, demonstrating and smiling as if this was the greatest day of his life.

Didn't he blame me for being so weak?

The baby shifted just a little and I sensed his father's touch soothed him.

"When can I hold him?" I asked as the nurse came in.

"As soon as possible," she replied. "Zachary's doctor will allow skin-to-skin, kangaroo cares in about three days."

"Three days?" I asked, my shoulders falling. That was an eternity.

Mike massaged my neck. "Everything will be okay. Our son just needs us to give him a little time."

"But it's my fault he's so little."

"No—if you'd tried to stick it out any longer, I could have lost you both." He kissed me. "But now I have a son and a gorgeous fiancée. You've made me the happiest man alive."

He wheeled me closer to the incubator so I could cradle our sleeping baby's head and feet. "Hi, bugaboo, I'm your mom."

Chapter Thirty-Five

Jane

Three weeks after Meg gave birth, Bob and I were sitting in my TV room scrolling through all the pictures of Zachary that Mike had shared with the grandparents via Google photos.

"Look at this, it's a video of him yawning," said Bob, completely rapt, Maya curled up on his lap and snoring.

"Oh, that's too precious." I marveled at how tiny Zachary was in comparison to his father who was holding him—how my grandson had been no bigger than Meg's three-and-a-half-pound Chihuahua.

To everyone's joy, the baby was exceeding all his benchmarks. They had sent his cord blood to the genetics lab and Mike called with the news that Zacary tested negative for vEDS. Thank God!

Meg had some issues with expelling her placenta, but that had been taken care of. Now that she had been discharged, she was still staying at the hospital to take care of Zach.

"When will he be able to come home?" Bob asked. "I want to give the little guy cuddles."

"I'll be first in line." I hated that the hospital regulations had become so strict that grandparents weren't allowed in, but I understood it, too. Premature babies were so incredibly fragile. "Meg said the doctors won't let him go home until he can eat on his own." I pointed to the feeding tube taped to his cheek. "And they're not even allowing her to breast feed him yet."

"Why not?"

"Because at his age, he hasn't developed the ability to suckle. They're tube-feeding him with her breast milk. Meg says he will be able to go home at the end of July at the earliest but a lot of preemie babies born at twenty-eight weeks aren't released until their due date."

Bob cocked his head. "August twenty-third?"

"Yes, it could be that long."

"Those poor kids."

"I don't know about that." I swiped through the pictures, smiling at the multitude of images of Zachary sound asleep. "Three weeks ago the unthinkable could have happened and now I have a daughter *and* a grandson. In my book, a few miserable months taking care of a preemie in the NICU is little price to pay."

Bob scratched Maya behind the ears. "At least you got off easy—taking care of Meg's princess."

"I've offered to spend a few days at the hospital to let her go home and get some sleep, but she won't leave Zachary's side." Mike was still spending as much time as he could at the hospital, but they'd both agreed for him to delay his paternity leave until the baby came home.

"Good for her." Bob kissed my cheek. "You know, we make a pretty good team you and I."

"We sure do."

He twirled some of my fly-aways around his finger. "Well, I was thinking..."

"Hmm?"

"Why don't we get hitched?"

Good Lord, of all the things Bob might have said, the idea of marriage hadn't even made a blip on my radar. I laughed out loud, then covered my mouth when I caught a glance of the hurt filling Bob's eyes. "Sorry, I didn't mean to laugh. It's just I've been single so long, the thought of getting married again has never occurred to me."

"No? Well, I hadn't really thought much about it either until I met you." Bob set Maya down and turned toward me, hitching up one knee on the couch. "Don't you think it would be nice to live under one roof, especially since the new exterior paint is nearly as picturesque as your garden? We have dinner together almost every night, lunch, too. Why not add breakfasts?"

I sat stunned for a moment. We did have a number of breakfasts together because of all the sleepovers we'd been having. But that's not what he meant. I liked him a lot. He was smart and funny and loyal. He was helpful, and thoughtful, and...*wonderful*.

Maybe I loved him.

And if I really thought about it, I couldn't imagine my life without him. Not now.

Goodness, I do love him.

"Breakfasts?" I asked, my fingers brushing his hair.

He nuzzled into my neck and nibbled my ear. "Yes, well, it's all your fault because you introduced me to lattes."

I chuckled, warmth spreading through me like sunshine. "I knew it was the lattes. It's always the lattes."

Bob took both of my hands between his powerful palms. "You don't have to give me an answer now, but I want you to think about it."

My breath hitched as I stared into those beautiful green eyes—green like a forest or a meadow—the color of luck, of hope, of stability. But could I burden him with FMD and vEDS? How could I expect anyone to want to be with me knowing of the aneurysms inside me like ticking time bombs, waiting for the opportunity to rupture?

I gulped. We couldn't sidestep the inevitable. "You know I'm damaged."

Bob's forehead creased. "What?"

I pulled out the comb from my little bun and showed him my scalp. "For starters, I'm losing my hair."

He rubbed his bald head. "If you haven't noticed, mine has already disappeared."

"Yes, but that's different."

"How so?"

"I'm a woman. Women aren't supposed to lose their hair. It's humiliating."

He tucked a lock behind my ear. "I can hardly notice, and honestly, I think you're too beautiful to let a little bit of thinning hair bother you."

"Thank you," I said, though it was hard to believe my scalp didn't repulse him as much as it did me.

"Hey." Bob kissed my cheek. "If it embarrasses you, why not get a wig—not for every day, but when you want to go out?"

"A wig?" I asked, not convinced.

"Sure. I know a hairdresser who can help."

"Who don't you know in this town? Every decent contractor that's come to this house has been recommended by you."

"It started with years of wearing the white coat and chatting with patients. I made a lot of connections then. Now, too, I guess." Bob took my hand and brushed his lips over my knuckles. "So, now that we have that cleared up, what do you say?"

Sighing, I ran my fingers down my neck. "I've already had a dissected carotid artery that nearly killed me. Are you sure you want to get involved with someone with health issues?"

"Involved—we're already majorly involved. I want to marry you, Jane. We all have things. I have high cholesterol and my father died from a heart attack when he was only fifty-seven. Don't think you are the only one who has drawn a short stick. You said yourself your gene mutation is the best of two baddies. I looked it up. A lot of people with your mutation only ever find out about it if they have an event like a dissection. You could live till you're a hundred whereas I might die tomorrow."

I stared at him, completely at a loss for argument. "You are amazing."

"No, you are—you're smart, and caring, and you have the cutest ass I've ever seen. Besides, you take fabulous care of yourself."

I didn't need to think about it any further. At long last, I had met my soulmate and I wanted to share whatever time I had left with him, be it two years or thirty. "Tell you what. Let's be trendy and move in together. Who needs a ceremony? Let's just be us. Do what we want."

Bob waggled his eyebrows. "Whenever we want?"

I kissed his cheek. "Absolutely."

He kissed my lips. "I think that's a great idea."

"Know what?" I asked after a deliciously long kiss.

Bob rested his forehead against mine. "Hmm?"

"I love you."

CHAPTER THIRTY-SIX

MEG

I looked into my baby's eyes and hummed *Brahams' Lullaby*, one of my early oboe solos.

Nursing at my breast, Zachary raised his leg as if he approved of my soprano, his little hand resting on my skin.

How blessed my life had become. Mike and I had endured ten weeks of torture while the baby was in the NICU, but he'd been home for a week now, and what seemed like a never-ending vigil in the hospital was now fading into oblivion.

"Do you know that you are a warrior?" I asked him. "You not only survived the odds, you kicked them in the teeth."

"He sure is a warrior." Mike came in and sat on the floor of the nursery facing my rocking chair. "In fact, I was just in my office writing a poem of sorts."

"Of sorts?"

"Well it doesn't rhyme perfectly."

"Not all poems have to rhyme. In fact, free verse follows the path of natural speech." I gently rocked the chair and gestured to the paper in his hand. "Is that it? Will you read it to me?"

Mike let out a long breath. "Well, if it's not any good, we can always use the paper for fire starter."

"I'll bet it is as profound as Walt Whitman's prose. Read it to me."

The man gave me a look with the corners of his mouth taut, as if he were completely unsure of himself. "Okaaay...here goes:

I thought my life was full until I met you,
But the first time I saw your face, a window opened to shining rays in every hue,
My world transformed from black and white into a kaleidoscope of color,
Surrounding me with a bouquet of new fragrances, a realm of endless wonder,
Your smile changed me forever because you were the one,

Until you gave me a son,
And now I am fulfilled in every way I can imagine,
My love is brimming with unending passion,
Because my family is paradisiacal,
Because I am yours, you are mine and together...we made a miracle."

I reached out to him and grasped Mike's hand. "That is beautiful. Perfect."

"Just like our baby."

Zachary unlatched and squealed, kicking his legs.

"See?" I laughed. "He thinks it's awesome, too. In fact, we should make a wall hanging out of it—entitle it *Contentment* or something."

"You really like it?" Mike asked.

I cupped his stubbly cheek with my palm. "I don't think anyone could have put it better."

"Thank you." He grinned. "So...since your birthday is in five days, what would you think about having Nana come over and babysit while we go to Digger's Sting for dinner?"

I shifted Zachary to my shoulder and patted his back. We'd only had him home for a week. "Oh, no. He's too young."

"All right. How about I order whatever you want from Digger's and bring it home?"

"That would be amazing."

⋈⫙⋈⫙⋈

Six weeks later, Elaine held out the skirt of a white taffeta bridal gown, examining it with a disapproving squint. "I can't believe he's already four months old."

"In birth months. In preemie months, he's basically still a newborn. It takes premature babies two years to catch up to their actual birthday."

All of the dresses I'd looked at so far had been built for a stick woman, yet my mother and best friend were searching through the racks of bridal gowns as if they could find something I'd be able to squeeze my post-pregnancy body into.

"What about this?" asked my mom, holding up a dress that looked like something Ursula from *The Little Mermaid* might wear.

"No."

"Hello," said a bridal consultant, floating into the room. "Do you have an appointment?"

"Yes." Mom patted my shoulder. "Corley. One o'clock."

I glanced at my watch. It was quarter past and we had better make it snappy because I needed to pump before my nipples started leaking. Now that my maternity and Mike's paternity leave was over, I had to milk myself every three hours. Mike and I had both negotiated four ten-hour days with our employers. I had Mondays off and he had Fridays. Mom and Bob had put their refurbishing business on hold and they were watching Zachary during the three days in between—at least for the next six months or so.

Elaine looped her arm through mine. "This is the bride to be. Can we get something off the shelf? The wedding is only six weeks away."

"Weeks?" The woman gawked. "Most brides give us a minimum of six months."

Though Mike and I had picked the date of September twenty-first shortly after we got Zachary's due date, I'd given no thought whatsoever about a dress or wedding planning for that matter. Only two weeks ago Mom had helped me send out invitations and I was ecstatic that my father was actually coming from Australia. We were doing everything entirely backwards—and had only ordered the rings last week. Mike's was a gold band and mine was a single solitaire with a wedding band that matched his.

"So, can you help us?" asked my mother. "I need a mother of the bride dress, and we'd also like to order bridesmaid dresses, but my daughter isn't going to change the date."

"We could always shop online," said Elaine.

I huffed out a sigh. "I don't like buying online because nothing ever fits."

"We do have a limited supply of gowns on the shelf." The woman eyed my waistline. "Let's measure you and see what we can do."

I groaned. "I'm no delicate flower."

"There is no judging here. We make brides of all sizes beautiful."

Was that meant to make me feel better? Because it certainly did not. It sounded more like she said, "Don't worry, Fatty, I'll squeeze you into something."

I was about to suggest we leave when both Mom and Elaine took an arm and pulled me into the back room which was filled with mirrors and a platform for gorgeous brides to stand upon and admire themselves.

Only because I wanted to look my best for Mike, I tolerated the measurements, then we sat and waited, tapping my foot while the attendant collected gowns.

"You don't look happy, Meg." Mom gestured to my nervous foot. "Would you rather we go to Minneapolis or Madison?"

"I'm fine. You know I'm always self-conscious when everyone is looking at my body."

"You have a complex, girl." Elaine backhanded my arm, a little hard if you ask me. "Even after your pregnancy you still look gorgeous."

"Maybe in a sweater and a skirt," I mumbled, looking at my mother out of the corner of my eye. Sure, I got her mutated COL3A1 gene, but why couldn't she pass on the slim figure to me?

"Hey." Elaine batted her eyelashes. "Remember the guy you and Mike set me up with last winter?"

"Yes, whoa, we've hardly talked about anything but baby stuff since then. Did you like him?"

"Uh huh." She twirled in place. "He's going to be my date for the wedding."

I grabbed her hands and squeezed them. "Oh, that's awesome."

"Here we are!" The woman came in with her arms full of white and sparkly things.

She held up one strapless gown after another. They all looked the same, though the skirts varied from princess to mermaid to the A-line, to the godawful column.

My head was about to shake off my neck. Maybe I loved color, but I didn't care for glitz. "Ugh. I guess I should have told you I don't want sequins or flashy crystals. I don't want my 'linebacker' shoulders bare, and there's no way in hell I'll ever be caught dead in a column dress. Not with these curves."

The woman puzzled for a moment before her face brightened and she held up a finger. "I think we might be in luck." She shuffled through a rack of dresses. "One of our brides cancelled at the last minute and her dress is stunning. We might need to size it down an inch or two, but that shouldn't take our seamstress too long, especially if you're okay with paying an upcharge to move your gown to the head of the queue."

Mom crossed her ankles and folded her hands. "If the dress is what Meg wants, then we'll work out the cost."

Ten minutes later, I was standing on the dreaded platform in the perfect gown. I even looked beautiful. I mean, *I* thought I looked beautiful, probably for the first time since I hit puberty.

The bridal attendant had taken a couple of tucks, fastened with pins, and the gown fit as if it had been made for me. With lace cap sleeves, and a pleated, crisscross bodice, the ivory chiffon flowed like a Grecian gown with a splay of beaded floral detail at the waist—no daisies, but the dress was stunning.

"I love the back," said Elaine, and I turned to examine the laced corset back.

"The question is how do you like it, Meg?" Mom pushed to her feet then walked around me with her fingers pinching her chin. "It's only the first dress you've tried on."

"It's perfect."

Elaine, ever not the subtle one, threw up her hands in victory. "You look like a goddess, girlfriend!"

The woman straightened out the train. "She does, doesn't she? That cut is so flattering and we hardly ever sell it. Most everyone wants something off the shoulder or weighed down with rhinestones."

"That's definitely not me."

I changed positions in front of the mirrors but no matter how I looked at it, this was the gown of my dreams. How did this dress make my cleavage look so hot? I mean, I never looked hot. Nice, passable, occasionally lovely perhaps, but not sexy.

I smiled. "Now, what about bridesmaid dresses and something for my Mom?"

"I think I have exactly what you need."

Chapter Thirty-Seven

Jane

Bob not only gave me the phone number of a hairdresser who supplied wigs, he drove me to my appointment. The care he took to make sure I found the perfect wig was adorable, even though he proved himself to be overtly opinionated. He didn't want me to buy a gray wig because he insisted my hair was blonde (um...maybe he needed new glasses?). He didn't like the longer wigs because I have a small head and my face got lost in the copious layers of hair. The bobs made my cheeks look too hollow.

He critically eyed the wall of wigs with his hands on his hips, insisting I needed something petite, and not white. Regardless of his opinion, I did try on a light gray wig I liked, but Bob pulled it off my head and said I was too "foxy" to settle for gray.

Foxy? I hadn't heard the term since I was in high school—maybe college, and definitely not since the eighties.

So, I ended up buying a rooted wig, which the hairdresser assured us happened to be all the rave at the moment. Who would have thought? I spent all those years dying my hair and covering up my ugly roots, and now that I'm mostly silver, being two-toned is in fashion. The wig's roots were a bit dark but the new look worked. Styled in a pixie cut, the tips were frosted with a light blonde and the hair laid in a tidy wedge in the back, contouring nicely with my neck. The best part? After two hours of wig shopping, Bob approved and I had a natural-looking lace front wig to cover up my thinning spots.

And I happily wore it today.

"What should I expect?" asked Bob as he pushed the stroller to the restaurant where Mike's parents were hosting the rehearsal dinner.

"Who knows? I haven't seen my ex-husband in twenty-three years." Bob and I did not attended the wedding rehearsal because as the mother of the bride, my role was to walk into the church with Bob on my arm and sit in the front pew. Besides, the kids needed us to stay home and babysit Zachary. I told Meg I could arrange for the teenager across the street to watch him during dinner, but she wanted the baby there.

Perhaps I should have been the one who stayed home. Before we left, I kept fooling with my wig, trying to make it look as nice as it had when the hairdresser fluffed it with her fingers, but I couldn't get it right. Then I smudged my mascara and had to start over with my makeup, smudging my lipstick when Zachary made a noise. I probably still looked like I'd been drinking fruit punch.

I had no idea why I was so ridiculously nervous about seeing Jack. I'd spent so many years trying to block the man from my memory, he hardly ever crossed my mind anymore. Yet, the fact that he was going to be at the rehearsal dinner had my stomach in knots.

"Should have brought your taser," Bob mumbled—I had told him about the time Jack choked on a bite of his drumstick at the dinner table. I jumped up and performed the Heimlich maneuver, making him cough up the chicken, sending it flying across the table. As soon as Jack stopped coughing enough to speak, he yelled at me for not making gravy that night. The scene was so typical of our marriage. Anything that went wrong was my fault.

The worst years had come after Meg was born. While I was pregnant, Jack retired from the Royal Australian Navy and took six months off before he "went back to work." The problem was six months turned into six years...then seven. I might have been able to put up with it before our daughter went to school, but as his drinking got further out of control, I was the one cooking, cleaning, taking care of Meg, and bringing home a paycheck.

I snorted and pulled the taser out of my jacket pocket. "I always carry the beast when I walk with the girls." Believe it or not, I got to talking with my next door neighbor this summer and she invited me to join her early-morning walking group—all ladies in my generation, which I've been enjoying immensely.

Bob reached for the taser, but I quickly slipped it back into my pocket. "Don't worry, Meg said she'd ask her father not to drink too much. Honestly, when Jack is sober, he's a decent guy."

"Great. Kool-Aid for the Aussie."

"Cordial," I corrected. At least when I lived down under, they drank cordial rather than Kool-Aid. "Regardless, we have to do our part to make a good showing for Meg. All smiles and love, no stress and guilt."

As soon as we walked inside, Jack spotted me from the bar. "Jane!" he hollered, pushing through the crowd with a beer in his hand and giving me a sideways hug as he scrubbed his knuckles over my head. "Look at you!"

I clapped my hands to my wig to keep it from falling off and took a giant step away. Then I ushered Bob in front of me and made the introductions.

The two men faced off like a pair of boxers, Jack several inches taller. But if you asked me, Bob's shoulders were broader and he had a lower center of gravity. If I were wagering, I'd put money on my sweetheart. After a brief stare-down, they shook hands and exchanged pleasantries.

"How was the flight?" I asked.

Jack took a long drink of his beer. "Bloody long and miserable." He punched my shoulder. "You've hardly aged."

He was lying.

"You, too." I was definitely lying. In addition to a head of gray hair and crow's feet etched down his face, his shoulders stooped and his nose had taken on a permanent red color characteristic of alcoholics.

He offered to buy us a drink (they were on the house) and introduced us to his girlfriend while Meg came over and took charge of the baby. Fortunately, the server came in and told us our table was ready and we all moved into the banquet room where Bob and I found chairs as far away from Jack as possible, just to make sure neither of us got the urge to break out my taser.

Meg and Mike were adorable, doting over their baby while the meal was served—a selection of beef or chicken and red or white wine. The kitchen was obviously ready for us because the meals came out shortly after we ordered.

I tried not to look down the table at Jack, but for some reason, the man kept catching my eye, talking loudly, and raising his glass my way. He'd switched from beer to red wine. I'd decided to drink water.

By the time dessert was served, I'd lost count of the number of glasses of wine Jack had consumed (old habits don't die, I guess, even if he was no longer my problem). My ex-husband stood and raised his glass, sloshing red wine on the white tablecloth. "A toast to the bride and groom!"

"Cheers!" everyone said, raising their glasses.

Bob leaned in. "Aren't the toasts supposed to be done at the reception?"

I eyed him. "You want to say something?"

Zachary decided to fuss and Jack pulled the baby out of his stroller. "This little fella has some pipes on him, I'll say."

I leaned forward watching like a hawk, but Jack cradled the baby safely in his arms. "The lad obviously has inherited his looks from Grandpa."

Everyone laughed except me.

"And he has the Corley red hair, bless him—good on ya, Meggie, for having a boy!"

"What's that supposed to mean?" Bob whispered.

I inclined my lips toward his ear. "During the divorce, he complained to his attorney that it was my fault because I hadn't given him a son."

"Does he know the sperm determines the sex?" Bob asked with a snort.

I clapped a hand over my mouth and tried not to laugh.

By this time, Zachary had worked himself into a dither, clinching his little fists, wailing as babies do when they're hungry or need their diaper changed. Jack handed him to Meg. "I have to add, the attitude he's showing is from Grandma's side." He hooted and raised his glass to me.

I glanced at Mike's mother. She wasn't smiling either.

Meg gave her father a look. "Thanks, Dad." She stood and lifted her glass toward me much like her father had done, but there was something in her smile that took the edginess out of the moment. "My mother might be a bit of a spitfire, but she gets most of the credit for turning me into the woman I am today. She single-handedly put me through college and took me to a gazillion lessons, and…" She paused, her shoulders shaking with her giggle. "No one can forget my mother taught me how to make the best slice-and-bake cookies in the world!"

The crowd laughed and applauded while Bob leaned in. "That was nice of her."

I raised my glass to my daughter and mouthed, "thank you." Maybe after all these years she had forgiven me for leaving her dad and subjecting her to all those winters. One thing was for sure, we had grown closer in the last year than in the last thirty.

After dessert, Bob stood and raised his water glass. "I want to thank Mr. and Mrs. Reynolds for hosting this delicious meal."

"Hear, hear," everyone said.

"Goodnight," Bob continued. "Get some sleep, and we shall see you all tomorrow."

"Don't do anything I wouldn't do, Big Bad Bob," bellowed Jack. He was always so original.

"Jeez," Bob mumbled, pulling out my chair and offering his elbow.

"Nice job, taking the high road," I whispered.

He threw back his shoulders. "Thank you."

"Though I am a little surprised..."

"Hmm?"

"That you didn't ask me for my taser."

Bob pulled the weapon out of his pocket. "Well, I borrowed this about the time the asshole scrubbed his knuckles over your hair, but I opted not to use it because you told me we had to make a good showing for Meg."

I slid my arm around his waist as we walked in stride. "That's why I love you."

"Why?"

"Because you you're kind and considerate."

He stopped at the crosswalk and gently flicked the bangs of my wig. "And?"

"Grown up?"

Bob shook his head. "Foxy."

I needed to help him move into the twenty-first century with that one. "How about handsome?"

"I prefer foxy."

"Hot?"

He frowned as if mulling it over. "Sexy?"

"Okay." I kissed his cheek. "I'll go with sexy."

Dressed in a flowing pink gown, I gazed down at my grandson sleeping in my arms and kissed his forehead. "Sleep little one and don't wake until your mommy and daddy have recited their vows," I whispered, though I doubted Zachary's parents would mind if he started to fuss during the wedding.

I was armed with a diaper bag containing two bottles of mother's milk and a pacifier. If none of that worked, the baby might steal the show. After all, he had become the center of our universe and I was pretty certain he knew it.

Incredibly, a year had passed since I moved to Wisconsin. I'd probably always have a sickly twist in the pit of my stomach whenever I thought back to the events that transpired at Bethany Plastics but can honestly say I harbored no regrets. I had performed my duty to the best of my ability and ended up being the butt end of a criminal's fraudulent scheme. The irony of it all was the fact that I'd found the flash drive in my purse, stuck to my guns, and in doing so, uncovered the depth of my boss' dishonesty.

I no longer thought about going back to the corporate world where I once had convinced myself that I'd "made it." I had been blind for too many years. If only I'd realized sooner how much my life in Denver had been as plastic as the bottles we made—pathetic, and empty as well. Sure, I'd made a good salary which enabled me to put Meg through school and build up my retirement. And for that I also have no regrets.

Maybe I was destined to arrive in La Crosse when I did. Perhaps Bob was destined to be the first contractor I met as well.

In the overall scheme of things, production quotas didn't matter. Balance sheets and net profits could go to hell. What mattered was family—Meg and Mike, and Zachary sleeping in my arms. What mattered was Bob, the man who had knocked on my door and smiled with shiny, friendly green eyes. Little did he know how far a small act of human kindness would take him. I certainly did not.

Meg and Mike's wedding was at the Episcopal church on the corner of Main and Ninth Street across from the library. The church was as old as my house and wouldn't look out of place in Europe. I know there were hundreds of churches built during the Middle Ages across Europe, but this one was iconic with arching, vaulted ceilings, exquisite stained glass, and an enormous pipe organ behind the altar.

Bob sat beside me, his hand resting on my thigh. "Is everything okay? They're five minutes late."

Earlier, I had been downstairs in the choir room helping Meg dress, and she was ready—her hair was done, her veil in place, her bouquet of brilliantly colored flowers. Jack had been pacing down there like a caged lion. He'd been cordial and probably hung over, but he looked showered and presentable in his tux.

I glanced over my shoulder just as the music began. Mike, his best man, and two groomsmen all dressed in black tuxedos came from the side and stood with the priest up in front of the kneeling rail.

My eyes stung as two bridesmaids approached, followed by Elaine, the maid of honor. She gave me a little wave as she took her place, and then the organ's volume ratcheted up with a fanfare announcing the bride.

Everyone stood as Meg appeared at the rear of the sanctuary, her arm looped through Jack's. He'd been a handsome man, though the years of alcohol abuse and the scorching Australian sun had taken their toll.

I suppose it came as a shock for him to see how much I'd aged as well. I wondered if he knew I was wearing a wig? Was that why he scrubbed my head with his knuckles last night?

My questions vanished as they started the march down the aisle. Meg's Grecian gown was absolutely stunning and Mike's gasp of approval twisted my heart.

"Waaaa," Zachary cried as if he knew he was missing out on something very important. I gently bounced him in my arms as Meg strolled past with an enormous smile, her gaze fixed on the groom. Jack, in his cavalier way, gave me a cheeky wink.

I glanced at his girlfriend in the pew behind, truly thankful that he'd found someone.

Throughout the rest of the service, the baby was miraculously well-behaved. As soon as he started to fuss in earnest, I gave him a bottle, love and contentment swelling through me more than ever before.

I had everything I'd ever wanted in life right here.

Bob was right. We all had our health issues. None of us could drink from the fountain of youth. Who really knew where we would be tomorrow? All we could do was take care of our bodies and educate ourselves about our weaknesses. FMD and vEDS were my Achilles' heels, but I've learned how to live with them. I'd learned not to let them control me. I accepted that it took a team of highly respected doctors to treat me—the vascular neurologist I'd been referred to after I hit my chin on the toolbox was able to get my dizziness under control and I hadn't had a debilitating migraine since he prescribed the right medicine. It amazed me how going to the appropriate specialists made such a difference in the quality of treatment.

I once abhorred doctor appointments. I guess I'm not ecstatic about them now, but I've come to understand that physicians in different disciplines provide distinct types of care and none of them knew it all.

Most of all, since moving to La Crosse, I've learned not to take for granted one single blessed minute. Every morning when I awake with Bob at my side, I thank God for the gift of another day, ever so grateful to have found a soulmate, ever so thankful to finally realize what is truly important.

My walking group met three times a week to power walk ten thousand steps. I think I've finally figured out how not to push myself—or push just enough.

One thing was for sure, I would never again allow any doctor to brush me off and make me doubt my symptoms or my sanity, and since I've found doctors who actually understand my condition, I doubt I will ever have to.

Bob rubbed his shoulder against mine. "What's going through that gorgeous head of yours?" he whispered.

I turned my lips to his ear. "I'm just happy to see Meg marrying such a wonderful man."

In that instant, my daughter glanced at me over her shoulder and gave a delightfully happy smile. While tingles skittered from the top of my head, down my shoulders and arms, I read her message loud and clear: *Life might be uncertain and woefully short, but these moments—finding love, creating family—make it all beautiful and worthwhile.*

Author's Note

Thank you so very much for reading *My Genes Don't Fit*. This book took me a long time to write. It also didn't fit in with any of the other books I've written prior, and thus the manuscript sat on my desk for a long time as I worked to decide what to do with it.

At fifty-eight years of age I did have a dissected carotid artery when I was on number twenty-eight of thirty pushups as I was practicing for my second-degree black belt test. The pain was the worst imaginable—a ten on that scale the doctors' offices always refer to. Two weeks later, my daughter suffered two dissections when she was in an incident in a car where her husband braked hard to avoid a collision. She often tells me she saved my life because it was her doctors who encouraged me to have a CT scan of my neck where not only the dissection was found, I received an initial diagnosis of FMD similar to what was described in this book.

I actually had my first vEDS-related incident when I was a teenager where my eardrum burst. Over the years I had many strange occurrences that, in hindsight, point to vEDS including hemorrhaging on an airplane (very embarrassing), nearly bleeding to death during a cesarean, leaky heart valves, numerous torn muscles and tendons, and a suspected carotid dissection at the age of forty-eight akin to the one I had at fifty-eight (except at forty-eight I was sent home from the ER without so much as a blood test and told I was merely having a migraine).

The journey to the diagnosis of vEDS could be described as an odyssey in self-flagellation from a vascular surgeon who took one look at me and diagnosed a perfectly healthy woman regardless of my radiology results, to being told that with FMD I wouldn't see any changes in unaffected arteries and they never needed to be looked at again (though this is false, it's a long story, so let's just go with it).

My diagnosis of vEDS came after my daughter's who didn't present with FMD and was subsequently sent for genetic testing. Though I wasn't thrilled, many puzzle pieces began to fit into place. But it was only the beginning of the fear that comes with being diagnosed with a disease where the average life span is fifty-one. My daughter was sixteen weeks pregnant when she received the news, and because of her high blood pressure, she was unable to carry the baby beyond twenty-eight weeks. Her son was in the NICU for three months and has since been diagnosed with cerebral palsy (a topic this book didn't delve into because it's a story in itself). The good news is the wee one doesn't have vEDS, thank God.

Along this journey, I have learned to slow down and embrace life. I am ever so happy to be here. Every day is a gift. Rain is a miracle. Snow brings not only beauty, but peaceful reflection. Sunshine is magnificent. My husband is my rock. Long walks are invigorating, and my two adorable dogs bring joy that abounds by the moment.

I wish you health and happiness as well as the ability to cope with whatever may come out of left field. God bless.

ACKNOWLEDGEMENTS

Heartfelt gratitude to all the caring physicians who have effectively treated or counseled me along this journey:

- David Deyle, M.D., Medical Geneticist, Mayo Clinic

- Eri Fukaya, M.D., Ph.D., Associate Professor Surgery, Vascular Surgery, Stanford Vascular Clinics

- Elizabeth Ratchford, M.D., Director, Johns Hopkins Center for Vascular Medicine

- Anette Faller, M.D., Internal Medicine, Vascular Medicine, Mayo Clinic

- Grace Paradella, M.D., Dixie Primary Care, St. George, Utah

- Ivan Garza, M.D., Neurologist, Mayo Clinic

- Jimmy R. Fulgham, M.D., Vascular Neurologist, Mayo Clinic

- Paul W. Wennberg, M.D., Cardiologist, Internist, Vascular Medicine Specialist, Mayo Clinic

To all the nurses and technicians who have provided care and counseling.

A special thank you to the members of the CT – Computed Tomography group on Facebook who helped me with terminology.

Thank you to my daughter Moriah Guy who provided many of the details involving Meg's diagnosis and pregnancy.

Thank you to the nurses in the NICU at Meriter Hospital in Madison, WI for their expert care of my grandson who was born at twenty-eight weeks gestation, weighing 2.5 lbs.

Recognition to Invitae for the critical work they do in genetics, their fast turnaround, and their detailed analysis.

Recognition to the members of the Facebook Groups: The VEDS Movement, Genetically Confirmed VEDS Group, and FMD – Fibromuscular Dysplasia Education & Support Group

Helpful websites:

Cleveland Clinic

Mayo Clinic

Fibromuscular Dysplasia Society of America (fmdusa.org)

The vEDS Movement

The Ehlers-Danlos Society

ALSO BY AMY JARECKI

Highland Force Series:
Captured by the Pirate Laird
The Highland Henchman
Beauty and the Barbarian
Return of the Highland Laird (A Highland Force Novella)
The Kings Outlaws series
Highland Warlord
Highland Raider
Highland Beast
Highland Defender Series
The Fearless Highlander
The Valiant Highlander
The Highlander's Iron Will (a novella)
Lords of the Highlands Series:
The Highland Duke
The Highland Commander
The Highland Guardian
The Highland Chieftain
The Highland Renegade
The Highland Earl
The Highland Rogue
The Highland Laird
Guardian of Scotland (Time Travel) Series
Rise of a Legend
In the Kingdom's Name
The Time Traveler's Christmas
Highland Dynasty Series:
Knight in Highland Armor
A Highland Knight's Desire

A Highland Knight to Remember
Highland Knight of Rapture
Highland Knight of Dreams (a novella)
Devilish Dukes Series:
The Duke's Fallen Angel
The Duke's Untamed Desire
The Duke's Privateer
The Duke's Secret Longings (a novella)
The MacGalloways series
A Duke, by Scot
Her Unconventional Earl
The Captain's Heiress
Kissing the Twin
A Princess in Plaid
Charmed by the Wily Lass
Blitzed series:
Defenseless
Unintentional
Tackled
ICE Series (romantic suspense)
Hunt for Evil
Body Shot
Mach One
Pict/Roman Romances:
Rescued by the Celtic Warrior
Celtic Maid
Stand Alone Titles:
My Genes Don't Fit
Time Warriors
Defenseless
Virtue: A Cruise Dancer Romance
The Chihuahua Affair
Boy Man Chief

ABOUT THE AUTHOR

An Image

Known for her action-packed, passionate romances, *USA Today* Bestselling Author Amy Jarecki has received reader and critical praise throughout her writing career. She won the prestigious RT Reviewers' Choice award for *The Highland Duke* and a RONE award from InD'tale Magazine for Best Time Travel for her novel *Rise of a Legend*. In addition to being a *USA Today* Bestselling Author, Amy has earned the designation as an Amazon All Star Author. She holds an MBA from Heriot-Watt University in Edinburgh, Scotland and now resides in La Crosse Wisconsin with her husband where she writes immersive historical and contemporary romance novels. Become a part of her world and learn more about Amy's books on amyjarecki.com!

www.ingramcontent.com/pod-product-compliance
Lightning Source LLC
Chambersburg PA
CBHW011556190726
48287CB00010B/2920